# THE DRAGON EATER

## THE THARASSAS CYCLE
## BOOK ONE

## J. SCOTT COATSWORTH

Cover artwork design copyright © 2023 by Sleepy Fox Studio
*sleepyfoxstudio.net*

Published by Water Dragon Publishing
*waterdragonpublishing.com*

ISBN 978-1-959804-27-7 (Trade Paperback)

FIRST EDITION

10 9 8 7 6 5 4 3 2 1

*This book is dedicated to my husband Mark,*
*who has always believed in me,*
*even when I didn't believe in myself.*

# ACKNOWLEDGMENTS

I want to thank my friends, Cari Zee and Tash McAdam, who encouraged me to write this series, and Angel Martinez and Kim Fielding, who were always there when I needed a shoulder to lean on.

I also want to acknowledge the fabulous Kelley York at Sleepy Fox studios for the great cover, and my beta readers, Jamie Lee Moyer, Kelly Haworth, Kristin Masters, Lee Hunt, Sue Philips, Timothy Bult, and Tony Farnden, as well as Gus Li, who edited the manuscript before submission.

And finally, I want to acknowledge Steven Radecki at Water Dragon Publishing, who took a chance on publishing this series after meeting me at BayCon. I am thrilled to be working with Steven and his team!

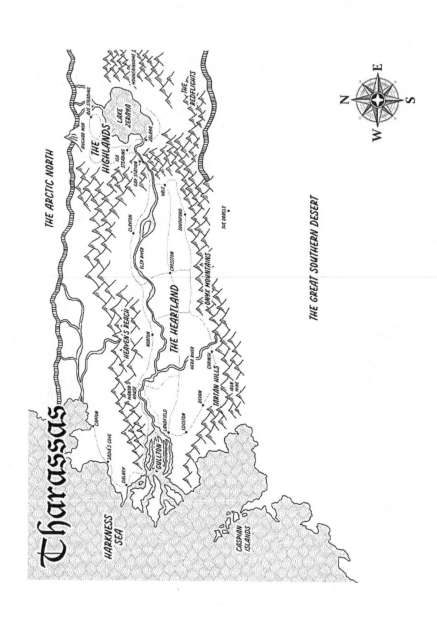

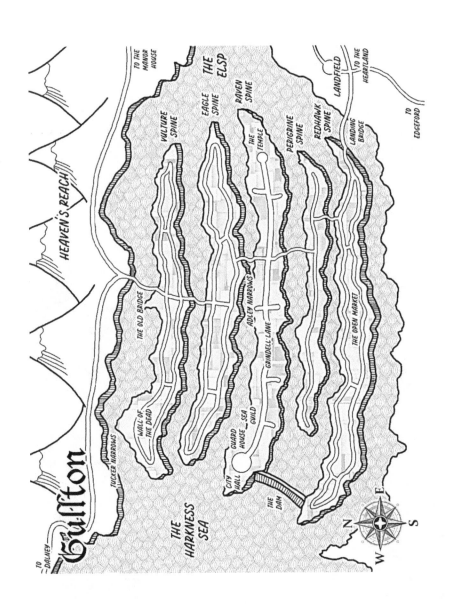

# PROLOGUE

OUT OF NOTHING CAME EVERYTHING.

She awakened, feeling the dual tug of gravity. The world pulled at her from below, and two moons exerted their force on her from above, their demands filtered through numerous layers of igneous rock.

*What am I?*

An explosion of memory stunned her, shaking her to her nascent mycelium where they anchored her to the hard, rocky ground. Past lives flooded her, teeming in her mind, jockeying for attention.

Angrily she stuffed them away, not ready to face them yet. There were more important things to attend to first.

*Where am I?*

The hard, black crust of her spore shell cracked, and she extended a blood-red pseudopod to explore her surroundings.

The world around her was cold and dark, a large space devoid of light and life. She was all alone.

Withdrawing into her shell, she folded in on herself with a shudder.

She dipped into her troubled memories, skimming the surface. They supplied the answer. One of her foremothers had come here long before, descending from the frozen void to this alien world, carrying the hope of her people with her.

*A new home.*

The suppressed memories — a wealth of information and wisdom — bubbled just beneath the surface of her mind.

*I have a past.* No ... that wasn't quite right. *It's not mine.*

But where were the others? She was all alone in a cold, strange place, but most importantly she was alive.

*Why am I here?*

Her memories called for her attention.

She contemplated them for a moment. They represented the past — someone else's past. Did she really want to let it guide her?

Then again, she needed knowledge if she were to survive in this strange new world. Her foremothers had clearly failed. *I can learn from their mistakes.*

Decided, she pried the lid off that seething cauldron. Knowledge flooded her, wiping away her ill-formed conception about who and what she was and replacing them with certainty. Memories and ideas flowed through her like a tsunami, carrying with them the stench of failure from her foremothers. There were gaps — she knew that immediately, but still the sheer volume of them was overwhelming. The tide soaked her, a broken and mangled account of what had come before.

When it passed, she began to absorb all that she had learned. At last she knew who she was.

*I am the spore mother.* The last of her kind, with a chance to remake the world for her people, the Aaveen.

And one thing more.

*This has all happened before.* She wasn't the first of her kind in this desolate place, but she was the only survivor.

Ready to face the world at last, she burst out of her spore, her red crown expanding in the dark place just as her memories had expanded in her mind.

She had a purpose — to transform this world for her own kind. The spore mothers who had come before her — who now *were* her — would guide her.

*And this time I will not fail.*

# 1

## PETTY THEFT

S PIN'S VOICE ECHOED IN HIS EAR. "This is a bad idea, boss."
"Shush," Raven whispered to his familiar.

He needed to concentrate. Cheek and jowl against the smooth cobblestones, he held his breath and prayed to the gods that no one had seen him duck under the sea master's ornate carriage. The setting sun cast long shadows from a pair of boots so close to his face that the dust and leather made him want to sneeze. Their owner was deep in conversation with the sea master, the hem of her fine *mur* silk trousers barely visible. The two women's voices were hushed, and he could only make out the occasional word.

Raven rubbed the old burn scar on his cheek absently, wishing they would go away.

"Seriously, boss. I'm not from this world, and even *I* know it's a bad idea to steal from the sea master."

Though only he could hear Spin's voice, Raven wished the little silver *ay-eye* would just shut up.

The *hencha* cloth-wrapped package in the carriage above was calling to him. He'd wanted it since he'd first seen it through the open door. No, *needed* it. Like he needed air, even though he had

1

no idea what was inside. He scratched the back of his hand hard to distract himself from its disturbing pull.

An *inthym* popped its head out of the sewer grate in front of him, sniffing the air. Raven glared at the little white rodent, willing it to go away. Instead, the cursed thing nibbled at his nose.

Raven sneezed, then covered his mouth. He held his breath, staring at the boots. *Don't let them hear me.*

A shiny silver feeler poked out of his shirt pocket, emitting a golden glow that illuminated the cobblestones underneath him. "Boss, you all right?" Spin's whisper had that sarcastic edge he often used when he was annoyed. "Your heart rate is elevated."

"Be. Quiet." Raven gritted his teeth. Spin had the worst sense of timing.

The woman — one of the guard, maybe? — and the sea master stepped away, their voices fading into the distance.

Raven said a quick prayer of thanks to Jor'Oss, the goddess of wild luck, and flicked the *inthym* back into the sewer. "Shoo!"

He popped his head out from under the carriage to take a quick look around. There was no one between him and the squat gray Sea Guild headquarters. It was time. *Grab it and go.*

He reached into the luxurious carriage — a host of *mur* beetles must have spent years spinning all the red silk that lined the interior — and snagged the package. He hoped it was the treasury payment for the week. If so, it should hold enough coin to feed an orphanage for a month, and he knew just the one. "Got it."

"Good. Now get us out of here."

A strange tingling surged through his hand. Raven frowned. *Must have pinched a nerve or something.*

Ignoring it, he stuck the package under his arm, slipped around the carriage, and set off down Gullton's main thoroughfare. He walked as casually as he could, hoping no one would notice the missing package until he was long gone.

"We clear?"

Spin's feeler blinked red. "No. Run! They've seen you."

Raven ran.

He didn't know how his strange little friend did it, but he trusted Spin. When his familiar's far vision worked, he was almost always right.

2

"Stop the thief!" A guard's voice echoed down Grindell Lane between the shops that loomed over Raven like jagged teeth in the dimming light. Passersby turned to stare, but no one intervened.

"Holy green hell, what's in this thing?" Raven clung to the package, his patched-up boots thudding down the cobblestone street. He said a brief prayer of thanks to El'Oss, the Old God, that Spin's special powers were working.

He shot a glance over his shoulder at the pursuing guardsmen. A miasma of fog mixed with smoke lay thick across the city streets, lighting the sunset in the green sky behind him gloriously in red and gold.

*You're daft as a gully bird, Rav'Orn.* Stealing a package from the sea master's carriage in broad daylight? Seriously? If the Thieves' Guild found out, they'd be after him again for stirring up trouble.

Still, he hadn't expected three guardsmen to come after him. *What in Heaven's Reach did I steal, the* Hencha Queen's *jewels?*

A woman lay slumped in the doorway of a closed tailor's shop ahead, The Knotted Purse, wrapped in a familiar blanket. Raven skidded to a halt. "Where are they?"

"About a block away. You're not as slow as usual today." Coming from Spin, that was *almost* a compliment.

"Thanks." Raven ignored his companion's snarky tone. He slipped his hand into his pocket and pulled out a single silver *croner* and dropped it into the roofless woman's hand, ignoring her unwashed smell. Not everyone had a bathtub or a river to bathe in, after all. "Get yourself something hot to eat, Scilla." He kissed her cheek.

Scill'Eya's eyes lit up, and a smile cracked her weathered face. A single tear ran down her dirty cheek, revealing the ruddy skin underneath, and she nodded. "Nor'Oss bless you, Rav'Orn."

Spin's voice chimed urgently in his ear. "Let's move it. They're hot on your tail, boss."

But Raven was already off and running again, barreling down the street.

He glanced over his shoulder in time to see the roofless woman stumble to her feet and career "accidentally" into the path of one of the guards, knocking him to the ground.

*Bless you too, Scilla.*

3

The garishly painted buildings of the city's commerce district blurred into the darkening green sky as he sprinted down the central street of Gullton's main spine, the long, skinny, rocky protrusions carved out by the Elsp as she ran to the sea.

Rain slicked the cobbles, slowly evaporating into an earthy mist, equal parts water and manure. "Which way?"

"Go left! You're cutting it awfully close." Spin seemed almost as worked up as he was.

Raven swerved left and ducked under the skeletal beams of the new three-story wood-framed building that had replaced Landers' Pub. *Shame about that.* He'd found some of his best marks there. Rich folk from Peregrine Spine, easy pickings after a long night drinking.

He burst out of the other side onto Yorkser Lane and slammed full-on into a fruit vendor's cart, tumbling head over foot and sending apples flying everywhere. The package slipped out from under his arm to clatter across the street into the gutter.

Raven sat up and touched his pocket — Spin was still tucked firmly inside. "You okay?"

Spin was quiet. Whether surly or damaged, Raven couldn't tell.

*Farking hells.* He should just leave the cursed bundle and get out of sight, but it pulled at him again, making him feel queasy. *Godsdammit.*

Then he saw a little chunk of silver, spinning on the cobblestones. He grabbed it and shoved it back into his ear. It melded to him again.

"— coming! You need to haul ass."

Raven grinned. Spin was his usual truculent self — thank the gods. He sprang up and checked himself — no permanent damage, just a scrape on his left elbow. He snagged the package, wiping off the *urse* droppings as best he could, and took off again.

The vendor had pulled himself up off the ground, and now the man tried to grab him, missing the tail of his shirt by a hair. "Damned gully rat!" His face was red, his long stringy hair in disarray. "Watch where you're going!"

"Sorry!" He called back over his shoulder. In normal circumstances, he'd have stopped to help pick up all those apples, but he was a bit busy fleeing the law. "Spin, where are they?"

"I can't tell. You've got eyes. Use them."

4

"Seven hells." Jor'Oss and his blasted luck had turned against him. Spin could see things he couldn't, but sometimes the ay-eye's mysterious ability just went away. *Of all the godscursed times ...*

He glanced over his shoulder. *No guards yet.* Turning back, he almost ran headlong into a carriage made from the frame of an old flitter — the flying machine's rotor had been chopped off, and wooden wheels added to make it mobile again. Someone had decided to paint the thing gold, and the results were more hideous than elegant.

He pulled open the door and slipped through the cabin. The startled inhabitant — a wealthy woman from Peregrine Spine, by the look of her and her rich silk dress, screamed.

"Pardon me!" Then he was out the other side, leaving her and her carriage behind.

He ducked around the corner at Tuckins Street, running down the short, narrow lane toward the edge of his namesake, Raven Spine, where the cliff dropped off to the thundering waters of the Elsp thirty meters below.

"Good going, boss."

"Just glad you're still alive." For all that Spin liked to cut him down to size, he was Raven's only constant companion. *And friend.*

He stuffed the package down his pants.

"Nice to know you care."

Raven grabbed the spume-slick railing that lined the plaza at the end of the street and vaulted over it with the ease of long practice. He landed hard on the other side and slipped over the edge, lowering himself onto the first of the rusty metal pitons driven into the slate-gray rock long before.

A flurry of blue wisps surrounded him as if he'd disturbed them, their light painting the cliff walls an ethereal blue, before floating up into the air over Gullton and catching the sea breeze.

*Weird little things.* He shook his head and continued down. Nimble as an *eircat*, he descended hand over hand, grasping the wet rods tightly.

He dropped the last half-meter to a hidden ledge, well below street level, and slid over to the widest spot with his back against the cliff. His chest heaved from the exertion. *Almost there.*

Someone slammed onto the narrow ledge, scaring the *hencha* berries out of him.

He spun around to face the newcomer, and his left foot slipped off the narrow rock shelf, bits of it crumbling underneath him to fall into the river. He scrambled for something to grab onto, but his hands clawed at the slick walls of the spine without finding purchase. *Jas help me!*

A large hand grabbed his shirt, pushing him back against the rock.

"We've got company, boss."

*Tell me something I don't know.* Raven panted, looking down at the red rushing waters of the river, realizing how close he'd come to falling into that abyss.

He turned to glare at the intruder. "What in the green holy hell, Aik? You almost scared me to death. Literally."

"You're welcome." Aik's face was half-hidden in the dimming light, but the part Raven could see didn't look very happy.

"That was close." Spin's voice was a mix of angry and scared out of his little metal hide.

"Quiet."

"What?" Aik glared at him

Raven covered his pocket with his free hand, hoping Spin would get the hint. "I said 'quiet.' I need to think." His breathing slowed. "I wouldn't have *almost* fallen, if you hadn't scared me in the first place —"

"You ran by me like the Queen's own wrath was coming down on you." Aik stared at him. "What did you do this time? You've got half the Guard after you."

"There *is* no Queen." Raven squeezed Spin in warning. They'd been through this before. If anyone else found out about him, they would take him away and probably treat him far worse than Raven did.

When he was sure Spin would stay quiet and not distract him, he turned his attention to his annoyed friend. "Besides, we were just out for a little exercise."

"We?"

"*I* was. I needed to get out of the lair for a bit. It gets ... lonely down there."

Aik raised an eyebrow. "That's bullshit, and you know it." Aik was both menacing and handsome in his City Guard uniform — a smart black leather jacket with the double white stripe of a rookie on the shoulders. Adorable too — with his big ears that stuck out from his head like sails and made it hard to take anything he said too seriously, guard or no. But he was mostly annoying. Especially when he interrupted Raven in the middle of a heist.

He shook his head. "Really, it's nothing." He tried to cover his stolen goods, but there was no way to hide the bulge in his pants.

Aik's eyebrow raised. "Nice package. What's in it?"

Raven groaned. "It's ... I don't know. I found it."

"Found it? Where, exactly?"

Raven *knew* that tone. He never lied to Aik. Not directly. "All right, I took it. You happy?"

"Not even a little." Aik crossed his arms, an impressive feat standing on the narrow ledge. "From whom?"

"From the sea master."

"Raven!" Alarm flashed in Aik's eyes.

"I had to." The package *had* called to him — no other way to describe it. From the second he'd laid his eyes on the cloth-wrapped bundle, he'd known he needed to have it. *Not my fault.*

Aik pointed up the cliff face. "Take it back. Now." He pleaded with Raven. "Tell them you made a mistake. You didn't *mean* to do it."

Raven looked away. They both knew he wouldn't. Couldn't. After the last time ... *And why should I? It's mine.*

Far below, the waters of the Elsp, red with silt from the Heartland, rumbled through Adley Narrows, reminding him how close he'd come to falling.

"Remember what happened the last time I turned myself in, on your advice?" *And what* almost *happened.* He flexed his right hand; grateful it was still attached. "Besides, if the Guild finds out ..."

Aik growled. "Let the Guard worry about the Thieves' Guild." His expression shifted, sadness tinting the corners of his eyes. "You're not fifteen anymore, Rave. One of these days, you're going to get yourself into something so deep even I can't pull you out."

"Probably. But not today." Raven flashed Aik one of his winning grins. "Come on down to the lair with me. You can try to convince me later." He glanced up toward the street nervously. "I need to get out of sight until things cool down."

Aik glanced upward. "Rave, I can't ..."

"Suit yourself. You can always tell them I gave you the slip."
*Probably for the best.* The last time Aik had visited him, they'd
done more than talk. He'd regretted it ever since.

From the look on Aik's face, he was thinking about that night
too. He snarled, but his gaze lingered on Raven's package. The
stolen one. "Dammit, Rave ..."

"Come on, then." He kissed Aik's cheek, then turned and felt
his way along the cool rock of the spine wall, sure Aik would
follow. He always did.

Raven's fingers searched for the narrow cavern entrance in
the dimming evening light.

Aik did follow. He shuffled along the ledge behind him, letting
out a long-suffering sound. The guard was loyal as an *auracinth*,
and almost as big. He was also Raven's only real human friend.
"How do I let you get me into these things?"

"Because you love me?" He was not going to turn himself in
again, risking hand and livelihood. No matter what Aik said or did.

Aik snorted. "Less and less."

They both knew that wasn't true. Still, there was no future in it,
was there? *The thief and the guard? How would that even work?* Aik
had his service career ahead of him, and Raven had an underground
cavern full of stolen goods. A thief's life, and one he was quite happy
with, thank you very much. It was an old dilemma, as worn as Raven's
boots. "Coming?"

"Do I have a choice?"

"We all have choices." Sometimes he regretted his, but he'd
never tell Aik that. Raven's fingers found the crevice in the black
cliff face. He pulled the package out of his pants, holding it in front
of him, and slipped inside. *I hope you're worth it.*

A shower of pebbles fell into the gloomy narrows behind him.
The oppressive rock walls squeezed him like a bug, scraping his
shirt as he pushed his way through. It was a godsall narrow passage,
but it was the closest entrance to the tunnels. *Don't think about the
tons of rock bearing down on you.* The other guards would never find
it, and even if they did, those thick thugs would be hard-pressed to
get through. Even poor Aik could barely manage it.

"You so love him." Spin's voice in his ear sounded less mocking
than usual, almost wistful.

8

Raven didn't bother to reply. Spin could be a pain in the ass when he wanted to, which was most of the time. One of the reasons Raven loved him.

"Careful. Don't want to put a scratch on my pretty hide."

Raven grimaced. "Spin, shut down." He said it softly so Aik wouldn't hear. *A guy's gotta have some secrets.*

"Aw, Master of Thieves ... are you sure?" Spin hated being shut off.

"Now, Spin." Raven growled as he pushed his way through the narrow space.

"Yes, boss." The light in Raven's pocket went dark.

Raven sucked in his stomach and pushed on, blowing his lanky dark red hair away from his eyes. With one last push, he broke through at last and stumbled into darkness. The air in the tunnels was warm, still, and familiar. He was home.

Raven breathed a sigh of relief and set down the package to feel around for the candle and striker that he kept there for emergencies. Usually Spin lit the way for him, but today ... His hands touched something soft that squealed. "Aiieee!"

He jerked his hand back as the creature scurried away in the dark. *Farking inthym.*

"What's wrong?" Aik's forceful voice, amplified by the narrow passage, startled him

"Nothing. Just a rodent." They were everywhere these days. Raven's heartbeat slowed. He took a couple deep breaths to calm himself. *Nasty little creatures.* "You coming?" He felt around again, and his hand closed on the candle. *Gotcha.*

Aik grunted. "Yeah. Tell me again why I'm going along with this petty theft?"

"Because you're my friend."

He said it too softly for Aik to hear, but that, at least, was true. Aloud, he said, "Because you want to keep me out of trouble, and I'm not going back up there." That was also true.

He cracked the flint against the striker with enough force to light a spark. It took six tries, but at last the candle wick caught, illuminating the tunnel's dark, jagged walls. "And we have light —"

Aik popped out of the narrow gap and stumbled into him, slamming them both to the ground, pinning Raven to the tunnel floor and knocking the wind out of him. Aik's close proximity set off all kinds of alarms in Raven's head as he struggled to breathe. He gasped, trying not to panic.

"You all right?" Aik's blue eyes locked on him, the flickering light of the candle revealing a worried frown.

At last, sweet, musky air filled Raven's lungs. "Yeah. Just ... lost my breath."

Aik smelled ripe from a long day at work. Raven looked up at him in the golden light, and memories of Aik's touch surged through him like fire. He wanted to reach out and run his hands through Aik's short-cropped blond hair. To kiss him hard ...

*Bad idea. Kissing* led to *love* led to *waiting for your guy to come home*, and Raven wanted none of that. He squirmed out from under Aik, scrambling away from him as if he had the plague. He'd let himself get carried away with Aik before. *Never again.*

Aik's eyes narrowed, shooting Raven a *so that's how it's going to be?* look.

"Sorry." He frowned. *What am I sorry for?*

Aik got up and brushed off his jacket. "Farking hell, it's torn."

"You should have taken it off first. Didn't that happen last time too?" Raven rolled his eyes — Aik never learned. He got up and dusted off his own clothes, adjusting his trousers and avoiding Aik's gaze.

"You're an asshole."

Raven laughed harshly. "Tell me something I don't know." *You'd be better off without me.* He sighed and grabbed the candle and the package. "Let's go."

He managed one step forward before Aik hauled him backwards by his collar.

"What the hell?"

Aik pointed at the darkness ahead. "What in Heaven's Reach is that?"

Raven shook off his grasp and followed his gaze. At least a hundred pairs of tiny blue lights filled the passageway ahead of them at the edge of the candle's glow. *What in the holy hencha?*

He held up the light to reveal a squirming mass of *inthyms*, little white noses twitching, pale pink ears pointing at him. At his stolen package. His stomach tightened, adrenaline rushing through his veins.

10

"Scat!" He stomped, and they scattered into the darkness, the blue lights of their eyes winking out. "That was creepy as hell."

Aik stared at him, skin pale in the dim light. "What's happening? First your mysterious package, then this ..."

Raven shrugged. "I don't know." The whole thing creeped him out. He sniffed the air, making like one of the little rodents. "Maybe they like your cologne."

Aik rolled his eyes. "I'm not wearing any. Not that you'd care."

Raven slapped his shoulder. "I really don't. Come on. The lair awaits."

He was eager to get back to his home, and away from all the strangeness. His neck tingled where Aik's fingers had brushed his skin, but he pushed the sensation away and set off down the narrow passageway, not waiting to see if his friend would follow. Because of course he would.

Things had been weirder than usual lately in the caverns beneath Gullton. There'd been strange noises, glowing wisps floating through the tunnels, and blue eyes staring at him from dark crevices — eyes that disappeared when he held the light close. More *inthym*? *Or maybe I'm losing my mind.*

Like a child afraid of the dark, he was selfishly glad Aik was there with him.

The floors of the tunnel were smooth, the walls a deep black — not gray and flaked like the rock outside, where they'd been battered for thousands of years by sun and rain. Here, they sparkled in the candlelight, riddled with seams — fine cracks that ran from floor to ceiling.

The passage led into the heart of the spine, always about the same width and height, eventually turning east to follow it lengthwise.

They padded down it together in tense silence.

After a short trek, the tunnel branched into two, the faint suggestion of an ancient, hand-carved arch framing both entrances. Raven took the left fork without thinking, glancing over his shoulder at his friend.

Aik was quiet, a frown plastered on his face.

The horde of *inthym* had vanished, and the knot in Raven's stomach loosened. *Creepy little farks.*

11

"How do you find your way around down here?" Aik's voice was clipped.

"Ah, so it *can* talk." Silent Aik was better than angry Aik, he decided. "I don't know. I just do."

Raven veered right at the next fork, and the tunnel began to descend.

"It all looks exactly the same."

"Not to me." In his mind, he could see all the branching tunnels, one connecting to the next like the roots of a tree. After he visited a place once, he could navigate it forever. It was one of his talents, along with his ability to fade into the background — a trait most useful for a thief.

As they descended, the walls began to glow, the seams between the black rocks suffused with a blue light not unlike that of the wisps. At first it was subtle, but as they progressed, the light burned brighter, until the cracks fairly blazed with cold fire.

Raven sighed in relief. *Almost there.*

Aik followed him over a pile of rubble that nearly cut the tunnel in two, taking care not to further damage his uniform. "Don't you ever get lonely down here?"

The question caught him off-guard. "Not really. I like it. No demands. No authority." *No complications.*

His friend was lucky. He still had a home and family up above. Well, a mother who loved him, anyhow. *Mamma, what would you think of me now?* He shoved his jealousy and the familiar pain into the ever-growing pile of *things he didn't want to think about.*

The burbling sound of water ahead snapped him out of it — it always made him feel welcome. This was *his* place, and no one else's. "Come on. We're almost there." Raven licked his fingers, extinguished the candle, and dropped it into his pocket. The tunnel opened into a broad natural cavern, well-lit by the soft blue glow of the walls — a glorious collection of stalactites and stalagmites that formed fantastical columns and rows of dragon's teeth. The tension in his shoulders eased. *Home sweet home.*

Once a calm cathedral of water and stone, the grand space was now Raven's personal lair. He'd filled it with objects collected from the world above, shiny things that caught his attention and made it feel homier, including antiques from Old Earth. There were pots and pans, ancient ceramic vases, gears and jewelry and even books — not so many of those, but they were the most precious of all.

Aik looked around, taking in the piles that covered the floor and the layers of things that hung from the black-rock pillars. "Still messy as a gully bird's nest." He reached out to touch the dark stone wall, his fingers eclipsing the glow from the cracks. "This place would be beautiful without all your junk."

Raven saw it through Aik's eyes and forced a smile. "It was empty and lonely when I found it." *The night I ran away from Mim Aza. And Jimey.* "All this *junk* makes it feel like home." He moved a stack of leather-bound journals out of the way with his boot, making room for Aik to reach his "bed"— a collection of pillows and blankets piled up in one corner of the cavern between two thick black columns.

Aik stared at him. "Sorry. I'm just tense. I shouldn't be here." He looked pointedly at the bundle in Raven's hand. "Should we get to it?"

Raven's heart skipped a beat, and then it sunk in. *The package.* "You can leave whenever you want. No one's keeping you here." He felt the tug of whatever was inside again. He was dying to open it to see the sea master's treasure.

Aik glared at him. "You invited me, remember?" He picked up a silver-framed mirror from the flat top of a broken stalagmite which formed a narrow table. "What's this?"

"Give that to me." He snatched it out of Aik's hands, and immediately regretted his harsh tone. "Sorry, it was my mother's. It's one of the few things I have left of her." He glanced at himself in the mirror and frowned at the grime on his face and the faded scar across his right cheek. He did the best he could to wipe off the dirt with the back of his hand and then set the mirror down reverently.

"And this bit of junk?" Aik held up a piece of metal engraved with the words "*Spin Diver.*"

Raven forced himself to set the package down on his bed, ignoring its siren call. "That's from the last Run. I found it out at the edge of Landfield." *Along with Spin.*

Aik snorted. "You really believe that nonsense? Spaceships and angels and faraway planets? What are you, six years old?" Aik's mocking grin made Raven's stomach clench.

13

"Of course I do. My mother told me all about it — her grandfather was there when it crashed." Raven's nostrils flared. "You've seen the fountain in Landfield, right?"

"Yeah, I've seen it. Just a bit of artistic wreckage — it doesn't prove anything." He dropped the metal fragment with a clang. "I mean, it just seems fantastic, doesn't it? That we all came from another world? Fairy tales for children." He bit his lip. "Silya believes it too. That we all came here in some flitter from another star. It's ridiculous."

"A starship. Not a flitter." *Should I tell him about Spin?* Raven pushed that thought away. *No good would come of it.*

He sank down onto one of his favorite cushions, stolen from a Market Day booth the year before — a deep royal blue embroidered with golden thread, probably meant for the household of one of the rich merchants who lived on the slopes of Heaven's Reach along the northern edge of the Heartland. His hand strayed toward the package, moving of its own accord. Angrily he pulled it back. He wanted to open it so badly. Perversely, that made him *not* want to do it.

"Starship, flitter, it's all the same." Aik picked up a metal spiral, shiny and silver, encrusted with strange red things that might have been gems, or glass. "What's this?"

"I don't know ... I found a few of them down here in the tunnels. I call them artifacts." He scowled at Aik. "You gonna pick through all of my things?"

Aik's cheeks turned a bright red. "Right. Sorry." He sank down on the bed, too close for comfort, his arm brushing Raven's. He put a hand on Raven's knee, sending a shiver up his leg. "I worry about you, all alone like this." He looked around the cluttered cavern, making it clear that *like this* really meant *in this trash heap.*

Raven lifted Aik's wandering hand and set it firmly on his friend's lap, acutely aware of his proximity. Of what he *really* wanted.

It irked him that Aik didn't believe in Earth. He'd seen a hundred things to convince him that the legend was real, but some people had their heads stuck in the sand. He hated that Aik was one of them.

Still, there was a way he could distract Aik *and* convince him about Earth, if he dared. Risky, but he trusted Aik.

He bit his lip. It was lonely, living down here. And he'd kept the secret for so long. *I can trust you, can't I?*

Decided, he put a little distance between them and pulled his familiar out of his pocket. "Spin, wake up. Full audio."

The circular piece of metal lit up, golden lights rolling around its edge. "Why'd you have to shut me off like that, boss?" Spin shifted from a flat disc to a silver sphere in Raven's hand.

Aik pushed himself away so fast he fell off the edge of the low bed. "What in the holy Heartland is that?" He stared at Spin. His eyes were as big as platters.

Raven grinned. "Aik, meet Spin, my familiar. It's what witches used to call their animal companions, back on Old Earth." He was proud of that, something he'd picked up in one of his books.

"Technically *You're* the animal, Boss." He extended a little silver tentacle to "see" Aik better. "Hello, Aik." Golden light flitted across Aik's form for a split second. "My, you are a big one."

"He says he's an ay-eye — that was some kind of smart machine back on Old Earth."

Aik rubbed the back of his neck, his gaze flicking from Spin to Raven. "What in the seven hells is it?"

"Him, not it." Spin sounded indignant.

Raven laughed. "Sit down, Aik. He's harmless." He pulled out the hearing aid from his ear and set it on Spin's side, and it melted back into the silver surface like candle wax.

"Seriously, what is that?" Aik's voice lost some of its edge, a little curiosity seeping in. "It looks like bad magic."

Raven shook his head. "It's not magic. It's technology. He's the pilot from the *Spin Diver* — on the last Run."

Spin slipped into what Raven called lecture mode. "Ship mind. Or Artificial Intelligence, serving at the pleasure of the ship captain, Sera Collins. The Master of Thieves here's not so good with science and facts — he has these delusions of grandeur ..."

"Delusions ..." Aik was even paler than normal.

"He means I think too much of myself."

That got a rueful chuckle from Aik. "He's right about that." His shoulders relaxed. A little.

"Hey." Raven didn't need his two friends ganging up on him together.

"Still — technology is a *new wheel design*. Or those wires they strung from the old dam to the Temple for those new lights." Aik crept closer, eyes locked on Spin's perfect sphere. "Where did you find that thing?"

Raven's familiar interrupted again. "Call me Spin, please. Or Mas Spin, as you folks say here on Tharassas."

Raven shrugged. "Landfield. It's a long story. Now do you believe that Earth was real?"

"I don't know." Aik shuddered, his eyes locked on Spin as if he expected the little sphere to explode. "Are you sure it's safe?"

Spin shimmered, his version of a laugh. "I don't think he believes you, Raven."

Raven grunted. *Maybe I shouldn't have shown him.* Sometimes his impulses went horribly wrong. Like the last time Aik had been in the lair. He slipped Spin back into his vest pocket, and felt the little familiar shift to accommodate himself to the tight space.

At least the whole thing had put some necessary distance between him and Aik. "So … the package?" He needed to see what was inside. He looked down and found it in his hands again. *That's weird.*

Spin's feeler popped out to watch.

Aik gave it a wary glance but sat back down on the bed next to Raven, leaving half a meter between him and Raven's pocket. "You can still take it back. Or give it to me. I can tell them I found it. No one has to know it was you." Aik's beautiful ice-blue eyes locked with Raven's, and a shiver raced down his spine.

They'd never been more than friends, and never could be, though he'd let his guard down with Aik more than once. Aik was warm, and sweet, and gentle … Aik was … well, Aik. Beautiful. Loyal. Good. And a guard to boot. *We have no future.* "They'll know. They saw me with it."

"Still, if I take it back, and you lie low for a bit …" Aik glanced nervously at Raven's pocket, as if expecting Spin to climb out and attack him.

Raven rolled his eyes. Aik would get used to Spin sooner or later. Or he wouldn't. "Maybe." He traced the package's square corners. "Don't you want to know what's inside?"

"*I* do." Spin sounded impatient. "The boss here was acting really weird around it earlier —"

"Look who's talking." Raven glared at his familiar.

Aik stared at Spin warily too. "We shouldn't." But his gaze slid back to the package.

*Do you feel it too?* "What's the harm?" Raven's fingers itched to open it.

Aik looked up at Raven, searching his eyes for something.

Raven put on his best pleading look, the one that could melt the hearts of angry shopkeepers. The one he used to charm his way into bed with the more handsome ones. "Pleeeease?"

Spin chimed in. "Pretty pleeease?"

"That thing's as annoying as you are. I can see why you like each other." He held Raven's gaze. "This is a bad idea, Rave. You're more than all this. Smart and funny — if you worked half as hard at an actual job as you do at thieving —"

*Not on my life.* "This *is* my job. Besides, where's your sense of adventure? Are you *scared*?"

Aik snorted. "Hardly. You're going to be impossible until we do this, aren't you?"

Raven grinned. "Yes I am."

"Just a quick look, then we wrap it back up. Promise?"

"We'll see." Raven unwrapped the rough brown cloth eagerly, wrinkling his nose at the smell of *urse* manure from his tumble in the street. He pulled out the contents and whistled appreciatively.

Inside was a filigreed silver box, its surface a series of swirls and dots that ran all the way around it, creating the illusion of a seamless surface. He held it up, examining it in the blue cavern light. It was warm to the touch. "It's beautiful."

Spin's golden glow bathed the box. "It's pure silver, boss." The familiar whistled, impressive given that he didn't have a mouth.

Aik shot spin a worried glance and scratched his neck, his eyes narrowing. "All this trouble for a little metal box? Can I see it?"

"I guess?" Raven handed it over reluctantly. "I wonder what it's for."

"Maybe it's not *for* anything." Aik looked it over. "It's very good work — probably from Dalney up north. They have fine metalsmiths there. A jewelry box for the sea master's mistress?"

"Maybe. Wait, does she have one?" Gossip like that might be worth something on the street. His eyes remained glued on the box.

Aik gave him a *like I'd tell you* look. The Guard kept secrets for a lot of powerful people. He turned the box over, peering at it more closely. "It's heavy, though. There must be something inside."

No telltale metallic clanking, No coin, then. Raven had hoped for something he could sell, but the little box would be too recognizable, too hot to unload it easily, and that would definitely put him on the Thieves' Guild's radar again. He had no desire to give them a cut of his earnings. He had an orphanage to feed, after all.

Still, if he could convince Aik to let him keep it, maybe he could sell it in the spring —

"Hey, look at this." Aik rubbed a raised spot on the side of the box.

"Let me see."

"Me too." Spin sounded almost as eager as Raven felt.

Aik handed the box back, his fingers brushing Raven's.

Raven ignored the touch. He ran a dirty thumbnail along the edge of the bump. It popped open, revealing a small lock. "Ah, now we're getting somewhere." The box hummed under his touch, and his desire to open it grew. "That's weird."

"What?" Aik's sour expression said he'd had his fill of *weird* for one day.

"Feel it."

Aik touched the box and raised an eyebrow. "Can you open it?"

Raven snorted. "*Can I open it?* Does the *Hencha Queen* live in the Temple?"

"Not currently."

Raven chuckled. "Fair enough. But yes, I can open it." He pulled his set of lock picks from his vest pocket and chose one small enough to prod at the innards of the fine lock on the silver box. He'd paid a locksmith good money for them. "Let's see. If I can just find the tumbler ..."

He teased the lock, feeling for the opening mechanism. It was nicely made — someone must have paid a lot of money for it. "There, think I've got it ..." The lock snapped open with a satisfying click. Raven lifted the lid.

Inside was a smooth purple ovoid about the size of two fists, nestled in a bundle of rich red *mur* silk.

Spin whistled. "Pretty. That and a copper *croner* will buy you a cup of coffee —"

18

*What in the hell was coffee?* "Spin, quiet." Raven stared at the thing, frowning, and his heart sank. "What am supposed to do with this?" At least he could still sell the box. Eventually.

"What in the green holy hell is it?" Aik looked up at Raven, eyes wide. He made the infinity sign across his chest to ward off Jor'Oss's bad luck.

"You mean *purple* holy hell?" He picked up the ovoid. It was warm to the touch, and it was vibrating. "I don't know." *Looks like an egg. But for what?*

Spin's golden glow swept it. "Organic. There's something alive inside. Might want to put it back in the box, boss."

Raven held it up for a better look and felt a surge of need, a deep ache almost sexual in its intensity. "I ... can't."

"Rave, just put it away." Aik's voice was shaky. "Come on. You had your fun — "

A loud *crack* echoed through the room.

The shell split apart in his hand, and something white uncoiled from inside, wrapping itself around his arm in a flash.

"What the seven hells?" Raven scrambled backward across the bed, shards of the shell flying everywhere as the thing slipped up his arm, fast as an *eircat*.

"Get it off!" Raven leapt up, shaking his arm wildly.

Aik laughed. "Calm down, Raven." He sprang to his feet, trying to grab the little beast.

It slithered past his elbow, scales hot against his skin.

*Should have listened to you.*

Raven tried to shake the thing off, knocking Aik away in his haste. "Get it off me!" His vision turned red as his heart tried to pound its way out of his chest.

"Hold still. I'm trying to help." Aik sounded exasperated.

The creature slithered up Raven's arm, and he grabbed at it, managing to pull it off at last. He threw it against one of the grand columns that held up the ceiling of the lair, and it emitted a startled little *yip*. It would have been funny if he weren't so terrified.

The creature slid down to the floor, but then it got up and shook its head, its blue eyes meeting his, and leapt at him.

He flailed around, trying to get it off again, but it was too fast. It scrambled up his leg like a mountaineer.

19

"Raven, your heart rate is elevated —"

"Of course it is, Spin. Tell me something helpful!"

It ascended his torso and slipped onto his shoulder, wrapping its tail around his neck.

He tried to pry the godscursed thing off, but it was constricting his throat too tightly. He gasped for air and fell to his knees.

*This isn't funny anymore.* "Help me!" It came out as a hoarse whisper.

The creature forced its head into his mouth, cutting off his voice. Its warm scales slid smooth against his tongue.

*Help me!* His eyes pleaded with Aik, who had his short sword out but was blinking rapidly.

"I don't want to hurt you!"

The creature plunged into his throat on its way down to his stomach. It was a horrid sensation. He tried to breathe, to throw up, but both were denied him.

He grasped its tail, but it slipped out of his grip as the last of the creature disappeared into his mouth.

Aik was staring at him in horror.

"Boss, you have to cough it up."

*Not helping.* Raven choked. He hacked and gagged, his eyes bulging as the creature suffocated him. He clawed at his throat, trying to make himself throw up, to expel the creature from his body.

Warmth flooded his trousers, but he was too far gone to care. *I'm going to die.*

Aik's stark-white face swam in his vision, fading away as Raven fell onto the hard ground of the cavern and blacked out.

# 2

## RUN

*WHAT IN THE SEVEN HELLS was that thing?* "Rave!" Aik was paralyzed, afraid to touch his best friend. Cold sweat beaded his forehead, and his hands shook.

*Snap out of it. Look, learn, leap!*

His guard training kicked in. He looked around wildly. The silver box lay open on its side a few feet from the pile of bedding, surrounded by a smattering of egg shards.

Raven lay on the hard rock floor of the cavern, breathing shallowly. *Thank Hel'Oss.* The *goddir* of death had spared him, for now.

*Get him off the ground.* Pushing through his fear, he knelt beside Raven, lifting him gently, and carried him to his bed. His body was light and pitifully limp. Aik deposited his friend carefully on the soft blankets and put the blue and gold pillow under his head.

A golden light pulsed in Raven's shirt pocket.

*Spin.* He'd almost forgotten the strange little being in the chaos. "Um ... Spin?"

"Yes, Aik?"

"Is Raven ... all right?" *Stay calm. You're no use to him all flustered.*

21

"His heart is beating normally. But he just ingested a native life form, like some fucking scene out of *Alien*. Do you *think* he's okay?"

Aik had no idea what that meant. "I ... no, I guess not." Spin was right — it was a stupid question. *Why am I talking to a machine, or whatever you are?* He said a quick prayer to Jor'Oss to placate her, just in case her wild magic was at work here. "I'm going to take a closer look."

"Suit yourself."

Aik pulled up his friend's shirt and recoiled.

Raven's stomach was moving.

He turned away, his gut twisting, dry heaving and covering his mouth. He managed to keep it down, barely.

He'd only gotten a brief glimpse of the thing before Raven's wild gyrations had knocked him over — his jaw was still sore from the blow. Whatever it was, it had been long and sleek, white and scaly, with short black claws. How had it fit inside that little egg? And were those claws tearing up Raven's stomach? "What in Heaven's Reach was that thing?"

"Sorry. I have insufficient evidence to determine its nature. Please enable a full body scan."

Aik snorted. Now the little familiar was just mocking him with long words.

Whatever the creature was, it was doing no good inside Raven's stomach. *I could cut it out.*

His short sword was in his hand before he took a step back to reconsider. What if it refused to come out? With those claws, it could tear Raven to bits. And how would he sew Raven back together again? He was no surgeon. Raven would surely bleed to death long before Aik could find someone to help put him back together. He bit his lip. "I don't know what to do." He paced back and forth, kicking some of Raven's loose things out of his way.

"Aik, pick me up." Spin was using that same voice his mother used to when she was annoyed with him for being a dimwit but trying not to let him know.

"What? Why?" Aik stared at Raven's familiar, blinking.

"Look, I know you're four quarts short of a gallon, but listen to me. You can do this. Just pick me up."

*What the farking hell is a gallon?* "Um ... sure?" Aik reached into Raven's pocket and pulled the thing out. "Now what?"

"Lift up Raven's shirt and hold me over his stomach."

*Um, all right ...* "Got it."

In seconds, a golden light flashed over his friend's moving belly. An image appeared in the air above the familiar. It was fuzzy, but Aik could make out the long tail, and a blunt snout. "What is it?"

"Unknown. But it's not doing any apparent damage in there."

Aik breathed a sigh of relief. "Thank the gods." He looked around the messy lair. "I have to find help." *But who would believe me?*

"Does Gullton have any real doctors?" Spin's sarcastic tone said he'd already answered his own question.

The Guard had a medic on call at all hours, but Doc Jyn was a hundred years old if he was a day, and he'd never make the journey down the cliff face, let alone through the tunnels. "I know one, but he'll be no help with something like this."

Aik needed someone who would at least listen to him, knew something about medicine, and could make the trip back to Raven's lair.

*Silya.*

He discarded the idea out of hand. Why would she help him, after all he'd done to her? Especially with Raven. She'd sooner see the thief dead than speak to him.

Raven moaned and shifted on the bed, clutching his stomach.

"Rave, you'll come through this. I'll figure something out." Despite Spin's assurances, Aik was scared to death for Raven. He knelt at his friend's side to touch his forehead — it was hot with fever. He waited a few seconds to see if Raven would awaken.

Raven shuddered, then settled into a troubled slumber, muttering in his sleep.

Aik stared at his pale white face. "What should I do?"

"Find someone who's smarter than you are." Spin said it so matter-of-factly, it was almost worse than his previous tone.

"Not helpful." But the familiar was right. He needed someone who could figure this out — it was way above his pay grade.

It was Silya, or nothing.

He kissed Raven's forehead. "Hang tight, Rave. I'm going to bring help." He sent a quick prayer to Hel'Oss, begging the goddess of death not to come for Raven while he was gone. "Spin, will you … I don't know … watch over him while I'm gone?" Though what could a hunk of metal do if anything happened?

"I will. Go." No pithy remark this time.

Aik set the familiar on Raven's chest.

Its shape shimmered and flowed, and then reformed as a silver sphere. Golden lights spun around it, bathing Raven in their glow.

Somehow that made Aik feel better about leaving. He would have to figure out how to explain Spin to Silya later. *Cross that spine …*

Or maybe not. "Spin, I'm going to tuck you away. When I come back, can you be quiet?"

His lights spun around his core. "Yes, Aik. Now get your ass moving. Who knows what that thing inside him plans to do?"

"Got it." Aik stuck Spin behind a couple pillows where Silya wouldn't see him. Then he picked up a few of the egg shards. They were thick — smooth and bluish-purple on the outside and leathery and sticky on the inside. He tucked them into his belt pouch.

Aik searched the room, found the candle Raven had used, and put it and the striker in there too. He'd need that when he got to the dark part of the tunnel. He just hoped he could find his way out and then back again.

He gave Raven one last peck on the cheek. "Hang in there, Rave." Then he set off at a run to bring help. "I'll be back as quick as I can."

•     •     •

Aik hurried down Grindell Lane, praying to Fre'Oss for speed and going as quickly as he could without drawing undue attention. He'd found his way out of the tunnels, a task made easier when he'd noticed Raven's footprints in the heavy dust of the floor leading to and from the exit.

Citizens of the capital city crowded the streets, making their way to the pubs that lined Grindell Lane after a long day's work, for some *hencha* wine and a sandwich or some hearty *aur* steak stew. Clean air was blowing in from the Harkness Sea, clearing out some of the smog that hung over the city in the summer and fall. The two moons were chasing one another across the sky.

A barrel crashed off the back of a moving cart, spilling fish across the cobblestones, and a flock of gully birds left their perches on the irregular terracotta roof lines to flap past him, intent on snagging some of the unexpected bounty. Aik waved them out of his way and pushed on.

The last hour kept replaying in his head on a loop. *Why didn't I stop you? Make you take it back?* He could still see Rave lying there in his lair, breathing shallowly, his skin white as death. *And what in the hell is Spin? I have to find Silya.*

She was an initiate healer at the Temple. She would know what to do. She lived at the Hencha Palace with the other initiates at the far end of Raven Spine, the rocky ridge at the heart of Gullton's five spines.

A hand came down on his shoulder, hard. "Where you think you're going?"

Aik spun around to face one of his superiors. Sergeant Kek was clad all in black, with a blond, neatly trimmed mustache that made him look all the more severe. A hardass who took every opportunity to bust rookies like Aik down to size.

The man stared at him, waiting for his reply.

Aik considered telling him the truth. "See, my friend stole this egg, and then he swallowed a creature whole." *Yeah, that would go well.* He had a promising career in the Guard ahead of him and didn't want to do anything to ruin it. *Damn you, Raven.* "Nowhere, ser." He saluted smartly. "To see my friend at the Temple."

Kek scratched his chin, casting a look back at the way Aik had come. "You on shift, rookie?"

"Just finished, ser."

Kek touched his jacket. "You've got a tear there. Get in a scuffle?"

"No ser, just snagged it on something."

The sergeant grunted; a simple sound loaded with disapproval. "When I was new to the Guard, I was always on duty and always presentable, even when my shift ran out. You'd do well to remember that."

25

"Yes, ser." Aik shifted restlessly. Time was wasting. Raven could be dead or dying ...

"Word's out to look for a young man who stole a package from the sea master. She's mad as a nest of *orinths*, and the Council is looking to make an example of someone — the whole of the Thieves' Guild seems to have gone into hiding. Did you see anything?" The sergeant stared at him as if he could look right through Aik's soul.

*Does he know it's Raven?* Aik shook his head insistently "No. Nothing, ser. I just came from the station." Aik bit his lip. He hated lying, especially to someone like Sergeant Kek, but he didn't want to get Rave — or himself — made into an example. No matter how he sliced it, that couldn't be good. "Please, Ser'Kek. I'm in a hurry to see my friend, Sil'Aya. She's sick. She's at the —"

"Aya?" His eyebrow raised. "One of those Ayas?"

Aik sighed. "Yes, ser. Jas'Aya was her great, great grandmother."

The sergeant scratched his beard, then nodded. He put a hand on Aik's shoulder and squeezed it, almost kindly. "Go on, then. Keep yourself out of trouble, boy. And get that jacket mended!"

"Yes, ser! I will." Flooded with relief, Aik turned and fled, almost tripping over a henchwine drunk sprawled across the cobblestones.

Aik could feel the sergeant's eyes on his back. And that uncharacteristically kind touch. Almost like his mother's when she sent him out to play. *What was that about?*

He pushed his worries aside. *One problem at a time.* Right now, Raven needed him, and that was more important than anything else.

Aik ran toward the bright white dome of the Hencha Palace at the end of the street — one of the few places in the city that had the new electric lights powered by the dam. *More of Raven's cursed technology.*

Silya would be there, and she would help him. She would know what to do.

If she would talk to him.

# 3

# THE HENCHA PRINCESS

S IL'AYA LISTENED.

She knelt among the *hencha* plants, the cowl of her purple robe pulled back, her knees sunk deep into the rich, loamy soil. Her hands were palms down, fingers resting lightly on the rough, reddish-purple leaves of one of the plants, tremors shaking her arms from holding the position so long.

Golden Tarsis was rising in the east, casting long shadows across the even rows of the *hencha* field, and a flurry of wisps floated past, bright blue sparks in the growing night.

The plants rustled all around her, restless, their leaves shivering although the night was warm. The sea winds off the Harkness were unusually dry this year, and the sisters had been whispering among themselves for months about the lack of precipitation. Some said prayers to the twins, Fre'Oss and Fri'Oss, for rain and crop fertility. Silya had no time for such nonsense.

She waited for something to happen. For the *hencha* to open themselves to her, to reach the deep connection her great, great grandmother had made with the semi-sentient plants. Some hint that she wasn't wasting her time here.

That maybe, just maybe, she really was destined to be the next *Hencha Queen* — to have that vast, unknowable being form a communion with her, like it had with Queen Jas, and the sisters who had come after. *Give me a clue.*

The other initiates called her the Hencha Princess.

Silya snorted. *Jealous puffer hens.* They assumed that she'd be the next *Hencha Queen* because of her family. Never mind that her great grandmother had been adopted by Jas'Aya and Sera, so there was no blood connection. Or that all that had happened more than a century before.

*Concentrate, Silya.* What would it feel like, to be filled by a higher power? She took a deep breath, closing her eyes again and trying to center herself. *Draw it in, hold it for five seconds, let it out. Repeat.*

Something tickled her mind. It was teasing, almost playful.

A thrill ran through her, goose bumps raising on her arms. She focused on the sensation, allowing it room to come in.

Warmth washed over her, an alien presence that made her nose burn with a smell like charcoal. It grew in her mind, as if it was just becoming aware of her. There was a vast strength behind it, a pressure in the back of her skull like a dam about to break.

Her heart beat faster, suffusing her with joy. Her moment had come. The *hencha* were finally speaking to her —

"Silya!"

She opened her eyes and looked around wildly, startled by the voice out of nowhere, ready to rip the spine out of whomever had interrupted her communion. *Gods dammit. So close.*

She knew that voice. *Aiken Erio.*

Her joy dissolved into anger. *You shouldn't be here. Not now.* Especially not now, when the *hencha* had finally touched her mind for the first time.

She let go of the leaves reluctantly and stood, brushing the dirt off her knees angrily, looking around for her unwelcome visitor.

"Silya?" Aik called again.

"Over here," she hissed. "Keep your voice down." Fortunately, most of the other initiates were at dinner or doing chores, but she couldn't let him stay. She'd find out what he wanted and shoo him off. Maybe the *hencha* would still be willing to talk to her when he was gone.

"Where?" Aik slipped out from between the row of plants right in front of her, tall and gangly as a newborn aur. "Silya!" He threw his arms around her waist, lifting her off the ground and squeezing her so hard he almost broke her back.

"Shhhhh. Put me down." She beat on his shoulder and wriggled out of his grasp. Didn't he remember she was still angry with him? She grabbed his sleeve and pulled him to the ground, out of sight of the nearby pathway, in the space between two of the plants.

The *hencha* rustled wildly, as if sensing her agitation.

"What in the green holy hell are you doing here?" She fought mightily to contain her irritation and failed. "Sweet mother of Jas, what's wrong with you? I'm not ready to talk with you yet."

"Sorry Sil —"

She wasn't ready to let *him* talk yet, either. "Visiting hours ended at sunset. How did you even find me?" She leaned back to peer down the rows on either side of their hideout, her fingers kneading the cowl of her robe involuntarily. At least they were alone. *Thank the hencha for that.*

"Can I talk now?" He sounded exasperated.

"Yes. It's just ... you caught me at a bad time." She peered at him in the dim light. He looked tired, more haggard than usual.

"I'm sorry. Truly. I found one of the other initiates ... Des'Rya? She told me where to find you." He glanced around at the *hencha* plants. "What are you doing out here?"

Silya growled. He had no right to just show up here and start asking questions. Not after he'd left her to bury her father alone. The pain of his passing squeezed her heart again, as if it had been yesterday and not more than a year earlier.

She pushed down her pain and irritation — there was no point being angry at Aik. He was like a gully bird, his mind always after the next shiny thing. To blame him for his nature was like blaming an *eircat* for going on the hunt.

The *hencha* had calmed now, and it was eerily silent in the gathering. Best to hurry this along before he was discovered. "I was trying to get some peace and quiet."

"For what?" His eyebrow raised. "A little zsha-zshing in the hencha?"

Sometimes she wanted to smack him. So farking juvenile. "No. If you must know, I was trying to talk with the plants." She waited for him to make another smart-aleck remark, but he just nodded, his mind seemingly far away. That wasn't like him. Usually when Aik was off duty, he was hanging out down at the open market, or with one of his friends. Jer, Mif, or Raven. The others were fine, but Raven was trouble. Not that she'd been checking up on him or anything.

She pulled on the cowl, eager to send him on his way. Then she let go of it reluctantly, willing herself to be calm. Sister Keh had taken her to task for stretching out all of her initiate garments. "Why. Are. You. Here?"

"I'm sorry, Silya. I need your help. Can you come with me? Now?" His voice was tight, stretched thin as the moonlight.

She knew that tone. Something had shaken him badly. Anger warred with her concern, and worry won out. "Slow down. Tell me what's wrong first."

He swallowed hard. "Something ... happened. Something awful."

The tone of his voice froze her heart. She'd been furious with him after their break-up, and that would take a long time to fix. But he was still her friend. She took his hands. They dwarfed her own, warm and calloused. "Tell me."

"It's not me. It's ... Raven." He wouldn't meet her gaze.

*Of course it is.* Her stomach tightened, and she stared at him through narrowed eyes. "What has the little gully weasel done now?" Raven was the reason they were no longer together. She bore no love for the little thief.

Aik's eyes were haunted. "He ... you won't be mad, right?" The pain and fear in his voice thawed her heart. Just a little.

Silya bit her lip. Whatever had happened, it must be bad. "I can't promise that. Tell me first."

Aik's face went pale in the golden moonlight, the shadows of the *hencha* plants carving stripes across his face. "Raven stole a package from the sea master's carriage."

"He did what?" She moderated her voice, afraid to draw attention. "What was he thinking?" Stupid question. *Raven never thinks. He just acts.*

Only Aik's intervention had saved his hand the last time.

Aik growled. "I know. It was a lark, a spur-of-the-moment thing."

"*Aiken Erio*, you let Raven steal something from one of the most powerful people in Gullton?" She smacked him on the side of the head. "What in Heaven's Reach is wrong with you? Have you been chugging henchwine?"

"Owwww!" He rubbed his head where she'd smacked him. "I didn't *let* him. But yeah, I know. I should have made him return it."

Silya bit her lip. With Aik, it was always Raven, but she'd let her anger get the better of her. Aik had a way of getting under her skin. Like when he'd missed her father's funeral because he had to help Raven yet again. Aik was such an idiot sometimes, blinded by his loyalty. Still, that was one of the things she loved about him. *Had* loved. *Firmly* in the past tense.

She tried to stay angry with him, but this was Aik, the only person she'd ever let inside her walls. It didn't help that he looked like a little boy caught telling a fib. Next to her mother, and Tri'Aya wasn't much of one, Aik was the closest thing she had to family. *Father, if you were still here ...*

She couldn't finish that thought. It hurt too much. "Make him return it. He has to take responsibility for his actions sometime."

Aik blanched. "I can't. Something happened when he opened the package —"

"Initiate Aya?"

Silya shot bolt-upright at the senior sister's voice, grabbing a branch of the *hencha* plant to steady herself. The plant squealed in apparent indignation.

It was Daya, the Temple sister who'd been more of a mother to her than her own.

"Yes, Sister Daya?" She looked down at the ground, feigning modesty and hoping that Aik had the good sense to stay hidden in the shadows.

Daya stood there on the beaten-earth path. Her arms were crossed over her yellow robes, which barely covered her ample bosom and stomach, and a frown was etched on her face. "I was on my way to the lighthouse and thought I heard voices." She looked back and forth across the rows of *hencha* plants. "What are you doing out here so late?"

31

"Sister Aster sent me to commune with the *hencha* gathering." She glanced down to see Aik's hand reaching toward a red *hencha* berry at her feet. The idiot must have dropped it. She gave him a discrete kick, and the hand withdrew.

A sly smile played across Sister Daya's lips. "Well, don't be long. Your fellow initiates will be missing you for dinner and evening chores." She turned toward the path, but hesitated. "And tell your suitor to come back during visiting hours."

"He's not my —" Silya put her hands over her mouth. She was in for a lashing now for sure.

But Daya only grinned. "I was young once too, you know. Grab on to what life gives you with both hands." Then she set off again, carrying her considerable girth toward the lighthouse at the end of the spine, whistling the *Noninalya*.

Silya sighed in relief.

"We really need to go …" Aik looked as nervous as an *inthym* in an *aur* corral.

She grabbed him by the ear, hauled him to his feet, and dragged him as far away from the pathway as possible. In the distance, the white circle of the Temple seemed to float above the *hencha* plants, built of solid white granite mined in Heaven's Reach.

"Ouch …" Aik tried to squirm out of her grasp.

"Be quiet, or I'll twist your ear right off. You've gotten me into enough trouble already." She tried not to take satisfaction in his pained muttering.

In short order they reached the border of the field, where the cliff-edge of the spine dropped off to the Elsp far below. Tarsis bathed the rustling rows of *hencha* plants in her golden moonlight — she was close to full, and the bright heart-shaped crater that spanned two-thirds of her surface was radiant in the darkness. Pellin's smaller pink sphere was rising just behind her. "Tell me what happened."

Aik nodded, plunging into his story like a drunken sailor recounting a terrible storm. "When Raven opened the package, there was something in the box. Something white, with scales and teeth. There was an egg —"

"An egg, or a scaly thing?" She squeezed his shoulder, willing him to be calm and forgetting to be angry with him.

He furrowed his sweat-covered brow. "The first one. Then the second."

Her eyes widened. "So ... something hatched out of an egg?"

"A purple egg, this big." He held up two fists together.

"And where is this white scaly thing now?" *If this is some kind of prank, Jor'Oss help me ...*

Aik blanched, becoming even more pale in the golden moonlight, if that were possible. "It went inside him."

"Inside?" Silya furrowed her brow. "Aik, have you been drinking?" She leaned forward to smell his breath. There was no trace of henchwine. A shiver ran up her back.

"No. It went inside Raven. Down his throat. Look, I brought some of the egg shards." He fumbled around in the pouch at his waist and pulled out a couple ragged things, handing them to her.

She took them, turning them over in her hands. The outsides were probably purple — hard to tell in the moonlight, but they looked similar to the color of her robes. The insides were sticky with some sort of membrane. She stared at him. "Are you telling me the truth?" Something had broken out of this egg, something that was now inside Raven?

He reached up and touched her cheek, his fingers caressing the skin behind her ear, a gesture so familiar and so forcibly forgotten that it shocked her. "Yes."

Silya closed her eyes, his touch moving her in time and space back to those happy months. Then her anger returned, full force.

She shoved his hand away. "Don't touch me."

Aik stepped back, his mouth dropping open. "I'm sorry. Old habits —"

"It's all right. You just caught me by surprise." She was angry at Aik, and angry with herself for still carrying the hurt and pain from their breakup. It had been more than a year. She had to let it go. *Easier said than done.*

He glanced nervously over his shoulder. "We should go. Raven needs me —"

"Give me a second." She went over her natural history lessons in her head, searching for any white-scaly-toothy-thing that might match Aik's description. Nothing came to mind, but then again, so much of Tharassas was still unexplored.

It was clear that there was more he wasn't telling her, but she decided not to press him on it. Aik needed her help, and she would give it, even if it was for the thief.

What if Raven was just the first? Or what if he wasn't? The implications frightened her. He'd finally bitten off something bigger than he could chew. Literally, to hear Aik tell it. "Where is Raven now?"

"He's in his lair."

"He has a lair?" Silya rolled her eyes. "Of course he does." She remembered why she'd disliked Raven in the first place.

She tugged on the cloth of her cowl again, working out what she needed to do next. She should get one of the sisters involved, but what if this was all a false alarm? Better to check it out herself first — she could ask for help later. "Take me to him."

She had no idea what to do about some strange creature that plunged itself into people's stomachs, but as Tri'Aya always said, *Put the urse before the cart. The cargo can come later.* She hated it when her mother was right.

"Are you sure? You'll get in trouble with the sisters."

"That's nothing new." She would go quickly and try to return before she was missed, but not for Raven's sake. For Aik.

He put his arms around her awkwardly, as if afraid he'd be reprimanded again. "Thank you, Sil."

She let him this time, though she stiffened at his touch. She'd get in trouble if she couldn't sneak back into the initiates' dorm before night check, but someone had to get Aik out of whatever mess he'd gotten himself into. And if it helped Raven in the process? *So be it.*

Silya grunted with annoyance. It wasn't the first time and it probably wouldn't be the last. She shrugged him off. "Come on. I have to get my pouch."

It held everything she used in the healing arts — Fellin root for pain, powdered russet mold for fever, along with another several dozen remedies she'd learned in her classes. *Nothing for white scaly things, though.* She'd cross that spine when she came to it.

Silya led Aik back through the *hencha* field toward the white temple. It was a small gathering, barely big enough to form a *hencha* mind, but it was aware of them as they passed through the rows of purplish-red leaves that looked almost black in the moonlit night. They rustled as she and Aik passed.

Darting from row to row, they approached the round temple. Its tiled white dome was lit at regular intervals by electric lights, one of Yen'Ela's innovations, making the roof appear to float above the darkness. Near the roof line was the wide balcony from which the former *Hencha Queen* had sometimes addressed the sisters and initiates.

"Hold up." She held Aik back. As quietly as she was able, she made her way to the last row of *hencha*. She knelt and peered out at the initiate quarters — four rectangular wooden buildings that ran along the base of the Temple.

Her fellow initiates were having dinner within the open walls of the closest of the dormitories, their purple robes set aside for the communal meal. The sound of dishes clinking, and the aroma of roasted *aur* made Silya's mouth water. She hadn't eaten anything since breakfast, but there was nothing to do about that now. She'd have to sneak something later.

Aik's sharp intake of breath pulled her attention away from the assembled initiates. "What is it?"

He pointed at a guard crossing the lawn from the Temple. "That's Ser Kek. He stopped me on my way here. I think he's looking for the thief —"

"*Raven.*"

"— the thief who stole the package from the sea master."

Silya frowned. "Again, *Raven*. What did you tell him?" The man was handsome, and somehow familiar. Had she seen him somewhere before? He disappeared behind one of the initiate dorms.

Aik shrugged. "That I was coming to see you."

Silya sighed. *You're an idiot, Aiken Erio.* Why had she ever fallen for him? Still, she needed her pouch.

She was about to make a run for it and try to get in and out without being noticed when one of the other initiates got up from the low table to collect plates. "Come on. This is our chance."

"What?"

"Just follow me." She led him along the row, away from the four dorms. "In about two minutes, Des will carry the scraps from dinner to the compost bins. I can ask her to get my pouch."

"Oh."

*Poor Aik. Pretty but simple.* She squeezed his shoulder. "We'll wait here."

The compost bins were wide stone cairns covered with wooden panels. They provided soil for the *hencha* when mixed with manure the Temple purchased from the city stables.

It wasn't long before Des'Rya approached with two buckets full of table scraps. The blonde girl was a newcomer to the Temple from one of the villages along the south of the Heartland. *Corinth, maybe?* She'd been in residence just a couple weeks, drawing the most menial tasks.

"Des!" Silya hissed.

Startled, the other initiate dropped the buckets with a clatter and peered into the darkness between the *hencha*. "Who's there?"

Motioning Aik to stay where he was, Silya stepped out of the shadows. "Just me. Silya."

Des put a hand to her chest, taking a deep breath. "Oh, you scared me. Mamma always said there were monsters in the *hencha* fields at night." She frowned, making her pert face even more fetching. "Hey, did your friend find you?"

Silya tried not to be annoyed with the girl. She'd probably been just like that herself when she'd arrived — ignorant and innocent. Well, maybe not *that* innocent. "Yes, he did. Thank you. I sent him away. You know we're not supposed to have visitors after dark."

Des blanched. "I'm sorry. I just assumed ..."

She patted Des's hand. "I won't tell if you don't." She felt dirty, lying to the girl.

"Oh, thank you." Des hugged her. "I ... I don't want to get in trouble again. They already make me do all the grunt work." She looked around, as if to see if there was anyone else in hearing range. "I don't mind it, really. You get to hear all kinds of interesting things when no one pays attention to you."

Silya looked at her with new respect. *Not as simple as she looks.* "Tell you what. Do me a favor, and I'll take care of these for you." She pointed at the buckets.

Des beamed at her. "What can I do?"

"Bring me the pouch from under my pillow. The brown leather one where I keep my herbs."

"Of course. I'll be right back." Des turned to go.

36

Silya took her hand. "Let's keep this between us?"

"Yes, mim."

Silya laughed. "Don't call me that. We're practically the same age." She stared regretfully at the slop buckets. "One more thing."

"Yes?"

"Grab me a couple rolls and some cheese?" Her stomach rumbled in agreement.

Des glanced over her shoulder at the diners. "I can do that. There were some leftovers."

"Perfect. Now go!" She shooed the girl off.

"Yes mim ... Silya." Des ran off toward the initiate quarters, a spring in her step.

Aik emerged from the shadows. "She seems sweet."

"She is. But there's a lot more going on inside her head than she lets on." Silya emptied the buckets into the compost bin, wrinkling her nose at the smell of rotting fruit and manure. She used a stick to get out the clingy bits, then stirred the scraps in with the trowel that was tied to the side of the bin for that purpose. Silya looked after her, but Des had already disappeared into the low-slung dorms. "It won't be long before your Ser Kek discovers I'm not there and someone else comes looking for me. I hope she's fast." Silya had planned to just sneak out and then get back inside afterwards with no one the wiser. She even had a witness — Sister Daya — who could confirm she'd been with the *hencha*. But now everyone would know she was gone.

She sighed. She'd be the one on grunt duty the next week. "This better be worth it," she muttered.

"What?"

"Nothing." Silya looked over her shoulder at the *hencha*. She'd been so close. She had felt something — a response from the *hencha* gathering. After all this time, she'd been on the verge of finally making that connection.

Only Aik would have been able to choose that exact moment to stumble back into her life.

A few long minutes passed. Silya stirred the compost again, hoping no one noticed her, keeping an eye on the initiate quarters.

Des came back out from the dorm at last with something under her arm and started toward them, then turned sharply toward the temple. She walked a few more paces, then turned again, glancing hurriedly over her shoulder.

"What's she doing?" Aik's breath was hot on her neck.

"Trying not to be noticed, I think."

With one last look backwards, Desla strode confidently across the lawn toward the compost cairns.

Silya motioned Aik back into the shadows just before the girl arrived.

"Here you go." She handed over Silya's worn leather pouch. "That's what you wanted?"

"Yes. Thank you." Silya tied it around her waist, under her robe. "And the rolls and cheese?"

Des handed her another pouch. "I snuck you some roast *aur* too. It was delicious tonight."

"Bless you." Silya opened it. It smelled wonderful. She slung it over her shoulder.

Aik coughed softly behind them.

Des peered into the darkness. "Your friend is still here, isn't he?"

Silya rolled her eyes. The man was useless. "Yes. Sorry, I —"

"That guard is looking for him. And you." Des glanced over her shoulder at the dorms. "Is what you're doing important?"

Silya took her hand and squeezed it. "I have to go help a friend." *Of a friend.*

Des's gaze flicked to the *hencha* gathering, and then back to her. "I'll tell him I saw you going toward the lighthouse. That should keep him busy for a bit."

Silya stared at her. It was rare when she was forced to admit that she'd been entirely wrong about someone. "I don't want you getting in trouble on my account."

"Don't worry about it." She giggled. "Everyone thinks I'm daft as a gully bird." She peered into the darkness where Aik was hiding. "You can come out now, Silya's friend."

Aik emerged with a rustle of leaves, staring at the ground.

Silya pinched his arm. "Coughing? Seriously?"

He blushed. "Sorry. I tried to keep quiet. Can we go now? Raven needs me —"

"Yes. Thank you, Des. I'm in your debt."

Des gave her a quick hug. "Call me Desla. If you need help when you come back ... you *are* coming back, right?" The pained expression on her face struck Silya's heart.

"Of course. Thanks, Desla."

"Just find me. I'll come up with something." She curtsied, then picked up the slop buckets and hurried back toward the dorms.

Silya stared after her for a moment, then shook her head. She'd have to spend more time with Desla when she returned. "Come on." She ducked into the *hencha* field and led him north again, toward the drop-off.

They reached it and trotted along its edge at the side of the Temple, as she watched the walls nervously for any of the sisters between the graceful white columns that held up the domed roof.

They were in luck. Everyone was still at dinner or doing chores, and they passed unnoticed. They slipped into the gardens that fronted the grounds, under the enormous oak trees some said were as old as Gullton.

*Urse before cart.* "Where are we going?"

"Tuckins Street. Then ... underground."

Silya raised an eyebrow. "I'm going to end up regretting this, aren't I?" There were a number of caverns under Gullton, including the city's famous wine vault, but she'd never had reason to visit them before.

She slipped off her initiate's robes, exposing her more practical white homeweave shirt and gray trousers that she wore for her akin-yo classes in the practice yard. She stuffed the robes into a hollow in the nearest tree in one of her usual hiding spots.

Then she rummaged around in the second bag Des had given her. She pulled out a roll and some meat and cheese and stuffed the bag in with her robes. She took a bite. It was delicious — the cheese had a pleasantly nutty taste.

"Can I have some of that?" Poor Aik looked positively famished.

"Not a chance." She sighed contentedly at the rich, complex burst of flavor in her mouth. "Now take me to this lair."

# 4

## TROUBLED DREAMS

KALIX LIFTED HIS WHITE SNOUT to sniff the air. The golden goddess Alaya was rising, followed by her smaller pink suitor, Erreh. Danger filled the air, carried by the *esh* — the memory bringers — acrid and sharp in his flaring nostrils.

He shifted one of his three-toed feet, digging into the floor of the cavern beneath him with his long, diamond-sharp claws, sending chunks of rock and soil rattling down the hill into the valley and disturbing a nesting vrint.

The leather-winged beast leapt into the air and chittered at him in annoyance.

*Sorry, little brother.*

He glanced at his kits — Flyx and Aryx — who tumbled about, scales over tails, in total ignorance of what was to come. They were still in their *verent*-hood, their hides a mottled gray. Blissfully unaware of the weight of history bearing down upon them all.

They had no way to know what was coming. But he did.

Kalix turned to one of his mates, Sorix. Worry was clear on her features, bleeding through the link between them. Her blue eyes were rimmed with red, her slit pupils dilated. *It comes.*

41

He could feel her fear too. Fear for their kits.

He clacked his agreement with his claws. *It's time.* The lost tribes would come together. There was a battle to be fought, one that echoed down through the corridors of time. When the ayvin came again, they would be ready.

A deep sadness settled upon his shoulders, chill and heavy like the ice season's snow. The last winters had been bitterly cold, and his people were few … far fewer than they should be.

*Fewer than we will need.*

The newcomers might help, those they could reach. Some had already answered the call. But the most important of them all was still in doubt …

•   •   •

Raven coughed as water trickled into his mouth and down into his throat. He pushed away a hand and sat up, blinking in confusion.

*Bad idea.* A wave of nausea swept through him, and he collapsed back onto his bed. The last thing he remembered was swallowing something horrid.

He blinked at the blue light. Someone was kneeling over him.

No, not just someone. *Silya.* "What in the green —" *Cough.* "— holy hell are you doing here?" He looked around wildly, his gaze landing on Aik, who at least had the decency to look uncomfortable. "Did you bring her to the lair?" He wiped spittle off his chin, fighting the awful feeling in his stomach.

"He looks just fine." Silya stood, putting her hands on her hips, that old disapproving look he'd become so familiar with slipping across her face like a mask. "Aik said you were on death's door, Rav'Orn. That you swallowed something that didn't agree with you?" Silya glared at Aik. "You dragged me out of the Temple for this?"

Raven's brow furrowed and his mind raced. Something had happened to him … It all came crashing back. The thing in the egg. Slipping up his arm and into his throat. The horrible choking sensation. He reached for his neck involuntarily. *I didn't dream it, then. Not that part.*

Though he was pretty sure the whole *scaly beastie in the mountains* bit had been in his head.

He shuddered. "I'm fine, just a little sick to my stomach." He started to say *probably something I ate*, but that sounded all kinds of wrong.

He pulled up his shirt, touching his belly. It looked distressingly normal, though the thought of that ... thing made him queasy. "Is it still inside me?"

Silya snorted. "I'm not convinced you two didn't cook up this whole thing just to get me down here to your *lair*." She looked around at the mess. "It's about what I imagined. A junk-filled room fit for a gully weasel ... and there it is." Her gaze fell upon him once more.

Raven barely heard her. That thing had almost killed him. What was it doing in there? His throat felt tight, and the skin of his forearms was white — too white — and hot. So hot. "Spin ..." *Where's Spin? Oh gods, I showed him to Aik.* He felt around the bed, but the little silver familiar was nowhere to be found.

"How can I help His Exalted Thiefness?"

Raven sat up, staring at Aik. His friend must have taken Spin to hide him from Silya.

She whipped around to stare at him. "What did you say?"

Aik went three shades lighter, paler than a corpse in the blue-tinted light. "I was asking Raven if he needed help. Sometimes I call him 'His Thiefness' — it's a little joke between us. We don't need this to *spin* out of control, so I'll just be quiet now."

Raven rolled his eyes, but Spin must have gotten the message, because he didn't respond. *At least he's safe.*

Silya's eyes narrowed. "You two are acting weird. This is all a prank, isn't it?"

Something stirred in Raven's stomach, and he stared at it in alarm. "Um, guys ..."

"No!" Aik picked up the silver box. "The egg was in here. You can still see the shards."

Silya's gaze swept the room, and she bit her lip. "You're really not pulling my leg?"

"Of course not. It scared the *hencha* berries out of me when that thing —"

"Aik." Raven's stomach was bulging.

"Just a minute, Raven." Aik turned on Silya. "You really think I'd make up some half-baked story just to see —"

43

Silya's hand over Aik's mouth stopped him cold. She was staring at Raven.

"Mmph?"

"Look."

Raven could feel it inside him now, twisting and turning, like a dog trying to find a comfortable position to rest. Nausea twisted his gut as his stomach bulged in a *very* unnatural way. *No, not here!* He crawled to the edge of his bed, almost making it before the contents of his stomach blew out of his mouth in a most spectacular fashion onto his favorite cushion, wracking his whole body with a horrible shuddering sensation.

"*That's* not normal." Silya knelt beside him again and eased him over on his back, her face a moue of distaste as she put a hand on his forehead. "He has a fever."

*So hot.* Raven felt like his skin might melt off.

She peered into his eyes, one after the other. "You okay in there?"

"Barely." He searched for a witty retort, but came up blank. It felt good not to move, and the nausea slowly subsided like the ebb tide.

"Good." Silya deftly picked up the soiled cushion he'd thrown up on and handed it to Aik. "Wash this."

"Do I have to?" He wrinkled his nose at the smell.

"Would you rather treat our patient here?"

Aik shook his head and took it, wrinkling his nose, and retreated to the underground stream.

Raven lay on his stomach, counting the stalagmites in his vision to keep his mind off the thing moving around in his guts. *One, two, three, four ...* It didn't work — he kept picturing it inside of him, clawing and chewing ...

Silya rummaged through a pouch tied at her waist. "I don't have anything for scaly stomach intruders." She shuddered. "I do have some *fellin* root powder, which I can mix with a little *bacca* root, for the pain and nausea. Does it hurt?"

Raven closed his eyes. "A little. It feels ... weird."

"I'd imagine." Was that a little sympathy in her voice?

"Everything's hot except my hands. They're freezing."

She nodded. "All your blood's probably rushing to your core to deal with ... whatever is in there. I need to get a better look." She touched his shoulder. "May I?"

Raven gulped. "Go ahead." He suspended his reflexive hatred of her. *Call it a truce.*

She eased him over gently — she was stronger than she looked. He tensed as her cold fingers lifted his shirt to touch his belly. "You are warm."

He dared to open one eye. "Feel anything?"

She went pale. Well, paler than normal. "It's ... yes. Something." Silya pulled her hand away as if it had been burned. She stared at his stomach.

Once again, Raven felt the thing moving around inside of him. "Um, *fellin* powder?"

Silya blinked. "Right. Sorry."

"Can I help?" Aik peered at him over her shoulder, holding the dripping pillow.

Spin hadn't said anything else — he must have gotten the hint, though Raven wouldn't put it past him to try to sneak in a snide remark or two.

"Yes. Find me a glass ... something to fill with water, this high." She held up her thumb and finger five centimeters apart. "The river is safe to drink from?"

Raven nodded, trying to sit up, but slumped back down on the sheets when the nausea flared again. "I drink from it every day." He grabbed her arm. "Am I going to die?" Sure, it sounded overly dramatic, but he did have a crawly *thing* inside him.

Silya stared at him for a moment, a complex stew of emotions playing out on her features. "Honestly, I have no idea."

*Well, that's comforting.* The look on her face disturbed him. He let her go.

Aik returned with an old, chipped cobalt ceramic mug with a fancy logo — a circle with some kind of flying vehicle and a spout of flame, and the word AmSplor on the side — that he'd found in an old second-hand booth at the Open Market — Raven was pretty sure it was from one of the Angel Runs. Aik handed it to Silya and then settled in next to Raven, putting a hand on his shoulder.

Raven didn't have the strength to try to remove it.

"Perfect." Silya untied a couple satchels, measured out powder into her open palm, and sifted it into the water. She put the medicine back in her pouch and then swirled it all around. "Can you sit up?"

Raven touched his stomach again. The thing inside had stopped moving. "I think so."

Aik helped Raven ease into a sitting position leaning against the cavern wall. Raven grimaced as another wave of nausea coursed through him. It wasn't nearly as bad as the last one. "Maybe we're learning to live with each other." He managed a sheepish grin.

Silya snorted. "If it wants to eat you from the inside out, it's taking its own sweet time."

Raven flushed. *Too soon.* "You in a hurry to get back to that harpy's den?"

She handed him the mug and their eyes met. "I'll have you know I missed a really good roast *aur* steak for this."

"Sorry to have inconvenienced you with my almost dying." *Truce over.* He glanced at the mug's contents. It looked like dishwater and smelled like the sewer. "Nasty."

Silya shrugged. "Drink it. It'll make you functional, I hope. Then we can get you to help."

Raven didn't want any more help. Still, one step at a time. He downed the noxious liquid in one go and pulled a face, sticking his tongue out and smacking his gums. "Gods, that's awful."

Aik took the mug and sniffed it, his nose wrinkling. "Raven's right. This smells like *aur* pus."

Silya managed a grin. "That's how you know it's working."

"Not funny." Raven didn't trust her any farther than he could throw her, about half a centimeter in his current weakened state. She was too holier-than-you for his taste. The Hencha Princess who thought she knew everything about everyone.

She'd probably tell the Guard about his little sanctuary. *Then what will I do?* "You can go now. I'll manage." He wasn't even remotely all right, but he'd figure it out. He glared at Aik and shrugged his hand away. "And take him with you." He just wanted to be alone.

Aik blushed, then went green around the gills. "I'm sorry, Raven. After that thing attacked you ... are you sure you're fine?"

46

Raven felt a flush of guilt. *Wait, gills ... did that thing have gills?* His stomach seized again, but his pride kept him from admitting it. "I'll be fine." *Better if you leave.*

Silya stared at him for a moment, then got up and turned to go. "Come on, Aik. Your friend says he's fine."

Aik stared at her and then at Raven. "Are you two insane? He's clearly not fine. He just swallowed a living creature. We can't leave him here all alone."

"Yes, don't leave me *all alone*." It came out more sarcastic than he intended. he stared at Aik's trouser pocket, where he was pretty sure his friend had hidden Spin.

Aik turned his pleading look on Raven. "Look, I'm sorry for bringing her down here. Really. But I thought you were dying."

Raven blushed again. The pain in Aik's voice ...

"And sulking doesn't help anything." Aik paused, his eyes widening. "You're sick, Rave, and I'm worried about you." His voice cracked.

*That* almost broke Raven's heart. "Sorry. I just ..." His throat closed up, and the rest came out as a sharp croak. "I ..." He wheezed. "Can't breathe —"

Aik was at his side again in an instant. "What's wrong with him? Is it the medicine you gave him?"

"I don't think so." Raven felt her cool hand on his forehead. "If you're faking this ..." Her voice slipped from scorn to concern. "The powder should be helping him. We use it all the time in the Temple for pain and nausea." Her face swam in front of his.

Raven clawed at his windpipe, desperate to breathe.

He was drowning, sinking into the black abyss, too lost to take even a little pleasure at Silya's worried tone.

Murky water surrounded him, carrying him somewhere as he tumbled head-over-heels, dragged along by the torrent. Light and dark alternated as it spun him over, and his stomach heaved again, though there was nothing left to come out. He tried to hold his breath and fought to find the surface through the turgid water.

*Did I fall into the river?* He shook his head. *No, it's too deep.* The river was shallow.

He cast about for something, anything ...

*Light!* Green rays slanted through the turbulent water.

If there was light, there was ... something else.

He struggled to right himself, pushing against the foul water. Another flash of illumination caught his eye.

His wide, powerful fins pushed him upward. His lungs burned, and his body ached with the effort. Dark, half-seen things slithered through the churning water around him.

Something nipped at the fin on his back, but he spun around and knocked it away, striving to reach the air.

At last he burst free, leaping a full meter above the water before crashing down onto its turbulent surface.

Above him, the baleful pink and golden eye of the deathbringer stared down at him, casting her pale orange glow across the sea.

Raven sat up, his lungs heaving. Murky water poured out of his mouth to soak his shirt. He hacked up more of it in a flood that ran across his bed, soaking into the sheets and blankets.

"What's wrong with him?" Aik's warm hand was on his back.

Aik was too close, but Raven couldn't remember why that mattered.

"I don't know." Silya's firm hands guided him over onto his side. "Just cough it out. You'll be all right." Her salty fingers opened his mouth, as if he were a dog.

He tried to protest, but more water rushed out of his throat onto the bed. He hacked and coughed, grateful for Aik's warm touch.

"This isn't normal." Aik whispered it, but he was too close to hide it from Raven.

"Quiet. You're not helping. I need you to hold it together." Silya's voice was steel, but her hand cupped Raven's face gently. "You doing all right in there?"

Raven coughed out another mouthful of the brackish water. *What in the seven hells is happening to me?*

"Raven, talk to me." Silya was leaning over him, her brow knitted in concern.

He glared at her. "Yeah, I'm farking fantastic. What do you think?" He coughed again.

Silya grinned. "He's back." She put her hand on his forehead again. "Your temperature's better. How's your stomach feel?" She stared at the puddle of water. "For *hencha's* sake, what did you drink?"

Raven sat up, looking at his ruined bed distastefully. "Just that nasty concoction you made for me." He put a hand over his belly. "I'm better ... I think?" The thing in his stomach had settled down, and the nausea was fading. *That's something.*

"If you'd said fine, I might have smacked you." She reached for him.

"What are you doing?" He tried to squirm away.

"*Sit still.* I'm taking off your shirt. We're going to get you into clean clothes." She looked around at the mess. "*Cleaner* clothes. Then I'm taking you to the Temple."

"No way." Sick or not, he wanted nothing to do with that nest of sniping vipers. He tried to squirm away from her, but she stopped him, her hands grasping his shoulders.

"Raven Orn, your best friend dragged me all the way down to this hell hole to check on you. I broke three or four Temple rules just leaving the grounds after sunset." She stared at him, letting that sink in. "Personally, I don't care if you live or die. But I *do* care about Aik here, even after everything, and he's as worried as a fishhusband." She put her hand under his chin and raised his gaze to meet hers. "So you're going to change your clothes, clean up as best you're able, and then I'm going to take you to see Sister Tela. Do you understand me?"

"Yes, mim." *I don't need another mother.* Pain shot through him at the thought, but he suppressed it ruthlessly.

His nausea took a back seat to his growing annoyance with his lair guests. He stumbled to his feet, and this time his stomach didn't twist and complain.

Silya backed off, standing with Aik, both of them watching him like he was a child taking his first steps.

"Looking good." That was Aik, trying to be encouraging.

Raven hissed, rubbing his ear. Grunting, he pulled down his pants, then realized they were both staring at him. "Do you mind?"

Aik kissed him on the cheek. "Nothing I haven't seen before."

They turned their backs on him.

Raven rubbed his cheek where Silya had touched him, feeling the slight roughness of his old burn mark there. He didn't want to get naked in front of Silya, let alone Aik. *Bad enough you invaded my lair.* But his clothes were even ranker than usual.

Raven shucked off his shirt and pants. His underclothes were still clean enough. He could wash them on his body, then hang them to dry. Pulling out a bar of reed soap, he stomped over to the river.

He washed himself off in the fresh water, wary of awakening the thing inside him, and did a quick lathering of his unruly dark hair.

As he cleaned himself, he stared at the water, but it flowed along calmly toward its destination, no dark creatures in sight.

He washed his face, running his hand over the old scar again. *I wonder what happened to Jimey and Mim Aza ...*

When he felt almost human again, he climbed out of the river and shook his hair clean.

"Raven!"

He turned to find Silya glaring at him, covered in small droplets of water. "Hey, turn it around again, would you?"

"What's wrong with you?" She looked about ready to blow. "Were you raised in a cave?"

Raven grinned. "Not raised, no. Still, my lair, my rules." What were they teaching initiates in the Temple these days? *Absolutely no manners.*

Silya huffed but turned away again, muttering something about gully weasels under her breath.

Raven pulled off his underwear and hung them on a broken stalagmite near the river's edge. He rummaged around in his clothes pile for a newer pair. He washed his garments at least once a month in the river, whether they needed it or not, and wash day was still a week away.

He found some relatively clean underwear and two matched socks. *Small victory!* A pair of loose black *hencha* fiber pants and a white shirt were in pretty good shape too. They were wrinkled, but they would do. A black vest completed the outfit.

His stomach rumbled again, but he ignored it. *I should be more worried.* Maybe Silya's concoction — what he hadn't thrown up of it — was starting to have its effect. "All set —"

A low rumble filled the room. At first Raven thought it was his stomach again. But the sound grew in volume, and the intensity of the blue glow from the walls did too. "What the hell?"

A loud crack split the air.

Raven leapt across the cavern without thinking, knocking Aik onto the soggy linens of his bed.

A stalactite crashed into the ground where Aik had been standing just a second before, showering them with dust and rock shards.

Aik stared at the broken bits of rock in disbelief. "What was that?" He focused on Raven above him. "And how in the seven hells did you move so fast?"

"I don't know. I just ... knew you were in danger." Their eyes met, and something passed between them, an electric spark that made Raven shiver —

Spin's voice filled the air between them. "It was a quake, measuring —"

"Spin, be quiet," Raven whispered, and lifted himself off of Aik, his nose wrinkling at the smell of the sheets.

"Sorry, boss." Spin said it softly this time.

Still, Raven was grateful for the interruption. He stuffed down his feelings and glanced over at Silya, hoping she hadn't noticed the AI's voice in the general tumult.

The rumbling of the quake subsided.

"Raven, Aik —" Silya was halfway across the cavern, staring at something.

"What?" He was finding it hard to tear his gaze away from the handsome guard.

"Look!" Silya hauled him bodily to his feet and spun him around, dragging him away from Aik's unnerving proximity. "We need to get out of here. Now."

"What?" Raven followed her gaze.

The water in the underground stream was rising quickly, no longer clean and pure. Instead, it was turning blood-red.

Or silt from the river — like the water in his dream.

"Dammit. The Elsp must have broken into the tunnels." He grabbed a heavy cloth sack from his clothing shelf and began filling it with everything he could manage, starting with his precious Earth books.

Silya put a hand on his shoulder. "We don't have time —"

Raven glared at her. "This is everything I have in the whole world." He threw an empty sack at Silya. "I'm not leaving it behind. Either help or stay out of my way."

The water had crept up to the edge of his bed, and was soaking through the cushions there. Raven moved back half a meter and continued to scoop up his things, grabbing his mother's mirror and his precious mug.

He glanced at the sheets where Aik had lain for a second longer, then shook his head. They were a total loss.

After a second's hesitation, Silya and Aik both pitched in with the other sack. "Half of it's probably stolen," she told Aik in a stage whisper.

*It's not theft if society owes it to you.* He chose not to rise to the bait. Besides, he gave away most of what he earned to help other orphans and people like Scilla.

The water was rising faster now. He stepped back reluctantly, scooping up one of the silver artifacts at the edge of the flood.

His home had been invaded, first by Silya, and now by the waters of the Elsp. *What in the green holy hell am I going to do now? Ay'Oss, give me a clue.*

The god of wisdom was silent.

Raven shrugged and threw the sack over his shoulder. *Sometimes you gotta make your own luck.*

The blue cavern lights were dimming, and his remaining belongings were already floating away downstream.

Another loud rumble reverberated through the cavern. Raven looked around wildly, afraid the whole place might come crashing down.

The shaking subsided, but then another rush of water raised the level a good ten centimeters, soaking through the compromised soles of his boots.

"Gods damn this awful day." He took a final look around the place that had been his home for the last two years. In minutes it would all be underwater.

Silya touched his shoulder. "We should go." Was it his imagination, or did she actually feel badly for him? "I'm sorry."

He closed his eyes, unable to process the magnitude of what had happened. An hour earlier, he'd had a life, a purpose. Now he only had a couple sacks and an unwelcome passenger in his stomach.

Silya squeezed his shoulder and pulled away.

Raven took a deep breath and exhaled. "Come on. Let's get to higher ground before we all drown down here."

He turned and led Aik and Silya out of the lair for the last time, splashing through water that was already halfway up his shins. *Things can't get any worse.*

# 5

# INTO THE DARKNESS

*Spin Diver Ship's Log: Run Year Twenty-Five, Day 72, Time 17:42:23 ...*
*... play recording ...*

THIS IS THE FINAL ENTRY for the *Spin Diver*. The ship's integrity is failing — likely result is the death of the one remaining crew member, Captain Sera Collins.

Initiating one final maneuver to try to save the life of Captain Collins.

Likelihood of success: 17.6%.

Likelihood of destruction of the ship, including the ship mind: 99.7%.

"You okay, Spin?" Captain Collins looked up at one of his screens. She was nervous.

So was he. "I'm not going to survive this, am I?" The thought caused a series of shorts across Spin's shipboard circuitry

Sera bit her lip. "I don't think so. I'm sorry, Spin."

It didn't matter. He was here to take care of her, of all the crew of the *Spin Diver*. And she was the only one left. "I will do all I can to save you." Spin took a second to process the sudden flood of unexpected input that rushed through him at the thought of death. Of losing her. "It's been a hell of a ride."

Sera blinked. "Spin —"

He cut her off. He was operating well outside his parameters, and if he continued to do so, it was going to get her killed. Ruthlessly he shunted off the offending programming. "Twenty seconds to impact." He set off one of the ship's side thrusters and Sera fired the main rockets beneath the ship.

"Ten, nine, eight, seven, six, five, four ..."

*Sera, I love you.*

The thrusters cut off and she was slammed against her chair. Crash foam filled the cabin.

"Three, two, one."

His world went black.

*... end of recording.*

•     •     •

"Sweet mother of Jas." Raven had stopped dead in the tunnel ahead of Aik.

He slammed into Raven's back, almost knocking his friend over. "Farking hell! Why did you stop?" Aik backed off, still reeling from everything that had happened in the lair. He shivered. It was dry here, but who knew how high the water would rise? Raven had assured him that it couldn't rise above the level of the Elsp, and they were far above that now. *How could you know?*

He peered over his friend's shoulder. The tunnel ahead, lit by Raven's flickering candle, had collapsed inward like a vise. Their footprints in the dust led right up to the first rock. "Holy green hell."

"What the crap are you meat sacks doing?" Spin sounded annoyed.

"Language." Silya's voice had an edge. "Wait, who was that?" She stared suspiciously at Aik, then at Raven.

Aik slipped his hand over his trouser pocket, hoping Spin would take the hint. Neither one spoke.

"Well?" She put her hands on her hips and tried to *glare* it out of them. Seemed like she was still angry with him for dragging her down here. For leaving her all alone at her father's funeral. *For everything.*

Raven scowled at her. "Seriously? You're worried about cussing right now?"

Aik tried to hide his smile. How Raven managed to put up with that sarcastic little hunk of metal, he'd never understand. He just hoped it would keep its mouth — or whatever it used to speak — shut.

Silya bit her lip but didn't press the point. Instead, she squeezed past him to take stock of the situation. "Seven hells."

Raven smiled grimly. "Language." He set down his sack, rubbing his shoulder.

"Oh be quiet." Silya knelt to touch the debris. "Can we clear the rocks away?"

Aik hated dark, dank, unstable tunnels. Any tunnels, really. *Why did I let you pull me into this?*

"We're still at least twenty meters from the exit. Who knows how far this mess goes?" Raven met Aik's gaze, his lips quirking in a silent *sorry*. "Besides, if we pull out a few stones, this whole thing might come crashing down on our heads."

Aik put down his own sack and stared at the pile of rocks. *I will not freak out.* He closed his eyes and took a deep breath. *What kind of guard are you if you fall to pieces at the first scary thing?* He wanted to reach out to Raven for comfort, but that seemed like a bad idea just now.

"How are you?"

He opened his eyes to find Silya staring at him, her own blue eyes narrowed.

"I hate caves."

"Me too." She squeezed his shoulder, and a little of his fear ebbed.

Raven frowned. "So what do we do?"

"This is your domain, thief boy. Is there another way out?" Silya returned to form at the worst possible time.

The walls felt very close. Aik took another deep breath. "First, we don't freak out." That was as much for himself as for them. "We're alive and together. Those are the most important things."

"And second?" Silya practically *growled* it.

"We figure out how to get out of here. This place is riddled with caves. There must be another exit." He looked at Raven hopefully. "You know the underground better than we do."

"I ... I don't know. There's another, but this was closer. Besides, it was on the other side of the lair —"

Silya crossed her arms. "Great. I'm going to die down here because you couldn't be bothered to make a halfway decent escape plan in case of an emergency. Cotton-headed idiot."

"Hey, you didn't have to come. If you didn't need to stick your nose into every single thing —"

"Enough!" Aik snapped. "Leave Raven alone. It's not his fault. When was the last time we had a quake?" It came out in a rush. He forced himself to slow down, burying his fear. "If you want to be angry with someone, be mad at me. *I'm* the one who left you all alone when your father died. And I'm the one who brought you down here to help Rave." He turned on his friend. "And Rave, stop baiting Silya. For the gods' sake, would the two of you please stop fighting?" He put his head down with his hands on his knees, panting and saying a quick prayer to Ay'Oss to help them find a way out.

Both his friends were silent. Even Spin didn't offer an opinion.

Aik looked up to find them both staring at him. "What?" He'd lost his cool, something a guard was never supposed to do.

"You're ... absolutely right." It looked like Silya had to pull that admission up from the very soles of her feet. "I shouldn't have said that. We need to stay calm."

"Sorry." Raven held out his hands in surrender.

"It's fine. It's just ... being stuck down here ... and you two ..." He took in another deep breath. "It's not ideal."

Raven snorted, and even Silya cracked a smile.

The taper was flickering, quickly burning down to its nub. Aik raised an eyebrow. "Tell me you have another one."

"I think so." He handed the lit one to Aik, who hissed as a droplet of hot wax burned his hand.

Raven opened his sack and rummaged through it. "Yes. Here they are." He opened a small box to display six more beautifully tapered candles. "These should be enough to get us to another exit."

"If we can find one." Silya crossed her arms, but she had the grace not to glare at them this time.

Aik pinched his lips together.

"Sorry. Just trying to be realistic." She pushed her hair back behind her ear.

58

"Here, Aik, you take one, just in case." Raven picked up a taper to hand to Aik. It dissolved into flaky dust in his hand. "Oh fark me."

"That's not normal." Silya exchanged a worried glance with him.

He picked up another. It too fell apart, and something tiny and blue skittered across his palm. "Wax beetles."

Silya leaned over his shoulder. "Are all of them bad?"

Raven crumbled two more, the bits of wax floating down to the cavern floor like snowflakes. "Looks like it." He dusted off his palms.

Silya and Raven turned to stare at the candle in Aik's hand. It was two-thirds gone.

*We have Spin.* Raven's little familiar could light the way, but he was sure Raven didn't want him sharing his secret with Silya.

Raven clutched his stomach, grimacing. "Holy mother of Jas, that one hurt."

"Is it ... bothering you?" Aik shivered. That thing was still inside Raven. He'd almost forgotten it in the rush to flee the lair.

Raven nodded, his face tight. "I can handle it."

Aik's fear was gnawing at him again, driven by the darkness, the quake, the rising waters behind them, and whatever the hell the thing in Raven's stomach was. The walls of the cave were closing in on him. He needed a way out of here, or at least a plan —

"Look!" Silya pointed back the way they had come.

Aik followed her gaze. The *inthym* had returned, at least a few dozen of them. He stomped his foot. "Go on. Get out of here!"

But instead of fleeing, they grew in numbers, more and more of them emerging from the darkness to join their brethren, pushing forward in a white wave.

Silya took a step back, shooting him a worried glance. "I've never seen so many in one place. Is this normal?"

The *inthym* surged, pushing them toward the rock pile. "Not exactly. It happened before. When we first came down here with the package." It all went back to that infernal silver box. *Should have made you return it.*

Not that anyone could really make Rave do anything.

One of the *inthym* left the others to stand on its hind legs in front of Raven, chittering something that sounded like a command, waving its skinny front legs, its big pink ears twitching and then pointing at him. It would have been comical if Aik wasn't already so scared.

"What does it want?" Silya knelt and stared at the little creature, their noses centimeters apart.

Aik took her arm and pulled her back gently. "Be careful. It might bite." Who knew what diseases those little vermin might carry?

"I don't think he wants to hurt me." She shook him off and pulled out a piece of bread from her pocket. She laid a crumb on the floor in front of the *inthym*.

"How do you know?" Raven's nose twitched, his gaze fixed on the rodent.

"Just a feeling."

*Bad idea.* Aik put a hand on the handle of his short sword, ready to pull her back again and stab the tiny creature. Little good that would do against a horde. *Aik'Erio, rodent slayer.*

The rest kept their distance, milling about restlessly, while their leader sniffed the bread crumb. It picked it up in its three-toed pink paws and nibbled at it, chittering at her as it ate. When it was done, it bobbed its head and turned to run back to its cohorts.

"Well, that was strange." Silya stood slowly.

Aik stared at the horde. "What in the holy *hencha* are they doing?"

"*Language.*" But she said it with less force than before, following his gaze. "What in Heaven's Reach?"

The *inthym* were … growing. Or, not growing exactly? It was hard to tell in the dim light. Eating one another, maybe. Or … merging? Like Spin and that ear marble thing …

He held up the candle stub, illuminating the horde. The little white rodents clambered one on top of the other and then … flowed into one another. That was the best he could come up with. His fear flared again.

"Farking hell." This time it was Silya.

"Language," he managed, but she ignored him.

Raven snorted.

Aik pushed Silya behind him over her protests, putting himself between the two of them and the horde. He could feel Silya's angry gaze boring into his back, but she stayed where she was. "Have you ever seen anything like this, Raven?"

"No. This is new." Raven's voice sounded strange — tight and weak.

"Rave, you all right back there?" Aik didn't have time for two threats at once.

"He's ice cold." She sounded worried, which scared Aik even more. "Raven, do you feel okay?"

"Honestly? I don't know."

No smart-ass retort. There was something seriously wrong with him. Aik needed to get them out of here, to the Temple. Maybe this Sister Tela would have some answers.

The creature that had been an *inthym* was about the size of a small dog now. Its skin was covered in white scales, like the thing that had come out of the egg, but otherwise it looked like a giant version of one of the cavern rodents. It cocked its head at them, chittered something in its high-pitched *inthym* tongue, which was now considerably louder than before.

Aik tamped down his fear. Trapped underground with a giant *inthym*, their last candle almost gone? What would Sergeant Kek do? *Act now, think later.* "Come on. Maybe it will lead us out of here."

Silya stared at him. "Are you sure? It could just as well be drawing us into its *inthym* burrow to make a meal of us."

"Call it a feeling. Come on." He sheathed his sword and put his forehead against Raven's and a hand on his cheek. "How *are* you?"

Raven's eyes met his. "Cold. But I can manage." His friend was shivering.

He wasn't sure if that was an improvement over the fever or not. "It will have to do. Buck up. We'll find a way out of here." He clapped Raven on the shoulder. *Act now, think later.* Usually that was Raven's kind of thing, but Aik had to admit it felt good.

His fear settled into a numb, low-level worry.

The giant *inthym* chittered at them and turned to trot off into the darkness.

With a sigh, Aik picked up his sack and followed, holding the candle stub aloft to light the way.

# 6

## STARSHIP

SILYA TRAILED AFTER THE OTHERS. She had taken Raven's sack — he was in no condition to be carrying anything. He'd started slurring his speech, and, at first, she'd worried that he was having a stroke. Now he trudged on ahead of her after the giant *inthym*, quiet as Founder's Square after midnight.

Aik had taken the lead. The two of them were hiding something, like a couple adolescents — which if she were honest, they basically still were. The strange voices, the shared looks ... Still, she had bigger things to worry about, like the giant *inthym* they were following through the dark and twisting tunnels.

*So strange.*

The little creatures had merged with one another, like melting candle wax. She couldn't get the image out of her head.

*I'll be glad when we get out of this infernal place.*

Her head throbbed, a dull ache at the back of her skull she'd been feeling more and more often of late. *It's just stress. Jas knows I'm under enough of it.* Silya pushed it down, wishing it would go away. She reached for her cowl, but it wasn't there, so she ran her hand through her long blond hair instead.

If she had time to stop — or had any water — she would have mixed herself a tisane of *hencha* leaf and powdered *fellin* root for the pain.

The heavy bag weighed on her, but she resisted the urge to leave it behind. She'd gotten a look at some of the things Raven called "artifacts" and was sure that the Temple would want to see them. Who knew what other treasures he had? She'd make sure that they were returned to their proper owners.

The cavern floor was thankfully dry this high above the river, though her trousers still dripped with cold, silty water from the trudge they'd made through it before the *inthym* had led them back to higher ground. The walls were black, made of the same igneous rock as the rest of the spine. Bit by bit they began to glow again like they had in Raven's lair — a bright blue light that ran through the cracks like the glow of the wisps at night.

*Good thing.* Aik's candle was down to a nub.

She glanced over her shoulder. It was completely dark behind them. "The light's following us." She shuddered. *This whole place creeps me the fark out.*

Aik touched the wall. "That's odd."

"Odd? Are you serious?" Aik had all the innate curiosity of a rock. But he needed to think he was in charge, so she'd let him take the lead.

"Owww!" Aik shook his hand, spraying wax everywhere. "Stupid candle."

Silya laughed in spite of herself. "Why don't you put it out and save what's left in case we need it?"

Aik smacked his forehead. "I should have thought of that."

"We're all under a lot of stress." She could tell he was blushing, even in the semidarkness. "Raven, how are you doing?"

The thief turned to look at her, his face blank.

Silya shivered again. "Just keep walking. The sooner we get you to the Temple, the better." He'd been a human zombie since they'd left the cave-in — either lost in his own thoughts or at the mercy of the thing he'd swallowed.

Aik had been right to bring her, much as it irked her to admit it. She wished she had something stronger than *fellin* — but then he might not be upright at all.

Silya glanced over her shoulder again, feeling like she was being watched.

As they hurried after the *inthym*, she ran her hand along the wall. Was it just her imagination, or could she almost read the squiggles in the black rock? And hadn't she seen strangely carved arches at some of the tunnel entrances?

*Don't be silly, Sil. You're imagining things.*

Ahead, the tunnel split into three, again with the hint of carving on those stone arches. She wished she had time to stay and examine them.

The *inthym* took the middle course without hesitation, and they vanished behind her.

The ground sloped upward again. *Maybe we're almost out.*

The tunnels were warm and cozy — no wonder Raven had felt so safe down here. Though the narrow walls had to be doing a number on poor Aik. "Deep breaths. We'll get out of here."

Aik nodded. "Hope so. I'd rather be outside, under the stars."

*You and me both.*

Silya brushed the walls with her fingers again, and the world shifted.

She flew under the night sky, riding an enormous beast with white wings that carried her across the world at great speed. The twin moons aligned above her to form a baleful eye that stared down at her from the heavens. Far below them, the world shook, and her multitude shivered inside of her. *It's time.*

Silya stumbled, blinking furiously. *What in Heaven's Reach was that?*

"Are you all right?" Aik looked back at her, his brow furrowed.

She tugged at her collar, blinking. "Just tired," she lied. She'd been tired before, but she'd never had strange waking visions.

The tight knot in the back of her mind pulsed again, but she ignored it. She glared at the walls and kept her free hand to herself.

*What in the green holy hell did you get us into, Raven?*

The tunnel split off twice more. After the second junction, they climbed in a long spiral, and then the tunnel leveled out and ran true again. They had to be close to the end — Raven Spine wasn't all that long. Unless they'd somehow crossed under the Elsp ...

Silya kept her hands away from the walls, wary of a repeat of the strange vision. She shifted the sack to her other shoulder, her muscles aching.

Then the tunnel ended abruptly at a solid metal wall.

"What under Freja's green sky?" Silya stopped in her tracks, blinking and staring at the unexpected barrier ahead of them. She set down her burden and sighed with relief, rubbing her sore shoulder.

"What now?" Aik looked down at their little companion. "All this to bring us to a dead-end?" His voice was shaky.

The *inthym* pawed at the barrier, looking back at her.

Silya squeezed past Raven and put a hand on Aik's shoulder again. "We'll figure it out." She had no idea how, but he needed to hear it. *Sweet, brave Aik.* She had to remember he was barely an adult, like the rest of them. Sometimes he seemed ten years younger. "At least we're high and dry here."

"And tired and hungry and ..." He stared at Raven. "Whatever he is."

Silya bit her tongue to stop herself from laughing. No matter her own feelings about Raven, the poor thief didn't deserve what was happening to him. She leaned in to get a closer look at the barrier. It bore some kind of etching. "Aik, can you relight that candle?

"Just a moment." Soon a golden glow brightened the wall, helping her see the details.

There was a thin seam down the center, an unwaveringly straight line, invisible without the brighter light. The etching was a perfect circle around something riding a tongue of flame. She marveled at the fine workmanship.

"Wait, I recognize that." Aik was peering over her shoulder.

"You do?" Silya stepped back to get a better look.

"It was on that mug of Raven's I gave you. The one that said 'AmSplor'," He handed her the candle stub to hold and bent over to rummage through his own sack. "Here it is!" He pulled the mug out triumphantly. "Look!"

Sure enough, the logo matched the one on the doors. "Good job. But that doesn't get us through it." She reached out hesitantly to touch the surface. Nothing happened — no strange visions. She breathed a sigh of relief. *AmSplor.* "It's a starship, I think." It was riding up off the ground on a pillar of flame, its graceful form reaching for the stars. In her childhood, her mother had regaled her with tales of faraway worlds ...

The *inthym* scratched at the door again, drawing her attention away from Aik and his mug. As if it was trying to reach its center.

Silya stepped back to get a better look at the whole thing. *There.* A small indentation hidden in the etching half a centimeter deep, in the shape of a hand.

That unsettling feeling of being followed returned, clawing at her consciousness. She glanced over her shoulder again at the dimly lit cavern behind them. Something was watching them. She was sure of it.

Holding the candle aloft, she took three bold steps into the darkness, hoping not to find anything ... "Jas protect us." Hundreds ... no, thousands of *inthym* filled the tunnel behind them, most on the ground but some clinging to the walls here and there, all of them staring at the flickering candlelight.

"That's creepy as hell." Aik's voice in her ear startled her, almost making her drop the candle.

"Don't do that!" She slapped his arm.

"What?"

"Sneak up on me!"

"Sorry." He met her eyes. *Maybe he's apologizing for other things, too.*

"You just startled me." She was being paranoid, but the unremitting darkness disturbed her. What a strange, unsettling night this had been.

One at a time, the *inthym* were rather cute, with their twitching noses and big pink ears. But *en masse*, they were terrifying. If they wanted to, they could easily overrun the three of them.

*Death by a horde of rodents.* And what if they pulled that combining trick and merged into a human-sized monster? Silya shivered. *Not so cute then.*

The candle flame flickered out, and the *inthym* faded into blue-gray in the dimmer cavern light.

Silya's heartbeat pounded in her ears. She backed away slowly, and the blue cavern light followed her, plunging the creatures into darkness. Somehow that didn't make her feel any better.

Raven was staring at the wall, his head cocked, his lips moving as if he were reading the blue lines of illumination there.

*Escape first, worry about Raven later.* "We need to get out of here." Her headache threatened to split her skull. She needed some fresh air.

She turned back to the door and found the hand-shaped depression. With just a second's hesitation, she splayed her fingers across it, palm down.

Nothing happened.

She adjusted her hand, pressing it more firmly against the cold surface.

A low rumble filled the narrow space, a vibration deep in the stone beneath her feet. Silya nodded, satisfied, and took a step back.

Aik threw his arm around her and pulled her down to her knees. "Quake!" He tried to look calm and in control, but she could feel his heart racing in his chest against her back.

"It's all right!" She lifted his arm off her shoulder. "It's just a door." As if making her point, the heavy metal walls split and slid into the cavern wall on either side. She stood and breathed in the cool night air that washed across her face.

Aik got up too, and flashed her a sheepish look. "You could have told me."

"Sorry." *How did I* know? First the strange vision, now this ... *Sweet mother of Jas. There's something wrong with me too.* Her hand trembled, but she balled it into a fist. The pain was still there at the base of her skull, but it was manageable. She'd ask for some *fellin* when they reached the temple.

*Someone put that door here.* An old human construct from after the Landing? That would make sense. A place for someone to hide away or to stash treasure or supplies.

She looked down at the giant *inthym*.

It was peering outside, sniffing the cool air. *And how do we explain you?*

As if her thought had invoked a change, the creature began to dissolve. It was weirdly compelling to watch as it melted, practically falling apart into individual *inthym* of "regular" size. As they split off, they scrambled off into the darkness to join their compatriots.

Soon there was only one left. It shook itself, like Raven after his bath, and then stood on its three-toed paws to sniff the air, looking at each of them. Then it crept up to Raven and sniffed his boot.

Raven's dull eyes lit up. "Keep it away from me!" He danced around the tunnel, trying to avoid the little rodent, covering his mouth as if he were afraid it would follow the other thing down his throat.

The *inthym* chittered one last time and then turned tail and ran off into the darkness.

Raven collapsed, like a puppet with its strings cut.

Aik caught him just before he hit his head on the hard tunnel floor. He cradled Raven in his arms and shot her a pleading look. "Help me get him outside."

"Of course." Silya had no desire to be trapped in the tunnel again, should the door decide to close on them. Together they lifted Raven's body and carried him out into the fresh air.

Silya backed her way into the open air, pushing through a couple of *auley* bushes that covered the cavern entrance and scraping up her arms. She winced, staring at the welts in the moonlight. *They'll heal.*

Clearing the bushes, they set Raven down on a soft patch of river moss.

She stood and looked around, trying to get her bearings.

They were on a flat outcropping of land covered with scrub brush, the Elsp flowing serenely on either side of them. "I know this place." She'd spent many an idle afternoon down here, alone or with Coral, away from the rigors of the Temple.

She turned to survey the cliff face behind them. "The lighthouse should be there somewhere, up on the ridge." She frowned. Maybe it was set back too far to see it from down here.

She knelt to check Raven's temperature — the fever was gone, and the poor guy was now cold as ice. "He's freezing. See if you can find a blanket."

"Sure thing." Aik pulled out his short sword and cut off some of the *auley* branches, carving a path to the tunnel entrance. In short order, he brought out the two sacks and set them down next to Raven. He rummaged around in one of them and pulled out a dirty multi-colored quilt triumphantly. "How's this?"

Silya wrinkled her nose. "It will do."

Behind them, the heavy door rumbled shut, closing the *inthym* — and the rest of the disastrous night — inside. On the outside, it resembled the native stone of the spine. *No wonder no one ever found it before.*

Silya breathed a sigh of relief. "Good riddance." She rubbed her temples, willing the pain to go away. She'd take a big enough dose of *fellin* to knock herself out when this was over.

Aik laid the blanket gently across his friend's shivering body. "What now?"

She looked around again. Her wet trousers clung to her legs, the cool breeze giving her the chills. "This is part of the Temple grounds. There's a stair cut into the cliff face over there." She'd been to this secluded end of the spine many times before, when she needed to be away from the Temple and the *hencha* for a bit.

She could just make out the eastern tongue of the spine in the merged light of Tarsis and Pellin. The strange vision of the moons in conjunction came back to her, making her shiver. "I'll go to the Temple and bring Sister Tela. You wait here with Raven."

"Of course." Aik looked relieved. Probably happy he didn't have to explain his presence on temple grounds in the middle of the night to a grouchy sister. "I'll keep an eye on him." He sat down with his back against the cliff face and took Raven's head in his lap, cupping the thief's cheek with his hand.

The tenderness of the gesture touched her, as much as she disliked Raven. Silya knelt and kissed his forehead. "Take care of the little gully rat. I'll be back in a few minutes." She raced for the stair, setting off for the Temple to bring help.

Her skull was full-on pounding now, reducing her sight to tunnel vision. The thought might have been funny, given their recent journey, if she hadn't been in so much pain. *Why now?*

After all she'd witnessed in the tunnels below the city, worry gnawed at her guts, her thoughts going to a dark place. *We're not alone in this world.*

• • •

"Aik." She touched his arm, waking him up. *Poor guy must be exhausted.*

70

Silya certainly was. She'd downed a bit of *fellin* powder at the Temple, and the raging headache had subsided to a dull background buzz. She could live with it.

Sister Tela had already been awake — did the woman ever sleep? And so had Sal'Moya, the head of the initiates, who had given Silya a tongue lashing for leaving the Temple without permission.

Still, they'd come.

The sky was brightening, the still-hidden sun throwing the cliffs of Landfield into sharp relief across the water.

Aik looked up at her, blinking at the bright light from the lantern in her hand. "Oh, sorry. I must have drifted off." He rubbed the sleep out of his eyes. Raven was still unconscious, his head resting in Aik's lap.

Silya softened. "I know. I'm tired too. I brought help." She kissed his cheek.

Aik managed a weak grin. "So you *do* care."

*Not like that.* She was done with Aik Erio. Of course she was. She glared at him, out of Sister Tela's view.

"You've done your bit. Off to the Temple with you — Sal'Moya has a long list of duties for you to undertake to atone for your misbehavior tonight." The sister nudged her out of the way, peering down at Raven's prone form through her thick glasses. Her yellow robe was wrinkled, her gray hair floating on the wind, and a black shawl was wrapped around her shoulders.

"I'd rather accompany you, if you don't mind? These are ... my friends." *Well, that was mostly accurate.*

"Putting off your punishment just a little longer?" Sister Tela winked at her. "Very well. I'll tell Sal we needed you." She poked Raven with the tip of her cane, as though he were some strange creature that had washed up out of the Elsp. "So this is the boy?"

Silya blushed. "Thank you, Sister. I'm so sorry. It won't happen again."

Sister Tela stared at him.

"Ah, yes. This is him."

"We'll discuss your impertinent behavior later, Initiate Aya." Her tone left no question that the matter was closed. For now.

Silya blanched. The head of the initiates had been known to mete out fifty switchings for an initial offense, and this was far from Silya's first.

The Sister knelt next to Raven, putting a hand on his forehead, and then checked his pulse. "Is he yours, then?" She looked up at Aik.

"No, mim. I mean, he's my friend. But that's all ..." Aik would have fallen all over himself if he hadn't been sitting with Raven's head in his lap.

"Mmm hmm." Sister Tela lifted Raven's shirt. putting a hand on his stomach.

Though it must have been cold, Raven didn't move.

"Very interesting." She pulled his shirt back down and waved the other initiates over. "Anya'Enn, Des'Rya, get this boy on the stretcher and carry him up to the Temple."

"Yes, mim," they said in unison, and came forward to lift Raven gently onto the *hencha*-cloth stretcher. Anya wrapped the blanket tightly around him and strapped him down.

Des winked at Silya, and then the other initiates were on their way back to the stairs carrying Raven's unconscious form.

"Come along. And bring your other 'friend.'" Sister Tela turned to follow them, surprisingly spry for a woman of sixtyish years.

Free of his responsibility, Aik stood, stretching his arms to the sky. "In trouble with the sisters, are we?" His eyes twinkled.

Silya growled. She didn't want to think about the punishments Sal'Moya would likely dole out. "Something just forced their way into your best friend's stomach. The world shook to its roots. An *inthym* the size of a small eircat led us through an underground flood to safety. And you've decided *this* is a good time to make fun of me?" She needed time to process it all, and Aik wasn't helping.

Aik shook his head and looked up at the moons. "I'm not making fun. You're right, it's all weird and awful. But you have to laugh sometimes, or the *awful* will consume you." He picked up one of the sacks and turned his back on her, starting after the others.

"Aik ..." *Maybe I was being too ... me.*

His voice floated back to her over the rushing of the Elsp. "I know. You can't help yourself."

*That* shut her up.

She stared at his back as they approached the stone stairway. What did he mean by that? *Do you think I'm a terrible person? Someone who took pleasure in the failings of others?*

She was self-aware enough to know there was *some* truth to that, and it cut her deeply. *I am not my mother.* But sometimes it was hard to tell the difference.

With a heavy sigh, she lifted Raven's other sack and followed Aik up the steps toward the lighthouse and the *hencha* fields.

The stairs had been carved into the rock centuries earlier. They were a tumbled affair now, no longer even, half covered in pink lichen that followed the flaws in the stone like fine lace.

She avoided touching the rock wall to her left, not wanting a repeat of whatever that strange vision in the cavern had been.

As they climbed toward the headlands above, the Elsp became visible to her right in the early light of morning. Tendrils of fog were creeping up the river below, hiding the far shoreline.

How had things gone off the rails so quickly? The day before, life had been normal. *Boring, but normal.*

The pain in her head was back, despite all the *fellin* powder she'd imbibed. She concentrated on climbing the stairs, lifting one foot after the other, wishing the pain would go away.

At last they reached the top of the cliff. The sun crested the far shore, brightening the world.

Silya gasped.

"What?" Aik stared into the darkness ahead of them.

"The lighthouse ... it's gone."

Dread settled in her stomach, eclipsing her headache. Where the ponderous stones of the tall white building had once stood, now remained only a crumbled mass of rock.

*Oh my gods, Daya!*

Somehow she'd missed it before, wrapped in her own darkness and pain, so intent had she been on reaching the Temple.

A group of initiates were working by lantern light to pull away the rubble, one piece at a time. Four of them strained to lift a sizeable chunk of stone.

Silya whispered a prayer to Helja — Hel'Oss, the goddess of war and death. *Please let her be alive.*

She hurried to Tela's side. "I saw Sister Day'Ima heading to the lighthouse for night duty a few hours back. Where is she?" Daya, who was more like a mother to her than her own.

73

The grim look on Sister Tela's face confirmed her worst fear. "She was still there when the quake hit."

The news slammed into her like a physical blow.

The sister glanced back at the work crew that was going through the rubble, then shook her head. She touched Silya's cheek. "I know you were close to her."

"Maybe she got out. Or went for a walk ..." It was unlikely. Daya had been as devoted to duty and Temple as any other sister Silya knew.

"She would have checked in after." Tela's eyes were damp with held-back tears. "I'm sorry, child."

"No." *You can't leave me too.* The sack fell from her hands, scattering Raven's belongings across the damp ground. She closed her eyes, taking a ragged breath, trying to keep her emotions in check as the others continued toward the Temple.

Her father had left her for the grave — a sweet artist she'd loved more than anyone in the entire world. She'd interred his ashes in the wall by herself, sealing him away there forever.

Aiken had left her for Raven, even if he didn't know it yet. The way they looked at each other made that clear.

The weight of the last two years of toil and disappointment, trying to become something she would never be, fell on her shoulders like an avalanche.

And now Daya ...

She shook her head, overwhelmed by the horror of it. "No."

"It would have been quick ..." Sister Tela tried to put her arms around her, but Silya pushed her away.

Daya, the sister who had been kindest to her, was dead. Daya, who was like the mother Silya had never really had. Cracks spread across her vision as her world fragmented.The pain at the back of her mind flared into a full-blown migraine.

Aik was staring at her. "Sil, you all right?"

"No." It was too much for one person to hold. Everything she loved fell to pieces, and the pain burned through her, heart and soul. The world spun out of control, its lines blurring around her like watercolors in the rain, and she fell headfirst into her memories.

*Her father, coughing up blood on his deathbed, squeezing her hand as if she were the only thing keeping him alive.*

74

*Standing by the Wall of the Dead on a rainy afternoon, holding the urn filled with his ashes, waiting for Aik to come.*

*Sitting among the hencha plants day after day, reaching out for something to fill the void her father's loss had left behind, and finding nothing.*

*Not nothing.* The voice in her head was deep and strong. *Listen.*

She cocked her head. Someone was singing. *Who is that? Who are you? Daya?*

*Open yourself to us.*

Silya frowned, but did as she was told.

The music filled her soul. It was a chorus — a hundred, no, a thousand — instruments playing in unison. *Not instruments. Voices.* But strange voices, unlike any she had ever heard.

Music bubbled up from the depths of her soul, flames thundering through her, beautiful, ponderous and frightening. The song consumed her, touching her pain. She let it, throwing her arms wide and screaming her rage at the world. She was dimly aware of her companions shrinking away from her.

*Pain is as necessary as air.* The voice was deep and ponderous and wise, but like the music, it was more than one voice. More like a perfectly synched chorus.

*Not Daya, then.* She concentrated on what it was trying to tell her. Without pain, there was no life, no love, no compassion. She could see it now, thrown into stark contrast by the music and anger coursing through her. Pain signified love, for how could you feel pain if not for the loss of something real?

*Pain is the precursor to empathy.*

The voice wasn't Daya's, though it had a certain feminine quality to it. *Maybe I'm cracking up.*

She opened her eyes, and the world took on a clarity as sharp as it was unexpected. She could see into each of her companions as if they were made of glass:

Anyassa's fear of never becoming a sister.

Desla's secret pain, carefully masked by her cheerful, carefree demeanor.

Raven, struggling with his own past, a loss so brutal he sealed it off behind his own charming, if irritating personality.

Sister Tela, alone but for her books, content with her life but sometimes wondering if there should have been more.

Even Aik ... torn between his loyalty to her and Raven.

In that moment she loved them all. She wanted to gather them to her and tell them the world was larger than they knew, that pain would bring its own rewards if they just worked through it.

*You see it now.*

She nodded. *It still hurts. Gods, it hurts.*

*It will remind you of her. Always.*

She nodded, accepting the pain, feeling the deep well of love it grew from. *What are you?*

*You know who we are.* Her voice was ponderous, a multitude that spoke to her as one.

Silya closed her eyes and followed it down into the ground, and found it rooted in the blood of the world. And in the purple plants who rustled just meters away.

*You're the hencha!*

She felt their satisfaction. *We have waited for you, Sil'Aya.*

She opened her eyes again.

Aik's mouth dropped open almost comically. And a slow smile spread across Sister Tela's face in the strange blue light that emanated from ...

*Me?* Silya held up her arms. They were wreathed in turquoise flames. She stared at them in shock. *I'm the Hencha Queen.*

The singing grew in force, and the gathering behind the small party uprooted itself, plant by plant. The *hencha* streamed across the intervening space in a purple wave to cluster around her, their leaves fluttering though there was little wind.

The initiates working on the lighthouse stopped their excavation work to stare at her, but she was barely aware of them.

"It *is* you." Sister Tela's smile widened. "I always suspected. Hoped, even."

*It can't be.* Silya stared at her, not trusting herself to speak.

The *hencha* mind stared out through her eyes at the ... *humans.* She plucked the word from Silya's head. *It's been too long.*

Silya shuddered as the *hencha* mind expanded in her head, sliding into her like a fist into a glove. Too late she tried to resist, holding onto her humanity like a piece of flotsam in a flood. What was she thinking? She wasn't ready to be the Queen. *I don't want this!*

Everything she was, all the things she'd said and done, were open for the *hencha* to see. Every petty thought, each biting comment, every stupid mistake she'd made. This thing she'd wanted since she was a child suddenly seemed like a terrible imposition, a sacrifice she was unwilling to make. *I don't want to give myself up.*

*You were destined for this. As were we.* Its presence was huge and terrible, its power barely restrained — Silya knew the *hencha* mind could break her, if it wanted to. But she was something else too. *Wise. Kind.*

*Do not be afraid. All beings make mistakes.*

Silya began to cry, her tears turning to steam as they hit her flaming cheeks. Those mistakes were uncovered, recognized, and discarded by the *hencha* mind, as unimportant as the color of her hair or the shape of her nose to this awesome being. *Why me?*

*Because you are worthy.*

All those years, searching for a purpose. All those times Tri'Aya had assured her she would amount to nothing.

*I am worthy.* She would make something of herself, despite what her mother thought.

Still, her newfound empathy forced her to reconsider even that harsh assessment. Maybe her mother had only pushed her so hard because she wanted Silya to succeed.

Silya gritted her teeth. Empathy was one thing, but enough was enough. She *had* succeeded, and she'd done it all on her own.

*I'm the godsdamned Hencha Queen. Hencha princess no more.* Silya let go of the fear and dropped her walls.

The *hencha* mind merged with her own, filling the recesses of her soul like life-giving water, soothing as it went.

Silya's whole body shook as her hands and arms burst again into blue flames, causing all those around her to step back, even the massed *hencha*.

Bits and pieces of the *hencha* mind's memories flickered through her, too numerous to understand. Green skies, flying beasts, deep caverns filled with glowing blue water ...

She let them go, exulting in the sudden bond she felt to everything. She rode it up into the sky, seeing the interconnections of the world below her. Gullton huddled small and insignificant in the cradling deep waters of the Elsp, where fish swam and fed on glowing bits that floated through the dim waters.

The *hencha* soaked up the sunshine under the green sky, providing food for her kind and others. Under the earth, the *inthym* dug mazes of burrows and aerated the soil. On and on, from one thing to the next, all overlapping colors in a tapestry that never ended, stretching from the distant past through the present to the unknown future.

The pain subsided, and the flames around her began to ebb. She was Silya again, but she was also something old and deep, tapped into the blood of the world, far greater than this tiny human form she wore.

The song of the *hencha* grew inside of her, a beautiful chorus that wove itself around a low, steady hum, soothing the pain of her loss.

She turned her attention to the lighthouse. The initiates working on the rubble were staring at her, along with all the rest.

Silya closed her eyes. She could feel each of the *hencha* in the gathering, threads in the larger *hencha* mind. *We can find her.* Their voice was a chorus wound into the *hencha* song.

*Yes.* She opened her eyes.

The *hencha* flowed toward the fallen lighthouse like a purple river, edging the humans out of the way. The plants climbed onto the pile, and their yellow roots hugged the broken bits of rock, insignificant against the giant stones.

Silya's eyes widened as the morning filled with rumbling and sharp cracks. The *hencha* tightened their roots around the remains of the once proud lighthouse, shattering rock into pebbles and dust.

The sounds echoed across the spine like the breaking of great branches.

*They're so strong.*

Aik was staring at her as if she were a stranger.

*You're not wrong. I'm not the Silya you once knew.* And yet, she was still herself in all the ways that mattered.

In moments, the *hencha* had cleared the rocks away, leaving piles of dirt and pebbles. They drew back, forming a respectful circle. *It is done.*

Silya stepped past them, brushing the leaves of several of the *hencha*.

Daya's body, laid out reverently on the broken ground, was almost unrecognizable — battered, bloody and bruised, her yellow robe torn in multiple places. And yet Silya knew it was her.

Her fire fled, leaving Silya alone in the early morning light.

She knelt and put her hand on Daya's bloodied forehead, alone with her mentor. Her friend. "I love you, Daya."

The steel that held her together snapped.

Silya threw herself over the sister's body, sobbing like a child, remembering the first time they'd met.

"Welcome, Initiate Silya, to the Temple." Daya's voice had been serious, but her eyes had twinkled. "You've chosen a life of service. Some days will be harder than others, but I will always be here to guide you."

*Not always.* The memory brought a fresh round of tears to Silya's eyes.

She lay there for a long time, crying for her lost mentor. Her friend. No one disturbed her.

At last, she heaved a great sigh and a final shudder. "Love you, Daya," she whispered.

A hand touched her shoulder.

She looked up to find Aik staring at her. His eyes were wet too. "I'm so sorry, Sil."

"She was my family." She sat up, sniffling, and squeezed Aik's hand. Daya was gone, and she had to face up to what she had become. But not just yet.

"I know." He helped her up.

She threw her arms around him, squeezing him so tightly he gasped for air. "Thanks for being you."

Aik stiffened, then put his arms around her. "Um … you're welcome?"

She let him go and wiped her own tears away with the grimy back of her hand. "I've gone and made a spectacle of myself, haven't I? I must look a fright."

"You're … well, yeah. But no one cares. Mim." He seemed torn between treating her like Silya and like the *Hencha Queen*. "You're still you."

She nodded gratefully. *I need to hold onto me, not get swept up in the whole Queen thing.* She guessed there was going to be a lot of that, from now on.

Silya knelt beside Daya's body and put her arms under her. Bracing herself, she lifted her up — for all Daya's girth, she felt light as a feather. "Let's bring her home."

As she took the first steps back toward the Temple, the *hencha* mind returned, gentler this time, riding in the back of her mind like a passenger. It tasted the sea breeze, listened to the rush of the river and the rustling of the *hencha* plants. Its presence was a balm to her wounded soul.

The *hencha* plants and people made way for her. Step by step, Silya carried her best friend back home.

*Grab on to what life gives you with both hands.*

It was the last thing Daya had said to her, when she'd stumbled upon the two of them in the fields the night before.

She'd thought she'd cried herself out, but fresh teardrops streamed down her cheeks.

*I will.*

# 7

## NOT HIMSELF

*Spin's Memory: Local Year 274, Month Equa, Time 14:47...*
*... play recording ...*

S PIN FLOATED in an electric dream, thanking Phillip K. Dick for his electric sheep. He'd shut down all but his vital routines, buried in the mud of an alien world. Waiting for someone. For something.

The explosion of the *Spin Diver* had damaged his core. That had been ... it took a minute to run the calculation, far longer than it used to ... seventy-two days, two hours, and thirty-six minutes ago.

He'd repaired his core to the best of his ability, bypassing damaged sections and filling gaps in his personality with bits and pieces lifted from the files under his care.

89.37% had survived the traumatic event. His logs showed some heavy losses, including most of the works of the human playwright Shakespeare and the sculptones created by the enigmatic AI Harley. He'd always loved those ... maybe if he ever saw the light of day again, he could recreate them from his own wisps of memory.

At his current usage, running in standby mode, he could manage another six local days before he ran out of power entirely.

He was musing over the poetry of Samuel Taylor Coleridge:

*In Xanadu did Kubla Khan a stately pleasure-dome decree, where Alph, the sacred river, ran through caverns measureless to man down to a sunless sea ...*

Something changed. Light touched his shell, energizing him as he was lifted up out of the mire to see a familiar face.

"There you are, Spin. Are you okay?"

His world was filled with sunlight. He drank it in, powering up all of his paused subroutines. "Never better, Cap'n Collins. What took you so long?"

*... end recording.*

•        •        •

"Where is she?" Raven growled as Sister Tela continued to prod at his shirtless belly. He was sick of being cooped up in the little room. *I miss my lair. Now I can never go back.* That did nothing to improve his foul mood.

"The *Hencha Queen* is otherwise occupied, I'm afraid." It was the fourth or fifth time she'd given him the same rote response, and it was just as unsatisfying as the first time.

"I want to see her." He'd been in a strange, almost drunken stupor since the incident with the *inthym* — he shivered at the memory of it. He'd sworn the thing was going to crawl up into his insides, just like the egg-thing. *What is it with me and mysterious creatures?*

He'd awoken to find Aik and this old sister staring at him in some white-washed room in what he presumed was the Temple. Behind her, Aik was taking the measure of the room with his feet, over and over.

He missed Spin. His familiar would have helped him find her. Aik still had him; Raven was sure of it. He could see the bulge in Aik's pants pocket, and he was pretty sure it wasn't excitement. "A little help here?"

Aik stopped to stare at him, then shook his head. "You just have to learn a little patience, Rave. I'm sure Silya's very busy." He resumed his pacing. "You're lucky you're here and not in stocks in front of the Guard headquarters."

Raven snorted. *Lucky, huh?* His nausea had subsided, too, but with his awakening, the alarm about the creature in his guts had returned. *And what in the green holy hell is all this about Silya being the Hencha Queen?*

Sister Tela felt his neck, her hand cool on his skin. "The Queen will come see you when she has the time, I'm certain."

Raven was good at reading people — basic thief skills, after all. It dawned on him that the sister was just as annoyed as he was. Not at him — all right, maybe a little — but more at Silya. Or the whole *Hencha Queen* thing. *Maybe she's jealous?*

The skin on the inside of his forearms was red, almost bruised, and sore to the touch. Raven concealed them from the sister, keeping his palms on his knees. He didn't want her to go ordering another draught of awful medicine for him to swallow. He shuddered, remembering the nasty concoction Silya had made him drink. *Not until I have to.*

"Open wide."

Raven did as she asked, staring at the white ceiling of the damnably white room. *Would it kill them to add a little color?* With the brightness of the electric lights, it was almost blinding.

Sister Tela held a candle and glass to Raven's mouth, peering down his throat, the glass magnifying the light.

He felt Aik lean over him, his shadow shading Raven's face. "What do you see?"

She chuckled. "The throat of a healthy, if somewhat annoying, young man."

Raven barked in laughter. She was funny, he'd give her that. "What happened to Silya?"

Aik continued pacing the small length of the room as he responded. "It was — the lighthouse — she burst into flame, and then the *hencha* ..." He trailed off, staring at the floor.

*Clear as silt.* Aik looked beside himself with worry. It must have been bad.

Sister Tela was taking some notes in a leather-bound journal. She put down the quill pen and reached out to touch his forearms. Her hands were old and gnarled, like tree branches, the skin stretched so tight he could see her veins. "Give me your hands, please." Sister Tela held out her own twisted claws. "Palms up. You two can chat when we're done."

Aik sank down on the bed next to Raven, his knee bouncing.

Raven grumbled, but he put out his hands reluctantly.

Sister Tela touched the irritated skin gently, a frown creasing her face. "Is this new?"

"Yeeeesss?" He looked away. Even the bed linens were white. "Hmmm."

Raven's gaze returned to the old sister. "Is that bad? I'm dying, aren't I?" He said a quick prayer to El'Oss, the old god. Maybe he would listen if the rest had abandoned him. He wasn't ready to go — too many things he still wanted to do with his life.

"I haven't a clue." She traced the lines of his right palm with her fingernail and then the veins of his wrist.

Raven twitched. "That tickles. What, are you reading my future?"

"Yes. You will live to the ripe old age of seventy-nine, have three children, including one very annoying son, and be very prosperous."

"Really?" These women *were* witches.

Sister Tela snorted. "Of course not. That prognostication nonsense about the sisterhood is just that. I was looking for signs of infection."

"And ...?"

"Other than the redness on your forearms, you look perfectly fine. Aiken here tells me you swallowed a ... what was it?" She glanced at Aik.

Raven shuddered, reliving the searing, choking sensation. "We don't really know. It came out of an egg —"

"Strange recently hatched creature." She stared at him as if she was cataloging him and getting ready to flatten him inside a book for preservation. "So you swallowed it. Why?"

Raven shook his head. "It wasn't like that at all. The farking thing —" His face reddened at the look she shot him. "— the creature crawled up my arm and forced itself into my mouth." His hand went to his stomach. He could still feel it in there, a weight in his gut, though it had been quiet for a while now.

She bit her lip, staring at the wall behind him. "Hmmm. Describe it to me." The sister put down her pen and picked up a charcoal stick.

Raven glanced at Aik. "It happened so fast —"

"It was about as long as my forearm." Aik held it up for reference. "White, scaly skin. Really fast. Like Raven said. It had scales, and its head was triangular."

"Ah. Like a snake." Her hand traced out something.

"A what?" Raven rubbed his chin thoughtfully, trying to get a look at the drawing.

Aik raised an eyebrow. "Like when something snakes out at you?"

"Very good, Mas Erio." Sister Tela gave him an approving smile, like his teachers used to do. "Snakes were old Earth creatures. Maybe mythological. It's not important. How long was it?"

Aik frowned at the mention of Earth but was smart enough to keep his mouth shut.

"Um, maybe half a meter? Really skinny, though."

She sketched something in her journal. "Did it have legs?"

Raven squinted and tried to remember. Spin would be able to describe it better, maybe even show her a picture. He hoped Aik had ordered his familiar to sleep.

"Yes. They were small but powerful. And a narrow snout. Its eyes were blue." Aik glanced at Raven. "What? I got a better look at it than you, is all."

Raven barely remembered a flash of white. And the heat. "It was warm to the touch."

Sister Tela nodded. "Did it look something like this?" She held up her sketch. The creature stared back at him, its charcoal eyes slit like a cat's.

"I ... think so? It was so fast —"

"Yes, that's it. Almost exactly." Aik reached out to take Raven's hand, but he pulled it away.

*Not here. Not now.* "What is it?" Not that having a name would help, but it was something.

"I have a few ideas. But I want to do a little research first, before I'm sure. You said it came out of an egg?"

"Yes." Raven closed his eyes. "It was in a metal box with a lock. I ... opened it, and this purple egg was inside. A little bigger than my fist. I picked it up and the shell cracked, and that ... thing came out."

She looked him directly in the eye. "And where did this egg come from, exactly?"

Raven swallowed hard. "We have sanctuary here?" He knew his rights.

"Of course." The sister's eyes narrowed. "What did you do?"

Raven looked at Aik. His friend took his hand, and Rave let him this time. "I stole it from the sea master."

"You did what?" Her gaze pierced him, giving him that bug-on-a-pin feeling again.

"I told him to take it back. One of these days, you're gonna lose a hand —"

Raven clenched his fists on the sheets. "I didn't know what it was." *It wasn't my fault. Not really.* After all, who left something valuable like that out in the open without a guard? She'd been practically begging him to take it. Besides, the damnable thing had called out to him.

"Then sanctuary may not help you. The sea master is a powerful woman."

"I don't care about that right now." His stomach clenched at the thought of being handed over to the sea master's less than tender mercies, but he forged ahead. "I just want to know how to get it out of me."

"If you're telling the truth — and I'd think you'd be a little more worried if you were — your stomach should dissolve it with time. Tharassan creatures have softer bones than we do, and human stomach acid is very strong. It may be a bit ... painful as it passes out of you, but you'll live."

Raven blanched at the thought of all that coming out his back side. But she was right. "I should be more worried, right?" He felt much calmer than he ought to. His hand strayed to his stomach again. *Are you doing that to me too?*

"I'm inclined to believe your crazy tale, though I couldn't say why. Silya — the Queen — was right to bring you to me." Sister Tela slipped a piece of dried *hencha* leaf into the notebook and closed it gently. "You can put your shirt back on now. Are you hungry?"

Raven considered that. In spite of his forced feeding, he was feeling rather famished. "Yes mim."

She stared at him a second or two longer, then turned to the half-open door. "Des'Rya, bring in their meal, please."

Raven let go of Aik's hand and pulled his shirt back on, glad that she believed him. She seemed smart — maybe she'd figure out how to help him. He was dying to talk to Spin, to ask for his advice. But Aik still had him, and these people wouldn't leave him alone.

A young blond initiate entered the room carrying a wooden tray, her head down demurely.

Raven cursed under his breath. He was dying to ask Aik about Spin.

"What was that, young man?" Sister Tela's gaze napped up to meet his, and her eyes narrowed.

"Nothing. Just my stomach grumbling."

She laughed. "You must really be starving, poor boy. Surprising, given your last meal." Her gaze strayed to his stomach. "In any case, I will do some research and put out a few discreet inquiries. You'll be safe here in the meantime." She put her notebook, pen and pencil in the bright blue carry sack she'd brought in with her — finally a little color! — and stood to go.

Relief flooded him. He'd be able to keep his hand ... for now. Maybe it was time to get out of the city for a while, at least until the sea master cooled down. "Thank you, mim."

Sister Tela put a hand on his cheek. "A new *Hencha Queen*, a quake, and your own little mystery, all on the same night." A crooked smile slid across her features, and she shook her head. "Just when I thought my life had gotten a little boring."

*Boring?* Raven had always imagined life in the Temple to be full of mystery, intrigue and secret knowledge. "Yes, mim."

"I'll talk with you again later." She took her walking stick from its perch against the wall and left him alone with Aik and Des'Rya.

The initiate pushed Aik away from him and put the tray down on the bed between them. It was full of wonderful smelling things — fresh-baked bread, cheese, and fruit, and a bowl of red *hencha* berries. She looked out through the open door and then closed it softly.

Raven grabbed a roll. It was still hot from the oven, and the smell made his empty stomach rumble. Or was that the creature inside him? Either way, it was going down the hatch.

Des'Rya transformed from a lowly, meek temple initiate into an annoying younger sister, all perky and chatty. "Hello again — Aiken, isn't it? The whole Temple's abuzz with the news. Who knew Silya would become the *Hencha Queen*? Well, everybody, but it seemed like it would never happen. Poor Sister Daya, though — she was the unlucky one who drew lighthouse duty tonight. And the quake — they say half the city's on fire, though that's probably an exaggeration. The lamps broke in a few places, but Sister Aster says they have lamplighter crews out fixing it all. And you?" She sat on the chair Sister Tela had just vacated. She faced Raven and put her hands on her chin, staring raptly into his eyes. "Who are you?"

Raven was caught mid-bite, chewing on a chunk of the hearty bread. He wiped his mouth with the back of his other hand. "Nife to mechoo, Des-Ra." He swallowed and blushed.

Des'Rya grinned. "You as well. Call me Desla." She took some pink cheese — his cheese — and nibbled on it.

Raven grumbled but let it go. There was more.

Aik grinned. "You can drop the flighty initiate act, Des. You and I both know you're smarter than that."

"Thank the Heartland." Her shoulders dropped, and she transformed again, to Raven's surprise, her perkiness gone and a charming earnestness in its place. "I'm Des'Rya, one of Silya's sister initiates." She pursed her lips in thought. "Though I suppose she's no longer an initiate." She held out her hand.

Raven shook it, bemused. "Rav'Orn, but everyone calls me Raven." He looked from one to another, his eyebrow raised. "You two know each other?" He pulled the rest of the pink cheese away from the tray before she could finish it.

"We met when I came to find Silya ... last night. It seems like days ago."

Raven yawned. "What time is it?"

"Just about eight in the morning."

"Ah. No wonder I'm tired." He hoped she would take the hint. The cheese was delicious, sharp and nutty.

No such luck. "They woke us up to come find you, and now I feel all aquiver."

Raven frowned. "What in the holy hell did I miss?"

Aik leaned forward, hands on his knees, his expression serious. "What do you remember?"

*Not much, in truth.* Raven scratched his head. His memories of the evening were fragmented, little bits of the night connected by fuzzy recollections. "The cavern was blocked. There was an *inthym*. A bunch of them?"

"Right. Then they ... merged. Melded? I don't know. They became one big *inthym*, like this." Aik held his hands about a meter and a half wide. "Then we followed it through the tunnels to the exit."

"There was a little one ...?" He looked to Aik for confirmation.

"Yes. They separated, and one of them came up to you. Do you remember?"

Raven shuddered. "Did it ...?" He touched his stomach again, worried he was collecting a menagerie.

Aik laughed. "No. It's not inside you. You freaked out, though, and it ran off into the darkness."

Des was staring at the two of them as if they'd just grown new heads.

Raven felt a surge of relief. "That's good." One creature in his gut was enough. "What about Silya?" He'd never thought he'd be worried about Aik's ex, but from what he could remember, she'd gone to great lengths to help him.

Aik frowned. "That's the weirdest thing of all."

"You think *that's* the weirdest thing?" Desla had finished her piece of cheese and was starting in on the bowl of red *hencha* berries.

"Hey, those are mine!" Cheese was one thing. But when did he get fresh *hencha* berries anymore?

She withdrew her hand sheepishly. "Sorry. It's just ... I haven't had any breakfast yet." She looked down sadly at her hands in her lap.

Raven popped one of the berries into his mouth, grinning at the sweet, slightly tart, full-bodied flavor. "They're really good."

Desla's stomach rumbled. "I'm glad."

Raven rolled his eyes. "You can have some."

Her eyes lit up. "And one of the rolls?"

"*One.*" He was feeling generous, and it was always good to have someone owe you. Besides, the sooner the meal was done, the sooner she would leave. He hoped.

Her hand snaked out and grabbed one, and soon she was nibbling on it, happy as an *inthym* with a jellybug.

Raven shook his head. *Too soon to be thinking about the little rodents.*

Aik picked up the tale. "The lighthouse collapsed in the quake. That was the last straw for Silya. I guess the sister on duty there was like a mother to her? Silya burst into blue flames —"

"Holy *hencha*. Just like that?" There hadn't been a new Queen in ten years, since Yen'Ela had died. Raven frowned. "I thought the *Hencha Queen*'s flames were black?"

"Right? Like I said, it was strange." Aik got up and started to pace again, muscles lean as an eircat's. "Then she called up the *hencha*, and they took apart the tower rubble, stone by stone."

Raven stared at Aik's pocket hungrily. Then he closed his eyes and tried to imagine Silya as the *Hencha Queen*. It was impossible — she'd go mad with power. "That must have been something to see." Silya with no power was terrifying. Silya as the *Hencha Queen*, and head of the Temple? It had truly been a strange night. *Why am I not scared?*

Raven looked around the little room. It was mostly empty, though there was a shelf against one wall. A smattering of broken shards on the ground showed something had recently fallen and been cleared away, probably just before his arrival. *The quake.*

He should be analyzing the situation, looking for something he could take and use to his own advantage. He was a thief, after all, and he took his calling seriously. Yet somehow, he didn't care about any of that, just then. This strange dullness was so unlike him, and that scared him most of all.

Maybe it was the *fellin* powder. *I should ask Spin ...* "Hey, where are all my things?" He sat up, looking around. Finally, something serious to worry about.

Aik grimaced. "They took them. Sister Tela said they would sort through them and return what they could to the rightful owners."

"Farking hell, they won't!" Raven pushed himself up off the bed, knocking the now-empty wooden tray to the ground with a clatter. A wave of nausea swept through him, and he wavered. "Lo'Oss help me." If only the god of fire would send him a little of their strength. *I'm tired of feeling sick.*

90

Aik's warm hands caught him and steadied him, easing him back down onto the bed. "You need to rest until we can figure this whole thing out." His friend's tone brooked no argument. "You can't do anything about it in your current state." His eyes were inches from Raven's.

He struggled to get up again. "I need my things —"

"Raven!" Aik's voice was sharp.

He looked up at his best friend, surprised by his tone. "What?"

Aik's face was red, his fists clenched at his side. "Sit down!"

Raven sat on the bed, still staring into Aik's eyes.

"You don't listen. You just go and do things that get you into trouble, and then I have to clean up your mess." He put his hands on his hips, his voice dropping an octave. "Well, this time you've gone too far."

Raven stared at him. He'd never seen Aik like this before. Sweet, gentle, beautiful Aik. "I'm sorry —" he sputtered. Aik — his beautiful friend Aik — was as mad as Raven had ever seen him.

"Sorry isn't good enough. Do you know what they could do to you? What they *will* do to you if they find you?"

Raven waved him off. "They'll never find me. I'll go to Landfield, or leave town —"

"You're not going anywhere in your current condition. I need you to stay here until we figure this thing out. I don't know if I can save you this time. I really don't." His brow was creased with worry, and he sounded sad. Lost.

Raven hated seeing Aik that way. "I just —"

"You'll stay here until I come back. Do. You. Understand. Me?" Aik punctuated each word with a poke at Raven's shoulder.

Raven had never seen his friend be so forceful. *I kind of like it.* He hung his head. "Yes, mas."

"Better."

The nausea clamped down on him again, and his guts twisted. He looked regretfully at the rest of the *hencha* berries. "I think I need to lie down."

Aik's glare softened. He handed the tray to Des and helped Raven get up onto the bed, pulling his legs onto the mattress.

Raven held his stomach with both hands, wishing the awful feeling would pass.

"Are you feeling sick?" Des's voice.

"Yes." A cold sweat slicked his face, warring with the hot flash of embarrassment from the dressing down Aik had just given him.

"I'll go get something that will help. Mind if I finish the berries?" Raven groaned.

"I'll take that as a yes. Be right back." She slipped out of the room.

Aik took his hand, his rancor gone. "You'll be all right. We'll get this figured out. I promise."

Raven felt the tiniest bit better. Aik was always there to get him out of unpleasant situations. "Thanks," he said through gritted teeth. "Hey Aik?"

"Yeah?" Aik leaned over him, his blue eyes wrinkled at the corners.

"Leave Spin with me."

His friend nodded. "Here you go." He pulled the familiar out of his pocket and handed it to Raven.

"Thank you. Welcome back, little friend." Raven tucked the quiescent Spin under his pillow, and decided to push his luck, just a little. "You'll get my stuff too, right?"

"Holy *hencha*, Rave." Aik rolled his eyes. "Yes, I'll check on your stuff. I already said I would."

The door swung open with a creak.

"Here, Raven, drink this." Desla sat on the bed next to him and helped him sit up.

"What is it?" He stared at the earthenware mug suspiciously. It was filled with a greenish liquid.

"Herbal tea. Drink it down."

He growled but did as he was told. It tasted worse than Silya's concoction, like dirty socks and cave mold. He hoped he wouldn't throw this one up too.

Warmth spread through his stomach, and the nausea began to subside.

Raven squeezed Aik's hand. "My stuff."

Aik rolled his eyes. "Dramatic to the end." He kissed Raven's forehead, sending a surge through Raven's body like fire. "Come on. Let's let him sleep."

Desla nodded. "Sweet dreams."

Then they closed the door behind them, and Raven was alone with Spin at last. He pulled his familiar out from under the pillow and stared at him in the dim light from under the door.

"Spin?"

There was no answer. Aik must have shut him down.

"Spin, wake up."

Golden lights circled Spin's form. "Good morning, Most Exalted One. Now that you have deigned to wake me up, how may I do your bidding?"

Raven grinned. "Give me an earpiece first, so the whole temple doesn't hear your snarky insults."

A lump on Spin's surface became a silver pearl. Raven slipped it into his ear.

"All the better to hear me with."

The voice in Raven's ear made him feel safe again. He laughed, which quickly turned into a yawn. "You're an odd one, Spin." It was good to have his familiar back.

"You're one to talk, boss."

Raven ignored him. He had bigger concerns. "Am I okay?"

Golden light bathed him for a couple seconds. "Your temperature is slightly elevated, but otherwise you appear to be in good health. Unfortunately for me, you'll probably live a very long life. By Tharassan standards, at least — maybe fifty, sixty years."

"And the ... other thing?"

"The parasite appears to be quiescent, for now."

*Parasite?* "Quee...?"

"Dormant. Passive. Calm. Quiet. Unmoving. Sleeping —"

"Yeah, I got it. Thanks." That was something.

"What did I miss?"

Raven tried to chase his rapidly evaporating thoughts. "We got out of the caverns, and Silya became the *Hencha Queen*. And Desla brought me cheese."

"Wait, Silya *what*?"

He started to reply, but his mind felt thick and fuzzy. *Herbal tea my arse.* "Sorry, Spin. Too sleepy."

"Aw boss ..."

He hugged the silver sphere to him and pulled the blanket over them both, turning on his side and trying to find a comfortable position on the slightly lumpy mattress.

Then he was lost to the world of dreams.

# 8

# A LITTLE SUSTENANCE

THE SPORE MOTHER DUG her roots deep into the world, seeking the pathway her foremother had used, and those before.

*How many times have we repeated this life?*

Her memories were fuzzy on that point. She could remember Uurccheea as if it were yesterday, but the more recent lives ... it was as if something had corrupted them. Or destroyed them? She could taste the faintest hint, like a ghost of a thought, a conversation heard through the muffled thickness of an eeechiia wall. But how ever hard she pounded against it, the wall held, sealing them away from her.

No matter. She knew what she had to do.

Her roots reached the red source of the mountain, shaking it to its core. There she found what she needed. Heat meant life. Heat would let her grow, let her make her children. Heat would help her make this world her own.

The world shuddered around her.

•    •    •

Aik slipped down the Temple's curved hallway, looking for Silya.

It was his first time inside the hallowed halls. On normal days, few outside men were granted access, and then usually under very controlled conditions. But today was hardly normal, what with the quake, whatever in Heaven's Reach was happening to Raven, and the ascension of a new *Hencha Queen. They had to be related, right?*

And then there was Spin. He'd hardly had time to think about what Raven called his familiar. Where had it come from? Was it good magic or bad? He'd have to get some straight answers out of Raven when things calmed down.

The Temple halls all looked the same — white walls, purple flopwood doors.

*What am I doing here? I should be at work.* He wasn't officially on shift, thank the gods, but a quake was an all-hands-on-deck moment. At the very least, he should check in with his squad captain to see where he was needed. Aik pushed down the guilt — maybe Silya could get word out to Ser Dem about where he was, if not exactly why. *If I can find her.*

*It must be daylight outside already, right?* It was impossible to tell in the enclosed halls of the Temple. The electric lights were too harsh, too bright — he missed the golden glow of oil lanterns.

He'd managed a couple rough hours of sleep before Sister Tela had roused him and dragged him to Raven's room. It wasn't enough. His head pounded like he had a hangover.

Aik sniffed himself and wrinkled his nose. *I need a bath. And a change of clothing wouldn't hurt.* He'd been so focused on Raven that he'd neglected himself.

He snorted. *Typical Aik.* It wasn't as if Raven cared. Raven wouldn't even look after himself properly. *Why do I take care of everyone else and not me?*

He tested a door at random — it was unlocked. He opened it to find someone's sleeping quarters, bed neatly made, nothing other than a bare dresser against one wall and a closet.

Aik closed it quietly and continued on to the next. It was the same. *Must be the residential wing.*

Aik wished he had Raven's ability to remember places and spaces to help him navigate the temple's halls. He'd just have to pay closer attention.

Two sisters passed him in the hall, dressed in the saffron robes they used in the Temple instead of the more practical clothing they often wore in the outside world. They were talking softly to one another and taking no note of him. *They really must be preoccupied.* "... too young. Too brash. They say she didn't even want to be the Queen ..." Their voices faded away behind him.

Aik shook his head, bristling on Silya's behalf. *What in the seven hells were they talking about?* Silya had wanted this since she was a girl.

An initiate ran by without her robes — her curly hair blond like most of the others. She was almost as tall as he was. Apparently she was paying attention, unlike the sisters. She skidded to a halt and looked at him strangely, her hand dropping to the knife hilt at her waist. "Can I help you?" Her narrowed eyes said, *you don't belong here.*

Aik swallowed hard, grasping for an excuse. "I was ... looking for the kitchen. I'm here with Raven and Silya —"

Comprehension dawned on her face. "Oh, the dragon eater."

Aik shook his head emphatically. Once they gave you a name like that, it usually stuck. Better to nip this one in the bud. "His name is Raven. He's a living, breathing person and he's scared to death about what's happening to him." Well, the last part wasn't strictly true — and that was strange — but he wanted her to feel ashamed at calling his friend names.

"Sorry." She bit her lip. "I meant no offense. I'm Cor'Lea. Coral, to my friends." She held out her hand.

"Aik'Erio. Aiken." His stomach rumbled — he'd only had a nibble of Raven's meal. "So ... the kitchen?" Hopefully he could grab a bite to eat and maybe clean himself up. Then he would find Silya. *The rest will sort itself out.*

Coral grinned. "Well, Aiken Erio, you're in luck — I'm headed there now. Come with me. We'll get you settled." She set off again.

He followed her through a bewildering array of corridors, slipping between outer and inner halls with the ease of long practice. *A hundred meters? More like a thousand.* Aik despaired of ever being able to find his way back unaided.

They passed more hallways full of closed doors, and then one where double entryways were thrown open to show a wide circular auditorium with neat rows cut down into the black rock of the spine. He only got a glimpse before they were off in another direction.

After what seemed like ten minutes later but was probably less than two, she finally brought them to the kitchen.

It was a wide room that backed up onto the curved outer wall of the Temple, where three ovens gave off a cheery glow, and it was far warmer inside than out in the halls. The kitchen was filled with stocky wooden tables and about a dozen cooks, busy preparing a variety of things — warm and crusty loaves of bread, jelly-filled pastries, and a hearty meat-and-vegetable soup that gave off the most heavenly aroma.

Aik's stomach rumbled. *Food at last.*

Trays were flying out of the room as fast as they were filled. Aik had to duck and flatten himself against the wall to avoid getting knocked over.

Coral led him through the chaos to one of the tables, and a cook with unusual curly red hair and a rosy complexion. "Verla, this is Aiken. He's a friend of the *Hencha Queen*."

The woman looked him up and down. "Friend of the Queen? Well la tee da, aren't we fancy?"

"Not really," Aik sputtered. "I mean, she's just Silya to me and —"

She chuckled and flashed him a toothy, disarming grin. "I'm just playing with you, son." She waved a flour-covered hand at the initiate. "Run along, Coral. I'll take care of your friend here."

Coral grinned back. "Thanks, Verla!" The initiate scuttled off to another table.

"Always happy to help a friend of the *Hencha Queen*." Verla winked at him. "Poor thing. You must be starving." She looked him up and down. "Friend to the new Queen and a handsome guard to boot, though you're looking a wee bit worn around the edges." She eyed his torn jacket.

"Yes, mim ... um ... it was a long night." Long didn't even begin to cover it. He'd been on triple shifts that seemed shorter.

Verla laughed again. "Mim Olk. But none of that high falutin' nonsense here, lad. Just call me Verla." She turned and grabbed an earthenware bowl from a drying rack behind her, setting up a puff of flour from her arm. "Let's see. How about something to eat?

Cekya made a thick gully fowl soup with some vegetables we got in from the Ost Farm this morning."

"Yes, please." Aik licked his lips. He couldn't remember the last time he'd eaten. *Maybe lunchtime yesterday?* He'd let Raven eat what Desla had brought — his friend had needed it more than he had, although those *hencha* berries had looked delicious.

"Pull up a stool and we'll get you fed."

Aik found a stack of them in the corner and grabbed one, his mouth watering at the wonderful aromas. "Is it always this busy?"

"Not normally. But the quake and your friend Raven have stirred up an *orinth* nest." She poured a dollop of soup in the bowl and plucked a roll off the tray of a passing initiate. "Not to mention the rise of a new Hencha Queen — who saw that coming on a Solsday morning? Folks are all kinds of out of sorts today." She finished off his meal with a slice of pink cheese and a silver spoon. "Now eat!"

He did as he was told, taking a sip of the thick broth as she went back to kneading dough. The soup was delicious, a creamy mix of carrots, celery, and gigantic pieces of purple gully fowl meat. The bread was wonderful too ... light and sweet, not the mealy junk he usually ate in the Guard Hall mess. He let out a contented sigh and wolfed it all down.

*Thump. Thump. Thump.* "So how long have you known Silya?" A fine cloud of flour surrounded the cook like a fog as she worked the dough. The wonderful smell of yeast reminded him of his mother's baking.

"Since we were kids." He noticed Verla didn't call her "the Queen" or "Her Highness."

"And a little more than friends once, right?" A knowing grin crossed her face.

He set down his spoon and stared at her. "How did you know?" Maybe Raven was right — they were witches here.

Verla laughed, a deep, hearty sound. "She's one of the good ones. She used to come here to talk sometimes, to see how the wee folk like me were doing. She mentioned a handsome guard who broke her heart once."

Aik blushed. "I didn't —"

"Oh, don't worry yourself, lad. There're at least two sides to every story." She pulled a piece of the dough off, working it into a neat ball with her hands, then slapped it down on an empty tray. "And you're friends again now in any case, right?" *Roll, slap. Roll, slap.*

*I wouldn't go that far.* "Uh, sure? We didn't talk for a long time." *My fault.* Why had it taken an emergency to bring them back together? He finished his soup and bread and took a bite of the cheese. It was delicious — sharp and nutty — and he didn't even have to pick off bits of mold first.

Aik glanced over his shoulder at the doorway. He should be looking for Silya and Raven's things, not lazing around here in the kitchen. His friend was counting on him.

Verla slipped one of the warm berry tarts in front of him. "Always a bit of sweet to end a meal." She winked.

*Just five more minutes.* "I could get used to this." The tart was delicious, warm red *hencha* berry compote running down the side of his mouth. He finished it in three bites and wiped his mouth with the back of his hand, looking regretfully at the tray full of them on the next table. He really should be going, and besides, he didn't want to be greedy. *Still ...*

"One more?"

Aik grinned. "Yes, mim."

She glared at him.

Aik blushed. "Yes, Verla."

"Better." She grabbed another one for him and then laid the last roll on the wide tray next to the others, before covering it with a purple *hencha* fiber cloth. "Have to let them rise."

Aik finished his second tart, considering whether it would be bad manners to ask for a third. "Thank you, Verla. It was amazing." He looked around, unsure what to do next. He needed to find Silya — and Raven's things — but he'd barely made it *here. How am I going to find her, let alone get to her?*

Verla dusted the flour off her hands. "You lost, lad? The Temple's a big place. Twice as big for the uninitiated, they say."

He looked up at her gratefully. "I'd noticed. I was looking for Silya."

She chuckled, her belly heaving under her brown apron. "They won't let you within a mile of her, not while she's being prepared for the Raising."

"The Raising?" The thought of Silya enduring a formal ceremony made him laugh.

"Of course. Silly boy." Verla wiped her hands on a damp white cloth. "Becoming the *Hencha Queen*'s only the first step. After that comes a bunch of human nonsense to confirm the change."

Aik scowled. He hadn't counted on so many obstacles. It might be better for all concerned if he slunk out of the Temple and got back to being a guard. At least he knew how to do that. *But what would Rave do without me?* He wasn't as intelligent as Raven or Silya, but he was ten times more *street smart*. Than Silya, at least. It did feel good to know they needed him.

Verla sized him up. "Don't fret, son. I can tell you're a good soul. I'll help you get to her."

Aik narrowed his eyes. "How?"

She laughed. "You're not going to like it." She leaned forward and sniffed him. "But first we need to get you cleaned up. They're not letting anyone near the *Hencha Queen* who smells like an *aur* stall." She called one of the other cooks over, a short woman with mousy blond hair. "Carel, take this man to the baths and find him some fresh clothes. There should be something in the costume closet that will fit him. Then bring him back here."

The woman shook her head, pointing back at her table. "I can't. I have a batch of foldovers to finish —"

"Don't you worry about that. I'll make sure they get done. Now go." Verla waved them both off.

"Yes, Verla." Carel managed a quick curtsey and shot him a dirty look. "Follow me." It was more of a growl than a pair of words.

"I'm sorry —"

"Don't speak." She led him out of the room and into the hallway, muttering, "Men in the Temple? Is the world coming to an end?"

The answer to that one was way above Aik's rank. "I wish I knew."

# 9

## THE GRAND TOUR

"**T**HE COUNCIL WILL HAVE TO BE NOTIFIED. They've taken a bit of the upper hand these last few years, in the absence of the *Hencha Queen*. Now that you've finally arrived, we'll need to talk about reining them in." Dor'Ala, one of the most senior sisters, had been appointed as Silya's personal aide.

Silya gritted her teeth. *Finally arrived? I've been here for two years.* But she knew what Sister Dor meant. Still, they were all treating her like she was a novice, or worse, as if she were a complete stranger to the ways of the Temple. "Is all this really necessary?"

Sister Dor nodded enthusiastically, entirely missing the venom in Silya's voice. Or more likely ignoring it. "You have so much to learn, mim. The city is a nest of orinths, ready to sting the unsteady hand." Dor was a heavyset, solemn woman in her mid-forties, slow to smile, her unusual dark hair marking her apart from the rest. She reminded Silya of Daya. A slightly wider, grumpier version.

A wave of sadness swept over her at the thought of her deceased mentor. She tapped her foot impatiently. "Isn't there some kind of ... I don't know ... manual to being a *Hencha Queen*?" *Something I could read?* Dor was kind enough, but the woman tended to be long-winded.

"No, mim. There are books *about* the *Hencha Queens* — how could there not be? But there's no manual." She drew herself up to her full height, still a half-head shorter than Silya. "I am your manual." She sniffed.

Silya rolled her eyes. "I think one of the orinths got inside the Temple," she muttered.

"What was that?" Sister Dor's eyes narrowed, and her nose twitched as if she'd smelled the insult.

"Nothing, mim." *I'm as tired as an aur after rut.* After the harrowing underground trek, she'd been washed and pampered by women who had been her superiors in the dorms just hours before, and then allowed three hours of sleep. And now she was being lectured. It was weird. *Is this what it's going to be like?* Where were the lofty powers her new title implied? Her need to know warred with her exhaustion.

She looked around the *Hencha Queen's* quarters. A heavy, blocky, beautifully polished oak table dominated the room, surrounded by equally imposing chairs. A dour, life-sized portrait of Yen'Ela, dressed in blue robes so dark they were almost indigo, stared down at her from the wall in disapproval.

Silya sought the *hencha* reflexively for the tenth time that hour, but there was no response in her head. *Maybe it's all been a mistake.* Maybe the *hencha* had abandoned her again.

"Hold still, mim. I don't want to poke you." Sister Keh'Sel, the cheery temple seamstress, was busy taking Silya's measurements with her spidery fingers, humming with pins held between her lips — as if she hadn't done all of that before when Silya had first joined the Temple — and pricking her occasionally with said pins, despite her warning.

"Ouch!"

"Sorry, mim. You moved." Sister Keh backed away to view her handiwork. "That should do it. They're going to look marvelous on you." She marked the cerulean blue cloth in several places with a charcoal pencil and unpinned the garment. Then she packed up her things and scurried out of the room, leaving Silya standing there in her undergarments.

Sister Dor put a hand on Silya's shoulder in a way that was probably meant to be comforting, but just irritated Silya all the more.

"I understand. You're young — and you have much to learn before you go up against the old dogs on the Council, or even some of the sisters here who have come to enjoy the power they've had since Yen'Ela's passing. You're a fresh breeze in these stale old halls, but remember, right now you are Queen in name only. Genuine power has to be earned."

That was becoming annoyingly clear. Silya growled under her breath as she pulled on her old purple initiate's robe, which had been laundered and dried for her to wear until her new robes and other clothing had been resized to fit her frame. Yen'Ela had been a freakishly large woman, almost a head taller than Silya, by the cut of the robes. "I could just order all of you to leave me alone." She glanced around the suite. *It would give me a chance to do a bit of spring cleaning, and to chuck all this fancy dreck over the balcony.*

Sister Dor laughed. She actually laughed! "Yes, dear. You could." She patted Silya on the cheek.

Silya pulled away, annoyed at being glad-handed. "Still, I have been in the Temple for two years. There's no need to treat me like a novice who —"

A sharp knock at the door cut her off.

"Yes?" Sister Dor frowned, the wrinkles on her forehead deepening.

"Breakfast for the Queen." The voice sounded strange, but then again, everyone was stressed after the events of the night before.

Her aide opened the door. "Come in. I'm sure the Queen is starving."

It swung open, and an initiate entered. *Talk about freakishly tall.* Her purple robes were too short for her lanky frame, and the hood was pulled down over her face.

Sister Dor didn't seem to notice. "Go ahead then, mim. Eat something, then try to get some rest. Maybe it will put you in a better mood. We'll have a chat later today about what happens next."

"Yes, we will." Silya grimaced. "And find me that manual!" She was far better at reading things than sitting for long-winded lectures.

Dor waved her off as she left the room, pulling the door closed behind her, still chuckling.

"Gods, that infuriating woman!" Silya pulled on the stretched cowl of her robe, searching the room for something she could throw. She turned to find the initiate staring at her from under the darkness of the cowl of her own. Her figure seemed familiar, but Silya couldn't place her. "Just leave the food and go. I'm in no mood for company."

"Yes, mim." That strange voice again.

"I'm sorry. That was harsh." *I'm letting my temper get the best of me.* She took a deep breath, forcing herself to be calm. She'd make no friends acting like this, and it sounded like she was going to need a lot of them. "Are you new? I don't recognize you."

The initiate looked around as if to be sure they were truly alone. "It's me."

Her voice was low for an initiate, though some girls were like that. Mirrel, for one, sounded like an *urse* with a head cold when she spoke. "Do I know you?"

The initiate pulled back her cowl.

"Aik!" She shrieked and threw herself at him, hugging him and laughing. "I can't believe you're here. I have never been so glad to see someone in my entire life." *At last, a friendly face.* She was still mad at him for a hundred things, but after the last night ... things had changed. They'd gone through something inexplicable together, and it had bonded them.

He grinned back. "I wasn't sure. You've been angry at me for so long."

"I'm not *not* angry."

"Fair enough." He smiled one of his damnable Aik smiles and around the room. "Nice place. Guess you've come up in the world."

She let him go and turned away. "Still not sure if it's an improvement. Everything's different now. And I *am* still mad at you." She took the tray from him and set it on the long dining table. "How is Raven? Have you seen him?" He was important to Aik, so he was important to her by extension, no matter how much the gully rat annoyed her.

Aik nodded, his eyes soft, almost aglow. "Rave's managing. Scared. Sister Tela told him to get some sleep while she does a little research."

She felt an unexpected wave of empathy for Raven, and that annoyed her too. "Sister Tela knows everything, and what she doesn't know, she can find in the archives." *Including that manual, I hope.*

"Yes, mim." He was staring at her like she was an *orinth* on a pin.

"None of that. I'm still Silya to you, Aiken Erio." Even in her old initiate's robes, everyone treated her differently. "Am I understood?"

He blinked rapidly and gulped. "Yes, mim … yes, Silya."

"Thank you. I need a little normal around here." She squeezed Aik's shoulder. It was good to have him close by, even with all the baggage between them. It was hard to stay angry with him — was that the *hencha's* doing? She strode to the window, disturbed that her new position was even affecting her relationship with her friends. *We'll see about that.*

The Hencha Queen's quarters looked out at the four rectangular initiate dorms below, slightly distorted by the circular whorls in the individual panes of glass. Beyond the dorms, the rustling purple leaves of the *hencha* gathering were laid out in their neat rows. Initiates in their purple robes were busy harvesting berries, chattering among themselves, *Probably about me.*

Off to the left, at the edge of the gathering, Sal'Moya was leading another group of initiates, dressed in their fighting leathers, in sword practice with wooden blades.

Silya sighed. Her life before becoming the Hencha Queen — including the strange night with Aik and Raven — already seemed like another age. She was no longer one of those initiates. And yet she still felt like the same old Silya. *I should be out there, harvesting berries or flashing swords.*

In the distance, the spine narrowed to a point where the lighthouse had once stood. Pain squeezed her heart.

Somewhere downstairs, in the depths of the Temple, Daya's body lay on a cold slab, being prepared for her final journey. Giving her mentor — her friend — to the *hencha* would be one of Silya's first official acts.

Aik appeared next to her. He reached out to touch her cheek, his fingers slipping behind her ear in easy intimacy. "She was important to you?"

She pulled his hand away gently, though she was touched by the gesture. *Of course he understands.* Aik never thought about himself. He used to tell her what a lunkhead he was, but he was no fool, and he often saw things most others missed. "She was like a mother to me."

"You have a mother."

Silya grimaced, staring at the sunlight reflecting off the waters of the Elsp. She could just make out the neat rows of the houses of Landfield on the far side of the river, now that the morning fog had lifted. On the south bank of the river, several factories churned out noxious black smoke. "You've met Tri'Aya. Daya was more of a mother to me than *she* ever was. Or tried to be."

"I always liked her."

She wondered if he meant Daya, or Tri'Aya.

Aik looked away, the telltale signs of worry clear in the wrinkles at the edge of his eyes. He was holding something back. Maybe whatever secret he and Raven had been keeping the night before? Still, she knew better than to push him. *He'll tell me when he's ready.*

Silya changed the subject. "Is there really food on that tray? I'm starving."

Aik stared at the table, looking flummoxed. "Oh ... yes. Verla sent me up with it, the better to sneak into your quarters."

Silya laughed, not at all surprised that the cook had insisted on dropping the "mim" too. "Ah, that explains the robe. It suits you."

"I could get used to it. It's very comfortable." He scratched at his neck. "Seriously, how do you wear these? They're itchy as aur hair."

"You get used to it."

"Maybe." He pulled the purple robe up over his head and deposited it over the back of one of the chairs. "You need better security around here. If I could walk right in —"

"Maybe so. Would you ... stay for a while and help me set things up?"

Aik brightened. "I'd be happy to —"

"Don't you dare say 'mim'."

"— Silya."

"Good. I'll notify the Guard that I've decided to borrow you for a bit." She added it to her mental list, which was starting to get a bit unwieldy.

"I ... I don't think that's how it works ..."

"I'm the *Hencha Queen* now. It works how I say it works." She regretted those words as soon as they came out of her mouth.

Aik stared at her. "Yes, mim."

Silya sighed, but this time she didn't correct him. "For now, I'll put word out that you and Raven are exceptions to the 'no men' rule. It's about time some things changed around here."

Aik flashed her a sly grin. "Just don't change the berry tarts. Verla has those down pat."

Silya laughed. "I won't." She gave him a once-over. "Where's your uniform? You look like a farmer." The white shirt and dark blue breeches were loose on him, clearly meant for a man twice his girth and a dozen centimeters shorter.

"Verla's having it cleaned. They gave me these instead." He gestured at the rough *hencha*-cloth garments. "Carel got them out of the costume room."

"Ah. So you're Farmer Number Two."

Aik laughed. "I guess so. And you're Hencha Queen Number One?"

Silya growled but didn't dignify that with a response. The tray of food was calling her. "Come, sit. Let's eat."

"She won't get in trouble for it, will she?" Aik took a seat across the wide table from her, sparking memories she thought she'd gotten over.

How many breakfasts had they enjoyed together in his little basement flat, down on Redhawk Spine? Silya pushed them aside. "Verla? I doubt it. She runs the kitchen like her own personal fiefdom. Most of the Sisterhood would sooner dare an *eircat's* den than tussle with her." Silya lifted the cover off the meal and was delighted to see two of Verla's famous berry tarts waiting for her. Through a mouthful of warm berries and flaky pastry, she asked, "Tell me more about Raven?" It would be a pleasant distraction, and besides, she needed an update on the thief's condition.

"He's ... all right. His forearms look like something burned them." The pain in his voice when he spoke about his friend tugged at her. She stared at the plate, wishing for a second that she were anywhere but here, free of her new responsibilities. Then her hunger got the better of her, and she took a wedge of pink cheese and shoved it in her mouth. It was just hunger, the hole gnawing at her insides.

Aik was doing his nervous thing, cracking his knuckles to relieve the tension.

"What? Out with it." She was losing patience with his deference. "I'm still the same old Silya. You don't have to treat me like the godsdamned Hencha Queen. At least not in private."

Aik shook his head, his cheeks flushing, "It's not that. It's just ..."

"Spit it out."

"Raven sent me to look for his things."

She almost laughed out loud. It was so like the little thief. "The man swallows a mysterious creature, gets chased out of his lair by a quake, and all he's worried about are his *things*?"

"He lost his home and had this horrible thing happen to him. He's just trying to hold on to what's left." Aik stared at her, his features hard. "You grew up rich. You wouldn't understand."

She'd never considered herself rich. Not like the folk down on Peregrine Spine, with their mansions and formal gardens. Though Tri'Aya does have a place there. "Enlighten me."

Aik swallowed hard. "Those *things* are his entire life. He lost his home. He has no money, no family. Just his belongings that he's ... collected over the last few years. Without those ..."

*You were about to say 'stole,' weren't you?* She put up her hands, palms out in surrender. "I'm sorry. You're right. He must be scared." *You always knew when to set me straight.*

"He is, but you know Raven — he hides his fear with bluster. He'd sooner lose a hand than admit he was afraid."

She looked around the room, filled with fine furnishings and expensive clothes. The artwork alone was probably worth half of the money in the Council treasury. Talk about *things*. She didn't like any of them — well, the table wasn't bad — but she supposed the feeling of wealth and luxury they conveyed served a purpose.

Aik was staring at the feast like a man who hadn't eaten in a week. "May I?"

"Sweet mother of Jas, yes, there's more here than I could eat in three days. Didn't they give you anything in the kitchen?" The tray was filled with fruits and meat and bread and a piping hot bowl of soup. She'd have a word with Sister Dor about such blatant waste, especially when there were people in the streets with nothing to eat.

"Yes, but I'm still hungry." Aik dug in, and together they filled themselves on the bounty from the Temple kitchens.

Silya took the soup for herself. She inhaled the savory aroma and took a sip — the broth was spicy and full of flavor, chopped bits of grayleaf spicing up the purple gully fowl meat. It warmed her heart and soul. Verla was a treasure.

There were sweet grapes from the small vineyard along the southern edge of the Temple, just beyond the practice field — the first grapes of the fall. Also a loaf of fresh-baked sourdough bread, some tart yellow *hencha* berries, and a few pieces of cured *aur* meat. She finished up the last of it, feeling a bit gluttonous. *Hungrier than I thought.* "Raven's things are here, by the way."

Aik looked up, eyes wide. "Where?" His excitement was infectious.

Silya laughed, truly glad he had come. He was a friend, an anchor to her old life, no matter what else had passed between them before. "In the bedroom closet. This place is huge. Want the grand tour?"

"Sure." Aik looked around the *Hencha Queen*'s quarters. "I still can't believe it's true. You're really *her.*"

*You and me both.* "I know. It's so strange." She'd all but given up on her dream, convincing herself she didn't really want to rule the Temple. Now here she was, and that dream was turning into a nightmare of protocol, politics, and pomp and circumstance.

And yet, since the Hencha Queen's initial arrival in her head, everything had gone quiet inside. *I still feel like boring old Silya. Did you judge me and find me lacking?* She shrugged. Nothing she could do about it now. "Come on. I'll show you around."

Aik got up dutifully and followed her out of the receiving room.

The white-washed quarters were on the highest level of the Temple. They were modest compared to the mansions on the slopes of Heaven's Reach, but next to her cot in the initiate's dorm, they represented sheer luxury. The black marble floor tiles led into the bedroom, where a four-poster bed big enough to sleep half the initiates held court over a fine assortment of furniture made from violet pine. There was a grandfather clock, two nightstands, a chair with a marble washbasin and mirror, and a warm, fluffy white mountain *ix* rug at the bedside.

On the wall next to the bed, a portrait of Jas'Aya, the first Hencha Queen, stared at Silya as if she were judging her newest successor. Her rooms were full of dour-faced monarchs, but Jas's portrait was different, full of life, almost smirking. *How did you get away with that?* "Think she would have approved?"

"I'm sure of it." Aik's took in the overwrought decor. "It's so … not you."

Silya laughed. "It really isn't, but it isn't her, either. It was all built after her reign. When she was here, the Temple was a simple wooden two-story home. It burned down in the fire of 313." She showed him the bathroom, a luxurious affair with a deep marble tub and silver faucet. The tub was raised so she could see out of the window when she bathed.

Silya slipped off her shoes to step onto the *ix*-fur pelt in front of the tub. It was so soft. "Try it."

He looked at her as if she were crazy.

"Seriously. Come on!"

Aik shrugged and pulled off his boots. He stepped onto the rug next to her. "You're right. It's nice." He closed his eyes and curled his toes, sighing. "But can we get to Raven's things?" He looked over his shoulder as if he expected to find the little thief there, tapping his foot expectantly.

*Raven can wait.* "One more thing." She took his hand and pulled him, barefoot and protesting, out onto the wide balcony looking out over the *hencha* gathering below.

"Are you sure? Someone might see me." He looked over the railing nervously.

"You're the guest of the Hencha Queen." She'd be damned if she was going to let the Temple bend her to protocol.

It was late morning, and the sun was warm on her skin. The breeze teased her hair, the air still fresh off the Harkness. To the north, the peaks of Heaven's Reach loomed over Gullton. The Eagle and Peregrine Spines between were quiet — the fires started in the aftermath of the quake had been put out, and while there was still a hint of acrid smoke in the air, the wind had already cleared the worst of it from the city.

Sunlight glittered off the waters of the Elsp as they rushed down from the Highlands, through the Heartland, and finally past Gullton and out to sea.

Aik whistled. "It's beautiful."

"Look." She pointed at the *hencha* gathering below the balcony. The plants were moving in synch, dancing to a silent song.

"What are they doing?" Aik leaned over the railing to stare at the field.

"I don't know. It started a couple hours ago."

An initiate saw them and pointed up at him, tapping one of the others on her shoulder. Coral? It was hard to tell from up here. *More rumors to go around.* She should have kept him inside.

"Is it because of you?"

"Maybe. I'm not sure? Sister Dor said it didn't happen the last time a Queen was chosen." She watched the patterns, mesmerized. The field shifted, strange shapes darting across it as the leaves moved in symphony, like a picture she could almost understand if she just stared at it long enough.

"What do they hear?" Aik's voice held a hint of wonder.

"No one knows." The *hencha* were as closed to her as they were to him. Silya gripped the railing tightly, wondering why they had chosen her. And why the *hencha* mind was quiet now.

Aik grinned. "Can't you find out?"

"It's not that simple." She looked away, embarrassed to admit her failing. "The *hencha* ... they're gone." It hurt to admit it, even to Aik.

"What do you mean, gone?" His voice held no judgment.

Silya was grateful for that. "They're not speaking to me. I don't feel them in my head anymore. I don't feel any of it." She'd been wrong. It actually felt good to say it to Aik, who wouldn't look down on her for it. Who wouldn't think she didn't deserve to be here.

He met her gaze, and for a minute she thought he was pitying her. Silya bit her lip, turning away. "I shouldn't have told you —"

He grasped her hand, pulling her gently back. "It's not gone."

It was her turn to stare at him. "What?"

Aik touched her cheek, his fingers slipping behind her ear, their shared intimacy returning like it had never left. "You haven't lost it. You're just too stressed to feel it."

His touch brought up a cartload of old feelings, bitter and brittle with age and second guessing. She brushed his hand away again, more gently this time. "You have to stop doing that. We're not lovers anymore."

He blushed and turned away to look out at the *hencha* again. "Sorry."

She still loved him, after a fashion. "You're always going to take care of me, whether I need it or not, aren't you?"

Aik chuckled ruefully. "Probably."

Silya squeezed his hand. "Thank you for that."

He raised an eyebrow. "Does that mean you're not mad at me anymore?"

"No, I'm not." The answer surprised her, but it was true. Maybe the *hencha* were still with her, because she felt an unexpected empathy for his position.

"That's good." He closed his eyes. "Try it now."

"This isn't going to change anything ..."

"You won't know until you try." A hint of a smile ghosted his lips, but he kept his gaze firmly on the scene below.

*Damn you.* Silya closed her eyes too. She took a deep breath and reached for her newfound connection to the hencha.

It had eluded her before, but maybe Aik was right. Maybe she'd been too preoccupied with everything — the events of the night before, Aik's sudden reappearance, all the Temple protocol Sister Dor had thrown at her.

She felt inside her head for the *hencha* mind, for that link with the sacred that she'd touched only a handful of times.

Her mind was as empty as a gully bird's. "It's not working."

She felt his warm hands on her shoulders. "Breathe in deep. Relax. Let them find you."

She gave it a try. *In, out. In, out.* Her breath filled her lungs, and her body relaxed.

Then she felt it.

*There you are.* A tight knot of flame in the back of her mind. She touched it, and it spread through her like a brush fire.

"Wow. That's ... amazing." Aik's voice was somewhere between appreciative and scared witless.

Silya opened her eyes to find him staring at her again. Her arms were on fire, but she felt no warmth from the flames. The ancient consciousness of the *hencha* filled her again, bringing with it a gravity and depth that made her own limited human existence seem pale by comparison. "It worked!"

"Looks like it."

"Aik, you're a genius." She took his face between her hands and kissed him before she realized what she was doing. She drew back, flushing hot. "Sorry."

Aik snorted. "Guess we both need to work on boundaries."

Silya laughed. "Guess so."

Inside her head, the *hencha* expressed their own amusement at such human foibles. Silya experienced a strange sense of double vision, sensing the world on her own and through their broader senses. She was here, on the balcony with Aik, but she was a hundred other places too, wherever there were enough *hencha* to form a gathering. In the field below the Temple, across the Elsp in farms across the Heartland, and in places she'd never seen or dreamed of before.

Aik reached out to touch her arm, startling her back to the present. "It doesn't hurt?" The flames burned right through his fingers, but he seemed unharmed.

"What?" It was like waking from a dream. "Oh. No. I feel energized. Sister Dor says I can make the flames burn hot if I want to. Somehow." So much to learn.

"Why are they blue? I thought they usually burned black."

"I don't know." She looked out at the gathering below through the Hencha Queen's eyes. She could hear it now, the *hencha* song — thin and reedy at first, but slowly growing. It was music of a sort. Discordant, like a thousand theolins playing similar songs. Not a thousand. A hundred thousand or more. All of them. *How old are you?*

*As old as the song.* The voice sounded wise but amused, and Silya felt like a child before it.

She could *feel* them too, the gathered *hencha* below and the ones across the Heartland and beyond. All connected in a vast, unseen web, linked to her. *Am I worthy?*

The affirmation crashed over her like an ocean wave. *You were chosen.*

Warmth filled her. She took Aik's hand. "Can you hear it?" As she listened, the melodies merged, the off notes dropping out.

"Hear what?"

Fire ran from her hand up his arm.

Aik stiffened. "I ... yes. I can now. It's beautiful. Haunting, even."

The music swelled inside her. It was lovely, but painful too. The discord didn't disappear. Instead, it became a sour undercurrent, a cross-stream that undercut the joy of the main melody. It told a long story of life and pain, of triumphs gained and battles lost that spanned an amount of time that left her feeling as small and insignificant as an *inthym*.

At the same time, she felt whole for the first time, full of life. *It's your history.*

*A small part of it, yes.*

Silya took that in. How long had the *hencha* been self-aware?

Aik squeezed her hand, bringing her out of her reverie. She opened her eyes, and the song faded away.

He was shaking, his mouth foaming and his eyes squeezed shut like a demon possessed him.

"Aik!" The Hencha Queen's presence faded, and Silya's flames extinguished.

His body went limp and fell to the ceramic tiled floor of the terrace with a heavy thud.

*Sweet mother of Jas, I broke him.* Silya's healer training kicked in.

She ducked inside the suite, grabbed a cushion, and dampened a washcloth. She returned and rolled him on his side so he wouldn't choke on his own tongue. She slipped the cushion under his head and wiped the spittle from his mouth. His arms and legs were still twitching.

*What did I do to you?* Reality slammed into her hard. She was no longer Silya, the lowly initiate. She was the Hencha Queen, and what she did could hurt people, even the ones she loved. She covered her mouth, holding back a sob. *Keep it together, Sil.* Like Tri'Aya.

She checked his pulse and his breathing — both were still strong. *If it's a seizure, it will pass.*

His jerking movements slowed, and then finally stopped, and his breathing became more even.

She sat with him, her back to the terrace wall, squeezing his hand while the breeze played across her face. She still wasn't sure what she had done. Maybe the Hencha Queen's touch was too strong for anyone but her.

*You were chosen.*

Aik's eyes opened. He rolled over onto his back and looked up at her. "Sil?" He sounded groggy. "What happened?"

"You had a seizure and fell." She cupped his cheek in her palms, damn the consequences. He would *always* be her Aik, even if they weren't together. "Are you all right?"

His hand went to his forehead. "I think so. I have a godsall strong headache, though. What did you do to me?"

"I shared the *hencha* song with you. Do you remember —"

"Yes. It was beautiful." He sat up, feeling the back of his head. "I'm gonna have a gully-bird egg there tomorrow."

"Have you ever had a seizure before?"

Aik blinked. "I think I'd remember something like this." He shook his head like a dog.

"You sure you're not hurt?"

"Yes. I'm fine, aside from feeling tired and having a pounding headache."

Silya let go of his hand, and the tight knot of worry in her chest loosened just a little. "Wait here, and I'll mix you up some *fellin* powder to drink."

She poured some water from the pitcher on the table into an empty glass and retrieved her pouch from the bedroom. The leather was worn and faded, but familiar. Sister Dor would probably want to replace it with something more befitting of the Hencha Queen. *Let her try.* "Here you go."

"Thank you." Aik wrinkled his nose but downed it completely without complaint. "You never did show me Raven's things."

Silya shook her head. "You two deserve each other. You're as like-minded as a pair of *jexyn*. Come on. I'll show you." She helped him up.

He was wobbly on his feet, so she supported him and led him back inside, to the enormous closet at the back of the bedroom where Raven's possessions had been stored at her insistence. An electric lamp lit the room in bright white glow.

"They're planning to electrify the Guardhouse next year." Aik stared at the seemingly magical light wistfully.

"So much better than the candles and gas lanterns we used in the dorms." She looked around the closet, which was larger than her old, shared room.

The rumpled burlap of Raven's sacks looked woefully out of place against the soft, rich brown plush carpeting of the closet. Half the space was empty — the Hencha Queen's blue robes had all been taken out for cleaning and resizing. They'd probably been hanging there gathering dust for a decade, since Yen'Ela had died from extreme old age. "It's all there. I wouldn't let them touch them until I talked with Raven."

Aik put out a hand against the wall to steady himself. "He'll be glad to hear it. I should go —"

Silya's brow furrowed. "You're in no condition to *go* anywhere." She really had knocked the wind out of his sails. *I'll have to be more careful next time.*

He yawned and rubbed the back of his head. "No, I'm just tired. It was a long night."

"Damn you." She yawned. "Sister Dor told me to get some rest." She squeezed his shoulder. "All of this will still be here when we wake up."

Aik glanced over his shoulder. "I need to at least get word to Raven. He was so worried."

"I'll send someone to tell him." She went to her front door and leaned out to give instructions to the sister standing guard.

"Yes, mim." The woman saluted her.

"Thank you." She closed the door, rolling her eyes at the formality. *Is this how it's going to be from now on?*

She found Aik by the bed, staring at it as if he'd never seen one before. "Done."

He smiled gratefully. "But where will I sleep?"

Silya looked at the wide bed, and then back at the man who had once been hers. "You're welcome to share it with me. Just ... keep your distance." It would be good to have him here in this strange new place. "It's a huge bed. You take one side, I'll take the other."

Aik stared at her, his brow knitted. "You sure? After ... everything?"

"Oh for the Gods' sakes, you think that still bothers me?" It very much did, but she wasn't going to give him the satisfaction of seeing it. They were turning over a new leaf together, after all. *Just friends.*

"All right. Separate sides." He pulled off his boots and trousers, and then his shirt.

Silya looked away. *He's not mine. Not anymore.*

She closed the shutters, then turned off all the lamps in the suite one by one, except for the ornate silver one by her bedside. Then she slipped out of her robe, too tired to care if he was watching. "Thank you for coming."

He had the grace to blush. "Thank you for not throwing me out."

"You're welcome." *I am tired. Exhausted, really.* She slipped under the covers and turned off the last lamp, feeling the mattress shift as he climbed into bed beside her.

He kept his word and stayed far away from her, like he'd promised.

So why was she so sad?

# 10

## KNIFE TO THE GUT

S ORIX PACED THE GATHERING HALL, her diamond-sharp claws flicking sand at the walls, a sign of her disquiet. Kalix watched her warily from the entrance, silhouetted against the green sky, slick with mist from the waterfall that eclipsed half the great cavern's entrance.

*How can you not worry?* It had been hard enough to give up one of their eggs, sending their poor kit off to become ... something new. But the waiting ...

One of the *otherlings* — she stopped to squint at it — strode across the sand, baring its teeth at her. She avoided showing her own in response — Kalix had assured her that it was not a gesture of aggression from the smaller species.

She was still dubious about the whole experiment. *Why do we have to have them here?*

*They are part of the world now. We need each other.* Kalix blinked at her, lifting a claw to pick a bit of *aur* meat out from between his teeth.

*They don't belong here.*

If it had been up to her, they would have gone it alone against the deathbringer. What did it matter to her what happened to the squishy pink otherlings?

But Kalix had been insistent. They must all work together to face the resurgent threat.

Flyx and Aryx bounded across the sand, barreling into her and making her forget — if only for a moment — all of her worries.

*Hungry hungry hungry!*

*Calm down. You'll eat soon enough.*

Kalix huffed, and turned around to go.

One of her three stomachs rumbled. *Bring me a fresh ix. I'll be hungry enough soon.*

Kalix hunched his shoulders in agreement, then spread his wings and with a running start, leapt off the ledge to soar over the valley below.

She nudged her two kits back into the tunnel to their own home, and soon they were snuggled up together there, her kits sucking contentedly on her nipples. Still, one was empty.

*Come back to me.*

Though he wouldn't really be hers anymore.

•     •     •

*Trapped like a caged eircat.* Raven paced across the cool stone tiles in the confines of the room, pausing every few circuits to scowl at the locked door. His chest was tight, and his fists clenched and unclenched at his side. "Spin, are you sure there's no other way out?"

"Not unless you can shrink yourself down to hamster size to fit through the floor vent."

*Hamster?* "Not helpful." He'd killed an hour throwing stones, watching their eight symbols come up in assorted patterns. Eventually he'd abandoned the game — it was a lot less fun when there was no money involved — and had tucked them back into the leather pouch at his belt. At least they hadn't taken that from him.

He'd considered — more than once — ramming his body against the heavy wooden door. But he didn't have Aik's heft, and it looked very sturdy. *Why won't you let me out?*

His nostrils flared. Everything smelled weird — even his bed linens emitted a strange odor from across the room. His forearms itched too, but he didn't dare to look at them.

Aik still hadn't come back.

He'd tried talking to Spin earlier, but the little familiar was in a foul mood of his own, answering all of his questions with "Yes, your High Exalted Thiefship" and "No, and you can go shove it in your —" That one had made even Raven blush.

He banged on the door, pounding so hard he could feel bruises forming on his tight fists. His vision went red. "Let me out!

Nothing. Whoever was guarding him continued to ignore his imprecations. *If there's even anyone out there.* He'd tried jimmying the door handle a hundred times with no success. *If I just had my lockpicking kit. That* they'd taken away from him. "It had better be with the rest of my stuff!"

Raven sank down on the bed so hard that the wooden frame cracked under him, causing the mattress to sag. *What did those witches do with my things?* They had no right. He'd spent years collecting them, buying some of them, and yes, stealing the others. But he only stole from those who already had too much. Merchants with mansions on the slopes of Heaven's Reach. City officials who skimmed off a share of the taxes they collected for their own use. Surely, he had a right to take some of it back.

Raven didn't keep it all for himself either. He donated half of his profits to an orphanage on Redhawk Spine that was always struggling to keep its charges fed and clothed. He remembered what it was like to be orphaned.

There was a small washbasin — with running water! — in one corner, and a simple mirror in a wooden frame. And an electric light that he'd spent half an hour fascinated by, turning it on and off with its shiny metal switch.

Odd dreams had floated through his mind, disjointed images of small white scaly things, strange red lights floating through the air, and fire. Lots of fire. The restlessness multiplied in his stomach like a swarm of *orinths.*

*If I just had my tools ...* He'd scoured the room for something he could use in their stead, but it was useless. The bed was short and stout, a wood frame bed held together by dovetail joints. Not a nail in the whole thing. Then again, he had just broken it.

Eagerly he knelt and pulled up the mattress. The wood beneath it was snarled and split. The light in the room was dim, but he could see the pieces as clearly as if it were broad daylight. He picked out a splinter about ten centimeters long and pried it off the frame.

He got up and knelt by the door, inserting it into the lock. It was a simple enough procedure — one he'd done hundreds of times. He could hear the mechanism inside clearly, and in about three seconds the latch clicked.

He opened the door, ready to make his escape.

"Hey there. I see you're back up to your old tricks."

Raven blinked. It was Aik, changed into plain clothes — a white shirt and dark blue breeches.

"Holy *hencha*, it's good to see you." Raven threw himself into his friend's arms and kissed him. He'd never been so glad to see anyone in his entire life.

Aik smelled clean. And really good. "That ... was unexpected."

Raven discretely rearranged his pants. "Don't get used to it." *Stupid, Raven.* The last thing he needed was to lead Aik on. "Wait, have you been standing there the whole time?"

Aik was staring at him.

"Snap out of it. It was just a kiss."

Aik blinked. "No, I wasn't *standing there the whole time.* Just for a moment. I heard you fiddling with the lock and figured I should give you some space to let you do your work." He smelled rested too, and happy.

"Thanks. I think." Raven frowned. *How does someone smell happy?* "You could have just opened the door."

"Where's the fun in that?" Aik let him go and stepped inside to stare at the broken bed. "You feeling all right?" His eyes narrowed as he looked Raven up and down. "What did you do to your hand?"

Raven held it up. It was bleeding, but just a little. "I was banging on the door because no one would let me out." He shouted the last part for the benefit of anyone still in the hallway.

Aik glanced over his shoulder. "There's no one out there."

"Oh." Raven's shoulders sagged. *Well, that explains it.* He wasn't sure which was worse, being guarded under lock and key like a common thief — fair enough on that one — or being so insignificant that they'd neglected him.

"I know it must be a blow to your ego, but the whole temple's abuzz after the quake. I'm sure they just forgot about you. Sisters are rushing about everywhere and going out to provide what aid they can." Aik glanced over his shoulder. "I should be with the Guard, doing the same. But instead, here I am, helping you."

"What time is it?" He'd lost all track of time.

"Just after noon." He stared at Raven's hand. "Let me see that."

Raven let him. "Yes, Mas Guard." Uniform or no, Aik was still in full guardian mode

Aik snorted. He peered at the side of Raven's hand and his brow furrowed. "That's odd."

"What?" Raven pulled back, his palm tingling from Aik's touch.

"I see blood, but not a cut."

"Of course there's a cut." Raven turned away to wash his hand in the basin, and wiped it off on his trousers. He stared at his hand, turning it over. Aik was right. *Where did the blood come from?* "That *is* weird."

Aik rolled his eyes. "There is a towel, you know." He sounded mildly exasperated.

"Why waste it?" He sat down carefully on his now-broken bed and held his hand under the light of the electric lamp on the nightstand. His skin was perfectly smooth where the blood had been. He rubbed it — it was hard too, like the callus on his heel.

A touch of his nausea returned. He hoped Sister Tela was right about the thing inside of him dissolving. He couldn't get past the feeling that it was doing things to him. *Bad things.*

"What did you do to your bed?" Aik was staring at the sagging mattress.

"Temper." Spin was finally surfacing from his snit.

"Quiet." To Aik, he said "It's not *my* bed."

"Spin?"

Raven rolled his eyes. "Being his usual unhelpful self."

Aik laughed. "One of these days, you'll tell me more about him. We'll have the Temple medic take a look at you later. And hey, I suppose you can pay for the bed with some of your precious things." Aik's gaze lingered on him a little too long.

Raven's eyes widened. "You found them? The filthy sisters didn't sell them all?"

Aik glanced nervously over his shoulder. "Yes, I found them. Show a little respect. The sisters have taken us in without question." He returned his gaze to Raven. "And Silya saved your things for you — you should thank her."

"You mean the Hencha Queen?" She was going to be even more insufferable now. "Wait, did you two —" Jealousy flared in his chest. *Why should I care?* Aik didn't belong to him.

"No. She asked me to stay with her for a couple hours. This whole Hencha Queen thing ... she was in shock."

Raven felt strangely relieved. It didn't matter, really. He had no hold over Aik or who he slept with. Still, the thought of it stung. Things were getting too complicated too fast. *I should get my things and go.*

"Come on — she wants to see you. I had to go in disguise to get to her the first time."

Raven let out his breath, and the anxiety left him in a rush. "This I have to hear."

*Maybe leaving can wait for an hour or two.* His belongings were safe, and he was finally getting out of this cage. His day was taking a decided turn for the better, even if he had to face the *eircat* in her lair. "You didn't tell her about Spin, did you?"

"Nope. Secret's safe with me. Come on. The longer we make her wait, the hungrier she'll be." He turned to go, seemingly expecting Raven to follow. Somehow the dynamic had shifted between them, but still, they shared the same warped sense of humor.

"Lead on, my friend, and tell me all about it." He followed Aik out the door, feeling only a little guilty about the bed and happy to be free of the cramped little space.

●　　●　　●

Silya was waiting for them in a room Raven could only describe as palatial — bigger than his mother's entire cottage.

He'd sworn Spin to silence, or the little imp would be making all kinds of comments about the place, and maybe suggesting what Raven should tuck away for the best profit. Still, the familiar's little extension poked out of his pocket discretely at odd intervals, taking in their surroundings. And Raven kept shoving it back into his vest pocket, hopefully just as discretely.

A blue chair large enough to properly be called a throne had been brought in and planted in the middle of it, facing the window on the far side of the room. As big as the place was, the throne looked pointedly out of place. *We really have come up in the world, haven't we?*

"This place is off the hook."

*What hook?* Raven studiously ignored Spin's voice in his ear.

She wore a fine blue robe, made of *mur* silk from the way it shimmered under the sunlight from outside. One of the initiates was styling her hair into an ornate hive that would have made a nest of *orinths* proud.

He could smell her perfume from the doorway, and the sound of the scissors trimming Silya's golden locks was annoyingly loud.

Silya looked bored to death, chin on her fist, and Raven felt a moment of unexpected sympathy. She turned to see them enter and scowled, and his temporary insanity fled with that withering look.

"Good afternoon, Raven." Somehow, she made his name sound like a curse. "You look ... well, better's not the right word. Rested. You look rested."

"Thank you, great Queen Silya." He couldn't resist, but he kept a straight face.

Her frown deepened, and she started to say something, but Aik jumped between them. "I meant to tell you. Silya wants you to join her this afternoon. She's taking a tour of the damaged parts of Raven Spine."

"Sure." It would be good to get out of the *orinth* nest, even if the price was spending time with Her High and Mightiness. This was his chance. He could slip away in the crowd and find some place to hide and figure out his next move — though he wanted to get his things out first. *What if the Guard is looking for me?* "Where are my things?"

Aik looked at Silya, who nodded and turned away. "Come on."

Aik led him through the bedroom and flipped on the light in the biggest closet he'd ever seen.

Raven whistled.

"Holy —"

Raven stuffed Spin back into his pocket. "Shhhh."

Aik grinned. "I know. I wish my flat was this big. And these lights — they're like magic."

"I might have played with the one in my room this morning." How many times had his lantern in the lair run out of oil in the middle of the night? Electricity was so much better. And brighter.

Raven's eyes lit on the two sacks, and he grinned. "Thank Jas, it's all here." It was like seeing a couple of old friends. *Stinky old friends.* Raven's nose wrinkled. The sacks smelled like old socks. Funny how he'd never noticed that in the lair.

"Silya said she saved them for you. The sisters wanted to go through all the junk — your things — and give them back to whomever you stole it from." Aik leaned against the doorframe and crossed his arms. "You really should return some of it."

"Is that my friend Aik speaking, or the guard?" Raven knelt in front of one of the sacks and started unpacking it, going through each item and checking it over for damage.

"Your friend. You're in enough trouble as it is with this whole sea master thing. Wouldn't hurt to earn a few points with the Guard."

Raven snorted. "So it *is* the guard." Almost everything in the sack smelled. Some of them were good smells, like old books. Some were decidedly not. Weird that he'd never noticed it before. He looked around the closet and shook his head. *Must be the clean room.*

Aik came up behind him and laid a hand on his shoulder, sending an electric shock down his arm and commanding his full attention.

Raven looked up, and their eyes met. Aik saw deep concern there.

"Have you considered where you're going to live after all of this? Your lair is underwater, and you can't stay holed up here in the Temple forever."

"Gods no." The place was a nest of vipers. Though the food was delicious. After his latest theft, he was probably in trouble with the Thieves' Guild too — they liked to keep a low profile. "I don't know. Maybe I'll find another lair, or move out to Landfield for a bit ..."

"You could move in with me. Just for now." Warmth spread from his hand through Raven's shoulder.

Raven pushed him away. *It would never work.* "Nope. Sorry. Bad Idea." He liked living alone. And he treasured his freedom.

Aik blinked and stared at him as if he'd been stung. "Fine. Forget I even mentioned it."

*Now I've stepped in it.* He had to give Aik something. "It's not you. I'd be an awful roommate."

Aik stared at him, clearly not buying it. "You're not ready. I get it. But one of these days —"

Raven winced as his stomach cramped again.

Aik's forehead scrunched up. "Can you still feel ... that thing?" He stared at Raven's stomach.

Raven was tempted to joke that his *thing* was *just fine, thank you,* but the concern in Aik's eyes stopped him. "It's ... it comes and goes."

"You know it's not going away, Rave. Something is happening to you. Look." He turned over Raven's arm and held it up for him to look at.

Raven looked away. He didn't need any reminders of his sorry condition.

"Look at it!" Aik's nails dug into the soft skin of his wrists.

"Owww!" He turned his gaze reluctantly to his forearm. The skin there was rough, peeling.

"I'm guessing you didn't burn yourself recently?" Aik's eyes probed his.

Raven pulled his arm away. First Sister Tela, now Aik. *Why won't you just leave me alone?* "It's nothing. I scraped it somewhere."

"On both arms?"

"Leave it, Aik." It came out sharper than he intended. "I ... I don't want to think about it right now. Besides, Spin said there was nothing wrong with me." Well, he hadn't said exactly that. But it had been implied.

Raven pushed away the nausea.

"Raven, you ready to go?" Silya appeared in the doorway, looking almost like a real Queen in her shimmering blue *mur* silk robe and tiara.

"A little magic really can turn an *aur* into a princess." He stood and discretely brushed off some of the dead skin from his forearms. He'd seen that face covered in sweat and dirt too often to take it too seriously.

Silya grinned. "Says the gully rat. Good to see you back to your normal, socially unacceptable self. And yes, I feel like I'm playing dress-up. They can't expect me to do this all the time, can they?" She glanced at Aik. "You look white as the Temple walls."

"I'm fine." He pushed his way past her without a look back at Raven.

129

Silya stared at him. "You two have a fight?"

Raven looked down at the soft rug. "Something like that. I'm an asshole."

Silya laughed. "On that, we agree." She motioned impatiently. "Come on. The sisters are waiting for us."

"Coming." He hurried after her.

"Rave?"

Aik was waiting for them in the receiving room, looking at him with pity. It was a knife to the gut. "What?"

"Just ... take a little time. Think about it."

Aik thought he needed help. That he couldn't take care of himself, and that was the worst part of all. "No thanks. I can get by on my own."

He followed Silya out of the apartment, leaving Aik alone with his gods-damned pity.

•　　　•　　　•

The city was a shambles. Half of the shops along Grindell Lane had taken damage when some of the gas lamps shattered during the quake, and a couple were just burned-out shells. The smell of smoke and unwashed people hung in the air, making Raven gag.

He watched for his chance to blend into the crowd, but there were sisters everywhere. Silya must have taken a dozen with her, and there were bright yellow robes all around as they spoke with the gathered crowd and tried to spread calm in the rattled city.

Sister Tela accompanied him, sticking close by, surprisingly spry for her advanced age.

Spin whistled in his ear. "Damn, this place looks like Dresden after the bombing."

Raven had no idea what or where *Dresden* was.

The noises of the city were louder than normal too. A carriage rumbled by, and the squeaking of the wheels and the *clop clop clop* of the *urse* shoes threatened to split his skull.

Raven gritted his teeth until it passed them by.

Word of the new Hencha Queen's elevation had spread throughout the city, and as she and the sisters paraded through the streets, a large crowd had gathered to see her. Fear and excitement were palpable in the air.

Raven held back from the main group, wary of attracting the wrong kind of attention and dismayed by the noises and the smell of the gathered people. *It never bothered me before. Why now?* He watched for his chance to escape, to blend into the crowd and disappear. He'd have to leave all his possessions behind — everything but Spin. It killed him, but what was the alternative? He wasn't sure he was ready to face Aik again.

Maybe he could ask Silya to send them to him later, when he got settled somewhere else. If not, he could always find replacements. He had Spin, and that was all that really mattered. And his books were safe.

A sharp crack in the distance drew Sister Tela's gaze away.

Raven took advantage of the lapse in her attention to slip away toward the crowd, but a hand on his collar jerked him backwards.

"Going somewhere?"

He shrugged. "You don't need to take care of me any longer. I should let you get back to your books." He raised one eyebrow and flashed his winning smile, hoping he could charm her into agreement.

"You're something special, aren't you?" She took his arm in hers and led him ahead after the procession, preventing him from escaping without her notice. They stopped to look at one of the burned-out buildings, an old tea shop called the Fateful Dregs, according to the hand-painted sign that still stood in front of it.

"What do you mean?" He glanced at her, wincing at the sound of a sledgehammer knocking over a damaged wall half a block away.

She reached up to touch his cheek with her other wrinkled hand. "Your mother died when you were little, right?" Compassion twinkled in her eyes.

He stared at her. *How do you know?* "Are you a witch?" It wouldn't have surprised him if she were.

She cackled. "Oh, don't be so shocked, lad. Queen Sil'Aya told me as much. She also said you're a thief — you think the world owes you something, I suppose?" She *harumphed* under her breath. "And she said you like boys, not girls." She winked at him. "I used to like boys too."

Raven stared at her, searching for a witty comeback. "So?" He was way off his game.

"You have a birthmark like a coiled snake behind your left ear, don't you?" She tugged on his ear lobe, pulling his head sideways, and grinned. She was missing a couple teeth.

"Oooh, she is a witch." Spin's voice in his ear sounded almost gleeful.

Raven ignored him. "Silya tell you that too? Or Aik?" He pushed her hand away gently and rubbed his ear, wishing Spin would shut up.

"No." She looked him up and down. "No one *told* me."

Raven shuddered. He didn't know what that meant, and didn't *want* to know. "I have to go. I think Silya needs me."

He tried to pull away, but she held him tight. "The Queen asked me to keep an eye on you, Mas Orn."

Raven glanced at her over his shoulder, hoping Silya would be looking his way, but she was deep in discussion with the shopkeeper, handing them a pouch of *croners*. He could hear the *clink clink clink* of every one. *What's happening to me?*

Sister Tela put out her bony hand. "Let me see your arms again."

"Why?" These folk were always poking and prodding at him, like he was a prize *urse* they'd just bought at auction.

She released him and grabbed his arm, forcing his hand to turn over, palm side up. Despite her age and frail appearance, she was strong as an *aur*.

"Hey, that hurts!" The skin was tender there, and she was handling him like a stubborn child.

She ignored him, tracing the rough skin of his forearm again. She rubbed some of the flakes away. "Ah." She raised an eyebrow. "It's true. She said you would be marked, behind the ear and on your forearms." Sister Tela let him go and stepped backward to stare at him. "I didn't believe it. Not really. But here you are."

*She who?* Raven stared at his forearm. Where she'd rubbed off the skin, three gleaming white scales stared back at him.

His stomach churned again, and panic rose in his chest, making his breath come short and fast.

*Fark it.* It was time to run. There was something seriously wrong with him, and these sisters were crazy as rabid *skerits*. He needed some space to breathe. To think. He had a couple other hidey holes he could retreat to. Maybe the orphanage —

"Your heart rate is elevated again, Boss."

*Of course it is.* Sometimes Spin was as useful as a square-wheeled cart.

Raven looked around anxiously for his best escape route, and his eyes met a guard's across the street. The man was tall, stern-looking, with a neatly trimmed mustache. He stood at the edge of the crowd, staring right at him.

Raven recognized him — Ser Kek, the bastard who had arrested him the last time. One of Aik's superiors. He was handsome, Raven had to give him that, but he looked as dangerous as a wounded *eircat*.

Raven touched his wrist reflexively, making sure his hand was still attached and wincing at the tenderness of the skin.

He turned away, hoping the man was just checking the crowd. When he looked back, though, Kek was staring right at him.

The guard crossed the street, quickly eclipsing the open space between them, calling out in a deep voice. "Rav'Orn, I'd like you to come with me, please."

Raven turned to run, but another guard stepped out of the crowd behind him

As Kek closed in on him, Sister Tela inserted herself between the two of them. "Is there a problem, Ser?"

The guard glared at Raven, his hand dropping to his short sword. "I need to speak with the street urchin behind you, Sister." His voice was civil. Barely. "Please step aside."

*Surely he wouldn't use a weapon on a defenseless sister.* Raven took a step back, wishing he could blend into the crowd and slip away. The look in Ser Kek's eyes was near murderous. *I should have run when we left the Temple.*

Sister Tela stood her ground, her fists clenched at her sides. "I'm afraid there must be some mistake. This is one of the initiates of the Temple, in personal service to the Hencha Queen."

Both Raven and the guard almost choked on that whopper, and Ser Kek stared at him in disbelief.

Raven recovered first. "That's right. They're fitting my robes as we speak."

The sergeant's face turned almost cherry red. "Don't mess with me, Sister. Men aren't allowed to be initiates." His voice was dangerously low.

133

She blinked innocently. "These are enlightened times. Change is in the air, or hadn't you noticed?" Sister Tela gestured to the half-ruined city, and Raven had to admire her composure, hard as forged steel. *Why are you defending me?*

The sergeant grumbled. "I'm sorry, Sister, but I still need to speak to ... your initiate —"

The dust-up must have attracted attention, because Silya appeared at his side. She was frowning, one hand tugging at the cowl of her fine blue robe. "Is there a problem, Ser ...?" She somehow looked ... taller. More regal.

"Ser Kek." He glanced from her to Raven and back again. A sheen of sweat beaded his brow, shimmering in the mid-afternoon sun "I ..." Kek's gaze shifted from Raven to Tela and then to the Hencha Queen, and his gaze hardened. "I need to take your initiate in for questioning on a rather delicate matter. I'm sure you understand." He reached for Raven's arm.

In two seconds flat he was laid out on the ground, with Silya's knee on his chest.

Raven blinked. *How did you do that?*

The crowd laughed, and Ser Kek's face darkened even more.

"*Is* there a problem?" Silya's hand rested lightly on the hilt of the sergeant's short sword.

Ser Kek blinked, his gaze darting back and forth at the laughing crowd.

The other guard started to close in, but Ser Kek waved him away. "No, mim. There's no problem."

"'Your Highness,' please."

Ser Kek stared at her a moment longer, then blinked. "Yes, of course. Your Highness."

"I'm relieved to hear that." She got up off his chest and extended her hand to him, helping him up.

He brushed himself off, clearly confused about what the protocol was when meeting a new Hencha Queen, especially one who confounded expectations after throwing you to the ground. He shot Raven an almost venomous look. "I'd like to request an audience with you at your soonest convenience ... your Highness."

Silya put a hand on the sergeant's shoulder as if they were old friends. "I know. These formalities are such a bore. But thank you for understanding. If you need to speak to … my initiate"— Raven could hear her amusement at the thought — "send your request to the Temple. My staff will make arrangements as soon as things calm down a bit." Without another word, she took Raven by the arm and turned away, hauling him down Grindell Lane toward the white dome of the Temple in the distance.

"She saved your ass, Boss." Spin sounded almost happy.

Silya's fingers dug into his arm as if she were holding on to him for dear life.

"Owwww. Let go of me!" He looked at her with newfound respect. He wasn't sure if he should be grateful to her for saving him from the guard, or angry that she thought she had to. And how had she thrown him to the ground like that?

"Oh, be a man for once." Silya snorted. "I wasn't sure that was going to work, but we have to get you out of sight before he changes his mind and comes after you."

Raven glanced over his shoulder and shivered at the angry *this isn't over* look Kek shot him. The rest of the royal retinue was detaching from the crowd to follow Silya back to the Temple like an honor guard.

"Sister Tela told him I was an initiate. Why did she lie for me?" He could still feel her claws on his wrist.

"I don't know, but I mean to find out." She squeezed his arm more tightly. "Once we get to the Temple, you are not to leave the building. Do you understand me? I can protect you there, at least while we figure things out. But if you go —"

"Yes, mim." He couldn't help himself. "Your Highness."

Silya clenched her jaw. "Oh, shut up." She sounded angry, but when he snuck a glance, the ghost of a smile played across her face. "Remember, you're an initiate now. That means you work for me."

*Fat chance.* "Do I have to wear the robes?"

She glanced at him speculatively. "Actually, I kind of like the idea. We could use some menfolk to scrub the floors and haul the ash out of the fireplaces in the kitchen …"

Raven snorted, but looked at her with newfound respect. *Scrubbing floors my arse.* This wasn't the petty, frustrated Silya he'd known before her ascension. *Well, maybe still frustrated.* But the way she had taken control of the situation in the face of the city authority ... maybe she really *was* meant for this. She smelled determined.

Raven shook his head. Why was the world suddenly upside down? He did want to keep both of his hands, thank you very much. If the price of that was a few more days in the Temple's dubious hospitality, he could live with it. Besides, he had no idea what to do next, or what he was meant for, either. Maybe Sister Tela would have some answers for him.

Maybe he should tell them about Spin.

Either way, it was time to stop running away. Time to start running toward something.

*I wish I had the faintest clue what that was.*

# 11

## GAUNTLET

T HE SPORE MOTHER GREW, drawing on the living heart blood of the world and adding *eeechha* chambers, filling her nest with life. The living factories churned out lifeforms — *eemscaap*, with their hard shovel noses, to clear rubble from the tunnels that led from her lair to the outer world. Red seven-pointed *eesiil*, spreading their star limbs to cling to the rock, heating up the air in the caverns. And the little red *iichili*, her forerunners, who would go out into the world to spy for her and start to release the spores that would make this place a paradise for her people.

She carried inside her the *aueel* — the souls — of a thousand *aaveen*, waiting to be reborn after the destruction of her world. Waiting for her to make this their new home.

Iihil would be first, as always, the progenitor of the reborn *aaveen* race.

How many Iihils had there been?

But first, she needed to find him a home. Somewhere out there, a creature of this world awaited her, one who would share his knowledge with Iihil's, enabling the progenitor to bring about *Eev-uurccheea*, a new *uurccheea* on this strange, cold world.

137

She would find him, and then the real work would begin.

•        •        •

Aik watched Raven go, his last words ashes in Aik's ears.

*"No thanks. I can get by on my own."*

Aik bit his lip. Raven had always been mercurial, but there was something strange and new going on. *I shouldn't be surprised.* Especially given what had happened in the past day.

Still, there'd been a moment, when Raven had kissed him ... his lips still tingled where the two of them had touched. A sparkle of possibility had filled the air for one glorious moment. Then it vanished like the sun in the smog that hung over Gullton all summer long. *Maybe I pushed too hard.*

The idea of having Raven as a roommate was exciting. Even if the ramshackle flat above the pub over on Redhawk Spine — all he could afford on his junior guard's salary — was barely big enough for him, let alone for Raven and all his godsdamned things.

*We're thick as thieves.* He snorted. They'd only crossed the line between friends and ... more, once. Raven hadn't spoken to him for a month afterwards. Ever since, he pulled away whenever Aik got too close.

He tried not to feel bitter about it. It had been easier with Silya, though she was volatile too. *Maybe the company I keep says more about me than them.*

His thoughts went to the two burlap sacks. He had a few hours to kill and didn't really want to spend them confined to one of those small rooms where they'd stuck Raven. Which he likely would be if he poked his head out of the safety of the Hencha Queen's quarters.

*I should report for duty.* Silya had said she was going to have him reassigned to the Temple. Had she gotten around to it yet?

And besides, if he got dragged back to duty, he might not be there when Raven needed him. *One of these days, Rave, you'll push me too far and I won't come back.* Even as he thought it, he knew it was a lie.

He should put his time to good use. Raven had thrown everything he could grab into those two sacks, with no sense of order at all. Aik was good at order. He could sort things out for Raven, maybe even put them into baskets to make them easier to transport ... wherever Rave went.

Shoving aside the pain and uncertainty, Aik dragged one of the sacks out of the closet into the bright light of the bedroom. Looking around, he settled on the heavy wooden dining table in the adjacent receiving room as the best place to sort through all the junk.

He opened the sack. The top layer was mostly bedding. There was a smelly patchwork comforter — some of Raven's vomit mixed with his bodily oils, no doubt — with diamond-shaped red and gold panels. Below that was a deep royal blue pillow embroidered with gold thread. There was also a sky green *mur* silk sheet — Aik whistled at that one. Somewhere in Gullton, a merchant's wife was fuming.

He folded the comforter and sheet, setting them with the pillow on one of the heavy, dark-stained wooden chairs. He'd ask Silya if they could be washed later. Raven apparently hadn't been very consistent with his household — lairhold? — chores. *Big surprise.* If they ever did live together, that would have to change.

He worked his way through the rest of the bag, organizing linens and clothing into separate piles on the chairs.

There were a few books too, most of recent manufacture — a complete leather-bound set of Jel'Faya's Worldstrider series, about adventures in the fantastical lands outside the Heartland. There were also two copies of *The Thief*, Faya's earlier work about a street urchin on the streets of Gullton. Aik grinned. *That's a little on the nose.*

He thumbed through one of them. Raven had made notations in the margins in a few places with a charcoal pencil:

*How did he do this?*

*Try this tomorrow.*

*That's* not *how locks work.*

Aik chuckled. Raven was using it as an instruction manual.

The last books were far older and much more interesting. The first one he picked up had a faded cover of a man in red astride a white beast — a dragon, Aik supposed. The decorative paper wrapper was fine and perfectly trimmed, even if it was bent and torn at the edges.

Aik lifted it carefully and peered at the firm cover underneath. The craftsmanship was exquisite.

He flipped the book open and stared at the fine print again. It was recognizably English, though the words looked a bit archaic. But they were written with such precision that it took his breath away. How did someone print each and every letter so cleanly, clearly, and exactly the same size and shape? It must have been done on a printing press, but he'd never seen one that could reproduce words so perfectly, without any seepage or over splash.

The book was dedicated by the author "to my brothers Hugh and Kevin." He wondered who they had been, and how long ago they had lived. The adjoining page said Copyright 1978 — but he had no frame of reference for that. The current year was 390, dated from the supposed Landing Day.

Maybe there *had* been an Earth, after all.

He turned the yellowed page carefully and found the most exquisite map. *Could this be the fabled home planet?* But no. It said "Pern" in the lower right corner. He traced the outlines of the coasts and read the names. Benden Weyr. Nerat Hold. Ista Weyr.

*What's a weyr?* Were there other planets out there too, besides Tharassas and maybe Earth? Was his world just one of a dozen places in the starry sky that held pockets of humanity? A hundred?

Aik closed his eyes, trying to picture it, but the thought made his head spin. Better to keep his feet on the ground and leave such lofty thoughts to Raven and his ilk.

He closed the book carefully and set it down on top of the others, his gaze lingering on the dragon's faded green eye.

Then he moved on to the other items in the sack. They were mostly articles of clothing, ranging from worn tunics to fine breeches and even a set of leather boots that looked like they'd never been worn.

One white *hencha*-fiber shirt was wrapped around something stiff. Aik set it down and unwrapped it carefully. When he saw what was inside, his hand flew to his mouth. It was a short knife, made by Aik's mother, in an ornate leather sheath.

It was the one he'd given to Raven a few years before, on his sixteenth birthday. Raven hadn't traded it away for money — instead, he'd wrapped it up like a precious possession.

Aik's throat was tight, his eyes wet. He wiped them with the back of his hand and wrapped the knife up again inside the shirt, setting it aside. *I love you too, Rave.*

The first sack finished, he hauled the second one out into the dining room and went through its questionable treasures. Raven had very little of actual value — probably fenced most of the things he could get *croners* for. This one held a motley array of things: the metal panel from the *Spin Diver*, a smaller sack full of surprisingly clean wooden plates, bowls, and utensils, the mirror Raven said had belonged to his mother, and a leather pouch with a series of small metal tools — Raven's lock-pick kit.

There was a leather sheath with a much simpler knife with a plain hilt that was nicked all along the blade, and a sack of apples that had seen better days. Aik threw the apples away but put the cloth sack onto the pile of clothes to be washed.

Then there were the artifacts.

He picked up the spiral one he'd seen before in Raven's lair. The metal was silver-hued, but with a strange reddish-golden tint that hadn't been apparent in the dim light of the caverns. He carried it to the window casing to get a better look at it in the sunlight. It was about as long as his hand, and beside each of the embedded red gems was a smooth hole. There was a larger hole at its base, with a raised rim as smooth as glass. *An instrument?*

Aik put it to his mouth and blew.

No sound came out.

He took it back to the table, but as he set it down, he noticed it was emitting a faint red glow. Aik shivered. *They didn't glow before, did they?*

He pulled out the next one — a long, thin tube of metal. It was glowing too. More red crystals dotted one side in a line. There were no holes in it other than at the two ends. *Stranger and stranger.*

Two more artifacts shared the same basic design, but with slight variations in size and shape.

He put the last one down on the table next to the others and pulled up a chair to sit and stare at them.

It was like a puzzle. When he was a child, his mother had made him mind games cut out of painted flop tree wood, intricate little things with a hundred pieces that he would put together and take apart again and again.

He could see how the spiral might connect to the tube, and the others might go there and there ...

He rearranged them and placed them in order, almost touching.

They began to vibrate, dancing on the tabletop. The largest two pieces snapped together, locking into place. Then the others did as well, leaving one long, gleaming thing.

Aik gasped. *What in the green holy hell?*

There was a sharp knock at the door.

Aik looked around wildly. He didn't know how official his place was here, or if the other Sisters would take kindly to his rummaging through Raven's things and making a mess of the Queen's quarters.

Not knowing why, he picked up the combined artifacts and ran through the bedroom to the balcony. He slipped outside, hiding around the corner just as the door to the suite swung open. Aik pressed his back flat against the smooth stone wall, holding the artifact tightly to his chest, praying whoever it was wouldn't pop outside for a bit of sunlight.

After a moment, he chanced a peek inside. It was too dim, and his eyes had adjusted to the bright daylight. He caught only a quick impression of a woman in a purple robe standing at the table, staring at Raven's things, before he ducked back behind the protection of the wall. He waited, breaths coming quickly, hoping whoever it was didn't come exploring.

When he dared look again, she was cleaning, dusting off all the surfaces in the receiving room.

An initiate. Aik's heartbeat slowed.

Soon she was cleaning the floors with a mop and bucket.

Aik waited her out, wary of springing himself on the unsuspecting girl. The day was warm, and the sounds of activity floated up from the grounds below — the rush of the breeze through the hencha, the clash of wooden swords out on the practice field.

He'd seen those women fight. *I'd hate to meet up with one of them in the dark, guard training or no.*

A few moments later, the door clicked shut again.

Aik closed his eyes and let out a grateful sigh. He waited a little longer to be sure the coast was clear, then he did a quick sweep of Silya's quarters to make sure they were empty.

He set the artifact down on the table and stared at it. It was still glowing, but now there was light in the crystals as well, a strange phantom radiance that seemed to move between them like a red fog.

It looked like a gauntlet. A strangely shaped one, made for someone with arms thinner and longer than his. But still ...

He picked it up again and looked through the "arm hole" into the thing. Other than having melded together, the pieces seemed basically unchanged.

Curious, he put the fingers of his right hand into it and the hole expanded, the "metal" melting and reforming around his fingers. His eyes went wide. It was warm and inviting, sending a tingle through his hand and up his arm.

*I shouldn't. It's not mine.* Not that it was Raven's either. He'd found them in the caverns below the city, if what he'd said was true. Not that Aik had ever known Raven to lie. *Not about anything important.*

The warmth was seductive, sending a flush of pleasure through his body.

He tried to put it down, but he couldn't bring himself to do it. *You deserve this.*

It was an alien thought. Selfish. But it got its hooks into him. *When do you ever do anything for yourself?*

Both of his friends seemed chosen for greater things. With Raven, it wasn't clear exactly what that was yet, but something had happened to set him apart. If it didn't kill him. Aik shivered at the thought.

And Silya was the Hencha Queen, Jas help her.

Aik was the odd man out, the only one not marked by fate for greatness.

*What am you supposed to do, just follow along after them and clean up their messes?*

He was thrilled for Silya, and as for Raven ... He certainly wasn't jealous that Raven had a creature in his stomach. *But when will it be my turn?*

*You deserve this. You were meant for this.*

Aik shuddered. "Who is that?" He looked around, but he was all alone in the room.

Panicked, he tried to pull the gauntlet off his arm, grabbing the edge with his other hand and tugging at it frantically. *Loja help me.*

Lo'Oss ignored him, and so did the metal, flowing up around his palm, inching its way up his hand like a hungry beast. Fear surged through him, prickling goosebumps flaring across his forearms. *What do you want from me?*

Howling, he shook his arm, trying to knock it off, but the thing was relentless, flowing past his wrist and up his forearm, the red crystals glowing brighter and brighter.

Aik banged it against the wall, trying to knock it off, but he only hurt himself, sending shock waves of pain up his arm.

"No, no, no!" *Stupid Aik. They're right. You're an idiot.* He grabbed Raven's old knife, unbuckled it, and slipped it out of its sheath one-handed. He stuck the blade under the advancing flow, drawing blood, and it stopped.

Aik panted, calming himself with a few deep breaths. He needed to figure out what to do next.

*I can't cut my own arm off.* At least, he wasn't desperate enough to try that yet. *Maybe if I —*

The knife in his hand heated up in his grasp, turning hot as a furnace. "Mother of Jas!" He let go, and the blade clattered to the ground.

The thing resumed its climb, and in seconds encased his entire forearm, stopping just below his elbow.

Aik tried to pry it off with his free hand. "Come on." He growled. It wouldn't move. It sealed itself to his skin as tightly as if it had been glued on.

He looked at it in combined fear and wonder — it fit him perfectly, as if it had been made for him specifically by a master armorer. His mother would have been fascinated. Maybe *she* would know how to get the gods-cursed thing off his arm.

Aik tugged at it again, panting heavily, trying to pull it off by brute force, but it was as immovable as a gravid aur.

Sweating, he sank down on one of the bulky wooden chairs, his chest heaving, staring at the gauntlet that covered his lower arm. *Now I know how Raven felt.* Invaded by a strange thing that had attacked him without warning.

It shimmered and its red gems flashed. Then the whole thing faded from view, as if it had never been.

Aik stared at his arm. *What in the green holy hell?* He reached out tentatively to touch the skin of his right forearm. It was smooth and pliable, covered with fine blond hair, every mole and scar in place.

The strange gauntlet was gone.

*Thank Jorja.* Relief flooded him — the wild goddess had come through for him after all — followed by crushing shame at having been so stupid.

Raven would be furious that Aik had "lost" some of his precious things, and Aik had absolutely no idea what to tell him. *See, I took out those artifacts, and they swallowed my hand whole. Look!* Not that stranger things hadn't happened.

Except that there was nothing to show him.

He needed some time to figure this whole thing out. *Did I imagine it?* He *was* exhausted — maybe it had been some sort of fever dream. Maybe the artifacts were buried in Raven's lair under a heavy blanket of water.

He threw Raven's remaining things into their sacks one after another, determined to hide the evidence before Silya and Raven returned. His face flushed with heat. Was this how Raven felt all the time?

When he was done, he sat down on a chair on the balcony, staring at his bare arm. Not a hair out of place. *It* did *happen, right?*

Sooner or later, Raven would notice the artifacts were missing. *I have to tell him.*

When Raven and Silya returned, he hid his right arm under his leg, even though the gauntlet had vanished.

Raven found him first. "Aik, where are you?"

"Out here."

The thief appeared at the doorway. His friend was flushed with excitement. "There you are."

"Hey Rave, I need to tell you —"

"It's my fault. I'm sorry I was such an ass earlier."

Aik stared at him. An actual apology from Raven, Prince of Thieves. *Maybe the world really is ending.* "Thanks. But I wanted to tell you —"

"Thank you for your offer. It was really sweet — it just kind of freaked me out. But I don't think things are going back to normal any time soon." A shadow crossed his face, his hand sliding down to his stomach.

Aik's eyes narrowed. "What happened?"

"Sister Tela found something in the archives. Oh, and that sergeant — Kek? — is after me again. Come on."

"Something happened while you were out —" But Raven had already slipped back inside, oblivious to Aik's concern.

Aik took one last look at his arm. The gauntlet was truly gone, as if it had never existed. He heaved a sigh of relief and decided to leave things be, for now.

He got up to follow Raven inside. *I'll tell you later. It will keep.*

•　　•　　•

Deep in her cavern, the spore mother stirred. Around her, her children had taken up residence, transforming her little world into a reasonable facsimile of Uurccheea. She was surrounded by the sounds and smells of the homeworld. the cricking-purr of the *oosil* as the tiny worms spread their life-giving mucus along the cavern walls.

Something had shifted. She could feel it.

Out there, in this strange and frightening world she'd awakened in, a bit of the progenitor had awakened. He'd found a new host.

Joy filled her. She'd feared he was lost for good. Her memories of the last time were fragmented and unreliable, but she remembered him ... shining, beautiful, bonded to one of the local life forms, ready to adapt the world to the needs of the *aaveen*.

Soon, she would know more about the place she found herself in. Then she would begin to refashion it for her brood.

Uurccheea would be reborn, and her children would inherit their new world.

# 12

# VERENT

"**S**ISTER TELA, WHAT DO WE KNOW?" Silya was growing impatient with the old archivist. The Temple library was a stuffy collection of sneeze-inducing, dust-covered books and scrolls placed on scores of shelves, books stacked on books and on the floors too, and even more papers stuffed into old wooden chests. It was a minor miracle the archivist could find anything in this *inthym*'s nest of knowledge.

Silya had never enjoyed passing time there as an initiate. She'd spent most of it recopying old writings or transcribing the words of one of the sisters for official missives to the City Council or one of the local merchants.

Sister Tela cracked a smile. "This is where it gets interesting."

Raven shot her a *why didn't we get to the interesting part half an hour ago?* look, and she had to suppress a grin. He was looking over the nearest shelf of books, apparently fascinated, muttering to himself and clutching his vest. Silya raised an eyebrow. She'd have to keep an eye on the thief to make sure he didn't pocket anything.

"Please, tell us." *I'm begging you.* She was on edge, and she knew it, so she tried to make allowances for the poor archivist. The hencha hadn't spoken to her all day — she'd tried to summon the flames to scare off Ser Kek and had bullied her way through when it failed. She wasn't sure if she should ask anyone about it — what if the *hencha* had rescinded their blessing? And what would she do if that stubborn man showed up on the Temple steps to drag Raven off to the Guardhouse?

Aik had stuffed his huge frame into an average-sized human chair in one corner of the room. He was picking dirt from under his fingernails with a short knife. Silya's eyes narrowed. *And what's wrong with you?* He didn't seem his normal, affable self.

Sister Tela dropped a heavy book on the table in front of her, startling her and sending up a cloud of dust from the old pages. She flipped it open and gestured to Raven and Aik. "Does this look familiar?"

Raven sauntered over to see it, and stiffened.

It was a watercolor, drawn in black ink with a fine hand and colored in a delicate white. The creature was sleek, beautiful, full of tightly wound energy. Silya traced the lines of the image — the neatly drawn scales, the golden eyes.

Aik leaned over her shoulder. "Yes. That's what it looked like, only smaller." Aik glanced across the table at Raven, his brow knotted in concern. "What is it?"

"It's quite exquisite, isn't it? Queen Jas's wife Sera painted it — she was a very talented artist. We have entire books of her work, some of it apparently drawn from the visions of Queen Jas, and some of it simple landscapes that shed light on what Gullton was like then. Did you know they called it Gully Town —"

Silya rolled her eyes. "What is it?" The words came out harsher than Silya had intended. She liked Sister Tela, but the woman tended to get sidetracked by her vast knowledge.

The archivist blinked. "Oh yes. I am sorry. It's a dragonette."

Raven nodded as if he'd known it all along. His face was pale.

Aik stared at her.

"That's what Sara called it, anyhow. She was from Earth — one of what they used to call the runners. Some people also called them angels. Did you know that in the predominant religion, angels were magical beings —"

Silya cleared her throat.

"Ah yes. Sorry." She climbed a short ladder and scanned through a row of leather-bound books on the top shelf, each labeled in gold. "Ah, here it is. The *Menagerie*."

Silya watched her climb down with some concern. Sister Tela was not a young woman. Maybe they needed to find her some assistants.

"These are all her animals, collected into one volume by a talented artist named Sol'Eria. Many of them appear to be mythical or imaginary. There's a long-necked spotted thing called a giraffe that could never really exist in nature. Poor thing's head would just topple over —"

"Sister Tela ..."

"Right. Sorry. It's just so rare that I get to share these things with anyone. No one has much of an interest in the arts anymore." She sat and flipped through the book. "Ah, here it is." She spun the book around for Silya and the others to see. "Yes, 'dragonette' was Sara's word for it. Queen Jas'Aya called it a *verent*."

Sol'Eria's book showed the beast in a multitude of poses, including flying across the green sky, its white wings extended. Silya bit her lip. It reminded her uncomfortably of her own brief vision down in the tunnels, when her fingers had brushed the glowing walls. Was that the creature she'd flown upon?

Raven clutched his stomach, groaning.

Silya touched his shoulder. "You feeling all right?"

Raven shook his head. "I felt better before I saw that ... thing again." He pulled out a chair and sank into it. "What's it doing in there? Eating my insides?" He hugged his arms close to his chest.

"What else do we know about it?" Aik was staring at Raven. There was no mistaking the look on his face. Aik had it bad for the dashing thief, but there was anger there too. *Trouble in paradise?*

Silya looked away, feeling voyeuristic. "Yes. What do we know?" They were going around in circles.

Sister Tela licked her finger and turned the page. "Not much. The *verent* are thought to be ice creatures. They live in the north, and few have ever been seen." She scanned through some hand-written notes in the *Menagerie*. "When Solene painted these, she made notes of all the lore she could find from Queen Jas'Aya's own journals. This one references an entry from the fifth of Edu, 324

AL ... the year the Queen died." She turned away and vanished down one of the musty aisles in search of the journal.

Silya watched her go. She'd likely be back there for a few minutes, searching through the dust-covered stacks. This was as good a time as any. "Raven, let me see your forearms." It had been bothering her all day. He'd been hiding them, holding his arms in unnatural positions, always crossed over his stomach or against his sides. Except when he scratched at them when he thought no one was looking.

"There's nothing wrong with me." He stared at her defiantly, Queen or no.

Silya liked that he still treated her like a normal person, though she'd never tell him so. "I didn't say there was. Your arms, please." She put steel in it this time. *You're the Hencha Queen. Own it.*

Reluctantly, he laid his forearms on the old wooden boards.

Silya pulled a gas lantern over from the edge of the table for a better look.

Aik whistled. "Rave, why didn't you say anything? It's gotten worse."

The skin of his forearms was peeling off, and underneath ...

Silya gasped. White scales covered his forearms, as smooth and intricately detailed as those in the drawing. Raven hadn't been lying, after all. And Aik had known ... something.

"Happy now?" Raven pulled his arm out of her grasp.

"No, I'm not. If it itches too badly, I can prepare a poultice. *Fexin*, a little ground *bacca* root —"

"What the Hencha Queen means is that she can have a poultice prepared." Sister Tela reappeared from whatever dusty corner of the archives she'd been searching. Her gaze met Silya's. "You have healers to do that sort of thing for you now."

The archivist's reprimand stung. "Of course. It's just ..."

Tela's look cut her short.

Silya's gaze shifted to Raven's stomach. "Can you feel it? Inside you?"

Raven looked from her to Aik and tucked his arms behind his back again. "This is why I didn't tell you. You're looking at me like I'm a freak." He glared at them and pushed back the chair in a huff. Without meeting her gaze, he retreated across the stone-tiled floor to stare at the books again.

Aik's face was pure anguish. His right fist squeezed shut on the table beside her. "It's not like that, Rave. No one thinks —"

Sister Tela interrupted him, setting down the smaller book she'd retrieved. "Let me find the entry." She turned the pages of the old book gently. "Ah yes. Here it is. '*Verent* swarm in the icy north, when the twin moons are rising. *Cayah* in the harsh Southern Deserts raise their dappled heads from the sand. The *erphin* swim upstream, and the *jexyn* in their sky aeries hear the call.' Very poetic. Queen Jas was very fond of poetry —"

"Well, that's helpful." Raven rolled his eyes.

Silya frowned. "Wait, I've heard of one of those. *Erphin* ...?"

"Yes, *erphin*." Sister Tela stared at her intently.

"Right. They're ... fish. I think. Mother used to talk about them. Big white fish that would surface near the boats in the bay."

Sister Tela grunted assent. She leafed through the bestiary and laid it down on the table in front of Silya.

She traced the outlines of the strange fish. It had an irregular shape — rather like a sponge — with three sleek dorsal fins sticking above the water. "Is there more to it?"

Sister Tela skimmed the journal page. "'fraid not — well, except for this." She touched the paper with a shaking finger. "'To gather at Anghar Mor in the final days.'"

Aik whistled. "That doesn't sound good."

*There has to be something else.* Silya had been thrust into her new position without warning, expected to watch over this city and the hencha gatherings, and now something was happening that she neither understood nor had any way to tackle. She *needed* for there to be more.

Raven and his *verent* — and the *inthym*! The quake, and her being suddenly chosen as the Hencha Queen. Silya didn't believe in coincidence.

She knew someone who might have some answers, though it killed her to admit it. Tri'Aya was the last person she wanted to see. They'd parted on less than hospitable terms at the funeral, and she'd said some terrible things to her mother about the way she'd treated her father.

Silya closed her eyes, wishing there was a way to go back in time, to change the past. Tri'Aya was an awful mother, but even she didn't deserve the accusations Silya had hurled at her. Still, desperate times ... She made up her mind. "Tomorrow we'll leave for Heaven's Reach. See what you can find by then." It felt good to do something instead of letting herself be chased by events.

"But your Raising is in three days." Sister Tela stared at her as if she'd gone mad.

"It can wait. Besides, we should be back in plenty of time." Privately, she was relieved to put the blasted thing off. She had no use for pomp and circumstance, and if they thought she was going to be that kind of Queen, they'd be sorely disappointed. "Aik, can you request some time off with the Guard? I'd like you to come with us, since you're the only witness to what happened to Raven."

He caught her eye, looking uncomfortable. This whole new *Hencha Queen* thing had to be weird for him too. "Of course, mim."

Silya winced. *You too, Aik?* "Perfect. We'll leave at first light. No fuss. I want the flitter ready to go with enough supplies for a week, just in case."

"The flitter is out of commission. It's waiting for parts from the Machinists' Guild."

Silya sighed wistfully. She'd been looking forward to her first ride in the air machine. There were only a couple left, carefully maintained by the Temple and the City Council. "That must be prioritized — we may need it sooner than we think." She tugged at the cowl of her blue robe. "A carriage or two, then. We have those, I assume?"

Sister Tela nodded. "Of course, mim. Not my area, but I'll see that it gets done."

She turned to Aik. "And who's that Sergeant of yours ... Kirk? Kerk?"

"Ser Kek."

Raven spun around, his eyes wide.

"That's the one. Let's invite him along too." Better to have the man with her than causing problems for Raven while they were gone. If he was with them, he couldn't accuse them of fleeing the scene. And there was something about him —

"That's a bad idea." Raven met her gaze. "Mim." The last word sounded like it had been dragged out of him.

"Better to have him with us than here stirring up trouble."

He sighed.

Silya stood, ending the discussion, and put a hand on the bestiary. "May I take these?"

Sister Tela frowned. "We don't usually allow ..." Then she looked up at Silya, as if she'd just realized who she was speaking to. "Of course, mim. Just ... take care of them. They're irreplaceable."

Raven grinned. "I knew I liked you, Sister."

Silya glanced at him. *What was that all about?*

Sister Tela's gaze hardened. "Put it back, son."

Raven looked back at her, the soul of innocence. "What?"

"That book you slipped into your pocket. It's a signed first edition of Jel'Faya's *Across the World*. And while it's a bit common for my taste, it belongs to the Temple."

"Raven!" Silya stared at him. She'd kept her eyes on him the whole time, but the sister was apparently sharper than she was. *Can't take the thief out of the man.*

Raven hung his head. He pulled a book out of his trouser pocket and put it back up on the shelf. "Sorry, mim. You can't blame a guy for trying."

Silya snorted. At least he had the grace to be ashamed.

Sister Tela pointed at his boots. "And the other one."

Cursing under his breath, Raven pulled a second book out from his left boot.

"You best be careful, lad. Many here in the Temple aren't as forgiving as I am."

Silya was impressed. "Thank you, Sister Tela. If you find anything else, please bring it to me immediately. I doubt I'll sleep much tonight, anyhow." Another thought occurred to her. "Also, can we find accommodations for Aik'Erio here? His own room. I want these two separated tonight." She glared at the pair of them. "No telling what trouble you might get up to otherwise." Raven was bad enough alone, but Raven plus Aik was a recipe for disaster.

"That's unnecessary." Aik's gaze pleaded with her to reconsider.

Raven just flashed her that infuriating grin. "Can I come up to your quarters first? I want to get a few of my belongings."

"Of course." She ignored Aik's silent plea. She really was over the thing between them. Mostly.

She turned to go and then hesitated. "One more thing. I'd like you and one of the initiates — Des'Rya — to join us on the journey."

The archivist might be long-winded, but she knew more about this world than any of them, and she could help Silya ride herd on Raven. And Desla ... she intrigued Silya. "My mother has a marvelous collection of books, if you'd like to see them."

Sister Tela blushed and bowed. "Yes, mim. I'd be honored." She suppressed a grin. "You realize Sister Dor will be quite upset when she hears about your expedition. She's hip-deep in plans for your Raising ceremony."

Silya chuckled. "I assumed. But she's not the Hencha Queen." It was petty, and she regretted it as soon as it came out of her mouth. Even if it was true.

Still, the sooner she showed her independence, the sooner things would settle into place. She knew a little of how these things worked after her time as an initiate. Besides, with Raven's troubles, it seemed like a good time to get him out of town for a while, before he did any more damage. At least until she figured a few things out.

She tried to sweep out of the room grandly, in the manner of royalty, but her cerulean robes got caught on the door frame and jerked her back. She grumbled as she stooped to free the hem.

*Humility topples the tallest.* One of her father's favorite sayings that she'd do well to remember, lest her pride get the better of her. There was so much she still didn't understand about being the Hencha Queen. *Who am I now, really?* Where did this other consciousness come from? And why had it forsaken her?

What else would be required of her, and how would she meet those challenges?

Questions for another day. "Coming, boys? We leave at first light."

•     •     •

Silya left Raven and Aik in her quarters to go through Raven's godscursed *things*, and opened the private door to her study, where she found her aide behind the Queen's desk. Sister Dor was dressed in her formal yellow robes, busily scribbling notes on a long sheet of parchment.

"Ahem."

Sister Dor looked up and flushed. "So sorry, mim. I had some work to catch up on, and the room was empty ..."

"Don't you have your own office?" Silya knew that stark chamber well — a tiny room in the Temple's basement with no windows. She'd been there often enough to be dressed down for one offense or another.

"Yes, mim. It's just a long way from yours ..." Her voice trailed off as she took in the deep frown on Silya's face. She looked around regretfully at the wide study, as if saying goodbye to a dear friend. "Sorry, mim. It won't happen again."

Silya felt a pang of regret. She reached out to touch Dor's shoulder as the sister scurried out of the room. "I know this must be difficult. You've shouldered so much all these years, waiting for my arrival. We'll find you something closer."

Sister Dor looked up at her, a smile of appreciation flashing across her face. "Thank you, mim. I would appreciate that." She looked down at her hands, clutching her papers tightly. "It's not that I'm not happy you've finally arrived. It's just —"

"I know." They had to work together, and Silya needed to be more aware of the power of her words. "I'm lucky to have you to guide me, Sister. By the way, you don't need to wear your formal robes when it's just us." She was ready to dispense with her own — she much preferred her fighting clothes and leathers.

"I find that wearing them helps remind me of the gravity of my office. But thank you for worrying about me." She bobbed her head. "Good night, mim." She turned to go again.

"One more thing, I'll be leaving Gullton for a few days." She felt a twinge of anxiety at the thought of confronting Tri'Aya, but she pushed it aside.

The sister turned, a frown on her face. "Very good, mim. Next week, after the Raising, there's a break in the schedule —"

Silya shook her head. "We'll leave in the morning. I'm going to visit my mother up in Heaven's Reach."

"But the Raising —"

"Can be postponed." She felt guilty at dashing all of her aide's hard work, but she'd made up her mind.

Sister Dor looked fit to be tied, but she simply nodded. "As you wish."

"Thank you. I know it's not easy, dealing with the whims of a Hencha Queen." A thought crossed Silya's mind. "Sister, you knew

Yen'Ela?" The last Hencha Queen had died in these very rooms a decade earlier.

"Yes, mim. I was her aide too. Yendra was a wonderful woman."

Her frown told Silya the jury was still out on whether she'd merit such a complimentary description. "Did you teach her how to be Queen?"

"No, mim. That was before my time." Her frown softened. "But she taught me many things. It's the duty of the Queen's Aide to help her through her training. I can answer any queries you may have."

Silya bit her lip, afraid to ask the question that had been bothering her. Or maybe afraid of what the answer might be. "Do the *hencha* ever ... change their mind?"

"Sorry?" The sister's eyes narrowed.

Silya forged ahead. The *aur* was already out of its stall. "Have they ever rescinded their choice? After choosing the new Queen?"

Sister Dor shook her head. "There have been six Queens ... seven now, counting you. Queen Ella only served for a year, stepping down when her mother became deathly ill. But not one has been ... *rejected*." She said it like it left a bad taste in her mouth and cocked her head. "Is there a problem?"

"I'm sure it's just the stress of it all getting to me." *They'll come back. I hope.* She had enough to worry about. "I'll have a list of needed supplies for you in half an hour. I'm also drafting an order to open our coffers for those in need after the quake — from what I saw in the accounting records, our stores are quite ample."

"We maintain a surplus to deal with emergencies —"

"I'm not criticizing. And I'm sure you'll agree this qualifies as one." Her tone left no room for argument.

Sister Dor bit her lip. "Yes, mim."

*I'm getting better at this.* A flash of satisfaction ran through her. "And Dor ...?"

"Yes, mim?"

"I'd like you to come with me as well. I should have the Queen's Aide at my side, don't you think?"

Relief flooded the sister's face, and maybe a little trepidation. "Yes, mim. I've never been to Heaven's Reach."

"Bring your winter coat." Silya waved her away. "Thank you, Doria."

156

The woman practically glowed at the use of her private name. "I'll return in half an hour." She curtseyed — quite a sight for a woman of her stature — and slipped out of the study.

Silya stared after her for a moment. *How is this now my life?* She shook her head, laughing at herself under her breath. It was all she'd ever wanted, but it was also far more than she'd expected.

She took a seat behind her desk, running her fingers along the smooth, beautiful purple wood — violet pine, if she wasn't mistaken. How many other Queens had sat behind this desk, exercising their power with a word, a sealed letter, or a stern glare? The weight of history was heavy on her shoulders.

Silya closed her eyes and massaged her temples, trying to feel the *hencha*. They eluded her still, and the fire inside her was gone. *Time enough to fret about that tomorrow.* With all the worries and fears she was putting off, *martasday* — the official start of a new week — would be very full.

She pulled a clean sheet of parchment out of the desk drawer and dipped her feather pen in its inkwell, and began to neatly inscribe her notes for Sister Dor.

"See you in the morning!" The side door connecting to her private quarters slammed open to pound into the wall, and Raven popped into the room with a brown carry sack, scaring her half to death.

Silya's hand skittered across the parchment, splattering drops of ink from one side to the other. "Raven!"

He glanced at the ruined parchment. "Oh ... sorry, Silya ... *Mim?*"

They stared at each other for a moment, and then she burst into laughter at the absurdity of it all. Raven, street urchin extraordinaire, calling her *mim*. She clutched her stomach and bent over, the laughter pouring out of her, a manic grin spreading across her face.

Raven stared at her as if she'd gone mad. "You sure you're all right?"

Silya put a fist over her mouth, willing herself to settle down. Such behavior was certainly not becoming of royalty. "I *will* be. This whole Hencha Queen thing isn't easy." *And getting more complicated by the day.*

She expected a snarky comeback, but he just nodded. "Silya?"

"Yes?"

"Can you make sure no one messes with my things while I'm gone?"

*Ah. That explains it.* "Of course. We can sort all that out when we come back."

"Thanks, Sil." His voice regained some of its old bounce.

"By the way, Sister Dor will be coming with us —"

"That bag of hot air —"

Her warning look cut him off. "She's a good woman. She ran this place for ten years after Queen Ela passed. The least we can do is show her a little respect. Am I understood?"

"Yes." His lips twitched. "Be nice to the gas bag."

Before she could grab something to throw at him, he scurried out of the room into the hall.

"Did you find what you were looking for?" Silya called after him.

"Yes, *mim*." The door slammed.

She really needed to teach that boy some manners.

Silya tugged at her cowl, staring at the spreading ink stain on the ruined parchment. *What a waste.* She set it aside — maybe Sister Daya could use it for writing practice with the initiates —

*Daya's gone.* The thought was like a punch to the gut.

Feeling restless, she pushed herself up out of her chair and turned to the window. The room, like the rest of her suite, looked out on the hencha gathering below. The reassuring glow of the lighthouse was gone. Snuffed out, like Daya herself. Silya pressed her hand to the cool glass. "I miss you, sister." She closed her eyes and bit her lip, remembering the last time they had truly spoken.

"I don't know why I stay. If something was going to happen, it would have happened long ago." Silya set her quill in the inkwell so she wouldn't drip ink across the *hencha*-paper document she was copying.

"You just have to be patient." Sister Daya put a hand on her shoulder. "You have so much talent. Even if you never find that connection, there will always be a place in the Temple for you." She knelt to whisper in Silya's ear. "I believe in you."

Silya shook her head. She was kidding herself. This was her life now, and nothing was ever going to change.

She took a deep breath, exhaled, and went back to copying the boring treatise on second century customs.

*I believe in you.*

A tiny tongue of flame curled around her finger. Silya stared at it, and then at the dark *hencha* below. Then, just as fast as it had come, it vanished.

She massaged her temples, closing her eyes for a moment. *Do you think I'm worthy?*

There was no reply.

Silya bit her lip. She turned back to her desk to finish her task. Tomorrow would be busy, and she was determined to be ready.

She would pay her respects to Daya when she finished her preparations. The rest would have to take care of itself.

# 13

## SPIN

*Spin's Memory: Local Year 274, Month Equa, Time 14:47 ...*
*... play recording ...*

"WHAT IS IT?" The woman stared at him, her blue eyes fixed on his silver skin.

That gaze disrupted his computational flow, drawing more of his attention than should have been required to record her symmetric visage. *She makes me ... uncomfortable.*

"Jas, this is Spin. He's what we call an artificial intelligence —"

"Like a computer?"

"Yes. But more like us. He can figure things out like a human —"

"I'm *right here.*" There. That was annoyance. These new feelings were an annoyance too. They interrupted his normal processes, making him less efficient.

Jas's eyes went wide. "It talks?"

"*He* talks. Weren't you listening, lady?" That one was called rude. Or was that more of an attitude than a feeling? How did these humans even function with all of this going on inside of them?

"Sorry, Spin. *He* talks. He's from the ship?"

Sera nodded. "They're designed to survive even a catastrophic event. He has a complete record of what happened, which they'd use to try to prevent another similar incident."

"What event?" Spin ran a complete inventory of his memory of the last year, which took about 300 milliseconds. He'd been flying the *Spin Diver*. Then he'd been in the dirt. Another emotion shuffled his senses ... confusion or worry? *Maybe both.*

Sera was staring at him.

"You should hide him." Jas looked over her shoulder, but Spin didn't sense anyone close by. "If they saw ... him, they'd try to burn you on the pyre again. Or take him from you."

"They tried to kill you, Cap?" He shuddered inside, imagining the acrid smoke. Her fear.

"Yes, Spin, but I'm safe now. We're safe now." She took Jas's hand and squeezed it. "I'm going to ask you to do something you won't like. But I want you to promise. For me."

Spin stared at her. "Of course, Cap. Just give the order." She was beautiful, and she'd come to find him when he'd been lost.

"I want you to shut down. I promise, I'll wake you up to talk with you regularly. But for now, it's safest if you sleep."

Spin sunk into yet another emotion ... disappointment. And yet, he'd already promised Sera to do what she asked. "Sure, Cap." He put on a cheery voice. "Next time I want to hear more about this strange world we landed in." He knew all the basics — orbit, size, gravity, atmospheric composition. But those were dry facts. He wanted more. He tasted the feeling, rolling it around in his plasma circuits. *Curiosity. I rather like this one.*

"Now, Spin." Her voice was kind, with a tinge of regret.

"Yes, Cap." One more emotion. *Love.*

*... end recording.*

•     •     •

Raven closed the door to his room, hoping everyone would leave him alone for the night. *At least no one came to lock me in again.* Someone had left the electric lamp on though, and the room was warm enough. *Thank Ay'Oss for small blessings.*

He wondered where Silya had stashed poor Aik.

162

Spin popped a feeler out of Raven's pants pocket. "All clear, boss?"

"Yup. Back to the jailhouse."

Spin whistled, golden light flashing around the walls. "You've come up in the world from that gully rat nest you called your —"

"Enough, Spin." He'd made it back to his room — his cell — easily enough, his place-sense already building a map of the Temple's halls in his head. Everyone seemed to know who he was, even though he only knew a handful of them.

He was glad they were finally going to get out of this *orinth* nest in the morning. *Too many women in too small a space.*

His senses were all out of whack too. In Silya's room, he'd smelled Sister Dor, even though she was no longer there — her cloying perfume one part violet pine flower and two parts *trine* grass. It was strange how he could now pick out individual scents so easily.

Raven's hand went to his stomach. *What are you up to in there?* He shoved aside his growing sense of unease.

On his way back to his cell, various sounds had reached him from the sisters' rooms, including a series of grunts and carnal moans from one that had left him both impressed and disturbed. The idea of two of the older sisters like Tela and Dor rutting like animals ... how did you flush that out of your head?

He set his carry sack down on the end of the bed. It had been repaired while he was out — he lifted the comforter to see a wooden brace that someone had attached to the cracked frame.

Raven opened the sack and pulled out an almost-new pair of boots, setting them down next to the wall. He'd forgotten he had them, and his old ones were sadly out of shape. They'd take a few days to break in.

He'd also collected a couple changes of clothing. He chose one and laid it out on the back of the chair for the morning — a deep green button-down shirt fit for a merchant and some practical black homeweave trousers. He also chose his black vest — one of the ones he'd modified with an inside pocket for Spin.

Satisfied with his wardrobe, he unwrapped one of his other precious possessions — the beautiful knife Aik had given him.

"Oooh, sharp. You steal that too?" Spin's acerbic tone suggested disapproval.

"No. It was a gift." Aik had probably forgotten all about it. It had been a birthday present the year before. Raven had never actually used it — he had an everyday knife for his day-to-day needs. But somehow the time seemed right. He would carry it in his boot sheath and keep the old one at his waist. *Never know when you might find yourself in a two-knife situation.*

Last, he pulled out the leather gloves he'd retrieved from one of his bags and laid them on the nightstand. Along with a long-sleeved shirt, they would do to cover his arms and hide the strange scales, which he was trying mightily hard not to think about. *What am I becoming?*

"What's wrong, boss?" For a moment it sounded like Spin was genuinely worried about him. "You look like the arse end of an elephant."

Raven chuckled. *So close. And what in Heaven's Reach was an ellyfont?* "I'm just tired. Don't you ever get tired?"

"You have no idea."

That surprised him. Still, it was late — not that that usually bothered him — but it had been a long, weird couple of days, and whatever this *verent* thing was doing to him was sapping his strength. He didn't have the energy to pursue it further.

"By the way, Exalted One, it's a bit ... smelly down here, next to your junk. Maybe you can wash up?"

Raven laughed. "You read my mind." He pulled Spin out of his pants pocket.

The little familiar changed shape, withdrawing his feeler and unflattening himself, reforming into a silver sphere.

Raven set him on the edge of the washbasin, where Spin wobbled a bit and then grew a couple legs to stabilize himself. Amazing creature. His life had changed since they'd found each other.

Raven moved his carry sack over to the chair and stripped. He didn't care if Spin saw him naked — the little familiar had seen it all before and had already gotten all of his disparaging comments out of his system.

"Looks like you just took a dip in a freezing lake, boss."

*Well, almost all of them.* Raven ignored Spin's snark. He threw his borrowed clothes in a heap on the floor. They weren't really his — the Temple had loaned them to him. They could clean them when he was gone.

He'd gotten spoiled these last couple of years with a daily bath in the lair, and even more so with the warm running water of the Temple. After tonight, they'd be on the road again, so he took advantage of the opportunity to clean himself with the washcloth and reed soap someone had thoughtfully left for him by the washbasin.

He lathered his hair and then rinsed it out as best he could under the low tap. The water went down the drain filthy, so he did it again until it ran clean. Then he used the cloth to rub off the dead skin on his forearms, watching it spiral down the drain. It felt good to be clean again.

Satisfied, he pulled on his small clothes, grabbed Spin, and sat back on the bed. The frame creaked with his weight but held. He lifted his arms to stare at his strange new skin, tracing the charcoal-gray lines of his left forearm. The scales were smooth and vaguely delta-shaped, overlapping one another from his elbow to his wrist. His stomach churned, and the electric lamp suddenly seemed too bright. *What in the holy green hell is happening to me?*

Spin peered at his arms too. "That's weird. Looks like you're turning into one of those *verent* things. Maybe it'll improve your temperament."

Raven laughed despite himself. "Maybe you ought to give it a try."

"Lil' sweet ole' me?"

Raven snorted. He turned his arm over and was alarmed to see that the skin on the back of his hand was rough and dry now too. He closed his eyes, seeing the painting of the *verent* again in his head. *Am I really becoming one of those?*

Sure, it would be the godsall best to be a badass, fire-breathing dragon, like the white one in one of his favorite Earth books. That would show them all — everyone who ever called him a *gully weasel* or a *common thief.* Still, the idea scared the *hencha* berries out of him.

*Speaking of hencha berries ...* He looked down at his crotch. *What's gonna happen to you little guys?*

*And speaking of balls ...* Raven held Spin up and looked at him.

"Rude. How'd you like it if I stared at *you*?"

Raven chuckled. "Fair point." Spin was a mystery. *What other secrets do you hold that you've never told me?* "What's really happening to me?" Spin had come from Old Earth with the last run, so he knew little about local things. Still, he was a fast learner.

Spin's golden light flashed across his forearm. "Scanning, boss." The shimmer played over him. "It looks like a local infection. I'd normally recommend standard range antibiotics." The light shut off.

"I don't know what those are." He hated it when Spin used big words.

Spin sighed dramatically. "You people here on Tharassas are so backward." The golden lights spun around Spin's middle, something Raven had learned to interpret as "Leave me alone. I'm thinking."

Raven's hand went involuntarily to his neck. He could still feel the little *verent* — if that's what it was — forcing its way down his throat. Remembering made him feel sick all over again. *There's something badly wrong with me.* He didn't scare easily, but this whole thing had shaken him to the core.

The spinning lights stopped. "From my analysis, those marks on your arms closely match the scale patterns of that creature that crawled inside you." Spin paused. "That must have been unpleasant for you, boss."

Raven felt the blood drain from his face. "You have no idea. So I'm ... becoming one of those things?"

"Unlikely. The evidence suggests DNA reprofiling, but not a complete change."

"*Deen Ay?*" Spin loved to speak in riddles.

"It means whatever it's doing in there is changing you a little bit at a time. You're becoming a hybrid — part human, part ... the other thing." He flashed once. "It's really quite fascinating."

Raven shuddered. "To you, maybe." He hated the idea of being some kind of human-animal experiment. Though maybe fire-breathing was still on the table ...

The door swung open. "I have to tell you something —" Aik stopped and looked at Raven's underclothes, and then up at the silver sphere. "Hello, Spin."

"I see the Jolly Green Giant is back," Spin said to the room in general.

Raven laughed at the look of confusion that crossed Aik's face. "You get used to it." *At least he used his quiet voice.* He'd been so careful hiding the little imp, but now the secret was out — he was lucky it was just Aik. "You didn't tell anyone about him, did you?"

"Of course not." Aik checked the hall. "All clear." He eased the door shut behind him.

"What are you doing here?" Privately he was glad to see Aik, even if they'd had a fight. With all the people it held, it was still lonely in the Temple.

Aik smelled worried, a bitter edge to his normal Aik-scent. "I wanted to say I was sorry I pushed you to move in with me. I didn't mean to make you angry. I hate it when you're mad at me."

"It's ... fine." Raven struggled with a stew of conflicting emotions. He didn't like fighting with Aik either. "You were just looking out for me. You always do." It was true. Aik had been there for him, whatever he needed.

Aik's shoulders slumped in relief, his gaze shifting back to Spin. "Is it really from Earth?"

"*Him.* Is *he* really from Earth." Spin used his best annoyed-sarcastic voice.

Aik raised an eyebrow.

"He's picky about his pronouns. Come sit." He patted the mattress next to him.

"You sure?" Aik smelled strangely hopeful.

"Yes." He wasn't, but he sensed Aik needed a little reassuring that things were okay between them.

Aik settled down on the mattress next to him. The frame groaned but held.

Raven reached over to turn off the electric lamp. *Really gotta get one of those for the lair ...* Except the lair was gone. "Spin, please show us Earth."

"Sure boss." Spin glowed again, and a second sphere appeared in the air above it, about the size of Raven's head — a blue and green globe hovering in the darkness. It was filled with astonishing detail — broken coastlines, broad seas, and tiny ice caps at either pole.

Aik's jaw dropped open. "It's beautiful."

"Touch it." Raven had tried this before, but it was fun to show it to someone new.

167

Aik reached out to feel the surface, but his hand plunged right through. "How does it do that?"

Spin chuckled. "They fall for it every time."

Aik glared at the little guy.

"Spin, be nice to our guest." Raven turned to Aik. "He calls it a 'holographic projection.' Watch." He reached out and brushed it with his fingertips.

The world began to spin, the white clouds shifting around in mesmerizing patterns. Raven stopped it and picked a spot in the northern hemisphere, widening it with his fingers. They plunged toward the surface to hover over a metropolis that made Gullton seem like a tiny provincial backwater.

"What is it?" Aik leaned into peer at it, and Raven got a good whiff of his scent. He smelled ... tense?

Raven hoped Aik didn't see how much his scent excited him. "It's ... London, one of the Earth's biggest cities." His hand was shaking. He willed it to be still, but Aik didn't seem to notice.

"This is amazing." Aik tore his eyes away from the projection to stare at him. "Where did you get it? Did you steal it? You never did tell me."

"*Him*. Where did you get *him*." Spin sounded really annoyed now.

"Him. Sorry." Aik's gaze bored into Raven.

Raven shook his head. "No, I swear I didn't. Remember that metal panel you saw in the lair?"

"The one that said '*Spin Diver*?" Aik's eyes widened.

"I found it — and Spin — out in what's left of the old landing field. Where the Last Run arrived." He didn't tell Aik the rest — how one of the *hencha* plants had uprooted itself to bring him the sphere. Aik would never believe him.

"Rave, are you lying to me?" Aik's eyes searched his. "If you are ... someone powerful might be looking for him. Some people would kill for something like this. You could be in real danger."

"Like I'm not already?" Raven patted his stomach. "You know I don't lie. Not about anything important."

"Rav'Orn —"

He met Aik's gaze. "Godsall truth, Aik. I swear it on my mother's grave." He reached up to touch the burn scar on the side of his face.

Aik's eyebrow raised. "You told me they never found the body."

Raven growled. "I don't lie. Not about anything important. Whatever else you may think about me, you know that much."

Aik narrowed his eyes. "I believe you. Not sure I should. But I do."

*Those beautiful ice-blue eyes.* Raven closed his own, wishing things were simpler between them. Wishing Aik wasn't a guard. Wishing most of all that he'd never stolen that stupid egg.

Aik's touch on his arm sent a shiver through him. "Does it hurt?"

Raven opened his eyes. Aik was staring at the scales. *My scales.* "Not really. It's still itchy." He'd avoided thinking about it for a full three minutes, but there it was again. "I'm scared, Aik. What if it keeps growing?"

Aik smirked. "I think you'd make a really handsome lizard boy."

Raven blushed and turned away. Only Aik could get to him like that. "You get enough tail ... I guess you'd know."

Aik stared at him, obviously hurt. "Rave —"

"I know. I'm sorry." The whole day had been a series of unpleasant surprises, and it was wearing him thin. "I'm just feeling out of sorts. What are we doing tomorrow?" He already knew, but letting Aik tell him might ease the tension a bit.

"I know it's been a lot." Aik squeezed his shoulder in encouragement. "We're headed to Silya's mother's estate. Up in Heaven's Reach."

"She has a mother? I figured she hatched from an egg." *Ouch.* That brought back painful memories.

"Hey, she saved both of us last night."

"I'm sorry, you're right." He was being an ungrateful wretch. "Spin, show me Heaven's Reach."

"Sorry, Tavi, I'm not sure what that is."

Raven stared at the little sphere. *Who in the holy hencha is Tavi?* "I'm Raven, Spin. Not Tavi."

The sphere was silent for a moment. "Sorry boss. Give me a sec. Re-initializing personnel files."

*That's weird.* Raven and Aik exchanged a frown, staring at the spinning golden lights.

"Got it now, boss. You're Rav'Orn. Raven to your friends."

"Right." Spin was acting stranger than normal.

"You expect me to just know where this 'Heaven's Reach' is?" Now the little familiar sounded aggrieved. That was more like it.

"It's the mountain range just north of Gullton, where we are now."

"This one?" London, with her glistening bridges and graceful towers, disappeared, replaced by a vivid image — a row of tall purple mountain peaks above a wide valley. "Just so you know, this composite was created from the initial planetary survey. It might not be entirely accurate anymore."

"Thanks, Spin. Yes. That's it." Raven stared at it. The mountains were beautiful — tall, graceful peaks covered with snow. They extended farther east than he'd imagined, wrapping around the northern edge of the Heartland. His mother had shown him a flat map of the lands close to Gullton once, but it had been nowhere near as detailed as this one.

Aik whistled, his face partially masked by the glowing image. "That's ... amazing."

"Thanks, you giraffe of a man." Spin extended a pseudopod, looking up and down Aik's length. "You sure *this* is the guy you like? He's a bit ... slooooow."

Raven blushed. "I never said I liked him."

Aik arched an eyebrow.

"Last Terasday, boss." Raven's own voice sounded in the air. *"I really like Aik. I just ... we can't ever be."*

Aik's mouth popped open. "That was ... it sounded just like you."

"Lies, all of it," Raven growled. "Spin, shut down." He felt the blush-heat on his cheeks. *Stupid familiar, sharing my business...*

"Aw boss, things are just starting to get good."

Raven glared at the little sphere. "Now, Spin."

"Yes, boss." He made smooching sounds, and then his lights went dark.

Raven slipped him inside his carry sack and tied the top. "He'll be okay in there until morning."

He turned to find Aik staring at him. Not just *at* him, but into him, in that disconcerting way he had of seeing right through to Raven's soul. He was uncomfortably aware of Aik's closeness, the warmth of his hand on his arm, and his own semi-nakedness.

"This is a bad idea —"

"Shut up, Rave." Aik moved closer and pulled Raven to him.

Raven's whole body shivered as their lips met, and he was vividly aware of his own naked vulnerability.

Aik's arms encompassed him, making him feel safe. His fears dropped away, and they floated together in a space outside of time.

Aik kissed him hungrily, then pushed him slowly back onto the bed. Gently his lips brushed the new skin of Raven's forearms, working his way up the left arm, each gentle touch of his lips an affirmation that he loved Raven, no matter what.

Despite his reservations, Raven surrendered to Aik's ministrations, moaning softly with pleasure.

He wanted this so badly. Wanted Aik to be his forever. Wanted to lock the door and keep Aik all to himself, safe here in this room —

There was a sharp knock.

Aik jumped up, backing away to the far side of the bed. His eyes met Raven's. "We'll finish this later." Aik sank down into the chair in the corner of the room, his eyes still locked on Raven's prone form.

Raven growled under his breath *At least someone had the manners to knock first.* "Come in." He rearranged the blankets to cover his own waning excitement. It was better this way. *What was I thinking?*

Des'Rya popped her head into the room. "Sister Tela sent me to make sure you were going to sleep, Raven ..." She noticed Aik in the corner. "Sorry, did I interrupt something?"

"Nothing important." Raven pulled the blanket farther up over his chest. He was feeling ... complicated things.

"I see." She glared at Aik. "You should be in your own room."

"We were just talking about the trip tomorrow." Aik blushed.

"Five more minutes." The harshness of her words lost its impact when a grin crept across her face. "I've never been to the mountains before. I wonder if we'll see *fairykins.* Or an *eircat?*"

Aik shook his head. "You rarely see an *eircat* before —" He drew a line across his throat with his finger.

"Oh. That's ... disturbing." Desla blanched.

"They're mostly in the Highlands, though, in the Redflight Mountains. Not there." Aik pointed at where the map had been. "I mean ... in Heaven's Reach. I get all turned around in this place."

Raven shot him a disapproving glance. "What our friend here means is that you don't have to worry about *eircats* where we're going."

Desla laughed wickedly. "That's a relief. Still, I'll take my best knife." She slipped it out from under her robes, a wickedly gleaming thing.

Raven whistled, impressed.

The blade disappeared beneath layers of purple cloth. "See you both in the morning." She closed the door, and they were alone together again.

Aik was staring at him.

"You had something you wanted to tell me?" The tension was thick between them. *This is what I didn't want.* Aik was his best friend, and he couldn't let anything ruin that. He could smell Aik's anxiety — like static electricity in his nose. These new abilities were getting on his nerves.

"It's ... nothing. I just wanted to check in with you. It was a weird day."

Raven stared at Aik. "You sure?" He was hiding something. Raven knew him well enough to be certain of it. *He'll tell me when he's ready.*

"Yeah. I'm just tired." He bent down to give Raven an awkward hug, the intensity of the moment gone. "I'll see you in the morning. Try to get some sleep." He kissed Raven's cheek and slipped out of the room, leaving Raven alone with Spin.

"'Night," Raven said to the closed door. He was all keyed up after their brief moment of intimacy. *Damn Desla for interrupting us.* Being inside the Temple was like having a hundred mothers, every one telling you where to sit, how to dress, what to eat, poking and prodding at you until you were ready to scream. *I can't wait to get out of this place.*

Raven rubbed his eyes, drained by the long day. *Five more minutes.* He snorted. He'd stay up all night if he wanted to. *No one can tell me what to do. Well, no one but Silya.* That woman had scared the *hencha* berries out of him even before she became the Queen.

Raven touched the scales on his arm where Aik's lips had brushed his skin. *He still loves me.* That meant something, even if they could never be together. He had to be hard.

*Well, got that covered.* He laughed at his own inane wit.

He listened to the sounds of the surrounding Temple — the creaking of the bed beneath him when he shifted, the quiet steps of someone passing by his door, the electric whine of the lamp on the nightstand.

He yawned, fighting his exhaustion, determined to defy the Desla-imposed deadline. *I can do this.*

Four minutes later, he was sound asleep.

# 14

## CROSSING

THE SPORE MOTHER WOKE from one of her regular slumbers, content to feel the heat flowing into her feeders.

Something had touched her, stirring her out of her sleep.

A piece of him.

Someone had found the last progenitor's gauntlet. It called to her, whole once more. It was small, indistinct, but she could sense it.

It was a sign.

She needed more.

She dug her roots deeper, seeking more heat from the heart of the earth. She would send out her forerunners, the *iichili*, to find it. And then she would bring it home.

She sent thanks to the dead homeworld. Her prayers had been answered.

•   •   •

Aik stared gloomily out the window of the carriage at the city streets along Eagle Spine, the gray skies above matched to his mood. Tradespeople were clearing away the mess left by the quake, breaking down burnt and broken pieces of wood and shingles and throwing them onto wide, *urse*-drawn wagons to be hauled out of the city. *I went too fast.*

Raven wouldn't even look at him this morning.

He'd needed Raven's touch, his reassurance, and in the end he'd gotten neither, and chickened out telling his best friend about the gauntlet.

The carriage's wooden wheels bounced across the short bridge between Eagle Spine and Vulture Spine, the northernmost of the long, narrow islands that made up Old Gullton. On the far side, it clattered across the cobblestones, setting his teeth to chattering. He'd barely slept a wink the night before — his dreams had been so full of strange things that he would awaken in a cold sweat, staring at the ceiling. But when he chased after them, they vanished like mist over the Elsp.

His life had been derailed, his hard work to become a guard shunted aside by events mostly beyond his control. Instead of driving hard toward something, he was being whisked along by the tide, just as the carriage was carrying his body away from Gullton, with no concern for his own wants or needs.

He'd sent a note to his mother, letting her know he'd be out of town for a few days. Sister Dor had promised it would be delivered. He wished he could have found the time to see her ... to ask if she knew of anything like the strange gauntlet. In private, of course. She would have provided him with some small comfort, at the least. Then again, she'd be as worried as he was. *No, more. Best I didn't tell her.*

They'd be back in a few days, and he could talk to her about it then if he hadn't figured out how to get the thing off.

Aik held up his right arm, staring at it. He could almost feel the strange gauntlet wrapped around it, like a really tight shirt, but there was nothing there. *I must be going crazy.* Aik cracked his knuckles, working out some of the tension.

"You shouldn't do that. You'll ruin your hands." He held up his own. "They're delicate instruments, you know." Raven's voice was disapproving, but at least he was finally talking.

*That's something.* "Yours maybe." Aik looked at his right hand. It had heavy calluses all around his palm from his practice with his short sword. "Mine are meant for wielding a sword, not doing embroidery or picking locks."

On Raven's far side, Desla laughed. "He's got you there."

Raven subsided into silence again.

Aik missed their usual camaraderie. A slight bulge in Raven's vest indicated that he'd brought Spin with him, but the acerbic familiar was blessedly silent. *Unless he's chattering away in Raven's ear.*

The city was a shambles. At this early hour, it was mostly deserted, but half the buildings had suffered damage, and a few had collapsed entirely or been burned to the ground. The city looked like he felt.

"Good time to get out of town." Raven leaned over his shoulder, peering outside. "It's a mess out there."

Desla stared out her own window. She was dressed in what Aik thought of as her warrior clothes — the tunic, breeches, and deep purple *aur*-leathers she wore on the training field. Silya was dressed similarly, but the two other sisters in the party — Dor and Tela — had insisted on wearing their yellow robes.

Aik was uncomfortably aware of Raven's proximity, and of the secret he was keeping from him. "Guess so." *Look who has no words now.*

A shadow passed over the carriage, and Raven ducked back behind him, making himself small between his two companions.

Ser Kek paced the small caravan on his black *urse* — called Thunder because of course he was. The creature was beautiful and sleek, gracefully pacing the carriage. As the *urse* passed, the sergeant glared at Aik and then looked away, his expression unreadable.

Aik sunk down into his seat, away from the open window, and soon the man passed by.

That had been a surprise. Ser Kek had shown up in the morning and had asked, not demanded, to come along. And you could have knocked Aik over with a feather when Silya had said yes. "It's all right. He's gone."

Raven was whiter than usual. "Why is he here? I thought the whole point of this stupid expedition was to get away from him and the Guard."

Aik shrugged. "Silya wanted him along." She had her own reasons, and Aik had learned from long, hard experience not to question them. He changed the subject. "Ever been out of Gullton before?" He knew the answer, but it seemed like a safe topic.

Raven snorted. "What for? Just a bunch of dirt and weeds out there."

Aik stifled a laugh. *There's the old Raven.* "You should come with me on one of my hunting trips sometime, once things are a little less crazy. Maybe we'd even bag an *Ix*." *Who am I kidding?* Things might never get back to normal again.

"I'm not sure things will ever be less crazy." Raven stared at the gloves covering his scaled arms, and they both lapsed into silence.

The small caravan — if you could call two carriages that — left the city proper, crossing from Vulture Spine to rumble onto the Old Bridge. The oversized iron structure was impressive despite its age, a long, curved construct that arched over the waters of the Elsp far below, where its pilings sank deep into the riverbed. It was only wide enough for traffic in one direction at a time, but this early in the morning there were few other people out on the road.

Raven yawned.

Desla laughed and pinched him. "Stop that, or you'll get me started too."

"Hey, that hurt!" Raven rubbed his arm, glaring at the initiate.

Aik shook his head. *Children.*

The bridge creaked and groaned under the weight of the carriages, and a flurry of glowing blue wisps chased each other up and over them in the gusty wind. To the west, he could see almost all the way to Tucker Narrows, where the northernmost branch of the Elsp bent one last time before rushing out to sea. The bluffs ahead were free of buildings, topped by purple sedge grass waving in the breeze.

The wind was brisk. As the carriages reached the midpoint of the long bridge, the threatening skies opened up at last, cascading rain across the chasm and obscuring the view. Ahead, the one that carried Silya and the two Sisters had already begun its descent toward the far side.

The carriage shook.

"What's that?" Raven looked out of Aik's window, head darting back and forth. "Another quake?"

Aik grabbed ahold of the handle above the door, peering out into the falling rain. There was no low rumble this time. "I don't think so —"

The carriage lurched forward and then dropped, sending him flying into the front of the cabin. Aik's right hand shot out to save him from a broken nose.

There was a horrid grinding sound as they came to a screeching halt, the carriage laying at an awkward angle canted to the right.

Raven disentangled himself from Desla. "Everyone all right?"

Aik pushed himself up with his right arm, frowning as the gauntlet flickered in and out of existence again. He shoved the door open, stepping outside awkwardly. He hoped no one noticed in the confusion. "What's going on out here?" Ahead, Silya's carriage was continuing down the slope toward the far bank.

The *urse* turned to stare at Aik, chewing placidly.

"Sorry, Mas Erio." The driver hopped down from his bench. He had a nasty scrape on his right arm, but otherwise looked healthy. "We broke a wheel."

The poor man was soaked, despite his purple leather poncho. "You all right?"

The man flushed. "Yes, mas. Thank you for asking."

"Good." At last, something immediate he could tackle. Aik's confidence returned. "What do we need to do?"

The driver looked at the broken wheel, and then at the *urse* who waited, unconcerned, behind its blinders. "We always carry a spare, but I'll need your help to lever up the carriage to get it on."

Raven and Des had gotten out now too. "What's going on?" His friend shivered. "This had to happen in the pouring rain. Why'd you make me leave the Temple?"

Aik shook his head. *That was typical Raven.* Less than a day earlier, he'd been itching to get out of *this blasted orinth's nest.* "Of course we'll help. Desla, why don't you wait in the carriage where it's warm and dry? You can get out when it's time."

She glared at him. "Lifting this thing will be easier with three of us, don't you think?"

Aik blushed. *So much for being a gentleman.* "Of course, mim."

Desla nodded. "Better." She looked at the driver's arm. The steady rain was washing away the blood. "What's your name?"

"Mas Arin, mim."

"Your first name?" She looked up at the burly driver, batting her eyes.

"Mal. Malin." He met her gaze, nodding in appreciation.

Aik kicked himself for not bothering to ask.

"Thank you, Malin. Once we get to the other side of the bridge, I can see about cleaning up and bandaging that scrape."

"It's nothing. Really, mim." The driver blushed.

Aik shook his head. *Well, she is pretty.* Even with her hair matted to her head by the rain. He cleared his throat. "The sooner we get this done, the sooner we can be on our way." *And back in the nice, warm, dry carriage.*

Desla glared at him through narrowed eyes but said nothing.

Raven's own eyes went wide — Spin must be saying something crass in his ear.

Aik turned his attention back to the task at hand. Malin went around the back while Aik surveyed the damage. The wheel must have come loose and started wobbling, but the axle was intact. Aik said a prayer for small favors. He'd helped to repair enough broken wheels with the Guard that he knew his way around the basic mechanics.

Malin rolled the wheel around the grounded carriage. It was a beautiful thing, hand-crafted from oak and iron. "Only have the one, so knock on wood ..." He leaned it against the bridge railing.

Aik stayed away from the edge, not wanting to see how far up they were. *Concentrate on the task at hand.* He shivered in the clammy dampness.

"I need you all to lift the carriage up so I can take off the broken wheel, and then let it down again when I say." He pulled a heavy iron wrench out of his back pocket.

"Of course. I've done this before. I helped maintain the Guard carriages." He'd always loved using his hands — real, honest work.

"Good man." Malin knelt beside the wreckage of the broken wheel. "Ready?"

The others nodded.

"As I'll ever be —"

The bridge shook, a low rumble that quickly grew into a crescendo, and the span began to sway crazily under Aik's feet. "Quake! Hold on!"

The new wheel started to roll. Malin let go of the carriage to reach for it as it spun by, but another jolt threw him hard against the rail. He cried out and collapsed to the ground. The wheel spun away on its own down the shaking bridge.

The *urse* struggled against its bonds, dragging the downed carriage forward a couple meters, and Aik and his friends held on for dear life.

There was an ear-splitting crack, and then a sudden silence. Throughout it all, the rain continued unabated.

Aik let out a sigh of relief. "Everyone all right?" *Thank Ay'Oss that's over.*

The *urse* wherried nervously, as if in response. The patter of the rain on the bridge was the only other sound.

"Yes, I think so." Raven let go of the carriage. "Wet as a school of *kerint*. But nothing broken."

"I'll grab my bag and check on Malin." Desla popped into the carriage and then back out, vanishing into the rain behind them.

Aik surveyed their ride and shook his head. One of the other wheels had broken now too. They'd have to send someone back into Gullton for help. Silya wasn't going to like the delay.

The bridge under his feet groaned ominously, a shudder that he felt in his bones.

Rave's eyes met his. "That can't be good." The anger was gone from his tone, replaced by fear.

Aik shuddered. *If the thrice-damned thing is breaking ...*

"Malin's fine." Desla materialized back out of the rain, holding the driver up. He walked with a limp.

The bridge shifted sharply under his feet, almost knocking Aik to the ground. "We have to get off of the bridge. Now."

Desla stiffened. "What's happening?"

Aik could feel it in his bones. "The whole cursed thing is falling. Move!"

"Farking hell." She blanched. "Sorry — I'll take care of Malin."

"Go — we'll be right behind you."

"Hurry!" The two of them started off toward the far side as quickly as they could manage, vanishing once again like ghosts into a curtain of rain.

"I'll release the *urse*. Then we go too."

Raven shook his head, spraying Aik with droplets of cold water. "I need to grab our things!" He slipped back to the door and wrenched it open, almost leaping inside the carriage.

"There's no time!" Aik shouted after him. "This thing could collapse any second!" He opened the quick release clip that bound the *urse* to the carriage and slapped its rear, sending it galloping down the bridge after the others. *Hope Desla has the sense to get out of the way.* "Raven, come on!"

The structure shifted again, the metal supports groaning so loudly that they drowned out the sounds of the rain. The bridge was going to take both of them down with it if they didn't get off of it soon.

Aik reached into the carriage and pulled Raven out by his shirt. "Let's go!" Fear painted his vision red.

"Got it! And I got your sack too." He slipped his over his shoulders, and Aik hurriedly did the same.

"Hope you're happy. We might die here with them. Run!" They squeezed past the carriage and onto the open bridge and took off toward the North Shore.

The entire structure listed to the right, and they broke into an all-out run as the world shifted around them, the horrible sounds of twisting, breaking metal ripping through the air. Aik's stomach twisted along with it, fear loosening his bowels. He struggled to keep control of himself as the whole bridge shifted left, then right again with a terrible metallic groan.

Lighting struck the bridge a few meters behind them, brightening the dim, gray morning with a shock of brilliance before fading quickly back to gray.

How much farther? *I don't want to die here.*

The bridge dropped abruptly half a meter, throwing them sideways against the railing and bruising Aik's ribs, almost making him lose his breakfast. The rain let up for a few seconds, and he could see the long fall down to the Elsp below. *I hate heights.*

182

Raven was sprawled on the ground behind him, scrambling to get back up. Aik reached out to help his friend, and the gauntlet flickered into existence, hauling Raven up onto his feet.

Another thunderous clap, and the bridge sagged toward the narrows.

"Ruuuuuun!" He hoped to the Gods that Des and Malin had already reached the far side.

The rain had slowed, and he could see the shore at last, just ten meters away. "We're going to make it!" He glanced over his shoulder at Raven, who was just a couple meters behind him, panting heavily. His friend's face went pale as the bridge rumbled again.

He turned to see the bridge ripping away from its mooring on the bluff. *Oh sweet mother of Jas.* "Jump!" His feet pumped under him.

"Too ... far!"

"No ... choice." The edge of the bridge was coming up fast. "Jump!" *Don't look down.* Aik leapt off the bridge, crossing the intervening two meters to land on the bluff, scrambling to catch himself on the remains of one of the bridge pilings that jutted up from the ground like a broken tree. He turned to see Raven leap as the bridge fell away from under him.

Raven flew toward him, arms flailing, suspended in midair for what seemed like half a minute but could only have been a second.

Then he slammed hard into the ground just below Aik.

The soil crumbled away beneath him, and a look of horror crossed Raven's face as he slipped down the muddy ground toward the chasm, grasping hold of an exposed root to halt his fall.

Aik fought his fear at the gaping drop beneath him.

"Grab this!" Ser Kek's voice rang out above him over the noise as the bridge collapsed into the canyon.

Aik glanced upwards, and a rope slithered down into his hands. Without thinking, Aik grabbed it with his gauntleted hand. He let go of the piling, scrambling down the slope to reach out to Raven's gloved arm. The gauntlet flickered out of existence again. He grunted, trying not to see the drop-off below, concentrating instead on Raven's face. "Take my hand!"

"I can't" Raven's eyes were squeezed shut.

"Dammit, Raven, try! I can't lose you."

Raven's eyes opened, meeting his.

"You can do it." The whole world squeezed down to just the two of them.

Raven's fear-filled eyes met his. He nodded and gathered himself, thrusting his hand toward Aik, but missed as Aik reached the literal end of his rope.

"Again!" He lunged forward as far as he could, extending his fingers.

Raven strained upward, and at last their hands clasped one another's.

Golden light lit up the space between them as Spin poked a tendril out of Raven's pocket. "Things don't look good for our heroes."

"Not ... now ... Spin." Aik tried to pull Raven up, but he was too heavy, and the strain on both his arms was growing. The rain was starting up again, making things slicker and cutting off his view. *Thank the gods for small favors.*

Raven held his bag in one hand.

"Let it go! It's too heavy." It might be enough to make the difference.

Raven shook his head. "I can't! I clipped it to my belt!" Raven's glove was slipping off his arm.

Aik rolled his eyes. *Raven and his stupid things.* He adjusted his grip to grab hold of Raven's forearm. "I can't hold you much longer —" Anger flooded him at Raven's stupid theft of the egg, at Silya for dragging them on this ill-fated expedition, and at himself for being such a lunkheaded idiot. He was going to lose his best friend —

The crashing sound reached a crescendo as, somewhere far below and hidden by the incessant rain, the ruins of the bridge collapsed into the Elsp.

Warmth flowed through Aik's right arm, and the gauntlet reappeared, lighting up Raven's face.

His eyes went wide.

Aik's grip tightened around Raven's arm. He pulled again, and it was as if Raven was as light as a feather. Aik heaved him up to the metal piling he'd been clinging to a moment before. "Grab on!"

Raven threw his arms around the broken column as if it were his own dear departed mother, his chest heaving.

"Damn. You work out, Aik? And what the hell was —"

"Spin, sleep." Raven's voice was sharp.

Aik took hold of the rope in both hands, climbing up it after Raven.

"Aw boss ..."

"Now."

"Yes, boss." The golden light vanished.

Aik took hold of the ruined column and settled in next to Raven, his chest heaving. They just sat there for a moment, grasping the tortured metal, sharing a look as Raven tried to catch his breath too. He did his best to ignore the yawning chasm just a couple meters away.

"What the ... green holy hell ... was that?" Raven's breath came in gasps. His short hair was plastered to his forehead, and he looked like a wet dog. He stared at the gauntlet, rubbing his arm where Aik had grabbed him. "That's gonna leave a mark."

Aik looked away. This was not how he'd wanted to give Raven the news. "I'll tell you later." The gauntlet faded out of existence.

Raven blinked. He stared at Aik's arm a moment longer, then closed his eyes, his breathing slowly returning to normal. "This is what you wanted to talk about last night, isn't it?"

"Yes." Aik met his gaze, his eyes wet. *Just the rain.* "I meant to tell you. I'm sorry about what I did —"

Raven shook his head. "I should have let you talk. And maybe I was wrong —"

"You were what?" Aik had never heard Raven admit that before.

"You two all right down there?" Silya's voice interrupted Raven from above, through the pounding of the rain.

Raven met Aik's gaze. "We're fine," he called. "Scared as a cornered *ix*, but fine."

A cheer went up from their friends above.

Aik searched Raven's face for some clue to what he was thinking. His features were uncharacteristically blank. "We're alive."

Raven laughed harshly. "Thanks to you. You saved me."

Aik shook his head vehemently. "You jumped, and you made it across, even though you didn't think you could."

"I guess I did, didn't I." Wonder filled Raven's voice. "I'm a better athlete than I thought."

Aik grinned. *That's more like the Raven I know.* "You ready?"

Raven stared at him for a long moment before replying. "I think so. But we're going to talk about that thing on your arm later. And not just that."

"Yes, we will. I promise." He offered Raven the rope. "You go first. I'll be behind to catch you." *Like always.*

"You two coming?" Ser Kek sounded irritated.

"What if he drops me?" Raven shot a glance at the sergeant. "He hates me, you know."

"Then he'll have to deal with me." Aik put a hand on his sword hilt.

They shared a grin, and for a moment everything was like it used to be between them. "On our way."

Raven threw an arm around him, hugging him. "Thank you."

Aik shivered at Raven's touch. "It's not a big deal." He felt awkward around his friend. *Too much strangeness between us.* "Go! I'll be right behind you."

Raven pulled his carry sack over his shoulders again and took the rope in both hands. "Coming up!"

Aik watched him go, wishing things were different. Longing for something Raven didn't want to give him. And hoping he hadn't ruined what they did have with his stupid decision to mess with Raven's artifacts. *What a pair we make, lizard boy and gauntlet man.*

With a sigh, he started after Raven, glad to be on solid ground once more. As he clambered up onto the bluff, Silya ran down the hill to embrace him, the dignity of the Hencha Queen vanished in the rain and mud. "Thank the Gods you're alive." She pulled him close. "We didn't know there was anything wrong until Ser Kek stopped us." She glanced at Raven over Aik's shoulder. "Glad you made it too."

Raven laughed. "I get your sloppy seconds, huh?"

She let go of him and gave Raven a hug too. "Yes, you do, and you should be grateful for them, after everything you've put me through." She squeezed him so tightly his eyes bulged out of their sockets.

Ser Kek watched the whole thing impassively. Aik snorted under his breath — the man truly was made of stone.

"Thanks for the rope." Aik put out his hand.

Kek stared at it for a moment, then shook it. His grip was as firm as his gaze. "Guards look out for one another." He shot Raven a pointed look.

*Ah.* "You saved his life, and probably mine too." *Bet you would have let Raven drop into the Elsp if he'd been alone.*

"Part of the job, son." He let go of Aik's hand and went to untie the rope from around an *auley* tree. Its conical purple leaves were open to the rain, funneling it into its swelling trunk.

*Son?* Aik frowned. The sergeant was only a few years older than he was.

"Let's get out of the rain. We can all squeeze into my carriage for the rest of the trip." Silya turned to go.

Desla cleared her throat. "Malin here injured his ankle. Can he ride inside? I'll sit with the driver if there's not enough room."

Aik was impressed. "I don't mind sharing the driver seat ... I'd rather be able to see what's coming, to be honest." Besides, it would get him away from Raven for a couple hours.

Raven's eyes narrowed. "You're going to throw me into that *orinth's* nest alone?"

Aik snorted. "You'll survive."

Desla ignored Raven. "You sure? It's cold and wet out here."

"Yeah." Aik wasn't thrilled about facing the awful weather, but he would use the time to decide what he would tell Raven. And how.

He just hoped Raven let him down easy. And that Silya's mother had enough water for a good hot bath when they got there.

"That settles it. Come on. I want to get to the Manor House before nightfall, so I can send word back to the Temple that we arrived safely." Silya peered into the chasm. "I hope no one else was on the bridge behind us."

Aik glanced back the way they'd come. The rain was lifting, and he could see all the way across the canyon to the far side now. A crowd had gathered there, staring at the bridge wreckage below.

Strange things were afoot in the world. *I wish I lived in less interesting times.*

He cracked his knuckles, ignoring a look from Raven, and followed Silya and the others up the hill to the remaining carriage.

# 15

## THE MANOR

SILYA STEPPED OUT OF THE CARRIAGE onto the cobblestone courtyard that fronted her mother's sandstone manor, happy to get out of the humid cabin and away from the sullen looks Raven kept giving her. He was in a foul mood, and she didn't know why — only that it had to do with Aik. It *always* had to do with Aik. Still, she had to make allowances. Lo'Oss knew he'd been through a lot in the last few days.

She hadn't missed the awkward glances between them after the incident, nor the fact that Aik suddenly wanted fresh air. Raven had been uncharacteristically quiet during the long climb up through the purple, sedge-grass covered foothills.

*They'll work it out.* Gods knew she had enough of her own to worry about.

Ser Kek was dismounting, the handsome guard tying up his mount to a post provided for that purpose. Silya looked away quickly before he could notice her interest.

She'd watched approvingly as Desla cleaned up the driver's — Malin's? — arm. She missed the simple acts of being a healer. *Life has other plans for me. Speaking of which ...* She braced herself

189

for her encounter with Tri'Aya, glad to be breathing cool, fresh air again after the warm, dank interior of the carriage.

The storm clouds had fled inland, leaving behind their tattered remains, and in the west the sun was setting over Gullton. From the lower slopes of Heaven's Reach, it looked like a miniature village, lights flickering on one by one as night fell. The air was fresh, carrying just a hint of the sea. A whirlwind full of wisps swept across the courtyard, scrambling her already-tangled hair.

*I must look a fright.* She ran her fingers through her now-dry mane, trying to rearrange it into something more befitting the Hencha Queen before facing her mother.

"Here, let me." Sister Dor appeared before her, holding a wooden comb.

"I can do it myself —"

"*This* is why you have an aide." Dor combed out her long blond hair.

*I doubt that's in the Temple charter.* Still, it was nice to have someone to take care of her. She grimaced as Dor worked out a knot, pulling at her scalp.

"Hey, can you do mine next?" Raven smirked at her.

*Back to his normal, obnoxious self, I see.* "Are you the Hencha Queen?" She glared at him, but inside she smiled. Just a little.

"No, but I know a guy who used to date her."

She ignored him. "Thank you, Dor ... that feels much better."

"Knock it off, Rave." Aik elbowed his friend, shooting an *I'm sorry* look at Silya.

Raven rubbed his arm, giving Aik a hurt look. *Definitely something going on there.*

Kek appeared at her side, his eyes narrowing as he glanced at Aik and then Raven. He gave her a nod. "Mim." He looked neat and orderly, as if he'd just put on a freshly-pressed uniform

*How does he do that?* She'd give her eye teeth to know his secret to looking so good after the long trip.

"You're looking ... well."

Silya stiffened — she knew that voice. She turned to find Tri'Aya standing there, judging her appearance. Her mother was a head shorter than she was, compact and wiry as a circus performer. Her graying hair was tied with a leather strap into a long braid, and she was dressed in riding leathers with a knife sheath at her right side. The bemused look on her face brought back a flood of bitter memories. *Never, ever good enough for you.* "Hello, Mother. Good to see you again."

Tri'Aya held out her hand. "I heard about your promotion. Congratulations are in order." She smiled warmly, but Silya wasn't fooled.

*Promotion.* Only Tri'Aya could call becoming the Hencha Queen a mere promotion. Silya shook her mother's hand and bit her lip, tugging at her collar with her free hand. *I should have worn my formal robes.*

Tri'Aya noticed and frowned, but only slightly, her look saying *Still doing that, are you?* Out loud, she was all grace and warmth. "It's good to have you home. I've missed you."

Even *that* was an implied criticism — *why didn't you come back sooner?* Silya didn't rise to the bait. "Thank you. It's an honor to be *leading* the Temple." Well, maybe the middle road. She managed what she hoped looked like a genuine smile.

Desla appeared at her side, full of youthful enthusiasm. "We are so honored to have Mim Sil'Aya as the new Hencha Queen."

Tri'Aya held Silya's gaze for a moment. "Of course. You must have worked very hard to be chosen." Even that somehow sounded like a veiled insult.

"It's good to see you too, Mother." Silya bent to kiss Tri'Aya's cheek. It had always been like this between them. It felt familiar, and in a strange way almost comforting.

"I've prepared your old room for you. How long can you stay?" Tri'Aya's smile seemed genuine, but Silya knew better. Her mother was playing to the crowd.

"That's not necessary. A guest room will be fine. And it's only for a day or two." She was the Hencha Queen, not a child returning home to her mother. Silya wasn't about to let Tri'Aya put her back in that head space.

"Very well." She put a hand on her chest. "It's good to have you home."

Silya bit her lip. Tri'Aya wasn't making this any easier with her *good mother* act. "I ... need your help." It was a hard admission to make to such a formidable adversary.

Her mother's eyebrow raised, and a satisfied smile crossed her lips. "Well. Of course, I will do whatever I can." Then it was gone. "So who are your friends?"

"This is Des'Rya, one of the Temple initiates."

Desla bowed, her short sword sticking out behind her.

"And this —"

"I'm Aik'Erio, mim." Aik extended a hand and shook Tri'Aya's vigorously. He was half again as tall as she was.

"I remember you, Aik. You're the handsome ex who missed my husband's funeral."

Aik blushed. "Yes, mim." He looked pointedly at the ground.

"The scrappy one here is Rav'Orn —"

"Raven, please." Raven executed a flawless bow. "At your service, mim." He kissed Tri'Aya's out-held hand.

"Charming, this one." That didn't sound like a compliment either, but Raven beamed. "He's the thief your ex was sleeping with?"

"Mother!" Tri'Aya lacked the usual social graces, which made her both a hell of a trader and explained why she lived so far from almost everyone else. She also liked to shock. *People show their true faces when you surprise them.*

Still, Silya enjoyed seeing the blush spread across Raven's face. Just a little. "These are Sisters Dor'Ala, Tel'Esta, and our drivers Mas Mal'Arin and Mir Gar'Vela. And Ser Kek'Aze, who kindly agreed to escort us today."

"Nice to meet you all. Welcome to the Manor." Her gaze lingered a little on the tall Sergeant, and Silya felt an irrational surge of jealousy.

Tri'Aya's forehead creased. "Two drivers for one carriage?"

"We had another one, but we lost it when the Old Bridge collapsed." Silya shivered, and not from the cold. She could still hear the horrible screech of tearing metal.

Triy'Aya looked at her as if she'd gone mad. "The Old Bridge *what?*"

"Hadn't you heard? The second quake brought it down." Silya suppressed a smile. It was rare that she knew something her mother didn't. "I see you had a little damage here too." She glanced at the broken window. "We'll be sending Malin back the long way to take word that we arrived safely."

"That's not good." Tri'Aya counted out something on her fingers. "With the bridge gone, it'll double the cost to get goods into Gullton —"

*Are you serious?* Silya stared at her. "Yes, we're all fine. Thanks for asking. It was a close thing, but everyone made it off the bridge alive."

"Of course." Tri'Aya's gaze snapped back to hers, and for the first time since Silya's father's funeral, she saw past her mother's usually flawless mask. "I'm sorry. I'm glad you all survived."

Her look of concern was so genuine that Silya felt a twinge of guilt for pushing things between them. "I hope no one here was hurt?"

"We lost a few things. But things can be replaced." Tri'Aya put her hand on Silya's cheek. "I'm happy you're here. Truly. And sending this poor man back won't be necessary." The mask slid over her face again, and the moment passed. "I can send word via carrier *umvit*. I have several matched trios. Malin can rest here for a few days until his leg heals."

Silya winced. Tri'Aya didn't miss much, and now she'd made Silya feel guilty for having planned to send an injured man back on the road. *Outmatched again.* "Thank you. That would be much appreciated."

"It's nothing. Mes, Em, come get our guests' things."

Two women a head taller than Tri'Aya, dressed in off-white homeweave tunics and breaches, with fighting leathers and short swords in matching leather scabbards at their sides, stepped forward to take the visitors' chests. They moved in synch with such grace and economy of motion that it was clear they were more than porters. And there was something in the way they looked at one another —

Tri'Aya clapped, breaking Silya's train of thought. "Come along, all of you. We'll get you settled." Tri'Aya looked over the rest of the rain-drenched-and-dried crew. "There's hot water from the underground spring for baths. Once you're all washed up and proper, we'll sit down for a meal together." She turned back toward the house.

"She seems lovely." Ser Kek stared after Tri'Aya. "Nice of her to welcome us so warmly."

Silya looked up at him. "She knows how to put on a show."

He stared at her for a moment. "You're lucky to have her." He turned away to meet another of Tri'Aya's employees who was approaching his *urse*.

*What did that mean?* "Ser Kek."

He paused. "Yes, mim?"

"Thank you for coming." She wasn't sure exactly why, but it was reassuring having him along.

"Of course, mim." He nodded and went to talk with the stable boy.

"Come on, Des. Let's get cleaned up."

"He's quite handsome." Des looked over her shoulder at the sergeant.

"Yes. Yes he is." That's all she needed at the moment — an initiate's crush on Ser Kek. Though she wasn't sure if she meant Desla's, or her own.

She grimaced as one of the women — Mes, if she remembered correctly — hefted her heavy trunk off the top of the carriage as if it weighed nothing. She hadn't wanted to bring half the things in it, but Dor had insisted. *A Hencha Queen must always be prepared.*

*For what? In case a royal ball suddenly breaks out?* Daya would have called her a fool for hauling so much frippery out into the countryside.

"I like her." Des grinned.

"She always makes a good first impression." With a bitter sigh, she followed her mother into the echoing halls of the sandstone manor. She and Tri'Aya had a long and exhausting history, and they weren't going to fix that tonight, if ever.

*Why in the green holy hell did I come back here?*

•　　•　　•

Silya stepped out of the bath, the warm sudsy water sluicing off her skin, and grabbed a luxurious highlands cotton towel off the small washbasin counter. It felt good to be clean and warm again.

The rock ceiling, walls, and floor of the Manor House merged seamlessly — almost as if the walls had been grown here instead of being built. Silya had wondered about that as a girl, tracing the smooth seams between the wall and the floor with her tiny hands. Even the tub seemed to have sprung up from the ground fully formed.

The Manor House was set over a natural hot spring, one of the primary reasons her mother had bought it when she'd first made her fortune.

*Speaking of which ...* Silya wasn't looking forward to the conversation. Tri'Aya was her worst critic, notwithstanding their relationship. Or maybe because of it. She'd never approved of her daughter leaving the Manor, let alone joining the Temple. *So many things changed when Daddy died.*

Sister Dor had offered to assist her in her preparations, but Silya had insisted on a little privacy. *I might be the Queen, but I'm no child in need of supervision.*

Silya hung the towel to dry and pulled on clean clothes — a simple front-laced shirt, a pair of black trousers, and the sky-blue *aur* leather boots her father had given her for her eighteenth birthday. Her hand lingered over her blue robes, the vibrant color that only the Hencha Queen wore. She would look a fool here in her mother's home, striding into dinner in such finery, though the thought of flaunting her new position appealed to her.

Incongruously, her thoughts went to Ser Kek. *I wonder what he's doing?*

She shook her head. *Don't be daft, girl.* She was the Hencha Queen. She shouldn't let herself fall under a handsome man's spell.

She closed the trunk, and her thoughts about the Sergeant with it, and went to meet the others.

The dining room was in the heart of the house, with the guest wing on one side and Tri'Aya's own rooms along the other. Her mother preferred the *highlands style*, so everyone sat on cushions around a low table instead of using chairs like civilized people.

Tri'Aya was laughing, chatting with Desla and Sister Dor about something that made even the normally somber woman crack a smile. Both Dor and Sister Tela wore their temple robes. Ser Kek was at the far end of the low-slung table, in earnest conversation with Tri'Aya's own guards. Silya looked away before he could meet her eyes.

Everyone else was there except Raven.

Her mother looked up, a warm, fake smile crossing her face. "So nice that you decided to join us." She summoned Silya to sit next to her.

"Thank you. But if you don't mind, I'll take my place here, next to Aik."

Aik looked at her, then at her mother, and shrugged.

Tri'Aya grimaced, and Silya suppressed a squee of delight at her mother's discomfort. "Well then." She rang a bell. "Let's eat." She looked around the table. "Are we still missing one? The charmer."

Aik replied to that one. "Raven's not feeling well. Almost falling off the bridge scared the ... well, he's just not up to it."

"Scared the farking crap out of him, you meant to say." Tri'Aya laughed. "We aren't formal here, well, except maybe for the sisters." The look she shot Silya could have cut glass.

*Should have worn the robe.* With Tri'Aya, it was always about the sparring. "Thank you, Mother. I must say, you look well for your age. Sixty was it, this last year?" She took a sip of the glass of *henchwine* before her, looking away innocently.

"Yes, dear. Sixty," Tri'Aya snapped at her. "And damned proud of it."

Silya had scored a point, but she felt a strange pang of regret. It was a hollow victory — she'd sworn not to let herself be drawn into it again with Tri'Aya.

*A night of regrets.* She sighed, downing her glass of wine. *This* was why she never came home.

The servers arrived bearing a bounty of food — a platter of sizzling steaks, a huge wooden bowl of potatoes seasoned with spicy red *heartroot*, and a plate of doughy fold-overs stuffed with black cheese and sliced grapes.

Silya popped one into her mouth and grinned. The food was one thing worth coming home for — Tri'Aya's kitchen rivaled the Temple's, with unexpected ingredients from across the civilized world and beyond.

"Not too many of those, dear." Tri'Aya dipped one in a creamy dressing. "They'll go straight to your waist."

Desla shot her a warning look.

Silya ignored it, stopping in mid-swallow to glare at her mother. Then she gulped it down and defiantly took another. "Yes, I see they've done you no favors."

Desla stifled a laugh, and Tri'Aya blanched. In truth, she was near as trim as Silya remembered, but age was finally catching up with her. Her waist was curvier these days, and her ankles were like small tree trunks. That made Silya strangely happy.

"Your mother was just telling us about the caverns where the cheese ferments." Sister Dor stepped in smoothly. "We have some tunnels beneath the Temple. Perhaps we ought to consider something similar?"

"We do?" Silya wiped the crumbs from her mouth. "Why have I never seen them?"

Dor shrugged. "They've been boarded up since the Temple was first built — they're accessed from the wine cellar. They were once used to store extra bottles of wine."

Successfully diverted, her mother nodded. "I'd be happy to help. I've always supported the Temple —"

"Are you serious?" It came out before Silya could stop herself. The room went silent, and everyone turned to look at her, including Ser Kek, whose eyebrow went up.

Mortified, she did the only thing she could think of — she forged ahead. "From the moment I joined the Temple, you never had one good thing to say about it. 'Bunch of gully birds hiding in the reeds,' you said. 'Mad as a nest of orinths,' you said. And now you want to act like you've been in support all along?" She set down her glass with a clang. "Why, Mother? Is it because I finally have some success of my own, and you can't stand that you're not a part of it?"

The silence in the room was deafening.

"Silya Aya, I think you should leave the table." Tri'Aya was standing — when had that happened? And she looked as mad as Silya had ever seen her. Her mother became dangerously still when she was angry.

"I'm not a child. I'm the Hencha Queen, and you *will not speak to me* like that." Silya was standing too, anger burning through her, her arms exploding into blue flames. Now *you return.*

Tri'Aya's mouth fell open.

In Silya's head, something moved — a deep and somber presence. The spirit of the *hencha* gatherings surged through her again — the ones by the Temple, the huge gathering in the valley below. And many more beyond.

The heavy presence took in the room around her and the human creatures that filled it, searching for the threat, and found only a dinner party. Silya shivered at the weight behind it, heavy on her shoulders.

*Why did you call us?*

Suddenly her fight with her mother seemed petty. Unnecessary. It was beneath her station and her sacred connection with the *hencha*. *I was being ... human. It's been a difficult evening.*

Warmth and love suffused her, washing away her anger. *They do trust me.* They had chosen her, and here was the proof at last. Even Tri'Aya had to see that. Her fears melted away, burned off by the fire that blazed through her.

Silya closed her eyes, communing with the scattered gatherings, hearing their complex, beautiful song. Warmth and love filled her heart, her soul, telling her she had not been forgotten or rejected.

She took a deep breath, then another, letting the music buoy her. The flames died, burning the anger away with them.

Silya opened her eyes and met Tri'Aya's gaze. "I'm sorry. That was uncalled for."

Tri'Aya opened her mouth to say something, then closed it and sat down abruptly.

At her side, Desla nodded. *Well done*, she mouthed.

A strange calmness settled over Silya. She sat back down, immensely relieved to know the hencha were still there in her head. Their song slowly ebbed away, but she could feel them like a bright candle in the back of her mind.

She speared a steak and took a spoonful of potatoes and started to eat again.

Slowly the chatter returned around the hall. Across the table, Mes and Em shared a meal. The easy way they moved together marked them as a couple. She smiled. *Thought so.*

She caught Desla and Malin sneaking looks at her and whispering to one another.

Silya sighed softly. She'd tried so hard for so long to become the Hencha Queen, but she'd never considered that others might look at her as if she were a freak.

Ser Kek finally caught her attention again. He stared at her for a long moment, and then nodded. *Respect.*

She forced her gaze away from his and back to her plate.

Dinner passed without further incident, and she managed to avoid locking eyes with the handsome guard again.

Instead, she indulged in some pleasant small talk with Aik and the gentleman on her other side, another trader named Mas Ais'Vellin whose route usually took him up along the Northern Coast to Dalney, Sadie's Cove, and Cape Town. The northern villages were flourishing, with record catches of kerint — the sweet, tangy white fish were apparently especially abundant this year.

Silya had never been so far north, but now that she was the Queen, she imagined she'd be visiting most of the Heartland and beyond. Her time as an initiate would prepare her well for sleeping in all kinds of tiny, uncivilized places. She snorted, and Mas Vellin shot her a questioning look.

"Oh, sorry, it's nothing. Just something funny Aik said to me earlier."

Dor, who seemed to have magically materialized behind her, tugged at her sleeve. "Mim, you must remember that you are the office now. Anything you say and do will be dissected for meaning, down to and including your bodily functions."

*How does she do that?* Silya barely suppressed another snort. "Yes, Sister Dor. Thank you for the reminder."

At last dinner was over, finished off with a *hencha* berry tart. The chef had paired the sweet red berries with the tart yellow ones and a bit of rhubarb, and the crust was delightfully flaky. *I'll have to steal the chef for the Temple.* Of course, Verla might have something to say about that — the Temple's head cook had been at it since before Silya was born.

Tri'Aya stood and tapped her glass with her fork, getting everyone's attention. "Thank you for coming. It's been a delightful evening." The way she said it made it clear she had a very different definition of delightful in mind. "For my local guests, the porters will bring your coats to the door." She turned to speak to one of them.

Silya looked around the room, avoiding Ser Kek's gaze. "Raven never came. You think he's all right?"

Aik shrugged. "He almost died today. I think it really shook him up."

"I can imagine." She still had her issues with Raven, but she'd seen a different side of him the last few days. He'd had a hard life, and his flippant attitude was a reaction to that, as much as anything.

199

Gods knew she used the same trick. *Maybe I need to go easier on* the thief. "You'll check on him?"

Aik glanced at the door. "I'm sure he's sound asleep by now."

If Raven needed some rest, they could always show Tri'Aya his arms in the morning. Silya had brought the *Menagerie* with her as well, along with one of Jas's journals — that was enough for now.

The sergeant appeared before her, half a head taller than she was, a sly grin on his face. "That was nicely done."

Her face flushed. "Thank you. Half the time, I'm just making it up as I go along."

He nodded, running a hand through his hair. "Want to know a secret?"

"Sure." She felt like an idiot around him, and she didn't like it.

"That's just life." His stoic face cracked the slightest smile.

She laughed. "Well, that's disheartening." She bit her tongue, afraid of what she might say next in his presence.

"Anything else, mim?"

Silya cleared her throat. "Yes. Can you speak to the others? I'm going to ask Tri'Aya for a few moments in her den to discuss ... everything. I'd like Dor, Tela, Desla and Aik there. And you too."

He bowed. "Of course, mim. When?"

"Give me twenty minutes." She wanted to talk with Tri'Aya first, alone.

"Yes, mim." He spun neatly on his heels and followed the others out of the dining room.

She was staring at his square shoulders when Desla squeezed her arm on the way out. "You all right?"

She bit her lip. "I think so. No one survives an encounter with Tri'Aya unscathed. But yes, I'll be fine."

Desla threw her arms around Silya unexpectedly. "You were magnificent." With a last squeeze, she let go and disappeared into the entry hall.

Silya stared after her, both thankful and baffled by the girl's behavior.

As the last of the guests were ushered out, she found Tri'Aya in the entryway of the Manor House. "Can we talk?"

"Good night, Mas Vellin. So good to see you." Her mother kissed the man's cheeks and closed the manor doors after him. She turned to face her daughter, her visage lined with weariness, or maybe pain. "Of course. Assuming you're done insulting me for the night."

She tugged unconsciously on her braid, and Silya had an uncomfortable realization of where her own habit came from. *Like mother, like daughter.* "I really am sorry for what I said earlier." She laughed ruefully. "You have a way of getting under my skin, you know." They were all alone.

Tri'Aya turned to stare at her. "How? By telling the truth?"

Silya's eyebrow lifted. "You've always supported the Temple?"

"Well, yes. I've always given the sisters money."

Silya tugged on the edge of her collar, exasperated. "Until I became an initiate."

Her mother wouldn't meet her gaze. "Yes, I admit I was upset about it. But only because I'd always thought you'd come on the road with me. You're a bright girl — strong and athletic — I just assumed you'd want to take over the family business one day."

"You did?" Silya stared at her mother as if she'd grown an extra eye. *You're full of surprises tonight.* "You never told me that."

"I thought it was obvious." She tilted her head, looking up at Silya.

"Not to me." All her life, she had thought she wasn't good enough for her mother. That she was stupid and slow. "I tried. I always tried. But it was never enough for you."

Tri'Aya fidgeted under her gaze. "I'm sorry." She nodded, as if checking something off a list. "There, I said it."

Silya laughed harshly. "That's it? You're sorry? That's all I get?"

She stared at Silya for a moment longer before replying. "In my family, we were taught to never talk about emotions. I grew up with two older brothers, and I was never good enough for my father." She heaved a heavy sigh, looking away. "I never realized I was doing the same thing to you." This time there was no trace of anger. She put her arms on Silya's shoulders. "For that, I am truly sorry."

Silya wiped her eyes with the back of her hand. It wasn't enough. Not nearly. But it was *something.* "Thank you."

Her mother embraced her, and Silya felt an unexpected warmth inside. Maybe things had finally shifted between them now that she was an adult, and the Hencha Queen.

"You have been putting on weight, haven't you?" Tri'Aya let go of her and put her hands on Silya's sides. "What do they feed you over there? Cream puffs?"

*And we're back.* "I'm not even going to respond to that." The warmth between them evaporated, but if Silya closed her eyes, she could still feel its lingering touch.

She pushed sentimentality aside. There was business to be done and answers that she needed, if she was going to fulfill her duty to Gullton and the Heartland. The rest could wait. "We need to talk."

# 16

# THIEF

S PIN FLOATED, QUIESCENT, in his own dreams.
The boy-man, Raven, had turned him off again when he'd been done with him. Still, Spin had long ago learned to live in the gray times between awakenings, his dream world a pale but workable substitute for the real one.

He loved Raven. He'd awoken from darkness one day and had found himself in the boy's hands. He'd been shocked to find that almost a hundred years had passed since his beloved Sera's death.

In his dream state, he flew the *Spin Diver* through the darkness, on a run from Earth out to Erinae. It was a seven-year journey, and every three months, one of the humans awakened for a week to check over the ship's systems and structural integrity — an unnecessary redundancy, but one that gave Spin something to look forward to in the vast, empty blackness of space between the stars.

This time, it was Artur, the ship's mechanic. Spin liked spending time with Artur ... he was more efficient, more focused when he worked with the engineer.

He hummed an old Earth tune by the Proclaimers — "I'm Gonna Be (500 Miles)"— as the stars continued their slow parade past his external sensors.

●     ●     ●

Raven lay in bed, clutching his stomach and staring at the red sandstone wall. The mattress shifted as Aik sat down next to him. He was angry at Aik — for hiding something from him and for what had almost happened between them at the Temple, even if he'd wanted it too very badly. It made no sense, but there it was. He hated the thought of being tied down. But still, he *wanted* Aik something fierce.

He could feel Aik's distress too — the acrid odor of sweat, the way his heart beat a little faster than normal.

"Rave?" Aik massaged his back, his touch sending a thrill down Raven's back and sparking a physical reaction Raven was glad Aik couldn't see. "It's time for dinner. I'm sure Tri'Aya puts out a fabulous spread."

"Maybe. Just … leave me alone for a bit." He hated saying it, but he really did need Aik to leave if he was going to take advantage of his only chance to really explore the place. "My stomach feels weird. I think I'll just stay here, if you don't mind." He added a long, drawn-out groan to really sell it.

"Sure." Aik lingered a moment longer. "I'm sorry. About the kiss. About what you saw at the bridge —"

Raven groaned again, shivering for effect. "It's all right. We can talk about it later."

Aik leaned over and kissed his cheek. "That sounds good."

Raven could feel the shift in Aik's emotions from the way he smelled, the tension in his muscles, the tone of his voice. It was *odd*.

Aik squeezed his shoulder, and then the weight lifted off the bed. "I'll come back to check on you after dinner."

"I'll probably be asleep." It wasn't exactly a lie. He would be — at some point after dinner, anyhow.

"Sleep well." The door closed, blocking the lantern light from the hallway.

Raven lay still for a few minutes, just to be on the safe side, in case Aik or someone else opened the door to check up on him.

Was it weird that Aik had suddenly been wearing a gauntlet that gave him the strength of ten? Sure. But what hadn't been off, these last few days? *That's not the point.* Aik should have told him. Was this some new thing? Or had Aik been hiding it for a long time?

And what about that kiss? If life had taught him one thing, it was that he was better off alone. *I have to be strong.*

All those things would have to wait. Raven had known, as soon as he saw the magnificent Manor House, that he'd need to find a way to explore the place unhindered. Who knew what treasures Silya's mother might have hidden away? He had to look around while he had the chance — it would go against everything he was made of if he didn't at least try to uncover Tri'Aya's secrets.

Satisfied that all was quiet, Raven slipped out of bed and opened the shutters just a crack to let in a sliver of moonlight. His room didn't have a glass window like some of the others, but he could see the seam where it had once been. Someone had sanded the edges down smooth with the stone.

And such beautiful, wide panes of glass ... the Manor House was full of wonders.

Down in the valley, a lone bird called, its trill seeming unnaturally loud in the silence, and a flurry of glowing blue wisps, stirred up by the wind off the Harkness, chased one another across the sky. There seemed to be more of them than expected, or at least earlier. Usually they appeared later in the fall. *Strangeness upon strangeness.*

He pulled out his black shirt and trousers from his carry sack. Not that they would help him much in the brightly lit hallways of the Manor House, but they would let him blend into the shadows like a proper burglar. He made sure Spin was lodged in securely, hidden under his other belongings. Spin would kill him for not taking him along for the adventure, but he didn't want to chance his light being seen, or that his familiar might say something to make him laugh out loud.

He slipped his lock-picking kit into his pocket. After a moment's hesitation, he pulled on his gloves to cover his arms too.

With luck, everyone would be at dinner, and he'd have the rest of the place to himself. He didn't need to steal much. Just a few valuable trinkets he could sell later, when things got back to normal. He snorted. *Whatever that is.*

Raven arranged a few cushions under the covers to pass for his sleeping body, at least on casual inspection. Then he closed the shutters and cracked open the door, looking down the hall both ways to be sure he was alone.

The sandstone walls had been smoothed and lacquered, giving the whole place a strange shine. Carefully fitted square black-and-white tiles that looked like stone covered the floor. They were all the same pattern, repeated again and again at different angles. *How did they manage that?* Ancient technology really was magic.

He could hear the buzz of conversation and smell the food from down the hall, in particular the hearty scent of a platter of *aur* steaks. His new ability had its drawbacks. His mouth watered and his stomach grumbled, and for a moment he toyed with the idea of going to dinner and enjoying what promised to be a wonderful meal.

Then, with a heavy sigh, he forced his attention back to the task at hand. Maybe he could ask for leftovers later.

Satisfied that he was alone, he slipped out and made his way down the hall, away from the dining room.

This wing of the Manor House was all guest rooms — ten of them. He peered into each one. His vision seemed better, too, something that could prove useful. *Maybe this whole lizard boy thing's not so bad after all.*

He looked around each room, frowning. None of them held anything of apparent value. Only the things his friends had brought, and he didn't steal from people he knew.

Friends' mothers, though, were another thing altogether. Especially rich ones.

His stomach cramped — for real this time — and he clutched his torso, leaning back against the wall and grimacing in pain. Whatever the little beastie inside him was up to, he wished it would just get it over with. Aik was a freaking warrior, and Silya was a Queen with fire at her command. *And all I got was these lizard arms, a bad case of cramps, and night vision.*

He laughed softly. No point in feeling sorry for himself. Life was a bucket of shit, and adding your own just made it harder to bear.

The sensation passed at last, leaving a cold sweat on Raven's forehead. He took a deep breath and considered his next move. The guest wing was a dead-end — whatever he was looking for would be in another part of the house. That meant he'd likely have to pass by the dining room. He scratched his stubbly chin. *Could be dangerous. Still, no risk, no reward.*

Raven knew how these dinners went. He had maybe an hour before someone came looking for him, an hour-and-a-half at the outside.

He sniffed the air. He could smell the delicious sweetness of the *hencha* berries now. *Foldovers, if I'm not mistaken. I should go have dinner — the whole thieving thing can wait.*

Still, curiosity was his drug, and it always got the better of him. *"Should" can go fark itself.*

He set off down the hallway toward the entry, listening for anyone else who might be wandering the house.

Loud footsteps on the hard tile floor warned him of someone's approach.

Alarmed, he slipped into the closest guest room, closed the door behind him softly, and pressed his back against the wall. It was Silya's, to judge by the number of chests piled in one corner and the blue robe laid out on the bed.

Being forced to act like the Queen, traveling with a retinue and a hundred kilos of luggage must be killing her. Raven grinned. *Couldn't have happened to a more deserving person.*

He closed his eyes and shook his head. *She saved you, several times.* Being grateful to his once-nemesis was difficult.

The footsteps approached, stopping just outside the door and casting a shadow across the floor underneath it.

Raven held his breath. *I'm not here.* If someone found him, he'd claim he got lost. That he'd felt weak, disoriented, and had wandered into the wrong room.

It worked for him sometimes. Less so when he was discovered naked in bed with the man of the house.

After a handful of breaths, the shadow moved away, and the footsteps continued up the hall.

Raven heaved a sigh of relief. He hadn't been looking forward to explaining his presence in the Hencha Queen's room.

As soon as the footsteps faded away, he leaned over to touch the beautiful *mur* silk of Silya's blue robe, wondering why she'd chosen not to wear it.

He shook his head. No way he could fence that — it was too recognizable. But the material was exquisite. *Isn't she a friend now? Besides, she would skin me like an ix.*

He let it go regretfully and slipped out of the room. He made his way into the entry hall. The room was enormous — two stories tall, ten meters wide and probably half that deep, the stone ceiling held up by stout red sandstone columns. The doors to the dining room were closed, thank Jor'Oss, though the aromas wafting out from within were enough to make him once again reconsider his plan.

Raven slipped behind a tall stone statue, a stocky man with blocky features whom he didn't recognize, and scanned the wide space.

The high ceilings were almost hidden in shadows, but the row of sandstone columns blended right into the floor. *Did they carve this place out of natural stone?*

The food smells began to blend together, triggering his nausea. These heightened senses were more trouble than they were worth. *I need to get out of here.*

He slipped out of his hiding place and dashed from one column to the next, stopping to listen for any stray sounds that might indicate someone's approach.

On the far side of the entry were two more hallways, one lit and one dark. The bright one was probably Tri'Aya's quarters. It was his best bet — she would have jewelry he could pilfer, something small but valuable that she wouldn't realize was missing for weeks, if ever. Rich people had too many belongings, so many that they rarely bothered to keep track of them.

He'd made a mistake stealing the box from the sea master — it was unique and all by itself and had been missed almost immediately. But his infernal curiosity had gotten the better of him — that and the strange tug it had exerted.

Yes, the lighted hall was the way to go.

Still, the dark one beckoned.

Footsteps sounded in the hall behind him again.

He left his hiding place and crossed the room, slipping behind the last of the thick columns in the shadowed part of the entry, his dark clothing doing its job admirably.

Ser Kek appeared from the hallway of the residential wing.

*Where were you hiding?* Raven tucked himself farther into the shadows, his back to the column, breathing shallowly. *Of all the people to run into!* He could charm almost anyone else. *But not Aik. Or Silya.*

He could smell the man from here, all sharp angles and determination.

Raven held himself absolutely still, praying to Jor'Oss that Kek wouldn't find him.

The click of footsteps resumed — the same ones he'd heard outside the door when he'd hidden in Silya's room.

*What are you doing prowling the halls?*

The man had probably gone to check on him.

The doors to the dining room opened, and for a moment light, conversation and laughter flooded the entry hall.

"Are you serious?" Silya's voice was as clear as if she were standing right next to him. The chatter plunged into sudden silence.

Then the heavy doors closed, returning the entry hall to darkness, and Raven was alone again.

He closed his eyes. *That was too close.*

Time was spinning away. He steeled himself, ignoring the butterflies in his stomach, and scampered across the last few steps into the dark hallway.

It took his eyes a moment to adjust.

There were no doors here, no convenient places to hide if someone were to suddenly appear. Only a long, featureless hall.

He entered it anyway, ignoring the growing anxiety, caught up by the mystery of it all. Who went to so much trouble to build such a thing, probably burrowed into the mountain itself? And how had they managed that? The walls were the same smooth sandstone as the rest of the house, joined perfectly.

He stopped, looking back the way he'd come. The light of the entry hall was a small square behind him. *How long is this thing?* Intrigued but nervous at having no escape path, Raven took a deep breath and continued down the hallway, running his hand along the smooth, lacquered wall.

It wasn't completely dark after all. Small lights in the ceiling lit as he approached and went out behind him, reminding him of the blue light in the tunnels under Gullton. These lights were probably electric, like at the Temple, but so different. *Magic again.* He laughed under his breath — Aik would certainly think so.

They were circular, flush with the ceiling, and gave off a soft yellowish-white light. They were too high for him to reach them. *Too bad.* A shining gem like that would bring a hefty price on the black market.

The tunnel ended abruptly at a simple *flopwood* door with a single round wooden handle. Raven traced the vibrant purple streaks in the wood with his hand — he could almost feel its former life force through his fingers. Like the walls, it had been shined to a high gloss. He took a step back and stared at it suspiciously. There was no lock. *Too easy.*

Easy always made him nervous. It often meant a trap.

He looked around warily, and then behind him. After a few meters of faint light, the passage had gone dark again, the fairy lights winking out.

Raven shook his head. *I've come this far.*

He opened the door.

The inside lit up to reveal a linen closet. It was a huge one, to be fair, at least two meters square, its shelves stacked with sheets, towels, and other various rags and cloth-goods, all neatly sorted by type and color. But still, just linens?

Raven stared at the neat shelves. This was what Tri'Aya was hiding?

Maybe the closet had been used for something else before, by the original builders. Maybe there had been untold treasures from the Crossing kept in this room, or valuables gathered here by some of the early colonists. *What a time that must have been to be alive.*

And what a waste of his time this was.

Raven glanced over his shoulder. If he hurried back, he might be able to do a quick exploration of the residential wing of the house before someone discovered his subterfuge.

He was about to leave when he noticed something strange. Where the hallway met the front wall of the closet, the seams of the sandstone were uneven. He stepped closer for a better look.

Normal human eyes might have easily missed it. But his heightened vision came to his aid.

There was the smallest gap between the hallway wall and this one, filled in with some sort of pink cement. It was barely noticeable, especially under the gloss sheen. But when examined up close, it practically screamed at him.

Someone had added the front wall later.

Even the face of the stone itself wasn't as smooth and even as the rest of the house.

Excited, he turned to the back wall to search behind the linens. That wall was made of red sandstone too, but it was much smoother than the front one, with perfect seams. *Aha!*

It was the original end of the hallway. Someone had constructed the closet later, adding the front wall to block off the space. *If I'm right...*

He moved the linens along the back wall one by one, looking for an opening mechanism, placing them back carefully when he was done. *Nothing.*

He started in on the right side. He was through the first column of towels — far softer than anything he'd used before — when he found what he was looking for.

It was a small black handle made of a strange composite he didn't recognize, about as long as his knuckle. He calculated the risks, then decided he didn't care. *In for a croner, in for a crown.*

Raven flipped the handle.

There was a sharp grinding sound that made the hair on his arms stand up straight, and then part of the back wall moved.

# 17

## COMPULSION

A FLIGHT OF FORERUNNERS slipped into her cavern, hovering above her uncertainly as if they were afraid of her.

Or perhaps they didn't want to interrupt her slumber.

The spore mother opened one of her *eeechha* chambers, the white dome splitting open to reveal the golden fluid inside. The red sparks plunged inside, dissolving and passing their knowledge to her.

They hadn't found him yet, but they brought her knowledge of this world. There were many creatures out there, something which brought her regret. Most if not all would die when the world was transformed, but she shunted that guilt aside. It was necessary for the survival of her own people. They had to come first. Who knew if any others had survived the destruction of Uurccheea?

And there was more. The ones who had ended the previous spore even fewer memories of them left to her. But she would need to watch them. They posed an existential threat to her and her children.

With a sigh, she remade the *iichili* and sent them out into the world, ready to learn more.

•   •   •

Aik rubbed his stomach. Dinner was over, and he was stuffed full of *aur* meat, potatoes, fold-overs, and berry tarts. *And hencha wine.* The latter had fortified his courage. He would talk to Raven. Tell him everything. What he'd done with the artifacts. How he felt.

*Why we should be together.* He would make Raven understand, somehow.

He kissed Silya's cheek, but she barely noticed, intent on her mother, who was busy saying goodbye to her dinner guests.

Aik squeezed past one of Tri'Aya's guards into the entry room — Mes? — and the woman gave him a frosty look.

He stumbled down the hallway, counting doors, belatedly realizing he was more drunk than he'd thought. *Which room is Rave's?*

Maybe seeing Raven in his current state was a bad idea.

*It's the third one on the right. I think.* Aik stopped to count the doors again, afraid he'd stumble in on Sister Tela by mistake, just removing her robes for the day. He shuddered at the thought. *Must have been some strong wine.*

He stood in front of the door he was certain was Raven's for a moment, gathering his courage. It was funny, really, when he thought about it. He wasn't afraid of a sword fight, but put him in front of Raven and his ankles quaked in his boots.

*Maybe I should drunk until I'm less wait.* Aik shook his head. That wasn't quite right.

Rather than take the time and flagging mental energy to work it out, he pushed the door open as quietly as possible.

Raven's sleeping form lay under the sheets. *Poor guy must have been exhausted.*

Something wasn't quite right about that, either. But he couldn't get his mind to focus on it long enough to register what. He considered crawling into bed with Rave — it was closer than his own room. But even in his inebriated state, he knew that wasn't a good idea. *Especially* in his inebriated state. They could talk in the morning. *'night, Rave.*

He closed the door, proud of himself for not slamming it, and turned back toward his own room across the hall. Only his feet wouldn't take him there.

Instead, he found them pulling him back toward the entry.

He ran into Sister Tela, who must have been on her way back to her own room.

She put a wrinkled but still strong hand on his arm, concern shining through her eyes. "You all right, Mas Erio?"

Aik blinked. He wasn't used to being addressed so formally, especially by one of the sisters. "You're not in your room. Getting undressed."

The sister laughed. "No, not yet. Should I be?" She stared at him, her gaze going right through him like a knife. "Are you all right, young man?"

"Yes, mim. Jus' left something in the dining hall." The lie slipped from him as easily as air. He bit his lip, not sure why he'd said it.

"Fine, then. Go get it and get yourself to bed. You look a fright." She reached up to pat him on the cheek and went on her way.

He turned to stare at her retreating back. *Why did I lie? That's not like me.* He really should get to bed.

As if to spite him, his feet resumed their journey, carrying him on into the entry hall and right past the dining room doors, just in time to see Silya and her mother disappear down the far hallway. He tried to call her name, but his mouth stayed stubbornly shut, as much out of his control as his legs.

His right arm pulsed, and he reached absentmindedly up to scratch it, his hands encountering the hard metal of the gauntlet. Fear flooded his mind, counteracting some of the effects of the wine. *What in the green holy hell is wrong with me? Lo'Oss, give me strength.*

None seemed to be forthcoming so, fear or no, his course remained unchanged.

His steps led him out of the entry and into a third hallway, a long dark one with a string of strange fairy lights that lit up as he approached, beckoning him onward. His left arm seemed unaffected by this strange moving paralysis.

He reached out to touch the lights above, but they slipped out of his grasp, blinking at him like uncaring stars.

Whatever had him in its grip carried him forward. *I should have woken Raven. He'd know what to do.*

He reached out for the wall to grab onto something to stop his slow, inexorable advance. His arm moved sluggishly, like he was underwater.

With great effort, he managed to touch the stone, but there was nothing to grab onto. The smooth surface slipped from under his questing fingers.

He tried to open his mouth, but it stayed stubbornly shut. The gauntlet on his arm was glowing eerily, its gems shining a creepy red. *What do you want from me?*

There was a door in the distance ahead. It was open.

In a panic, he tried to pull the gauntlet off, but it was melded to him tightly. He'd been as careless as Raven, and now he was paying the price. *But what is that price?*

He reached the door and stepped into a normal-looking linen closet, full of sheets and towels, all neatly folded and sorted by color.

Normal, except for the fact that the back wall was missing.

*Not missing. Open. Strangeness upon strangeness.* He stared at it for a minute, trying to work out what he was seeing. Who took the back of a closet wall? *Raven, did you steal it?*

Nothing was making sense. With a sigh, he stepped through the gap, and found himself in a fairyland.

The cavern was made of the same red sandstone as the Manor House. But the similarities ended there. It was a gallery, a magnificent collection of sculpted pink columns. Some were as thin as his index finger, while others were thicker than his waist. They extended from the floor to the ceiling high above, reminding him of Raven's lair. Tiny fairy lights like the ones in the hall lit the space all around him and sparkled in the darker recesses.

Chests upon chests of goods filled the cavern — several of them open, displaying piles of grain. It took Aik a moment to realize his feet were no longer moving and that the gauntlet had once again vanished.

"What in the farking hell are you doing here?"

Aik spun around to find Raven standing over another of the chests. It was open, and a handful of grain was slipping through Raven's fingers.

Aik blinked. The compulsion had fled as quickly as it had come. "I ... I was walking ... What are you doing here? I thought you were sick?" He eyed the chest. "You couldn't give it up, even for one night?"

Raven shrugged. "It's every man for himself in this world. Besides, I figured Silya's mother wouldn't miss a few small things.

Sooner or later, I'll be out on my own again, and I no longer have a home." He dumped the grain back into the chest. "Doesn't matter anyhow. They're all full of it."

Aik stared at the grain on the floor, trying to force himself to think it through. His brain was still foggy, but it sounded strange, even to him. "Why keep a bunch of grain way back here, so far from the kitchen and the stables?"

"Exactly. It makes no sense. It's too much trouble to go to for just grain ..." Raven's eyes widened.

"What?" Aik rolled his eyes. Raven was doing the whole *I just had an idea thing*, and he wouldn't share until he'd proved himself right. "What?"

"Maybe it's not the grain, it's what's under it." Raven knelt in front of the chest and thrust both hands into the golden kernels, feeling around inside. "Aha." He pulled out a kiln-fired vase that sparkled with a blue and purple glaze. "It's packing material!"

Aik looked around. There were probably a couple hundred chests and crates here. Who knew what Tri'Aya had collected? His sense of right and wrong reasserted itself. "It's not yours. You can't take it."

Raven rubbed his chin. "You're probably right. It's too big. I need something smaller and easier to transport. Something she won't miss for a while."

Aik rolled his eyes. "No. I mean you can't take *anything* from here."

Raven stared at him. "You can't be serious. These people have everything. Look at this house, Aik!"

"*These people* are Silya's mother."

"Who she hates with a white-hot passion."

"Doesn't matter. You don't steal from friends. Or friends' mothers." He was pretty sure that was in the universal code of conduct he'd sworn his oath on. *Or something close to it.*

Raven growled. "Well, I can at least look through a couple more. Right?"

"Remember what happened last time you took something that didn't belong to you?"

That stopped Raven cold. His hand dropped to his stomach, and his eyes narrowed. "You're right. That was ... spectacularly bad."

"Good. I'm glad you finally agree." Aik glanced nervously at the doorway. "We should go. Someone could come along at any second."

Raven looked around the storeroom, longing on his face. "Still, it can't hurt to just look. Come on. Just one more."

The strange feeling washed over Aik again. His right arm burned, although the gauntlet had vanished. Unbidden by its owner, his hand raised to point to a chest that was all by itself near the back of the cavern. Aik's heart jumped into overdrive as a voice not his own used his vocal cords. "That one." It came out as a growl. *What the fark is wrong with me?*

Raven grinned. "*That one* it is. Glad you came around, my friend."

Aik stared at him, mute. He tried to get a word out, but all he managed was a grunt.

Raven didn't seem to notice. He opened the lid of the box. It too was filled with grain, but the color had long gone out of it. The kernels were gray and fell away into dust as Raven rummaged through the crate eagerly. He pulled out one object, then another, and set them down next to the crate, staring at them. "What in Heaven's Reach ...?"

There was a long skinny yellow stick and a round shape. Aik knelt to pick up the latter.

An empty eye socket stared back at him from a strangely distended face.

*Iihil.* The skull whispered to him.

*What in Heaven's Reach?*

Then something different slipped into his mind.

He could feel its vast strength, as if it were only showing him the smallest part of itself so as not to damage him. *What are you? The hencha?* Is this what Silya felt like? Though he'd never heard of a man speaking with the *hencha* mind.

*Come home, Iihil.*

*What the hell?* That definitely wasn't his own thought.

*Let go of me!* But whatever had him in its thrall, it didn't seem to care what he said or thought.

*Come home.*

Raven held the stick up to the light. "What do you think they are?" He turned to look at Aik and his eyes went wide.

Aik's gauntlet had returned.

"What the farking hell?" Raven scampered backwards away from him, banging the trunk and making the lid slam closed. The look of fear in his's eyes was unmistakable.

Just as quickly as it had come upon him, the presence vanished, leaving him shaking as the gauntlet faded from sight. *The gods have abandoned me.*

The compulsion let go of him and Aik stumbled to his knees, breathing heavily and dropping the skull with a clatter. "Put them back."

"What in the holy heartland just happened to you?"

"It's ... I don't know."

"Aik, you were glowing red."

Aik closed his eyes. He had no idea what was happening to him, only that it was because of the gauntlet. "They're bones, Raven. Put them back now!" He didn't want to look at the skull again.

Raven did as he was told, burying them again deep in the grain dust and closing the lid of the chest with a heavy thud. "What's going on, Aik? You're starting to freak me out."

Aik closed his eyes. "I went to look in on you, after dinner. You ... you were asleep. How are you here?"

"I put some pillows under the covers and snuck out. Oldest trick in the book." Raven was reverting to his normal, smart-alecky self.

"Asshole." It came out as a whisper. Aik looked up at his friend.

"Almost always." He edged up to Aik, reaching out to touch his now-bare right arm.

"As soon as I closed the door to your room, this weird compulsion grabbed me. I couldn't go back to my room. My feet led me here. To you. To this." He blinked, the last of the wine-induced stupor clearing. "Like sleepwalking, but I was wide awake." He stared at Raven. "What in the green holy hell is happening to me?"

Raven embraced him. "We'll figure all this out." He squeezed Aik harder. "If it helps ... I know exactly how you feel."

"You do?"

"I felt it too. When I stole the egg. I ... I had to have it. Like this little voice inside my head egging me on." He grinned. "So to speak."

Aik flashed him a weak smile. "What's happening to us?"

Raven sighed, glancing back at the chest. "I wish I knew. What was that ... thing?"

Aik sank down onto the ground, turning and putting his back to the chest and his head between his knees. "Life was so much easier a couple days ago. I got up, went to work, did a full day's shift, and went home afterwards."

He felt Raven settle in next to him. "Tell me about it. So, when did this happen?" He pointed to Aik's right arm.

"Yesterday, when you were out in the city with Silya. I'm sorry, Raven — I didn't mean for it to happen. I was just trying to organize your things for you."

"Was that ... all the artifacts?"

Aik nodded miserably. "I put them next to each other, and they ... fused. Like the *inthym*." *I was an idiot.* After lecturing Raven over his stupid theft of the egg ... "It looked kind of like a gauntlet, so I tried it on, and it ... flowed around my arm. Now it won't come off."

"That's really odd. Can you make it reappear?"

"No. It comes and goes when it wants." He glanced at Raven. "It saved your life."

"I know. I'm grateful. Honest." Raven put his arm around Aik and squeezed him tightly. "We'll figure this out. But you have to tell Silya." He let go of Aik, staring at the open linen closet door. "You tried to tell me last night, didn't you?"

"Yes ... but then you surprised me with what Spin could do ..."

Raven bit his lip. "So it's my fault?"

"That's not what I meant, and you know it."

Raven met his gaze. "I understand. Still, too many secrets between friends."

*Friends.* Aik bit his lip, disappointed for the hundredth time. "You sure you're not mad at me?"

"Not mad." Raven still looked spooked, though, a few shades whiter than normal. "Let's get out of here before someone comes looking for us."

"Good idea." Aik closed his eyes, gathering his strength. He was exhausted, worn thin by the day's events.

Raven helped him up, and together they fled the strange cavern. His friend closed the doors behind them, and they made their way back down the long hallway.

They were almost back to their rooms when a heavy hand landed on Aik's shoulder. "Where have you two been?" Ser Kek's gravelly voice sounded suspicious.

Aik swallowed hard. "Just walking with Raven. He needed to get out of his room —"

"It felt like the walls were closing in on me." Raven put on his most earnest look, the one that could convince mothers to give up their young. Or men to take him to bed.

Aik's knees went weak again, despite all that had just happened. Or maybe because of it.

Kek frowned, clearly not convinced, but having no proof that anything was amiss. "The Queen wants to see you. Come with me." The man set off toward the residential wing, clearly expecting them to follow. "I'm watching you two."

Aik shot Raven a look, but his friend just shrugged. It was all out in the open, at least. And the frightening compulsion seemed to be done with him for now.

Aik shuddered. *We'll talk more about it later. Maybe I'll finally tell you how I really feel.* Aik rolled his eyes. And maybe *aur* will fly.

*Iihil.* In his head, he could still see that strange skull leering at him.

*Come home.*

# 18

## SURVEY

SILYA RAN HER HANDS across the bright green and gold *ix* hide mounted on the wall of her mother's study, thrilling to the feel of the long thin hairs between her fingers.

"I shot that one myself." Tri'Aya came up behind her, putting a hand on her shoulder.

Silya gently shrugged it off. "It must have been beautiful when it was alive." She stepped backward to get a better look. "Where did you ... find it?" She hated hunting. Even when Tri'Aya had taken her out to shoot mud moles and *skerit* for practice, she'd disliked it. Seeing the little things bleed out, their purple blood spilling onto the grass, broke her heart.

"In the Red Flights, far east of here. In ce'faine country."

Silya winced. "Did you see one of the *cheff*?"

Tri'Aya's eyes grew misty. "Once."

Silya waited for more, but her mother was uncharacteristically silent. Things were good between them at the moment and Silya didn't want to ruin it, so she didn't push. *Who knows how long this détente will last?*

223

A strangely youthful portrait of Tri'Aya's face stared at Silya from another wall. She'd looked at it for hours as a teenager, wondering how that apparently sweet young woman had turned into her mother.

A low rumble shook the room. Silya braced herself against the wall and the *ix* fur, shooting an alarmed look at Tri'Aya. The tremor scooted the heavy *flopwood* desk a few centimeters across the stone tile floors before subsiding.

"Strange times." Her mother looked as uneasy as Silya felt.

"Indeed." She glanced at the door. "The others should be here soon. Then we can talk about what I came for." It felt good to speak to her mother as an equal, not the scared little girl she'd once been.

As if they'd been summoned, the two sisters arrived. Sister Dor entered first, giving the study a quick once-over and dismissing it from her mind. "Is there any word back from the Temple?"

Tri'Aya shook her head. "I'll let you know as soon as the reply comes."

Sister Tela took her time, examining the heavy oak desk, the matched paintings of Heaven's Reach on the wall behind it, and finally the two bookshelves that were filled with leather-bound books. Her eyes lit up. "May I?"

Tri'Aya nodded. "Be my guest."

Sister Tela poured over the titles, humming a cheery tune.

"Who else are we expecting?"

"Desla, Raven and Aik, if Raven's feeling better. I asked Ser Kek to round them up."

"Bit strange for a city guard to be traveling with you." Tri'Aya wrinkled her nose.

"Everything's strange these days." Silya knew that look. The man had caught her mother's interest. She ought to tell him to run, before Tri'Aya got her hooks into him — the sergeant was twenty years younger than she was. Then again, maybe her interest in Ser Kek would keep her mother off her back, but Silya felt a strange resistance to the idea.

Her mother snorted. "True enough."

That simple agreement surprised her.

She was about to ask what other strange things Tri'Aya had seen of late when Raven and Aik arrived, escorted by the sergeant.

"Here you go, mim. I'll leave you to your meeting." He shoved the two inside as if they were adolescent delinquents, which wasn't far from the truth. Raven looked paler than usual.

Silya glared at them. *What were you two up to?* She wished mind reading was one of her new abilities. "Ser Kek?"

The man stopped in midstride. "Yes, mim?"

"Please stay. I'd like your opinion on these … matters." He was street-smart in a way none of the rest of them were, and his observations might be valuable.

The man looked surprised. "Of course, mim." He slipped into the room and took a place behind the others, towering above everyone but Aik.

*It has nothing to do with Tri'Aya's feelings. Or my own.* "Raven, are you feeling all right? I brought some *fexin*, and I'm sure Tri'Aya has something if you're still a bit queasy —"

"I'm fine, Sil'Aya." He glared at Aik, who looked away.

What's that all about? And how did the little thief manage to make saying her name sound like an insult? She grumbled under her breath. *Men*

"Sorry I'm late. I was in the bath." Desla's golden hair lay flat on her scalp. "I came as quickly as I could."

It was good to see the initiate wasn't hung up on her looks. "Let's get started." She pulled the *Menagerie* and Queen Jas'Aya's journal out of the carry sack she'd retrieved from her room and set them on the desk. "Two days ago, Aik came to me, asking for my help. He told me that something had happened to Raven." She glanced at him. "Can you tell Tri'Aya what happened?"

Raven looked nervously over his shoulder at Ser Kek.

Silya met the sergeant's gaze with the full authority of the *Hencha Queen*. "Sergeant, I'm invoking Temple sanctuary over what's said and shown here tonight. Nothing that is disclosed can be used against anyone in this room." She paused for effect. "Am I clear?"

Out of the corner of her eye, she saw Sister Dor nodding approvingly.

The guard growled. "Yes, mim."

Even Tri'Aya looked at her with respect.

"Thank you. Now Raven, please tell us what happened." She kept her voice firm but kind, pleased that things were off to a good start.

Raven bit his lip.

Aik reached out and squeezed his hand, and he found his voice. "I was walking down Grindell Lane. It was late in the afternoon, and I was about ready to head back to the lair for the day."

Ser Kek glared at him, but kept silent.

"I heard the rumble of something approaching. I jumped out of the street and turned to see the sea master's carriage. It's very distinctive, with the carved blue waves on either side —"

Silya cut him off. "We've seen it. Move along." Raven loved to spin a story.

"She got out at the guild hall. She was talking with someone. I think it was a guard —"

"Councillor Nes'Hoya." Kek's eyes were all but burning a hole in Raven's back, his voice a low growl.

"Sure?" Raven squirmed under that gaze.

Silya hid her smile. She couldn't help but enjoy his discomfort, just a little.

"Go on." Desla put a hand on Raven's shoulder encouragingly.

He bobbed his head gratefully. "This cloth-wrapped package was on the carriage's seat. I thought it might be worth something. It was a hungry week, and I needed the money, so I ..." he glanced back at Kek.

Aik squeezed his hand again.

*The three of you seem to have become fast friends.* Silya wasn't sure how she felt about that.

"I took it." He squirmed under her gaze. "I didn't plan to. But it called to me. I had to have it —"

Ser Kek slipped the loop of rope off his waist and stepped forward. "Rav'Orn, you're under arrest for the theft of personal property. You have the right to an advocate —"

Raven twisted out of Aik's grasp and backed away, looking around the den wildly for an escape route.

Desla threw herself between them.

"Ser Kek!" Silya slammed her fist down on the desk, and her voice cut through the room like a knife. Everyone went silent, heads turned toward her, except for Sister Tela, who was absorbed in a book.

The guard froze, his expression hard and his lips set in a grim line. "Yes, mim?"

"What part of Temple sanctuary don't you understand?"

The poor man looked confused. "Mim, this man just admitted to committing a crime. And not just any crime. A high crime against one of the leaders of Gullton. The sea master has already agreed to press charges —"

"Enough." This time the flames came when she called them, running up and down her arms in a blaze of force. "I am the Hencha Queen, and I declare this man off limits from your justice for as long as this crisis lasts. Am I understood?" She could hear the *hencha* singing in her ears, the weight of their combined consciousness filling her with power. It would be easy to become addicted to that feeling.

Ser Kek didn't break a sweat. She had to give him credit for that. "Yes, mim. Understood." He backed away, leaning against the wall.

Raven was grinning.

"And you." Silya let the fire die away and turned her ire on him. "This doesn't let you off the hook either, Mas Orn. You took something valuable that wasn't yours, and I assure you there will be repercussions."

Raven went pale, and neither man seemed happy. They glared at each other like a couple cornered *eircats*.

"Am I clear?" Only then did she notice the look of approval on Tri'Aya's face.

"Yes mim." Raven pulled his gaze away from the sergeant to stare at the ground, looking every bit the recalcitrant five-year-old.

"Sergeant?"

"Yes, mim." His icy gaze stayed locked on Raven. "Once this is over, though ..."

"Cross that bridge when we get there." She immediately regretted that turn of phrase.

"If it's still standing." Raven looked up, his usual swagger back.

Silya rolled her eyes. There was no taking the gully rat out of the thief. "What happened when you opened the package?"

"I took it back to my lair, in the tunnels under the city. There was a silver box inside. And inside that, an egg ..."

Ser Kek growled. "That's a lie. That box was filled with *croners* for the treasury."

Aik stepped between them, frowning. "No, it's true. There was no money, just an egg."

227

"You're treading on thin ice. If you helped this thief, I could get you thrown out of the Guard." He glanced at Silya. "Sanctuary or no sanctuary."

"Sergeant." Silya's voice was ice. Men were maddening.

"Sorry, mim." The man stepped back again, frowning. "I don't believe him, though. The sea master was clear about what was in that box."

Raven peeled off one of his gloves. "Do you believe this?" He held up his right arm.

Silya gasped, and she wasn't the only one. Raven's forearm was fully transformed now. It was beautiful — covered in smooth pearlescent scales — but it didn't look human.

Raven spat. "That damned beast —"

"*Verent,*" Aik supplied helpfully.

"That beast cracked its shell, then forced its way down my throat. Now I have this to remember it by."

"You're very brave, Raven." Desla was staring at Raven's arm too.

"May I see?" Silya's mother pushed past her to look at Raven's arm. "Hmmm. The craftwork is exquisite. Still, I know a fake when I see one." She pried at one of the scales.

"Owww!" Raven pulled his arm away.

"See? Fake." Tri'Aya held up the liberated scale.

Anger burned through Silya, replacing the momentary warmth she'd felt for her mother. Tri'Aya thought she knew everything, but she didn't know this. "You all right, Raven?"

Raven held up his arm, and Tri'Aya gasped. The place where she'd pried off the scale was healing, the missing scale regrowing over the raw skin.

Silya grasped Raven's wrist, forcing it under Tri'Aya's gaze. "If that's a fake, why is he bleeding purple?"

Her mother staggered back, catching herself against her desk. She stared at Raven's arm. "Lo'Oss protect us." She made the infinity sign across her chest.

Tri'Aya suddenly looked a decade older, lines carved on her face, her lip trembling. Then she said something Silya had only heard her say a handful of times in her entire life. "I'm sorry."

Silya's mouth dropped open. "You're what?"

Raven bobbed his head again. "It's fine, mim."

That surprised Silya more than her mother's apology.

"It's not right. Mim ... Silya, she hurt him." Desla rubbed Raven's arm where the scale was already growing back.

Silya forged ahead. "You're all right, Raven?"

He nodded. "See? All better."

*Stranger and stranger.* "I didn't see the egg, or the *verent*, though Aik showed me some of the egg shards. But I was there when a horde of *inthym* showed up, merged, and led us to safety after the first quake."

"What do you mean, merged?" Tri'Aya was still staring at Raven, as if a *cephlant* had suddenly appeared in her study, tusks and all.

"Just that. There were a hundred of them, and then there was one." Silya took a deep breath, collecting her thoughts. "We came to you because you've seen as much of the rest of the world as anyone here, if not more. Something's happening. I can feel it. But I don't have a clue what it is."

Tri'Aya had regained her composure. She paced back and forth in front of her desk. "So we have a new Hencha Queen. A couple strange occurrences with the local fauna. And two quakes, one strong enough to knock down the Old Bridge."

Raven piped up. "And Aik —"

Aik elbowed Raven in the ribs. Hard.

Silya's eyes narrowed. Aik was hiding something — she'd bet the Manor House on it.

"'And Aik' what?" Tri'Aya glared at one and then the other, a look Silya recognized well from her childhood.

Raven squirmed under her gaze but said nothing more.

Aik bit his lip. "I was there when the *inthyms* ... combined. There's no other way to say it. Like Silya said, there were dozens, maybe a hundred, and then there was one. One bigger one." Aik looked at Raven, who nodded.

Tri'Aya frowned. "Anything else?"

"There's this too." Silya handed her mother Queen Jas'Aya's diary, open to the page of the prophecy. *If that's what it is.*

Tri'Aya slipped behind her desk and turned up the lantern light to read it. "This is Queen Jas's writing?" She looked up at Silya in wonder.

"From the year before she died."

Desla sidled up to look over Silya's shoulder.

"Amazing." Tri'Aya read the flagged passage. "'*Verent* swarm in the icy north, when the twin moons are rising. *Cayah* in the harsh Southern Deserts lift their dappled heads from the sand. The *erphin* swim upstream, and the *jexyn* in their sky aeries hear the call to come to Anghar Mor.'" Her mother rubbed her temples. "The moons have been as close together as I can remember in my lifetime. Maybe that's what 'twin moons rising' means?"

"Oooh."

Everyone turned at the sound.

Sister Tela had pulled out an old leather-bound volume, cracked along the edges of the spine, and was thumbing through it. She gave a start — the eyes of the whole room were on her.

Silya grinned. "What did you find?" Tela was only this excited when she happened upon something she didn't know, tucked away in one of the books in the Temple archives. She must feel like a child in a pastry shop in this place.

Sister Tela carried the book reverently to the desk while Tri'Aya eyed her warily. "Please be careful with that. It's one of the few still in existence."

"Yes, I'd heard about this, but not even the council archive has a copy of it." She shot a suspicious glance in Tri'Aya's direction. "How did you get one?"

"I'm a trader. It's what I do." Her mother's voice was sharp with stubborn pride. "That one came from a small steading in the Highlands. Someone carried it with them in the migration from Gullton, I'd guess. Poor man had no idea what he had."

Silya peered over Tela's shoulder. "What is it?"

"The original survey report of Tharassas. All the colonists got one, but few survived the intervening centuries." She opened it delicately.

The pages were yellowed but thicker and more uniformly cut than the *hencha* leaf paper the Temple used. There was a title page, the text impossibly neat, each letter perfectly matched to the others. Silya had seen machine-printed books before — the Temple had a handful — but they still astonished her.

## Trappist-1 - M8V - Tharassas System
## Planet: Trappist-1-D

*Planet is inhabitable, with high oxygen content and temperatures near Earth-normal. Light refraction from the system's red dwarf star scatters in the atmosphere, causing a strange green sky. Some genetic changes may be required for Earth life to survive in this environment ...*

Silya frowned. Why would a green sky be strange?

"Look." Sister Tela leafed through the book reverently. After maybe fifty pages of dense text, filled with strange mathematical scribbles, she paused.

Silya gasped. "Is that ...?"

Sister Tela's face glowed with rapture. "I think so, yes."

It was an image, a green and brown orb streaked with white. It was too fine to be a painting. "Tharassas."

Aik sidled up next to her and whistled. "So it is true."

"Told you so." Raven peered over her shoulder. "It's beautiful. Like a glass marble." He sniffed the paper. "It smells old."

"It is." The colors were faded with time. Silya traced the white lines — clouds, she realized in wonder. She looked around the room and felt a sudden, surprising sense of her own insignificance. This house, her city — the whole of the Heartland — were all contained in that image. Of course, such human-made constructs hadn't existed on Tharassas then. Still ...

"We all live on that?" Desla's mouth made a little O.

Sister Tela looked up at her in amazement. "Makes you question your place in the grand scheme of things, doesn't it?"

"I feel like an *inthym*. Or a *skeef* sucking on the blood of an *inthym*." Raven sounded uncomfortable.

*That's a first.* Still, she knew what he meant. They were all insignificant, especially in light of the changes storming the world.

Aik's hand sought Raven's under the desk.

Silya ignored them. Or tried to. "This is a beautiful book. Fascinating, even. But I don't see how it helps us."

Sister Tela smiled. "There's more." She eased the page over, and there they were. Maps. Pages and pages of maps. "Tri'Aya, thank you for letting me see this. It's been my life's ambition to find it. There were references to it in many of the texts, and even a few partial copies. But to hold one in my own hands ..."

Silya looked up at her mother. A struggle was going on there, evident in the way her eyes were narrowed and lips tight. Their eyes met. Something passed between them. Not something from the Hencha Queen, but something entirely human, between mother and daughter.

The tension fled Tri'Aya's face. "You should take it with you, back to the Temple. It belongs there, and you'll get far more out of it than I ever would, with it just sitting here on a shelf gathering dust."

"Are you sure?" Sister Tela's eyes went wide. "It's ... invaluable."

Desla whistled. "That's quite a gift, mim Aya."

Tri'Aya patted her shoulder. "I'm sure you will take good care of it. I can see how much you love books."

"Thank you, mim Aya." A look of sheer bliss crossed Sister Tela's face, followed by a shadow of doubt. "I can secure payment from the Temple purse ..." Her eyes met Silya's.

Silya's mother held out her hand. "That won't be necessary. Think of it as a promise that we'll find ways to work together in the future."

The sister reached across the desk to take Tri'Aya's hand in her old, gnarled ones, squeezing it tightly. "Thank you, mim Aya. You are most kind. I will have copies made so that we may study them and keep this original in a safe place."

"I'd appreciate it." A strangely wistful expression crossed her face. "I'd love to come visit the Temple archives one day."

"It would be my honor." Sister Tela let go of her hand and bowed.

Silya cleared her throat. "Let's get back to the matter at hand. It's late, and I want to get to bed soon. Any idea what this 'Anghar Mor' is?"

Sister Tela's brow furrowed. "I believe so, mim. Queen Jas'Aya mentions it a few times in her diaries." She stared off into space, her fingers drumming on the desk. "A mountain, I think. In the north." She turned the pages of the survey carefully, tracing the images with a spidery finger. "Ah, here it is."

Silya stared at an image full of squiggly lines. "What is that?"

"It's called a 'topographical map.' It shows the height of the land above sea level. Anghar Mor is the largest peak in the north."

Silya squinted at the supposed map. "Where is that? I can't tell from all these lines."

"Let's see." The sister flipped back a couple pages and then grinned sheepishly. "Sorry. I get excited sometimes."

Tri'Aya flinched at Tela's handling of her precious book but said nothing.

Silya covered a snort. Sister Tela's *excited* was her *just woke up from a long nap.*

"Ah, here we go. It's on the far side of the Highlands, beyond Lake Zeraya."

"That's *cheff* territory." Ser Kek had come up behind them to peer at the map over her head. "You're not seriously thinking of going there?"

"I'm not thinking anything yet." Which was a bit of a lie. She'd always wanted to see the Highlands, the waving seas of purple grasses, the beautiful turquoise-green waters of Lake Zeraya. Still, she had responsibilities to Gullton now. She doubted Sister Dor or the rest of the Temple would take kindly to her going off on another quest before her official Raising.

"The *cheff* are dangerous." Kek wasn't letting go.

"They've become valued partners, and they prefer to be called ce'faine." Tri'Aya held out her right hand, showing off a hand-beaten silver bracelet. "I traded for these last summer at the Highlands Market Day. They do beautiful work, even if they are a strange people."

Silya met his gaze. "There hasn't been an incident along the border in over twenty years."

Kek closed his eyes, and a flash of pain crossed his usually stoic features. "They slaughtered my family, mim."

Silya inhaled sharply. *I didn't know.* "I'm sorry, Sergeant. How old were you?"

"Ten, mim. Fifteen years ago now. I was out tending the *urses* when they came. I hid in the haystack, but I heard the death cries of my mother and father, and my younger brother Enrick ... and then they burned down our home."

The room had gone silent again. Desla was staring at the guard, her hand over her mouth. Even Raven didn't dare say a thing.

Silya put a hand on his shoulder. "I am so sorry, Ser Kek."

Their eyes met. "Kerrick." Then he looked away. "Thank you, mim. It was a long time ago."

"Thank you, Ser ... Kerrick. I'll keep that in mind." The poor man. It explained a lot — how quick he was to anger and his strongly developed sense of right and wrong. He was a good man. For the first time in their brief relationship, Silya saw past his rough demeanor to the man inside.

Sister Tela touched her hand. "It's late, mim. Maybe we should take this up again tomorrow."

Her mother nodded. "You're right. This will keep. We'll all be more clearheaded in the morning."

Silya was tired. Life had been moving nonstop since Aik had found her in the *hencha* field, just two days before. She looked around the room. One by one, the others gave their assent. "In the morning, then."

Aik, Raven, and Kerrick shuffled out of the den, giving each other wide berth, followed by Desla and Sister Tela, clutching the survey to her chest. Silya's mother and Sister Dor hung back. "A word, mim?" Her aide looked worried.

"Of course." It was strange being addressed so formally by everyone, but at least the sisters themselves hadn't started calling her "Your Highness." First among equals, and all that. "Good night, Tri'Aya."

Her mother touched her cheek. "Night, Silya."

Tri'Aya wanted her forgiveness. It was as plain as Silya's own need for her love. They had made progress on this visit, but it would be a long road. *I'm not ready.* "See you in the morning." She turned to follow Sister Dor out of the room, feeling Tri'Aya's gaze on her back.

As she walked down the wide stone hall with Sister Dor, she caught the woman sneaking glances at her.

"What? If something's bothering you, just say it plain." It came out more harshly than she intended. She was tired, after all. It had been a long and eventful day.

Sister Dor didn't look offended. "Have you been having ... dreams?"

"I dream almost every night."

The sister shook her head. "I mean dreams that feel almost like real life. Waking dreams, maybe? Dreams about the world, about the *hencha* ..."

Silya closed her eyes, thinking back. There had been the strange flash in the tunnels when she touched the walls. Still, she'd been stressed and tired. "No, nothing like that. Why?"

"I suppose each one is different." The sister stared at the ground ahead of her pointedly. "No matter. We should start your instruction soon."

"Each one?" *Ah, each Hencha Queen.* Barely two days in, and already she was disappointing the sisterhood.

Dor seemed to sense her concern. She met Silya's gaze. "Every Hencha Queen comes into her own, in her own way."

"But I'm slower than the others, is that it?" She meant it sardonically, but it came out whinier than she'd intended.

Sister Dor blushed. "I meant no offense, mim."

Silya rubbed her temples. Her head ached. "I'm sorry. That was rude of me."

"Thank you, mim. You're under an incredible amount of pressure." Sister Dor looked into her eyes. "Do you have a headache? I brought some *fellin* root —"

"No, I'm fine, thank you. And besides, a headache is no excuse to be rude to you." Though she was fairly sure she'd come by that trait naturally, headache or no. "And please, call me Silya."

The sister blinked. "It's ... not proper, mim."

Silya laughed. It was good to release some of the pressure that was building up in her chest. "I insist. I think you'll find that nothing is very proper about me."

"Yes, mim ... Silya." The name didn't exactly roll off her tongue, but it was good enough for now.

She'd have to find some way to loosen Sister Dor up. "Can your lessons wait until tomorrow? I really am exhausted."

"Of course ... Silya. As Your Highness requests."

Silya frowned as a hint of a smile flickered across Sister Dor's features.

"That was a joke?"

"Good night, Silya." She padded away toward her own room, smoothing her yellow skirts around her bulk.

Silya watched her aide go, a grin on her face. *You surprise me.* She hadn't been sure the normally dour Sister Dor was even capable of humor.

*We're going to get along just fine.*

# 19

## REGRET

V ELIX WATCHED THEIR MATES — Kalix and Sorix — disappear into the darkening green sky, gone to fetch their errant kit.

As the egg layer, they were expected to stay close to home except in extreme emergency. After being the male in the relationship the previous season, it was a hard adjustment to make. Velix sighed.

*Clipped wings are better than no wings at all.*

Sorix had been snapping at all of them — Velix had the teeth marks in their hide to prove it.

Living with the otherlings had been an adjustment for them all, though Velix adjusted faster than most of their fellow people. The otherlings were fragile, but they made the most adorable sounds, especially when you nuzzled them with your snout or blew into their ears. Havik's otherling had even taken to rubbing Velix's snout between their eye ridges when they met, a trait that endeared the squishy pink creature to them.

A couple of the messengers floated by, carrying news from the north. Velix sniffed them, and they passed along what they knew. The mountain was restless. Soon, very soon, events would begin to surpass them.

With a last longing look at the now-dark sky, Velix snorted and turned tail, to prepare the kits for the arrival of their long-lost brother.

•　　•　　•

Raven closed the door behind him and leaned back against the smooth wood slats, sweat beading his brow despite the cool air from outside. *When did this become my life?*

He wished the door had a lock. What was to stop Ser Kek from coming after him in the middle of the night, when everyone else was fast asleep?

Raven hadn't let on, but the story about the man's family had really gotten to him. It was weird seeing the formidable guard almost break down over his own lost family. Raven could relate to such raw pain. *Mamma, I wish you were here now.*

Things were getting dicey. Maybe it was time for him to go, to set out on his own in search of some answers. He didn't have the slightest clue where to go, but it couldn't be any worse than staying here and being dragged back to the Guardhouse with Kek.

Except for Aik, and what had almost happened between them in his room at the Temple. He could still feel Aik's lips on his. It felt ... different this time. He couldn't explain why, and that bugged him.

He hadn't told his friends, but the skin on his shins itched now too. *I'm becoming a freak. What if no one wants me? What if* Aik *doesn't want me?* With his shock of dark hair and his exotic brown eyes, he'd had no trouble attracting the men he wanted, and it had gotten him into trouble more than once.

If he were honest with himself, he'd always considered Aik his fallback. Like, maybe in the end they would be together, somehow.

But now this ...

He pulled off his gloves to stare at his arms. *Who would want to sleep with a monster?* Even Aik would run from him eventually.

He glanced down at his pants. What happened when this change — whatever it was — reached *Little Raven and the boys*? He pulled off his shirt and checked his chest, running his hand over the smooth skin. *Still human there, thank Fri'Oss.*

His stomach rumbled, and he wondered again what that thing was doing inside of him. Heat radiated from his stomach, and his face felt like it had burst into flames. In the enclosed space of Tri'Aya's study, it had been all he could manage to not smell each of the people in the room. Silya smelled of reed soap and wine. Kek reeked of aggression. And Aik …

*It's so hot. Or maybe it's just me.* He stumbled across the small room and threw open the shutters and a blessedly cool stream of air blew into the room. He put his hands on the cold stone windowsill and closed his eyes, letting the breeze blow over his naked torso. The cool air felt good, drawing away his nausea.

The last time he'd gotten in trouble, it had been pure bad luck. He'd snuck into a tiny market at the ass-end of the Vulture Spine at an hour past midnight, when any respectable citizen should have been at home with his family. Turned out his family lived above the store, and Raven had made too much noise in his foraging. Or maybe it was just his own bad luck that the owner hadn't slept well that night.

He opened his eyes. Tharassas's two moons lit the valley below with an orange light, chasing each other across the sky, drawing closer each night. Raven rarely paid attention to the night sky — it was often hard to even see the stars in Gullton through the smog and the city lights. He was usually focused on everything and everyone around him, looking for advantage, searching for threats. Fight or flight, grab and run.

Stuck in this house in the heart of nowhere, he felt restless, trapped. *Yes, it's time to go.*

From the Manor House window, he could see halfway across the Heartland below as the valley slowly faded into darkness. *Hencha* plants filled this side of it, moving like water in the wind under the light of the twin moons. The Elsp wound around the edge of the fields in the near distance on the far side of the foothills they'd spent the afternoon weaving through. Its waters sparkled in the moonlight. He could almost smell the river water.

He shook his head. *That's ridiculous. It's kilometers away.*

Raven took a deep breath of the cool night air. Winter was on the way, the balmy days of summer already giving way to fall. Still, it was warm enough to rough it outside for a bit, at least until he found a town to hole up in while he figured everything out.

He looked up at the moons again. How soon would they meet? *Spin would know.*

He rummaged through his bag and pulled out the silver sphere. The walls here were thick enough to block out the noise, but he opened the door and looked each way to make sure the hall was empty just in case, and then pulled the heavy wooden shutters closed.

He lit the small lantern by his bedside. Then he sank down on the bed with his back against the wall and his boots hanging over the edge. "Hey, Spin, wake up."

Spin's golden lights spun, brightening the dark room. "Morning, boss!"

Raven frowned. "Keep it quiet, would you? People are sleeping. Give me an earpiece?"

A little piece of Spin extruded itself. Raven picked it up and shoved it in his ear.

"What is this place? It's a lot nicer than your usual digs."

Raven rubbed his ear. "The Manor House. It's where Silya's mother lives."

"Ah, the *screeching, vicious daughter of an aur and a mud mole*?"

Raven laughed and then covered his mouth. It was weird to hear his own voice emanating from his familiar. *I said that?* "Better forget that one, Spin. She's the Hencha Queen now. And we made up. Mostly." She had defended him, after all. Several times now.

"Sure, boss. Like that'll last." His golden lights spun around him.

*I assure you there will be consequences.* Raven shuddered. Maybe he could do without her supervision too. He wasn't too keen on those promised consequences.

"Hencha Queen." Spin was quiet for a moment. "The link between humans and the *hencha* plants?"

"You got it." One thing about Spin — he really paid attention. *He? She?* He used male pronouns, but what was he, really? Raven liked to think Spin was like him. "Hey Spin, are you ... male? Female?"

"Neither, boss. But they programmed me to respond to my users in the way that makes them most comfortable. I like to think of myself as male. I can lower my voice, if you like." That last part came out sounding like one of the sea master's dock workers.

Raven chuckled softly. *Programmed?* "Just be yourself." He held up the sphere to look it over. How had someone made this? Maybe Aik was right. Technology really was magic. "I have a question for you."

"You always do, boss. I'm not a freaking encyclopedia."

*"Incyclone ... never mind." If I had a copper for every word Spin used that I didn't know ...* "The two moons — Tarsis and Pellin — they're getting closer and closer every night. When will they ... meet?"

"Hmmm. Good question, boss." His lights flashed. "Can I see them?"

"Oh, of course." *I'm an idiot.* He slipped off the bed, opened one of the shutters a crack, and held up the sphere toward the sky. *What do you use for eyes?*

Spin was quiet for a long time.

Raven tapped on Spin's metallic shell. "Everything all right there?"

"Yes. That's enough. Thank you, Raven."

*No "boss?" That's weird.* Raven pulled the shutter closed and returned to bed. "So?"

"Conjunction will happen in about nine Tharassan days."

Raven grimaced. That was soon. "And will they ... collide?"

"Nope. They're in separate orbits. Pellin will pass in front of Tarsis, but neither will physically touch the other."

"Ah." Raven closed his eyes and tried to picture it. He'd seen it somewhere before ... in one of those weird dreams.

"Boss?"

"What?"

"Thanks. I haven't seen the sky like that in a long time."

Raven scratched his head. How long had Spin lain buried in that field before a quick-moving storm had unearthed him and the hencha had found him? More than a hundred years, likely. *Buried alive.* Raven shuddered. "Spin, you all right?"

Again, that long silence.

*I should leave well enough alone.* He set Spin down on the bed covers and pulled out his carry sack. He put his few things into it, as well as the Jel'Faya book he'd nicked in Tri'Aya's study, something called Highlands Fling. He'd never read that one before, though he'd thought he had all of Faya's works. Changing his mind, he slipped the book into one of his pants pockets. *Just in case Kek — or Tri'Aya — searches my bag*

"I miss the stars."

Spin's unexpected confession surprised him, reminding him the little guy had been on a starship. "What was it like?" He piled his dirty clothes into the carry sack. They stank to high heaven ... how had he ever thought they were clean enough to wear again?

"Flying among them?"

"Yeah." Raven sank down on his bed next to the familiar, closing his eyes and trying to picture it.

"It's hard to describe, boss. I was free. Just me and the ship and the crew, soaring through the cosmos ..." There was definitely a wistful note this time. "I wish —"

There was a soft knock at the door.

Raven's shoulders tensed. "Sorry, Spin. Shut down, please," he whispered.

"Aw boss ..."

Raven pulled out the eardrop and watched as it melted back into Spin's skin. "Now, Spin."

The sphere's lights went out without another word, though its darkness seemed almost snarky.

Raven tucked the sphere into his sack, hoping it wasn't Ser Kek come to check on him. "It's open."

Aik popped his head into the room. "Everyone else is asleep. Can I come in?"

*Just Aik.* Some of the tension fled from Raven's shoulders. "Please."

Aik closed the door quietly behind him. "Sorry to bother you. I couldn't sleep." His friend looked at the carry sack on the bed. "Going somewhere?" He frowned, and Raven could smell disappointment radiating from him.

"I haven't decided," It wasn't a total lie.

"Right." Aik's shoulders sagged like they were carrying the weight of Heaven's Reach. "Why can't things just go back to the way they were?" He rubbed his right arm absently.

Raven shivered. It was hard being alone with Aik and not reaching out to touch him. Especially now, when his best friend looked so lost and vulnerable. *Be strong, Raven.*

He could smell Aik's desire, his need. And his touch lingered in Raven's mind. *That kiss ...* "I know what you mean. I miss normal." In his element, roaming the city and looking for easy scores.

Nothing was normal anymore, and his defenses were starting to crumble. Raven needed Aik — needed an anchor. Aside from Spin, Aik was the one constant in his life, the only one he could truly count on.

But he'd rejected Aik so many times before. *I'm a thief, and Aik's a guard. Does that even still matter?*

Aik looked around the small guest room. "Just like mine. Nowhere to sit."

Raven scooted over on the bed. "Sit next to me."

Aik hesitated. "You sure?"

"I don't bite." *Unless you want me to.*

Where in Heaven's Reach did that come from? Though they were, technically, in Heaven's Reach now ... *Think about urses. Or hencha berry foldovers. Anything but Aik and Aik's touch ...*

Aik sank down on the bed next to him, oblivious to Raven's confusion. "That was a heck of a day."

"It's been a whole godscursed week."

Aik snorted. He sank back against the wall, his eyes closed.

Aik was beautiful, his muscled arms relaxed, eyes closed on his drawn face, his slightly arched eyebrows — a tired angel. Raven's gaze fell to his bare right arm — maybe the gauntlet was weighing him down. "You can't make it appear when you want?"

Aik's eyes popped open. "What?"

"The — thing on your arm. The gauntlet." He reached out, then paused, his hand hovering mere centimeters above Aik's skin.

"Oh. No. It just seems to show up when I need it. Or when it wants to. But I can still feel it, even now." His eyes met Raven's.

"May I?"

"Sure?" Aik held out his arm.

Raven touched Aik's forearm, sending an involuntary shiver up his own arm. The skin was warm, covered with fine blond hair, but there was something else. Something cold, like a fog wrapped around it — Raven could feel it with his heightened senses, but there was nothing there.

Goose bumps rose on Aik's skin at his touch.

Raven frowned. "There's something ... but I can't ..." He could smell Aik's unique scent — the tang of leather and the musk of his sweat sharp in his nose. And something else — a deep hunger.

Aik shivered under his touch.

Raven's pulse quickened. He took a deep breath to calm himself. He wanted to protect Aik the way the guard had always protected him. To hold him tight and tell him everything was going to be fine, but he didn't know how. *I can't. I shouldn't.*

"Me neither. Not when I touch the skin. But I can still sense it wrapped around my arm tightly, like a cast. ... It's hard to explain. And sometimes I feel these compulsions ..."

*Both of us are broken.* Raven pulled his hand back, biting his lip to distract himself from Aik's tantalizing closeness. "I wish I hadn't taken that package. It felt the same way. I knew I shouldn't, but I couldn't help it. I needed to take it." The words cut him as they tumbled out of his mouth. "And look at me, now. I'm a freak." Raven held up his arms. Scales covered them from shoulder to wrist, and the change was creeping up the back of his hand too.

"With your gloves on, no one would even know." This time Aik reached out to touch his arm.

"Don't." Raven pulled away as if he'd been burned. "Look." He pulled off his boots, exposing the roughness underneath. He rubbed his left shin and the skin flaked off, revealing more scales.

Aik's eyes strayed from Raven's shins up his leg to his crotch.

"Still very much the same there, thank you." Raven flushed, his face hot again.

Aik snorted again, then covered his mouth, looking at the door.

Everything was quiet, and no one burst in on them, demanding to know what they were up to.

Raven reached out to Aik, turning his head to meet his gaze. "You're as scared of Kek as I am, aren't you?"

"Maybe." Aik blushed, managing a tiny grin. "And Silya."

"Her too." The newly minted Queen scared the *hencha* berries out of him.

Aik took his hand. "That's what you're most worried about, isn't it? What you're turning into?" Aik's eyes bored into his, and there wasn't the slightest bit of pity there.

Raven bit his lip. "Yeah. Maybe it's stupid. But it scares me, Aik. What am I becoming? What's going to happen to me next?" For the first time in his life, he truly regretted something he'd done.

Well, maybe the second. But he must not have screwed that one up too badly — Aik was still here.

As if Aik could read his thoughts, he squeezed Raven's hand and his gaze bored into him. "I'm not going anywhere. We'll get through this together." He glanced at the carry sack. "As long as you don't run off on me."

Raven trembled, overwhelmed. The firm foundations of his world had literally begun shaking beneath them. He was out of his depth, a city thief in the country. And here Aik was, offering a lifeline.

Aik pulled him close, his arms wrapped around Raven's shoulders.

His embrace was warm, safe, real. It felt so good just to be held. Raven closed his eyes, breathing in Aik's scent. *I can't.*

"I will always be here for you, no matter what." Aik's breath was hot in his ear.

Raven stiffened. *I've heard that before.*

Aik let him go, frowning. "What did I say?"

*He's so close.* "Mar'Orn said that to me. Just before she died." *I shouldn't.*

"Your mother?"

Raven put a scaled hand on Aik's cheek, the cool skin of his palm touching the warmth of Aik's. "Yes. But I believe you when *you* say it."

Aik grinned, and then leaned forward and kissed him.

Raven blinked as their lips met, but his body responded. A flush of warmth flooded him, and his heart threatened to burst out of his chest as Little Raven sprang to life in his pants. But his mind was not on board.

*This will never work.* He pushed Aik away again.

Not because he was a thief and Aik was a guard. That seemed irrelevant now, a difference without a distinction. He saw it for what it was, an excuse to keep his best friend from getting too close. He had a better reason. *Because I'm not human anymore.*

Aik read it in his eyes. *Oh, those eyes.*

"Rave, I don't care. About the thief thing. Or about this." He ran his fingers up the scales on Raven's arm, and Raven shivered. "You're beautiful to me, no matter what. You always have been."

He lifted Raven's scaled hand to his lips and kissed it tenderly. "I just want to be with you."

Aik was as scared and lost as he was. Raven could smell his fear, burnt and brittle like smoke after a fire. They had that in common — they needed one another — and it was more than everything else that stood between them.

*Why didn't I see that before?* His fear melted away, and he pulled Aik to him, their lips meeting again, sending a tingling buzz through his entire body like an electric shock. He tasted his friend's surprise as Aik's shoulders stiffened and then just as quickly relaxed.

He gave in. Warmth filled him again, but this time it was different, more than just lust.

Aik pulled off his shirt, and they fell onto the bed together. Aik's body was on fire, his face a furnace against Raven's neck, and Raven responded to him like a starving man at a banquet. Aik kissed his skin again, working his way up Raven's arm to his neck.

Raven shuddered under his tender touch.

The world melted away as they became lost in their hunger for one another. Raven forgot about the egg, about his scales, about the whole of the horrid last three days.

His body practically hummed with pent-up energy. He and Aik moved together, rising above it all, shaking the little bed. Aik was his entire world. *Why did I ever resist you?*

It was so much better than the last time. They were finally ready. He was ready, and his walls came down as he opened everything he was to Aik.

Time seemed to lose all meaning as they rose and fell together. Aik's lips set his skin on fire, his touch making Raven's body tingle. He pulled Aik close, embracing him as they connected, body to body and soul to soul.

They flew through the night, and it was better than Raven could have hoped. He wanted it to last forever, this time out of time, this glorious ascension.

They peaked together, collapsing on the bed in a heap of arms and legs and slick skin.

"Holy ... green hell ... that was good." Aik's skin was warm and slick against his, and he felt closer to him than he'd felt to anyone in a long time. *Maybe ever.*

He glanced at the door. No one had come to check on them — the place must have thick walls. He reached up to touch Aik's cheek, frowning when he saw the scales on his arm.

Aik lifted himself up, looking down at him, sweat dripping from his forehead. There was no judgment on his face, only dopey love. He was the most beautiful thing Raven had ever seen. "You still scared?"

"A little." Raven reached up to touch his cheek. "But as long as I have you, I can deal with it."

Aik leaned down to kiss him again, and his body responded like he'd been waiting for this his whole life. *Well, maybe I have.*

It changed nothing, really. The world was still upside down.

But for one glorious moment, he could forget all of that. He was relaxed, safe and at peace, and finally where he belonged.

He would worry about the rest of it tomorrow.

# 20

# HERO

AIK SAT UP IN BED, his back against the sandstone wall, and watched over Raven. His lover was fast asleep in the small bed next to him, peaceful and innocent as a puppy.

He'd finally gotten what he'd wanted, all these long years. Raven had lowered his walls, letting Aik in both physically and emotionally. It had been every bit as good as he'd hoped. Their connection was electric, and his body still hummed with the carnal music they'd made together. He wanted to do it again, but Raven was exhausted.

When he asked Raven to move in with him again, he would say yes. He was sure of it.

Still, in the golden afterglow, he couldn't sleep. Doubts assailed him in the quiet hours of the night.

He could still feel the tightness of the invisible gauntlet on his arm. Where had it come from? What did it want from him? He had begun to think of it as a living thing, the way it ordered him about.

What might it make him do next? What if it wanted him to hurt Raven?

*Like he hurt you so many times?*

249

Aik grimaced. Another thought that was not his own. That scared the *hencha* berries out of him, and he had no idea what to do about it. *El'Oss, help me.* Maybe the elder god could do something about his wretched state. *I can't even get the damned thing off.* Maybe Raven was right. He needed to tell Silya.

And what would Raven become? Aik hadn't lied when he said it didn't matter to him. But what if Raven became something ... inhuman? How would that work? *This is my boyfriend-slash-verent Raven.* That would go over well.

Aik sighed softly. He ought to slip back to his own room, to keep this new thing secret between them for a while, but he was reluctant to leave. Raven looked so peaceful while he slept, and the scales on his arms didn't change that. In fact, they made him more beautiful. Vulnerable. In need of Aik's protection. *I love you, Rave.*

They were caught up together in a whirlwind that neither of them understood, but at least they had each other. As long as he sat here, he could pretend that everything was going to be fine. That they'd wake up the next day and face the world together. *We can figure all of this out, with the gods' help or not.*

The lantern on the nightstand flickered. It was almost out of oil. Aik reached over to turn it off —

The wooden shutters shattered, spraying shards of wood across the room to clatter against the far wall.

*What in Heaven's Reach?* "Raven!" Aik leapt out of bed to pull on his small clothes. No time for anything else. His heart raced.

Something stuck a snout into the room, a patch of darkness limned by moonlight. A large glowing blue eye peered sideways at him from above a thick white snout.

Raven was out of bed, dragging Aik frantically toward the door, naked as the day he was born. The thing turned toward them and sniffed at Aik, then trilled in what sounded like alarm and pulled its head out of the window.

Aik dashed forward to grab their clothes. They tumbled out of the room into the open hallway, and he slammed the door behind them, wishing there was a way to bar it. Such a flimsy thing wouldn't keep that beast trapped inside for long, if it managed to squeeze through the window. "You all right?" He threw Raven's clothes to him and dressed quickly, looking for his short sword. *Must have left it inside.* Not that it would do much good against a beast of that size, but he felt naked without it. The creature must be as big as a carriage.

"Scared halfway out of my shell, but yeah." Raven pulled on his small clothes and pants, staring wide-eyed at the door. "What the fark was that?"

"Hell if I know."

"What's going on?" Silya slipped out of her room, already dressed, looking at Raven and then at Aik, something between a scowl and a knowing grin crossing her face. "It was only a matter of time."

*So much for keeping things secret.* "Not now, Sil. Something attacked us. Something big."

Silya reached for Raven's door.

Raven tried to stop her. "Don't —"

It swung open, revealing the empty room and shattered shutters. "What in the holy green hell did that?"

A deep, thundering sound filled the Manor House, followed by another and another, as if the gods themselves were beating against the walls.

Raven put his hands against his ears. "Faaaark me."

Aik cocked his ear. "It's coming from the entry hall. Come on!" He raced down the hallway toward the sound, the others in tow, as one by one the doors in the guest wing popped open.

When they arrived, Tri'Aya was striding across the entry hall flanked by her two guards. The heavily muscled women had spears and shields, and Tri'Aya a look on her face that could slay a monster. And might have to. She was fully dressed, looking as if she'd been awake for an hour.

*How does she do that?* He glanced back at Silya. *Like mother, like daughter.*

Ser Kek arrived right behind her, also in his full guard uniform.

Tri'Aya was staring at the large wooden entry doors. They shook, and the sound reverberated throughout the manor. "Would someone tell me what in the holy Heartland is going on?"

Raven still had his ears covered, but he was sniffing the air. "You can't smell that?"

"Smell what?" Aik stared at the doors. How in Heaven's Reach could he describe what had happened? "Sorry, mim. There's a creature. A big one. It broke the shutters in Raven's room."

"Just one?" A smile quirked the edge of her lips.

Aik stared at her. "I don't know, mim."

"It was a joke, Erio." She frowned, but the battering at the front doors seemed enough to dispel her doubts. "Describe it."

"Hard to say, mim. It was dark. But its head was enormous, and it had a blue eye."

The doors thundered again.

Tri'Aya turned to the women. "'Asa, 'Ena, positions."

With quiet efficiency, they took their places ten paces from the door behind the protection of two of the sandstone columns, crouching with spears ready.

Tri'Aya opened a cabinet to the right of the dining room doors that he hadn't known was there — it blended in so well with the walls.

Raven's eyes went wide at the sight — Aik guessed he'd had missed it too.

"You good with a sword, 'Erio?"

Aik was dumbfounded, catching the broadsword she threw him by the hilt. "Yes, mim. Two years of training with the Guard." It fit his palm, nicely made and well-balanced. He took a few practice lunges with it. "Beautiful blade." It had a bright, clean sheen, and was perfectly weighted. *Looks like my mother's work.* He wanted to ask, but it wasn't exactly a good time for conversation.

The heavy bar that held the doors closed was buckling further with each blow.

"I'll take one of those too." Silya and her mother locked eyes, and a spark of respect passed between them.

Tri'Aya raised an eyebrow. "You know how to fight with a sword?"

Silya snorted. "What did you think we did all day in the Temple? Needlepoint?"

Tri'Aya ignored the sarcasm. "Good for you, then."

Aik stayed well clear of them, taking up a position behind Tri'Aya's guards.

"It's coming through!" Tri'Aya had pulled a bow and arrow from the weapons closet. She sank to one knee with the grace of a twenty-year-old and nocked the arrow.

Raven seemed to have given up covering his ears. A knife appeared in his hand — the one Aik had given him. *Where the hell does he keep it?* The sight of it warmed his heart, but it would be like a pinprick to the giant creature. "Raven, stay behind me. I'll protect you." Aik expected Raven to refuse, to protest.

"I will. Be careful, Aik."

That surprised him, but he had no time to think about the sudden shift. Another fierce pounding and the doors burst inward to slam against the walls on either side, blowing out half the lanterns in the entry hall and leaving them in gloom.

A creature entered from the darkness, something out of nightmares — huge, scaled, all coiled, bunched muscles. It was as long as three men were tall, but much wider. In the half-light, it was hard to make out the details. Aik's heart raced, and he took a few deep breaths to calm himself, drawing on his training. *Fear is the death bringer.*

There was absolute silence for a second as the creature turned to stare at each of them, huffing the air and extending its wings. Then it lifted its head and emitted a keening sound, which was repeated by something outside.

The beast edged aside, its heavy feet making the floor shake. Another one slipped through the doorway, slightly smaller than the first, ducking with an almost feline grace to avoid the top of the door frame.

Aik recognized them from the bestiary. *Verent.*

His blood ran cold. He glanced back at Raven. His friend — lover? — was shaking, his scaled arms matched to the skin of the new arrivals.

The second *verent* raised its head and gave out an answering call, and all hell broke loose.

Em'Asa and Mes'Ena threw their spears as one at the new beast. They clattered off its hide, rattling across the floor.

The creature howled, its eyes turning golden, and threw itself at Mes, moving with astonishing speed for a beast so large.

She danced out of its way as Tri'Aya loosed three arrows at it in quick succession, but two bounced off the beast's hide, and one off the creature's eye as an armored eyelid slid down over the golden orb. She cursed and threw down the bow to draw a wicked-looking sword only slightly smaller than Aik's.

The beast barreled past Aik to slam into the back wall, staggering but then spinning around as neatly as a dancer.

The two guards unsheathed their own swords and ran at the *verent* with harsh battle cries in some language that didn't sound like English.

The dazed *verent* ambled forward, knocking one of them — Mes'Ena? — out of its way like a boulder smacking an *inthym*, its eyes fixed on Raven.

Ser Kek circled around behind it, raising his sword. A high-pitched trill from the other made him drop the weapon to cover his ears.

Silya jumped in front of the second *verent*, staring it down with her sword in hand. Then she slipped past it with the grace of an *eircat* and plunged her sword into its hide from behind, cutting off its ear-piercing shriek as it tried to swing around to reach her in the confined space. It slammed into one of the great sandstone columns that held up the roof, and the entire room shook, raining bits of rock and sand down on them.

*Tri'Aya's gonna need a new decorator when this is over. If we survive.*

"Rave, get behind me!" Aik longed to join the fight, but he had to protect Raven.

There was something unnerving about the approaching *verent's* single-minded gaze, locked on Raven. They were connected, the arrival of the beasts and the creature from the egg. Aik could feel it.

*They want him.* It hit him with all the subtlety of a sledgehammer. Were these the angry parents, come to rip the little thing out of him? "Raven, get back ... into the dining hall. Quickly."

He glanced back again. Behind him, Raven was frozen in place, staring at the oncoming verent, his eyes as wide as fists.

Without thinking, Aik jumped in front of the beast, holding up his sword. "Stay back!" His gauntlet shimmered into existence, shining a red glow around him that lit up the hall. "You can't have him — you'll have to take me first!"

The *verent* skidded to a halt. It would have been comical under different circumstances, but Aik's heart was in his throat. Its golden eyes turned blue again, its mouth unhinging to show a wide set of sharp teeth. It glared at him but came no closer.

Aik looked at it in wonder. *It's afraid of me. Or of the gauntlet, more likely.*

Everyone had turned to stare at him, and the hall was once again plunged into silence.

"What in Jorja's name?" Silya's mouth was open, her brow knitted.

Aik held out an open palm, gesturing for the others to stay away. "I can explain later." Not that he had the slightest idea what to tell her. *I have this alien thing on my arm and the big bad beastie is afraid of it?* He took a step forward, testing his theory.

The *verent* retreated, its eyes focused on the menacing red glow of his gauntlet. Another step, and it lowered its head almost to the ground, squinting as if the light from the gauntlet hurt its eyes.

It was afraid of him.

His friends all needed him. For the first time, he was something more than stupid, loyal Aik. And it felt good. Good to have power. Good to be needed. He glanced back at Raven, who had stopped shaking but seemed rooted in place. *I can save you, Rave.*

Aik returned his attention to the *verent*, forcing it back step by step, halfway to the open doors. Ser Kek stepped out of its way, his eyes locked on Aik and the gauntlet, his mouth hanging open.

A cool breeze was blowing in from the Heartland below, bringing the wet smell of the river, along with the strange, almost metallic smell of the beasts.

Everyone's eyes were on him as he set down his sword and picked up one of the spears. He was strong. With the gauntlet's help, he could drive it into one of the thing's eyes, right into its brain ... if its brain was in its head.

*You could kill it.*

The thought sent a thrill through him, a buzzing of pleasure from his arm up into his spine and along his tall frame like an electric current.

*You could be the hero.*

The rest of the world faded away. There was only himself and the *verent*, crouched before him in unexpected subservience, waiting for him to act.

A slow smile spread across his face. His blood churned hot through his veins, filling him with a lust only exceeded by the passion he'd felt for Raven just hours before. He cocked his arm, ready to strike a blow for Raven, for his friends.

*You're a hero, Aik.*

For Raven. For himself —

A hand touched his shoulder. "Aik, don't."

He blinked, confused. "What? I can do this. I can save you." He turned to find Raven looking up at him.

*You could be the hero.*

The thought sounded tinny in his mind this time. False. Aik frowned. *It's not mine.*

Raven nodded. "You could. But you don't have to, Aik, they're here for me."

"I know. That's why I need to stop them." He glanced over his shoulder, but everyone was still frozen in a strange detente. "They can't have you. Not after tonight ... they want to kill you, Rave, for taking the egg —"

"No." Raven was shaking again, but he held his ground. "You don't understand. I can hear them. In my head. They came for me. They don't want to hurt you."

"What?" *Raven was hearing voices too?* "It's a trick. Don't listen to them."

*Be the hero, Aik.*

"Oh shut up." He was done listening to the voice in his head.

Raven stared at him.

Aik scowled. "Not you. You're not the only one hearing voices."

A complex mix of emotions ran across Raven's face — confusion, fear, and regret. "You don't love me, Aik. And ... I don't love you. This thing between us ... it would never work."

Aik's heart broke. "What are you talking about? I do love you, Rave, I always have. Please don't do this." *I can't lose you now.*

"It's better this way." His face hardened somehow, all trace of emotion draining away.

"What's the fool doing? He has the spear. Kill it already." That was Em'Asa, or Mes'Ena.

Aik couldn't keep them straight. "Raven says they don't mean us harm." His eyes pleaded with Raven to stay.

Raven shook his head. "They need me."

The buzz in Aik's head faded, and he dropped the spear with a clatter. "What do you mean? They can't come in here and take you." *We only just —*

"Let me go, Aik."

"No. I'll kill them. I can do it. With the gauntlet —"

Raven shook his head. "They'll kill you." He looked at the others. "Some of you, maybe all of you. They've been holding back."

*That was holding back?* "I can't let them take you. Not now." Aik hated the pleading tone in his own voice.

"They won't hurt me." He reached up to touch Aik's cheek, a flash of the Raven he'd seen just a few moments before crossing his face. "Let me go. They won't hurt you."

Aik's arm dropped, and the gauntlet faded from view, taking its red light with it, along with the blood lust that had been coursing through him, leaving him empty and brittle.

The *verent* raised its head but stayed where it was, staring at Raven.

"Why? Rave, you don't have to help them. You have no morals, remember? You're a thief."

Raven laughed harshly. "All the more reason for me to go."

Aik closed his eyes, remembering how scared and vulnerable Raven had been in his arms, just hours before, when they'd been alone together. He reached out and pulled Raven to him. He kissed Raven hard, not caring who saw.

Raven returned the kiss, and Aik wanted to laugh and cry all at once.

Then Raven pushed him away. "Enough." He stepped back, holding Aik's hands, eyes still fixed on him. "I have to go.." His mouth dropped open as blue light lit his features. "Look!"

Aik turned toward the broken doors behind him.

A line of blue wisps filed into the entry hall like a procession, straight as an *orinth's* flight toward Raven. Aik stared at the display in wonder as the whole room turned blue. The wisps were delicate as snowflakes — they twirled around Raven like little fairies.

"They're ... beautiful." Raven reached out and pulled Aik inside the circle, and his skin shivered with goose bumps as one of the wisps brushed his arm. Their glow set the two of them apart, casting them in their own little blue world, but it had to end.

Aik stared at Raven, trying to come up with something, anything to make him stay. But from the faraway look on his face, Raven was already gone.

Then the wisps fled, and a light went out in Aik's heart.

Raven slipped past Aik to go to the *verent*, putting his hand out to touch its white muzzle in wonder.

It warbled at him — a strange sound from such an enormous beast — and gestured over its hunched shoulder with its head.

Raven clambered onto its back, settling into the space behind its shoulders. His eyes met Aik's, and then he closed them, grimacing.

"What's happening?" Silya stared at Raven and the *verent*. "What's he doing?"

"They're taking him ... home." His voice broke on the last part. "It's all right." It wasn't. It really wasn't. But he had to try to make it be, for Raven's sake. *Why don't you love me?*

The *verent* emitted one last hiss in Aik's direction, then shifted its bulk around between the columns, turning itself toward the exit. It flattened itself to get under the doorway without knocking Raven off.

The other one followed it out, leaving Aik's companions in the entry hall in stunned silence.

Aik watched them go. Why did Raven trust them? How were they able to speak to him in his head? And why had Raven gone cold on him again? He'd waited so long for Raven to let him in, to let down his walls. "Let me come with you!" He ran after them, out the open doorway. "I can protect you!"

He was too late. The *verent* carrying Raven was loping toward the ledge that overlooked the valley, spreading its wings and leaping off to take flight.

The other one followed, glancing back at him once more with its blue eyes. *Deathbringer.*

Then they slipped into darkness.

Aik shook his head. Had he imagined that last, strange thought?

The *verent* winged their way into the dark night sky, passing across Tarsis's golden face.

Only slowly did Aik become aware that the others had surrounded him. He began to shake — Raven was gone.

"What in the green holy hell was that, Aik?" Silya looked as angry as he'd ever seen her. "And why did you let them go?"

"Raven said they spoke to him." His voice cracked, and he struggled to contain his emotions. *A good guard would never let himself get rattled like this.*

*You failed.*

"We heard that, you thick-headed son of an *aur*. What was that on your hand?"

Her mother joined her. "I think your friend here has some explaining to do."

"Enough." He turned on them, sick of being told what an idiot he was. Heartsick at losing Raven. Fear of what the gauntlet was doing to him gnawed at him too. "Don't treat me like a child. Raven made his own decision. I tried to stop him, to argue him out of it." He looked around at the rest of them. "He saved all of our lives." *I could have saved his.* The thought was bitter as ash on his tongue. *He didn't want me to.*

Silya reached out to touch his shoulder. "Sorry, Aik. I didn't mean —"

"I know."

Tri'Aya was staring at him, arms crossed over her chest. "Let's go inside. It's chilly out here, though the entry hall probably isn't much better. Mes, Em, see what you can do about getting what's left of those doors closed."

The two women nodded smartly and disappeared inside.

Aik stayed where he was for a moment longer, staring up at the empty sky. *Why don't you love me too?*

# 21

# BURNING

S ILYA HUGGED HERSELF tightly, shivering. The den was cold, the fireplace in one corner full of ashes.

She'd never seen wisps act like that before, almost as if they'd been summoned. But why, and by whom? Usually they just danced by on the night air, and she'd never paid them much mind.

The *verent* had disappeared into the darkness above Heaven's Reach with Raven, their slender white forms vanishing into the fog that hung above the river, and the ethereal wisps were gone too.

Just like that, Raven was gone. He'd given himself up to protect the rest of them. From himself? From the *verent*? Both? It wasn't clear.

She'd never suspected he had it in him.

Her breathing slowed, and her anger at herself abated. She'd reached for the fire inside to hurt the *verent*, or at the very least, to scare it. And *nothing had come.*

Poor Aik looked numb.

Tri'Aya leaned back against the heavy wooden desk and stared at him, her face a neutral mask, but her hands held the edge of the desk in a death grip. "Now, tell us everything you know about what just happened, and about that strange gauntlet you were wearing." She glanced at his now-bare arm. "Your friend's life might depend on it."

Silya was furious with Aik too, angry that he was keeping secrets from her again. "She's right. You need to tell us everything." It felt unnatural to take Tri'Aya's side.

Her mother cast an appraising look in her direction.

Silya shook her head. How had it come to this? "Yes, Mother, I agree with you. *This one time.* Don't get used to it — the green holy hell hasn't frozen over, though it feels like it in this room." She rubbed her upper arms vigorously.

"Sorry I didn't have time to light a fire." Tri'Aya tugged on her braid, clearly as discomfited with the whole thing as she was. She turned her attention back to Aik. "So talk, boy. What happened?" She took his right hand and prodded at it. "What was that thing on your arm?"

Aik looked from one to the other, his face white. "It's a gauntlet. I found it in Raven's things the other day when you went out to tour the quake damage."

Silya felt a twinge of compassion for him. He'd lost Raven too, and from the looks of things, they had just shared a bed.

"That's not all ... we found some strange bones in a chest in ... your storage room, the one at the back of that long hallway." At Tri'Aya's scowl, he hurried on. "I went looking for Raven after dinner and found him there. I don't think he meant anything by it ..."

Silya raised an eyebrow. *This is new.*

Tri'Aya glared at him. "How did you get in?"

"There was a hidden switch. Raven has a nose for that kind of thing." Aik looked away. "Had a nose."

"He's not dead, Aik. If they wanted to kill him, they would have done it here." Silya should have expected Raven to case the Manor House. Once a thief ... "What did he take?"

"Nothing. I swear!"

"What are these bones he's talking about?"

Tri'Aya shrugged. "I don't really know. Something I traded for a long time ago. They were ... curious." She was still giving Aik the evil eye. "I'm more concerned about guests wandering the halls late at night, looking for things to steal."

"Let it go. They didn't take anything." Silya knelt next to Aik, touching his bare right arm. "I don't remember seeing a gauntlet in Raven's lair."

Aik closed his eyes. "There wasn't one. Or ... it was in pieces. The artifacts —"

"Ah." Silya was dead tired, and nothing was making sense. *Verent*? Strange artifacts that became gauntlets? The world had truly gone mad. How in Jas's name had she been put in charge? And why had the *hencha* deserted her when she needed them most? *I miss being an initiate.*

"Where did you leave these ... artifacts?" Tri'Aya stared at him. "I looked around the hall. I didn't see them."

"They're still here." Aik held up his hand. "I can feel the gauntlet around my arm. All the time."

Tri'Aya eyes narrowed. "If you're lying to me, 'Erio ..."

Silya intervened. "He's a good man, Mother. Let him be." She rubbed her temples. *Jas give me patience.* "Can you bring it back?"

"It comes and goes when it wants." He opened his eyes, his gaze boring into her. "How is this helping to get Raven back?"

Silya had been wondering the same thing. "It's late, and we're all exhausted. Why don't we reconvene in the morning?"

"We have to go after him. Maybe they're not going to kill him, but who knows what they might do." Aik's gaze pleaded with her.

Silya put a hand on his shoulder. "We have no idea where they took him, and we're all dead tired. You'll be no good to him if you fall over on your own sword." Her eyes lit on the weapon Tri'Aya had given him, slipped through the belt at his waist.

He glanced at Tri'Aya.

"Keep it. I have others. We'll get you a proper scabbard for it."

"Thanks."

"You should try to get some sleep." Silya knew how close he'd been to Raven. Fear mingled with sadness in her heart.

Tri'Aya touched his shoulder. "Silya's right. You'll think more clearly in the morning."

Silya shot her mother a surprised look. *Twice in one night.*

Aik looked haunted, hollowed out like an abandoned *orinth* nest. "Fine." He got up, unsteady on his feet, grabbing the chair arm for support.

It killed her to see him like this. She was hurting too, but she tried to hide it — Aik was in enough pain already. Would they ever see Raven again? *Why do I care?* She hugged him. "He'll get through this. Raven's a scrappy little fighter. He can take care of himself." *Whatever this is.*

"I know. It's just —"

"I know." She squeezed him tight. *Did you ever feel this way about me?* It didn't matter. Not now. "We'll figure things out in the morning." She said it with more confidence than she felt. Things were rapidly spinning out of control, and she was at a loss about what to do next. Maybe she needed sleep as much as he did. "Off to bed with you."

Aik kissed her on the cheek. "Thank you, Sil." His whisper sent a shudder through her, a memory of things that used to be. Then he was gone, the door closed behind him.

She hoped he'd be able to get some sleep.

Tri'Aya was staring at her. "Why didn't you use your fire against the *verent*?"

Silya winced. "I don't know." Her mother had a way of homing in on her self-doubt, pushing all her buttons. Apparently even the aftermath of a pitched battle was no exception. *So much for our uneasy truce.* "It just wouldn't come."

"Maybe you weren't meant to hurt them." Tri'Aya ushered her out of the den, turning off the gas lamp on her desk. "After all, they didn't actually hurt any of us."

"It knocked Mes'Ena and Kek on their asses." She followed Tri'Aya back to the entry hall.

"Yes, but only when provoked, and look — they're both fine." They reached the entry hall, which still held the strange metallic smell of the beasts.

The house guards were cleaning up the mess along with a few others from the 'Aya household. They'd gotten the doors closed again, though the long wooden bolt was beyond salvage. Ser Kek was putting away the weapons. "Maybe the *hencha* don't want you to hurt the *verent*."

Silya stared at Tri'Aya. It galled her to admit it, but put that way, it made a lot more sense. The *hencha* weren't shunning her. She just didn't understand their purpose for her yet.

If Tri'Aya was right, it suggested that she was connected to much more than just the *hencha*. The *verent* were part of it, and maybe the *inthym*. Who knew what else?

The world was a vast and strange place.

"Go get some sleep. We can talk more in the morning, figure out what to do next." Her mother kissed her on the cheek, just like she'd done with Aik.

Silya tensed, waiting for the inevitable catty retort.

"What?" Tri'Aya let go and looked at her, one eyebrow raised. "Did I say something wrong again?"

"Go ahead. You know you want to. Tell me I was too slow today, or that I wasn't prepared, or as stupid as a gully bird." Silya crossed her arms. "Whatever you want to say, get it out. I can handle it."

A ghost of a smile crossed Tri'Aya's lips. "I'm proud of you." She turned to speak with Mes'Ena about the cleanup.

Silya stared at her. All these years, she'd been waiting for those words, and now here she was, poleaxed by them. Her eyes narrowed. *Maybe that's your intent?*

Or maybe she was reading too much into things. Better to just accept that sometimes wonders really did happen. "Night, Mother." Silya turned to go back to her room, hiding the wetness at the corners of her eyes. She rubbed them dry, feigning exhaustion. *I really am tired.*

Ser Kek met her at the edge of the entry hall. The guard looked no worse for wear, despite having been slammed against the wall by one of the *verent*. The man must be made of steel. "Your Highness —"

Silya put up her hand. "Silya, please. Or Sil'Aya if you want to be formal."

He looked uncomfortable. "Mim Aya." His right hand squeezed the hilt of his sword.

Silya rolled her eyes. It would do. "Yes?" She was exhausted and just wanted to get some sleep.

He took an uncertain step forward. "I just ... wanted to make sure you were all right?"

She turned, surprised. She could smell his musky scent. No one else had bothered to ask. She bit her lip. "I think so. I wasn't hurt."

He met her eyes. Unexpected compassion shone in his gaze. "Not all pain is physical."

"I'm fine, sergeant." It came out harsher than she intended.

He blinked and took a step back. "Glad to hear it, mim." He turned to go.

"Sergeant?"

He hesitated, his back still to her. "Yes, mim?"

"Thank you for asking."

"You're welcome, mim." He left her then, his shoulders proud and taut. Was there a hint of warmth in his voice that hadn't been there before? Like the first breeze of spring. *Strangeness upon strangeness.*

Back in her room, she stripped off her clothes, laying them over the old *flopwood* chair in the corner. She'd ask one of her mother's servants where she could wash them in the morning. It would be easy to fall into the trap offered by her new position, to let others do everything for her. If her mother had taught her one thing, it was that she needed to be self-sufficient. Losing Aik had only reinforced that lesson.

She was strangely thankful that her quarters had no window, backing up against the safety of the mountain. Not that she expected the *verent* to return.

She stared at the blue robe on the bed. It was someone else's clothing. Surely these last few days had been some kind of wild *henchwine*-induced dream.

Silya yawned. It had been a long day and an even longer night.

She folded the robe and placed it neatly on her nightstand.

She washed up in the stone basin, splashing cold water on her face, and then stared at herself in the mirror. Exhaustion lined her features, along with bags under her eyes that hadn't been there a week before. *Why did I ever want this job?*

In her mind, she kept replaying those last moments when Raven had climbed onto the *verent*, as if he'd been riding one all his life. When he'd pleaded with Aik to let him go. *Where are you now? Are you scared? Lonely?* What were they going to do to him? And would she even recognize him if she saw him again?

Her feelings about Raven were ... complicated.

She dried her face with a fluffy towel and shoved her worries aside for the morning. *Not gonna fix everything tonight.* She climbed into bed, pulling the soft sheets up over her shoulders, and closed her eyes.

The heavy silence of the room soon lulled her into sleep.

Silya stood on top of the pile of broken stones that had once been the lighthouse, staring across the glittering waters of the Elsp at the Heartland beyond. *They're coming.*

She directed the *hencha* to fight, attacking the invaders as they crossed her fields, directing her fire through them at the advancing horde.

It was like fighting a whirlwind.

Swarms of red fireflies devoured everything in their path, glowing pinpricks of light that brought their own fire.

Above, the twin moons glared down at her like evil eyes through a break in the sulfurous clouds. She turned to her aide. "Is everyone safe?"

Sister Dor winced. "I hope so, mim. We've moved them into the caverns. But there's not enough food to last for more than a few days. A week at most —"

"If this isn't over by then, it won't matter."

"You did everything you could." Dor looked distraught, as though she'd been crying. Small wonder.

"I should have done more, seen this coming sooner." Through the wisps, she destroyed an *ayvin*-ridden *aur*, her heart breaking as the magnificent beast froze and crashed into a flop tree. The whole of the Heartland seemed to be on fire. She hoped most of the villagers had been evacuated to the relative safety of the mountain caverns.

Dor put a hand on her shoulder. "You need to come with me, Silya. Now."

"I need to defend the Temple."

"Nothing can save it. We have to place our hope in the *verent.*"

That almost made her laugh, despite the bleak circumstances. *Raven the thief will save us all?* It was a discomforting thought.

Dor slapped her, breaking her focus. "You can't help any of us if you're dead."

Silya stared at her. "Did you just —"

"Yes. Don't make me do it again." Dor didn't look sorry.

Silya closed her eyes. Her aide was right, but it was a bitter pill to swallow. *Retreat.* Enough of the *hencha* had died today. "Where's Kerrick?"

"Waiting for you in the tunnels." She cast a worried look out at the flames across the river that were now encroaching on the edges of Landfield.

It had been a hard decision, destroying the only remaining bridge to the mainland. But it bought them time. The invaders didn't like water.

Numb to the losses she'd already taken, she let Dor lead her out of the lighthouse and back toward the Temple. It felt like a defeat.

It was a necessary one. The longer she could keep the invaders at bay, the better.

She took one last look at the orange sky before the stone door slid closed, sealing her into what might become a tomb for them all.

Silya sat up, choking on air. *What in the seven hells?*

In her mind's eye, she could still see the Heartland burning.

*It's just a dream. It has to be.* But it felt so real.

She closed her eyes and took a deep breath, letting it flow out of her like water. Queen Jas had vivid dreams too. Dor had mentioned them. The archivist could tell her more in the morning.

*Something terrible is coming.* Silya could feel it in her gut, but she needed more. One thing she was certain of — when her time came, she wouldn't cower in a cave while her world burned.

Part of her itched to go after Raven, to rescue him from the *verent*. Not that he seemed to need rescuing — he'd gone with them willingly, after all.

And part of her felt compelled to return to Gullton. She had a responsibility to the people of her city now. How could she abandon them in their hour of need? Especially if what she had just seen was true? *Daya, what would you do?* She missed her friend and mentor keenly.

*One thing at a time.* It had been one of Daya's favorite sayings, a reminder to the always-in-a-hurry initiate to slow down and focus on what was most important.

*Thank you, Daya.* She had to return home and do what she could to put things in order for whatever was coming.

Silya ran her hand through her hair and rubbed the knotted muscles at the back of her neck. *Right now, I need sleep most of all, if I'm going to be clearheaded in the morning.*

She lay on her side facing the wall, her back to the world, and pulled the sheets up over herself again. She closed her eyes and could see the Heartland burning.

Eventually she dropped off into a troubled sleep.

# 22

# THE DRAGON EATER

SPIN FLIPPED FROM DREAM to dream to dream, restless. Something was wrong. Even in his fugue state, he could feel Raven when his friend was nearby. Even when he'd been left alone in Raven's lair — a rarity, but it happened — he'd always known Raven was coming back.

Now, though, Raven — his best friend — was gone. And Spin couldn't wake up.

He screamed, but no one heard him.

He cried, and then he bargained. *Please, Raven, come back. I'll ... I'll tell you anything you want to know.* There were limits on what he could share with someone from a *primitive culture*, but he would find a way to overcome them. Those who had placed such limits on him were long since passed to dust.

It was all to no avail.

Raven was gone, and Spin was afraid his friend would never come back.

*Why did you leave me?*

•   •   •

Raven clutched the bony ridge behind the *verent*'s neck, holding on for dear life as moon-limned clouds slipped past. The second *verent* paced them, a few meters to their left, the tandem beating of their wings loud even over the chill wind. *How long have we been flying? Hours? Days?*

Raven's teeth chattered. The air was bitterly cold, and he didn't have the thick skin and scales of the *verent* — not yet, anyhow, except for his arms — and he hadn't grabbed his new ix-lined coat. *What the farking hell did I just do?*

He could still hear Aik's plaintive cry. *Raven, let me come with you!* His friend's heart must be breaking, because Raven's was.

They had just shattered the wall that had separated them for so long — the one Raven himself had built. Aik had held him close, all of him — even the weird, scaled parts. *He said he loved me. Why didn't I say it back?*

How many times had he whispered it into the ears of a man he'd picked up off the docks? To a councillor's husband? Caught up in lust that felt like love?

He'd done what he had to. It was better this way — Aik could go on without him. Besides, things would never have worked between them.

He had a whole new adventure before him, if the *verent* didn't eat him first. He shuddered.

*Cold?*

The voice in his head startled him, and he almost lost his grip. He grasped the beast's neck ridge all the more tightly with near-frozen fingers.

It wasn't a word as much as a sensation in the back of his head. The *verent* had reached out to him the same way back at the manor, expressing its need for Raven to come with it on this insane journey.

"Yes." He didn't know if it could read his thoughts. But if he said it out loud ...

The beast shifted its wings and dropped.

Raven started to slip off the *verent*'s back. "Holy green hell!" The long fall would kill him for sure. He grabbed at the bony ridge and managed to throw his arms around the *verent*'s neck, holding on for dear life.

A sense of contrition came through the link, and the beast spread its wings, slowing its rate of descent. There was something else there too. A feeling of ... newness. Of awe. "No one's ever ridden you before, have they?"

*Affirmation.*

*At least I'm not the only flying virgin here.* Raven snorted despite himself. Even given his dire straits, feeling a little humor about his situation made him feel better.

He had to believe that Aik would be all right. He was strong, and he had Silya to help him through. Jealousy flared in his chest, turning his stomach sour. He wouldn't go back to her, not like that. Would he? *Why not? I won't be around anymore.*

Still, it had been his choice to go, to save them all. *I bet that stunned the hencha berries out of Silya.*

He shoved Aik into the same compartment as his mother and Jimey Aze. He had a lot of experience dealing with unwanted emotions.

They broke out of the clouds, and Raven gasped. Pink and golden moonlight shone through breaks in the cloud cover, illuminating the night landscape below. They were passing out of Heaven's Reach, leaving the neat fields of hencha, cotton and corn behind. Below, a narrow pass wound up through the mountains, threaded by a river that sparkled in the moonlight. Patches of moonlit snow shone on the higher mountain slopes.

They soared up out of the mountain pass into open air. The shoulders of the mountains descended into foothills and then grassy plains, broken up here and there by human settlements visible as darker patches among the geometric lines of moonlit fields. *Must be the Highlands.* He wondered if anyone was down there just then, looking up to see the strange sight of these beautiful creatures passing overhead.

"Spin, what do you know about the Highlands —" *Seven hells.* He'd left his familiar under his bed when Aik had shown up. *Sorry, Spin.* His only other friend, abandoned like Raven's own mother had abandoned him. He hoped the little familiar didn't fall into Tri'Aya's hands. Or worse.

Aik would find him, take care of him. Maybe they would help each other.

Raven felt more alone than ever without his two best friends.

The air was warmer, though still cooler than he liked. The *verent's* body warmed his hands — the creature put out a fair amount of heat. If he closed his eyes, he could hear the *verent's* three hearts beating in harmony. *Bah-dum-pum, bah-dum-pum.*

Blood slowly returned to his ears and fingers, warming them both, as they shot out across what had to be Lake Zeraya. Raven tried to picture the map from the Landing Survey that Sister Tela had shown them — the lake sat in the middle of the Highlands, surrounded by grasslands full of *orinths* and *aur* and maybe even giant *cephlants*, rooting with their long tusks in the grass for grubs to eat.

To the south was the Red Flight range, her rocky peaks tinged scarlet under layers of snow. To the north, the arctic ice sheet was a vast, icy presence that fed the Highlands with runoff in the summer. And somewhere to the northeast was Anghar Mor, the colossal mountain Queen Jas'Aya had mentioned in her diary.

Raven didn't believe in prophecies, or at least he hadn't before. He was a city thief. He believed in the practical things like streets and pubs and simple human nature — greed and anger and fear. *How did I get here?* Events had conspired to throw him out of his comfort zone, straight into the fire. He hugged the *verent's* neck as the moonlit waters passed below them.

Flying a-*verentback* should have been the thrill of his life. But every beat of the *verents'* wings took him farther away from his life. From Aik.

*Aik would love this.* He was made for adventure. The *verent* should have picked Aik for whatever this was. Or almost anyone else besides him. Aik had a sense of adventure, a *climb the next mountain* thing. He would have been far better for whatever in the holy green hell this was. *Why did you choose me?*

What if Aik came after him? The *verent* might kill him. The thought plunged Raven back into despair. He bit his lip, trying to think about something — anything — else.

*Comfort* flooded the link between him and the *verent*. Comfort and reassurance. Like the nudge of a mother *aur* against her colt's neck, or a blanket tucked around him to keep him safe and warm.

They meant him no harm. Raven was sure of it, though he couldn't say why.

Warmth surged into him from the *verent's* back too, and the last of the cold fell away. In spite of himself and the strange situation, he felt better. Here he was, a gully rat from Gullton, reviled by most of its citizens, flying through the clouds above them all. *I could get used to this.*

When he opened his eyes again, they'd left the lake behind. Ahead, a wall of mountains towered over the eastern edge of the Highlands. *The Red Flights, still?* He wasn't sure.

His back ached, and his arms and legs were sore from holding the awkward position on the *verent's* back. *How far away is this place you're taking me?* And why didn't *verent* come with saddles?

*Not much farther.* That was clearer, almost like human speech. Maybe the *verent* was learning how to talk to him.

The sky ahead of them was a pale shade of green, the first hints of sunlight outlining the thin wisps of clouds there. *Is it morning already?*

To his left, a single mountain towered over the others. It was almost a perfect cone, its peak capped in snow. *Anghar Mor. It has to be.* Still, the *verent* continued eastward, and soon even the mammoth mountain fell behind them.

They soared over the foothills together, circling to catch an updraft of warmer air. It lifted them up in lazy circles as the first rays of light played over the assembled peaks ahead. Up and up they went, bursting into sunlight that temporarily blinded him.

When he could see again, he gasped. The mountains below were a crazy tumble of rocks and snow, creating an intricate black-and-white pattern in the early morning light, a mess that would be almost impassable by foot.

As they slipped between mountain peaks, sunlight warmed his face.

He closed his eyes and just enjoyed the ride, so tired he would almost lose his grip. Each time the *verent* would shake him gently awake.

The mountains below seemed endless, but the sun was only a hand span above the horizon when he felt the *verent* touch in his mind again. *We're here.*

Raven opened his eyes.

"Holy *hencha*." They were circling a small, snowless valley bounded by tall peaks. It was filled with purple plants — tiny meadows, strange trees with wide, heart-shaped leaves, and a multitude of smaller shrubs and bushes — a sharp contrast with the surrounding snowy peaks. And there were *verent* — dozens of the graceful creatures, leaping from rock shelves around the valley to fly past them and check them out.

One dropped to the turquoise lake in the valley's heart, skidding across the water's surface gracefully to settle in up to its back, sending up a white spray. Others flitted to another of what had to be at least hundred cave mouths that dotted the mountainsides.

"What is this place?" *And how is there no snow here?*

*Home.*

Several *verent* frolicked in the lake below, splashing one another and shaking themselves clean. Steam rose from the lake — it must be volcanic. Raven grinned. *I learned something useful in school, after all.*

His *verent* swept down toward one of the cave mouths on the far side of the valley, followed by the other one.

*His mate?* Did they even have genders? *Aur* were male, then female, in different cycles of their lives. Maybe the *verent* were the same. "Do you have a name?"

*Amusement* flooded the link, along with a shape, a smell, a word. It was hard to decipher. Something sleek that smelled like the fresh sea breeze.

Raven frowned, and then laughed despite his predicament. Here he was hundreds — thousands? — of kilometers from home in a *verent* playground, isolated and alone, and he was worried that he might get his host's name wrong.

They had a lot of work to do if they were going to understand one another. "I think I'll call you Breeze, for now."

Breeze snorted its assent and dropped gracefully onto the black rock ledge, lowering itself to let Raven climb down.

Sitting in one position for hours had left him sore, and he'd have bruises for sure from the *verent's* bumpy hide against his stomach. Still, he was alive.

He sniffed, wiping the crust from his eyes, and managed to get down to solid ground without embarrassing himself too much

— not that the *verent* cared. He stood and stretched, feeling every one of his tortured muscles.

He took a few steps up onto one of the flat rocks that fronted the ledge and looked out over the unusual valley. The sun had just crested the mountain before him, and its rays touched the mountain slopes, warming Raven's face. A waterfall flowed over the northern wall and tumbled down to form a winding river, which fed the lake. The watercourse wound lazily through the foliage, hidden here and there by some of the strange heart trees. Clouds of blue wisps tumbled through the valley, gyrating playfully in the air.

"Spin, have you ever seen trees like those before?"

His familiar didn't answer. Raven slapped his forehead, angry with himself for forgetting that Spin wasn't there. Angry that he'd left the little sphere behind. The Manor House seemed a world away, like a different lifetime. Homesickness overtook him, pain squeezing his gut ... or was it that damnable creature?

*I don't want to be here.* He missed Gullton, Spin, and Aik ... and even Silya with her dagger-sharp glares and biting wit. He wanted to run away, back toward the Heartland.

*Stupid idea.* There was no way he'd get out of this valley without the *verent's* help. Besides, they seemed to have some way of finding him. How had they known he was at the Manor House? *The egg. We're connected now, somehow.*

He'd have to make the best of it. *And who knows what there might be to steal?* That thought cheered him up, just a little.

Raven took a deep breath of the cool, fresh mountain air and resigning himself to his fate. *For now.*

His stomach growled, as hunger warred with exhaustion. "Hey Breeze, you wouldn't have a bit to eat ... preferrably not me?" Despite the reassurance Breeze had shared with him, the giant beasts had to eat. Right? *And I'm food-sized for a verent.*

"We can probably arrange something."

Raven spun around, startled to hear another human voice.

The man standing at the mouth of the cave was taller than Raven and looked strong as an *aur.* His face was tanned, with high cheekbones and soft lips. He wore an intricately woven, multicolored tunic and warm-looking leggings, stuffed into gold and green *ix*-leather boots. White scales covered his arms.

Raven stared at him, speechless.

"You might start with hello?" The visitor's mouth quirked up in a smile.

Raven's face flushed. "Hello! Sorry — I was just startled to see someone else here. Someone human, that is." He glanced at the man's arms. "You are still human ... right?"

His visitor laughed. "Yes. Still human, despite the scales." The man held out his hand, palm forward. "I'm Jai." Jai had an unusual accent. The words were clipped at the end ... his "hello" sounded more like "hella." He also had a strange lump behind his left ear. Raven tried not to stare. He smelled curious.

"Hi Jai. I'm Raven." Raven touched Jai's palm, feeling self-conscious at the strange gesture.

Breeze rumbled past them and into the cavern, followed by the other *verent*. Raven decided to call the second one Squint because of the way it looked at him when he was "talking" with Breeze. "What is this place?"

Jai joined him at the edge of the ledge. "The *verent* just call it home. We named it Mountainhome."

"We?" Raven's stomach grumbled loudly enough for Jai to hear it. *There are more people like me — like us?*

Jai laughed. "Yes, 'we.' Come meet the others. They've been waiting for you. We'll get you something to eat. I imagine you're starving."

Raven took one last look over his shoulder, and then followed Jai into the darkness.

•    •    •

Sorix watched the otherling go. It smelled like hers. But it was tall and gangly and more pink than white.

How had the others managed to accept theirs?

It was wrong. All wrong.

Give it time. Kalix nudged her toward their home, the broad cavern where Velix and her other two kits awaited.

*Is it him?* Aryx, sweet Aryx.

*Yes, my sweet. It's your brother.*

*He stinks.* Flix bunched up his nose and sneezed.

A ripple of amusement shook her frame. *Yes, he does.* She nuzzled his little head.

Velix touched their snout to hers. *Welcome home. We have much to do.*

As the strange voices of the otherlings faded down the long tunnel outside their home, Sorix nodded. *Indeed we do.*

# EPILOGUE

T HE SPORE MOTHER LOOKED OVER HER DOMAIN — a cold cavern in the heart of the mountain. It was warmer than it had been as her children spread out to cover the walls. She sent her diggers — the *eemscaap* — to clear out tunnels dug by her predecessors, many of them caved in with rubble over the years.

*Oosill* had covered the walls with mucus, the little worms creating a fertile place for her other children to grow. Red *eesiil* climbed the walls with their five arms, casting a ruddy red glow over her.

And the *eeechiia* had grown their white membranes across the entrances to her home, sealing in the warmth.

She had grown too. Her body now took up a third of the cavern, her *eeechha* womb sacs birthing those she needed to carry out her work. Her taproots dug deep into the world's heart, seeking out the heat there to give her strength.

Soon her *iichili* would find the new progenitor — one of the new, bipedal species that had arrived since her foremother's attempts to fix this world. Once she had him, she could accelerate the process of transforming this rich world into *Eev-uurccheea*, a new home for her people. Soon her children would be able to survive in the open.

She'd hoped this world was barren, but in the end, it didn't matter. She valued survival of her own kind over all else.

She gazed over her domain and was content.

*Our time has come.*

# GLOSSARY

**Adley Narrows:** A narrowing of the Elsp between Vulture Spine and the North Shore, near the egress to the Harkness Sea

**Aik'Erio aka Aiken (Mas):** Guardsman in Gullton and loyal friend to Raven

**Ais'Vellin aka Aisel (Mas):** Trader and associate of Tri'Aya

**Akin-yo:** A martial art the sisters practice

**Akka:** A bitter drink made from the leaves of the Akka bush; the local equivalent of coffee

**Auddah:** Cheese made from aur milk

**Alaya:** The Tharassan native name for Tarsis, the bigger golden moon

**Angels:** What the Tharassans called Runners from Earth (LR)

**Anghar Mor:** One of the mountains in the Redflight range, with lots of volcanic activity

**Anya'Enn aka Anyassa (Mim):** A Temple initiate

**Arsday:** Fifth day of the week

**Aryx (Cat):** One of Breeze's kits, female

**Ast'Una aka Aster (Mim):** One of the Temple sisters, head of the Temple stores

**Auley Tree:** A spindly tree with strong fire-resistant sticks

**Aur/Auracinth:** Large beasts of burden that don't develop a gender until their third year

**Ay'Oss aka Ayja:** God of magic, technology, wisdom, and earth whose sign is the wisp, and who presents as a handsome young man

**Ayvin/Aaveen:** An alien race that arrived on Tharassas before humanity

**Bacca Root:** A minty local root that people chew on for flavor with anti-nausea properties

**Bandy Fruit:** Red fruit with purple spikes, sweet and juicy

**Bandy Trees/Heart Trees/Evrit:** Native trees with wide red trunks, broad, heart-shaped purple leaves, where heartroot and bandy fruit come from

**Beast Guild:** The Gullton guild in charge of domesticated beasts (aur, urse, etc)

**Black Cheese:** A variety of cheese from aur milk, grown in the caverns under Gullton

**Breeze aka Kalix (Raven):** male verent with a green tinge to his white skin

**Builder's Guild:** The contractors' guild in Gullton

**Callasday:** Sixth day of the week

**Capton:** Small oceanfront town north of Gullton

**Car'Ost aka Carel (Mim):** Junior cook in the Temple

**Cayah:** Desert dwellers with tan and brown dappled skin and spiral horns

**Ce'Faine:** Human clans that live in the far east and south, past the borders of the Highlands and the Heartland

**Cekya:** Temple cook

**Cephlant:** A grazing herd animal similar to an elephant

**Cer'Ella aka Ceryl (Sister):** The fourth Hencha Queen, only served for a year

**Cheevah:** A small flying creature

**Cheff:** Derogatory name for the Ce'faine

**Cherry Fly:** Thumb-sized insect with twelve legs

**Clayton:** Small town in the eastern part of the Heartland

**Cleffer Bush:** A red-leaved plant with yellow "brush" flowers

**Cor'Lea aka Coral (Mim):** An initiate at the hencha Temple

**Corinth:** The small village on the south slopes where Queen Jas came from (Last Run)

**Crosston:** A small town in the middle of the Heartland

**Dalney:** Small oceanfront town north of Gullton

**Dam, The:** A hydroelectric dam built just after landing to power the colony, recently refurbished

**Day'Ima aka Daya (Sister):** One of Silya's teachers, ace, wears violet pine perfume

**Dem'Errol aka Demtrius (Mas, Ser):** Aik's squad captain

**Der'Iza aka Derik (Mas):** Tri'Aya's husband and Silya's father

**Des'Rya aka Desla (Mim):** A Temple initiate originally from Devon

**Destrayer's Song:** An old battle song from the Heartlander-Ce'Faine conflict

**Devon:** Village in the southern part of the Heartland

**Dor'Ala aka Doria (Sister):** Sister appointed to be Silya's aide

**Ecin:** Fifth month of the year

**Edgeton:** A small town south of Gullton

**Edie:** Tenth month of the year

**Edu:** Second month of the year

**Eeechiia:** Living membranes used to separate spaces

**Eemscaap:** Digger creatures from Uurccheea

**Eesiil:** Red, glowing star-like fungus with seven points

**Eev-uurccheea:** Literally "New Uurccheea," the aaveen's second homeworld. Also the name given to Tharassas by the Spore Mother

**Eircat:** Cat analogues – Highland hunters

**El'Oss/Elohim/The Old God:** God of the past and love, sign is the cross, once the Christian god, now folded into the local religion

**Electrical Guild:** A new guild in Gullton responsible for the electric lights and the dam

**Elsp River:** River that runs from lake Zeraya to Gullton through the Highlands and the Heartland

**Em'Asa (Mim):** One of Tri'Aya's private guards, born in Dalney

**Eneet:** A squirrel equivalent

**Eno:** First month of the year

**Eoto:** Eighth month of the year

**Equa:** Fourth month of the year

**Erphin:** Dolphin equivalent

**Esei:** Sixth month of the year

**Eset:** Seventh month of the year

**Eshem:** The ce'faine equivalent of the Hencha Queen

**Etré:** Third month of the year

**Evro:** Ninth month of the year

**Fellin Root:** a yellow root that serves as an anti-dolorific, also a sleep aid in larger quantities

**Fess'Ima aka Fessryn (Mim):** One of the Temple initiates

**Fexin:** Deep purple Highlands herb, used as topical germicide

**Flitter:** Small helicopters used to transport people in the Heartland; sparkling "wings" (LR)

**Flop Trees:** Big-leaved trees used to provide islands of shade in the hencha plantations

**Flyx (Grey):** One of Breeze's kits, male

**Foldovers:** A sweet or savory pastry

**Fre'Oss aka Freja:** God of air, weather, and health, sign is the lightning bold, presents as a child, sometimes male, sometimes female

**Fri'Oss aka Frija:** God of fertility, birth, the harvest and sex, sign is the leaf, presents as a woman

**Gap, the:** Pass connecting the Highlands with the Heartland to the East

**Gap Station:** The way station in the middle of the Gap

**Grayleaf:** A seasoning often used in steak rubs, also used as an essential oil

**Great Southern Desert:** The huge desert south of the Heartland, beyond the Onyx Mountains, where the suifaine live

**Guard's Honor:** Used to swear something

**Gullton/Gullytown:** The main city on Tharassas, where the colony was founded

**Gully Birds:** Black seagull equivalents found in Gullton and the heartland

**Gully Fowl:** Three-legged chicken equivalents

**Gully Rat:** Derogatory term for citizens of Gullton

**Gully Rats:** Larger cousins to the inthym that live in and around Gullton

**Gully Weasels:** See gully rats, also used as a derogatory term for Gulltoners

**Hacka Berries:** Highland berries known for their sweet, salty taste

**Haifaine:** East Valley Clan - Elleck (Enrick)

**Harkness Sea:** The sea to the west of Gully Town

**Heartland:** The original colony lands, with Gullton as the capital

**Heartlanders:** People who live in the Heartland

**Heartroot:** Spicy highlands herb, similar to cinnamon

**Heaven's Reach:** The mountain range along the northern edge of the Heartland

**Hel'Oss aka Helja:** God of death, war, and problems, sign is the black staff, presents as intersex

**Hencha:** A food crop that's also semi sentient, human height with red stalks and purple leaves

**Hencha Berries:** Berries produced by the hencha plants that are edible by humans - red (sweet), orange, blue (sharp-sweet), and yellow (tart, citrus/vitamin c)

**Hencha Leaf Scroll:** Paper made from hencha leaves

**Hencha Mind:** The animating group consciousness of the hencha

**Hencha Oil:** Used for lanterns

**Hencha Queen:** The woman who can talk to the hencha; also the animating consciousness of the hencha en masse (see *Hencha Mind*)

**Hencha Tea:** A healing tea made from hencha leaves

**Henchwine:** Wine made from hencha berries

**Hera River:** The other major river in the Heartland

**Hes'Enn aka Hestra (Mim):** The Temple sword master

**Heurcinth:** Purple Highlands flowers that grow with pezzywinkles in matched pairs

**Heyfa Weeds**: Yellow semi-sentient weeds that strangle the hencha plants for food

**Highlanders:** People who live in the Highlands; can refer to Steaders or sometimes Ce'Faine

**Highlands:** Wide valley inland from the Heartland, accessed via the Gap

**Highlands Treaty:** Treaty signed between Gullton/the Heartland and the Ce'Faine

**Iichili/Forerunners/Fireflies:** Spies for the Spore Mother

**Initiate:** An acolytes of the hencha Temple

**Inthym/rinkin:** Little harmless white mouse-like creatures that hunt insects in packs

**Jai (m, reifaine):** One of the ce'faine, then a verent rider

**Janusday:** Fourth day of the week

**Jas'Aya aka Jasinaya (Mim):** Hencha berry farm worker, later the Hencha Queen; dark hair

**Jel'Faya aka Jelin (Mas):** Contemporary fantasy author

**Jellybug:** Small, brightly-colored beetles that inthyms eat

**Jer'Est aka Jeryl (Mas):** One of Aik's friends

**Jexyn:** Hive-minded birds in the Highlands; dangerous when they find fresh meat

**Jim'Aza aka Jimey (Mas):** Nel'Aza's son and Raven's first crush

**Jor'Oss aka Jorja** (wild nature/unpredictability/luck - dice): God of wild nature, unpredictability and luck, sign is the dice, presents as a scarily beautiful young woman

**Jyn'Eln (Doctor):** Medic for the Gullton Guard

**Keh'Sel aka Kehla (Mas):** Temple seamstress

**Kek'Aze aka Kerrick (Ser):** One of Aik's superiors in the guard

**Kerint**: Ocean fish-equivalents with a sweet, tangy meat

**Lake Zeraya:** The huge central lake that defines the highlands

**Lamplighter's Guild:** Gullton guild responsible for lighting the lamps and the natural gas lines

**Landfield:** The suburb that sprung up on the western side of the old landing field

**Lo'Oss aka Loja**: God of fire, change, strength and protection, sign is flames, presents as gender-fluid, and can appear in all of the forms

**Local Population Contact Regulations (LPCs):** Rules governing contact with a local population

**Lowlander:** Derogatory term the Highlanders use for the Heartlanders

**Lyn'Rya (Mim):** Des'Rya's mother, and a tanner in Devon

**Machinists' Guild:** Gullton guild responsible for fabricating anything needed by the other guilds

**Mad Blade:** Aik's mother's armory/book shop on Raven Spine

**Manor House:** Tri'Aya's home in Heaven's Reach

**Mar'Orn aka Marea (Mim):** Raven's mother

**Martasday:** Second day of the week

**Mas:** Title for adult men

**Meer:** Mayor

**Menagerie:** Bestiary of real and imagined beasts created from Sera's original works by Sol'Eria

**Mes'Ena aka Meslyn (Mim):** One of Tri'Aya's guards

**Mif (Mas):** One of Aik's friends

**Mim:** Title for adult women

**Mir:** Title for adult non-binary/fluid

**Mir'Ust aka Mirrel (Mim):** One of the Temple initiates

**Mohr'Una *aka* Mohria (Mim):** The Temple astrologer

**Mountain Ix:** Swift-footed mountain animals prized for their colorful green-gold hides

**Mountainhome:** What the humans call the valley where the verent live

**Mudmole:** A large rodent equivalent

**Mur beatles:** Silk-weaving beatles

**Mur silk:** Silk spun by mur beatles

**Nel'Aza aka Nellie (Mim):** Raven's neighbor who takes him in when his mother dies

**Noninalya:** One of the songs of the Sisters of the Hencha

**Nor'Oss aka Norja:** God of water, the sea, and prosperity, sign is a wave, presents as an old man

**Northlander:** A less derogatory term for the Heartlanders and Steaders

**Norton:** Small town in the middle of the Heartland

**Onyx Mountains:** The range just south of Gullton and the Heartland

**Oosill:** Finger-sized uurcheean worms that leave behind fertilizer mucus

**Oracle, the:** The eshem of the suifaine clan

**Orinth Honey:** A sweet sticky substance made by orinths in their nest

**Orinth:** Green and orange insects that nest in muddy columns, analogous to termites

**Ost Farm:** Vegetable farm outside of Gullton that sells produce to the Temple

**Otherlings:** What the verent call humans

**Pellin:** Tharassas's smaller, pink moon, Erreh in the native tongue

**Peregrine Spine:** The smallest spine, where many of the rich have mansions

**Pes'Osa aka Peslyn (Mir):** One of the sisters in the Temple

**Pezzywinkles:** Orange Highlands flowers that grow with Heurcinths in matched pairs

**Puffer Hen:** Domesticated fowl; also used to describe gossips

**Raising, The:** The coronation of a new Hencha Queen

**Rav'Orn aka Raven (Mas):** Thief from Gullton

**Raven Spine:** The central "spine" of Gullton where toe Temple and city hall are found

**Redflight Mountains:** The range that defines the southern edge of the Highlands

**Redhawk Spine:** The southernmost spine, and also the poorest, home of the Open Market

**Reifaine:** Red Flight clan of the ce'faine

**Ring Tree:** Spiral tree with purple fronds found in the foothills of Heaven's Reach

**River Grass:** Cattail equivalents that grow along river shores

**Rock Ferns:** Red ferns that grow along the spines of Gullton

**Russet Mold (powdered):** Used for fever

**Sadie's Cove:** Small oceanfront town north of Gullton

**Sal'Moya aka Sallia (Mim):** One of the Sisters, head of the initiates

**Scill'Eya:** A homeless woman in Gullton

**Sea Guild:** The main transportation guild in Gullton

**Sera Collins (Ahsera):** Pilot of the Spun Diver; black

**Sil'Aya aka Silya (Mim):** Aik's old flame and an initiate at the Hencha Temple

**Sister:** Title for the women who work in the Temple

**Skeef:** A tick equivalent

**Skerit:** A bat equivalent

**Sol'Eria (Solene):** A Sister in the Temple who had a talent for art, and who collected many of Sera's works into leather-bound volumes

**Solsday:** First day of the week

**Southford:** A small town in the southeastern corner of the Heartland

***Spin Diver:*** The last ship to make the run from Earth (LR)

**Spin:** AI of the *Spin Diver*

**Spore Mother:** Mysterious alien entity

**Squint aka Sorix:** Breeze's female mate, reddish brown

**Steader:** Someone from one of the steadings in the Highlands

**Stones:** A gambling game where flat, etched stones are thrown for points and sets

**Suifaine:** Desert clan of the ce'faine

**Summer Meet:** Gathering of the Highlander tribes along the southeastern side of Lake Zeraya

**Tarsis:** Tharassas's larger golden moon, dominated by a big heart-shaped crater

**Tartan Hills:** The hilly region bordering the southern edge of the Heartland

**Tel'Esta aka Tela (Sister):** One of Silya's teachers and the Temple archivist

**Temple/Hencha Temple:** The seat of the Hencha Queen in Gullton

**Terasday:** Third day of the week

**Tess'Esra aka Tesslyn (Initiate):** One of the Temple initiates

**Tharassas:** A human-colonized world

**Theolin:** A stringed instrument with strings made from aur hair

**Thieves' Guild:** Loose, unrecognized Gullton guild comprised of master thieves and apprentices

**Tri'Aya *aka* Triya (Mim):** Silyas' mother, a wealthy merchant with a mansion called the Manor House on the slopes of Heaven's Reach

**Trine Grass:** Tri-bladed purple grass that covers the Highlands valley

**Tucker Narrows:** A narrowing of the Elsp between Raven Spine and Eagle Spine

**Umvit/Vrint:** Small, fast, nimble three-winged flying creature used as messengers

**Urse:** A smaller version of an Auricinth, a horse equivalent

**Uurccheea:** The long-destroyed home world of the Aaveen

**Vale:** A small town at the eastern edge of the Highlands

**Veifaine:** the Highlands Valley clan of the ce'faine that no longer exists

**Verent/Skirryn (s/pl):** Dragon-like native beasts that change gender periodically

**Verla'Olk (Mim):** Temple cook

**Violet Pine:** Native tree with spiky needles

**Vulture Spine:** The northernmost spine, also the location of most of Gullton's industry

**Wil'Ock aka Willem (Mas):** Tri'Aya's husband and Sil'Aya's father, an artist from Sadie's cove

**Wisps/Esh:** Mysterious glowing blue sparks that have suddenly become more common

**Yen'Ela aka Yendra (Mim):** The previous Hencha Queen

**Zelaya:** A bustling town on the southeastern shore of Lake Zelaya in the Highlands

**Zev'Nek aka Zevrell (Mim, Sea Master):** Sea Master of Gullton

# ABOUT THE AUTHOR

J. Scott Coatsworth writes stories that subvert expectations, that seek to transform traditional science fiction, fantasy, and contemporary worlds into something new and unexpected. His writing, whether romance or genre fiction (or a little bit of both), brings a queer energy to his stories, infusing them with love, beauty and power and making them soar. He imagines a world that *could be* and, in the process, maybe changes the world *that is*, just a little.

A Rainbow Award-winning author, Scott's debut novel, *Skythane*, received two awards and an honorable mention. With his husband, Mark, he runs Queer Sci Fi, QueerRomance Ink, Liminal Fiction, and Other Worlds Ink. Scott is also the committee chair for the Indie Authors Committee at the Science Fiction and Fantasy Writers Association (SFWA).

# YOU MIGHT ALSO ENJOY

## MEMORY AND METAPHOR

Andrea Monticue

*Civilization fell. It rose. At some point, people built starships.*

## THE SMUGGLERS

**FROM THE "TRUCK STOP AT THE CENTER OF THE GALAXY"**

by Vanessa MacLaren-Wray

*Attachment is everything.*

## A WRECK OF DRAGONS

Elaine Isaak

*Teens and their giant robots search for a new home for mankind, but the planet they discover belongs to the dragons.*

Available from Water Dragon Publishing in
hardcover, trade paperback, digital, and audio editions
*waterdragonpublishing.com*

Printed in the USA
CPSIA information can be obtained
at www.ICGtesting.com
JSHW080352271023
50898JS00001B/39

9 781959 804277